Discover the
WRITER'S LIFE
in New York City

Over more than six decades of steady innovation, The New School has sustained a vital center for creative writing. Study writing and literature with The New School's renowned faculty of writers, critics, editors, and publishing professionals—in the heart of Greenwich Village.

Master of Fine Arts in Creative Writing
The New School's distinguished MFA program offers concentrations in fiction, poetry, nonfiction, and writing for children. Fellowships and financial aid are available.

Bachelor's Program in the Liberal Arts
Writing students seeking a BA may apply to the **Riggio Honors Program**. Students who are accepted into the program are eligible to receive a partial scholarship.
The Riggio Writing Honors Program is offered in conjunction with the Leonard and Louise Riggio Writing & Democracy initiative at The New School.

Summer Writers Colony, June 1–19, 2009
Join workshops and literary salons with renowned New School faculty members and visiting writers, including **Joan Acocella, Don Brown, Mark Doty, Linda Gregg, Sarah Manguso, Joseph O'Neill, Benjamin Taylor, and Elizabeth Winthrop**. Undergraduates can earn 6 credits. Open to noncredit students. Housing is available.

For more about the programs, call 212.229.5630 or visit us online.

www.newschool.edu/writing25

THE NEW SCHOOL

2008–2009

Director: Robert Polito

MFA FACULTY
Jeffery Renard Allen, Jonathan Ames, Robert Antoni, Susan Bell, Mark Bibbins, Susan Cheever, Jonathan Dee, Elaine Equi, David Gates, Jennifer Michael Hecht, Ann Hood, Shelley Jackson, Zia Jaffrey, Hettie Jones, James Lasdun, David Lehman, Suzannah Lessard, David Levithan, Phillip Lopate, Patrick McGrath, Honor Moore, Sigrid Nunez, Meghan O'Rourke, Dale Peck, Darryl Pinckney, Robert Polito, Helen Schulman, Tor Seidler, Laurie Sheck, Darcey Steinke, Benjamin Taylor, Paul Violi, Sarah Weeks, Brenda Wineapple, Stephen Wright.

Associate Director: Jackson Taylor

MFA VISITING FACULTY
Max Blagg, Deborah Brodie, Patricia Carlin, Marilyn Goldin, Vivian Gornick, Fannie Howe, Gary Indiana, Dave Johnson, Joyce Johnson, Mary Lee Kortez, Wendy Lesser, Sharon Mesmer, Marie Ponsot, David Prete, Lloyd Schwartz, Susan Shapiro, Jackson Taylor, Frederic Tuten, Susan Van Metre, Vicky Wilson.

Associate Chair: Luis Jaramillo
Associate Director: Laura Cronk

RIGGIO HONORS
PROGRAM FACULTY
Jeffery Renard Allen, Catherine Barnett, Mark Bibbins, Patricia Carlin, Elizabeth Gaffney, David Gates, Shelley Jackson, Zia Jaffrey, Suzannah Lessard, Greil Marcus, Sigrid Nunez, Honor Sachs, René Steinke, Lynne Tillman, Paul Violi.

GRANTA

12 Addison Avenue, London W11 4QR
email editorial@granta.com
To subscribe go to www.granta.com or call 845-267-3031 (toll-free 866-438-6150)

ISSUE 106

EDITOR	Alex Clark
AMERICAN EDITOR	John Freeman
SENIOR EDITOR	Rosalind Porter
ONLINE EDITOR	Roy Robins
ASSOCIATE EDITORS	Helen Gordon, Liz Jobey
INTERNATIONAL EDITIONS EDITOR	Simon Willis
CONTRIBUTING WRITERS	Andrew Hussey, Robert Macfarlane, Xan Rice
DESIGN	Lindsay Nash, Carolyn Roberts
FINANCE	Geoffrey Gordon, Morgan Graver
MARKETING AND SUBSCRIPTIONS	Anne Gowan, Joanna Metcalfe
SALES DIRECTOR	Brigid Macleod
PUBLICITY	Pru Rowlandson
VICE PRESIDENT, US OPERATIONS	Greg Lane
TO ADVERTISE CONTACT	Emily Cook, ecook@granta.com
IT MANAGER	Mark Williams
PRODUCTION ASSOCIATE	Sarah Wasley
PROOFS	Lesley Levene
MANAGING DIRECTOR	David Graham
ASSOCIATE PUBLISHER	Eric Abraham
PUBLISHER	Sigrid Rausing

Granta USPS 000-508 is published five times per year (Feb, May, Jun, Aug & Nov) by *Granta* 12 Addison Avenue, London W11 4QR, United Kingdom at the annual subscription rate of $45.99
Airfreight and mailing in the USA by Agent named Air Business, C/O Worldnet Shipping USA Inc., 149-35 177th Street, Jamaica, New York, NY 11434. Periodicals postage paid at Jamaica NY 11431.
US POSTMASTER: Send address changes to *Granta*, PO Box 359 Congers, NY 10920-0359.

Granta is printed and bound in Italy by Legoprint. This magazine is printed on paper that fulfils the criteria for 'Paper for permanent document' according to ISO 9706 and the American Library Standard ANSI/NIZO Z39.48-1992.
This magazine has been printed on paper that has been certified by the Forest Stewardship Council (FSC).
Granta is indexed in the American Humanities Index.

ISBN 978-1-929001-36-1

Cover illustration by Andy Bridge

CONTENTS

Energetic failure

In 1979, when Bill Buford introduced his first issue of *Granta*, a penetrating, bravura survey of American fiction, he proclaimed his efforts to be 'a kind of energetic failure'. Thirty years later, I know what he means. Gathering together a magazine of new writing requires a certain amount of energy, although of an almost entirely pleasurable kind; sifting through short stories and novels-in-progress to provide an entertaining and illuminating sample of today's literary landscape is hardly work, by most people's standards. The prospect of failure is a different matter. But failure to do what?

That first issue of 1979 – a blend of fiction, interview material and critical writing – set out its stall clearly enough; to challenge the cultural hegemony and shortcomings of the contemporary British novel ('characterized by a succession of efforts the accomplishments of which are insistently, critically, and aesthetically negligible') by introducing the magazine's readership to writers from the United States who had, by and large, not yet garnered widespread attention.

Buford's tone was insistent, polemical, occasionally table-thumping; his line of argument at times academic, at times more impressionistic. His rather laudable demand – request, or suggestion, is too mild a word – was for British writing to notice the conversation that was going on in America, and to join in. Subsequent issues of *Granta*, most notably 'The End of the English Novel' (*Granta* 3), 'Dirty Realism' (*Granta* 8) and the once-a-decade 'Best of Young British Novelists' and 'Best of Young American Novelists' have attempted to encourage and to extend the

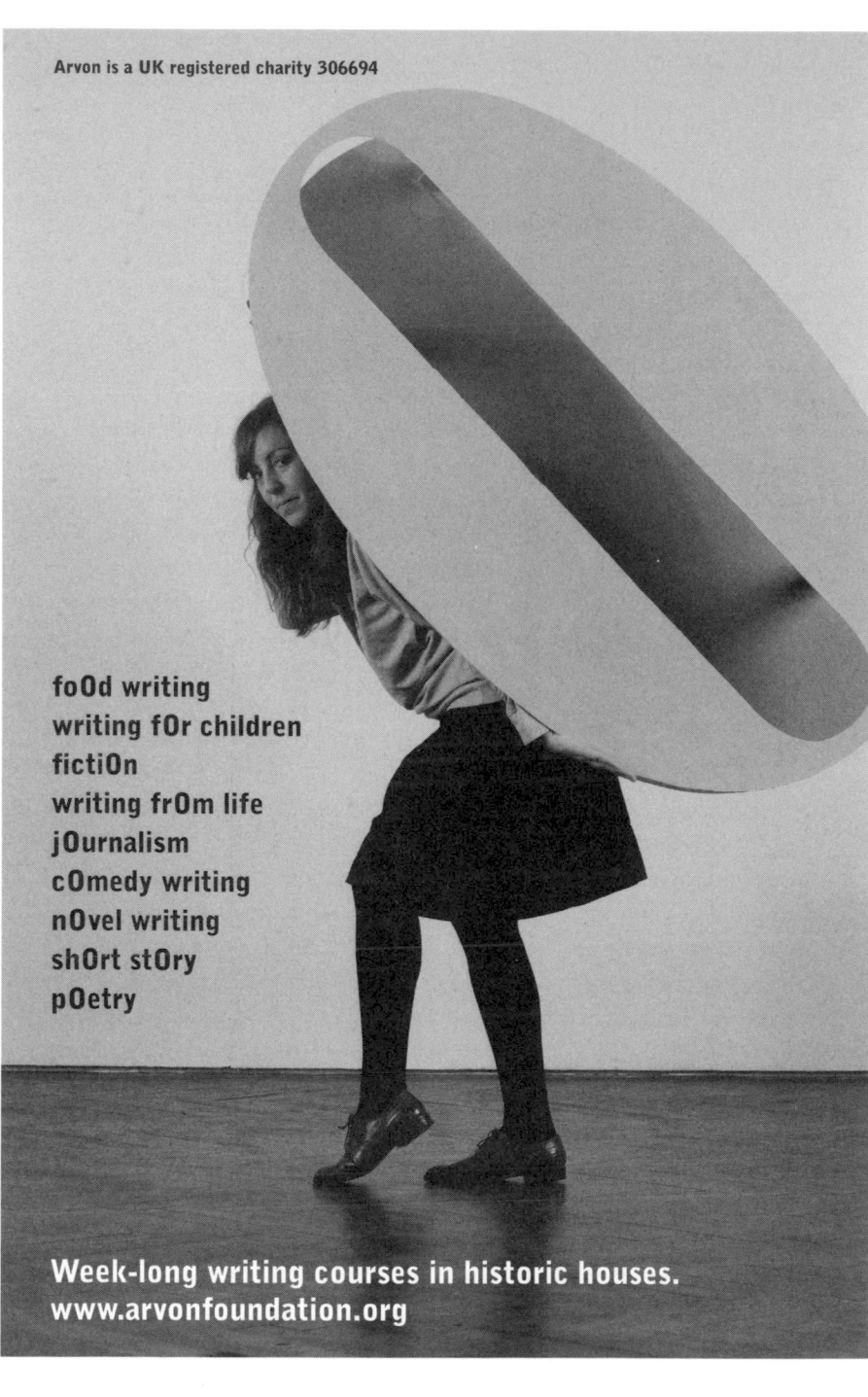

foOd writing
writing fOr children
fictiOn
writing frOm life
jOurnalism
cOmedy writing
nOvel writing
shOrt stOry
pOetry

Week-long writing courses in historic houses.
www.arvonfoundation.org

dialogue by providing snapshots of particular moments and by isolating emergent trends and movements.

This particular conversation has, of course, developed, not least because our literary discourse now encompasses far more readily writing that originates beyond the twin poles of America and Britain. But it might also be the case that the grand statement about literature, its provenance, its direction, its nature and its aim, has begun to seem anachronistic. Have we given up the idea of defining and characterizing contemporary literature because it has itself given up on the idea of a fictional project?

The counter to this argument is that the New American Writers, the Dirty Realists and so on, probably didn't see themselves as part of a group, and that writers – usually solitary, contemplative, dedicated to the expression of an individual sensibility – rarely do. Its reinforcement is that all writers work in a historical context, and their work will inevitably be inflected to a greater or lesser degree by the social, political and cultural climate of the time as well as by their personal circumstances or inclinations.

But labelling and categorizing have their perils as well as their undoubted uses. In the interview that Jhumpa Lahiri conducted with the great short-story writer Mavis Gallant for this issue, a portrait emerges of an artist determined to pursue her vocation at all costs, for whom the first step was to move continents and embark on a lifetime of what could be described as self-imposed exile. Her work subsequently draws heavily on the experience of emigration, isolation and cultural dislocation and disconnection; and on the specifics of French life and society following the Second World War. Gallant's fiction, and the perspective she provides on it here, bubble with glimpses into the period (the hostility of the English, for example, the first taste of French butter, the portrayal of Parisian cafe society as a flight from freezing apartments), with intriguing nods towards the shifting tectonic plates that form a writer. A question, however, remains: what would Gallant have written had she never moved from Montreal to Paris?

It is unanswerable, of course, although one feels that the attentive intelligence and commitment to language that characterize her stories mean that a different setting would have produced different work, but not necessarily an unrecognizably different writer, or no writer at all. But what the encounter between Gallant and Lahiri reveals is the extent to which a writer must first establish their own corner of ground from which to speak.

The stories we've chosen for this issue do not define an era nor encapsulate a literary movement. We have included work by several established writers – Paul Auster, Helen Simpson, Amy Bloom, Ha Jin and Nicola Barker – but we also alighted on writing by those who will likely be less familiar to our readers, for example the New Zealand writer Eleanor Catton, whose eerie story 'Two Tides' opens the issue, and William Pierce, who brings us a tale of mutual cultural incomprehension in the workplace in 'American Subsidiary'. We also feature a short graphic piece by Chris Ware, and an extract from a forthcoming novel by Adam Thirlwell, one of the last crop of Best of Young British Novelists. Beyond a certain kind of antic humour in evidence in several of the pieces, I would be hard pushed to identify a connecting thread, but that itself does not seem to constitute failure. It may turn out that fiction succeeds best when it represents nothing but itself. ■

Seen

A real bungalow is stone
and snow white mud
on the inner walls,
a large grate
and a slate floor
and a picture of itself.

Every cupboard is old,
every glass and cup
wiped clean.
The wind cannot get in
so the flies are free
to buzz against the glass.

Outside, blue twine
is tied to a telephone pole
and a gate
to keep the brown cows
in their field.

Fuchsia hedges, clover
in full juice:
purple clover, purple heather.

There's a silver line
on the sea between
green sheer islands:

Now the sound of the wind
playing a foghorn,
enters forgotten.

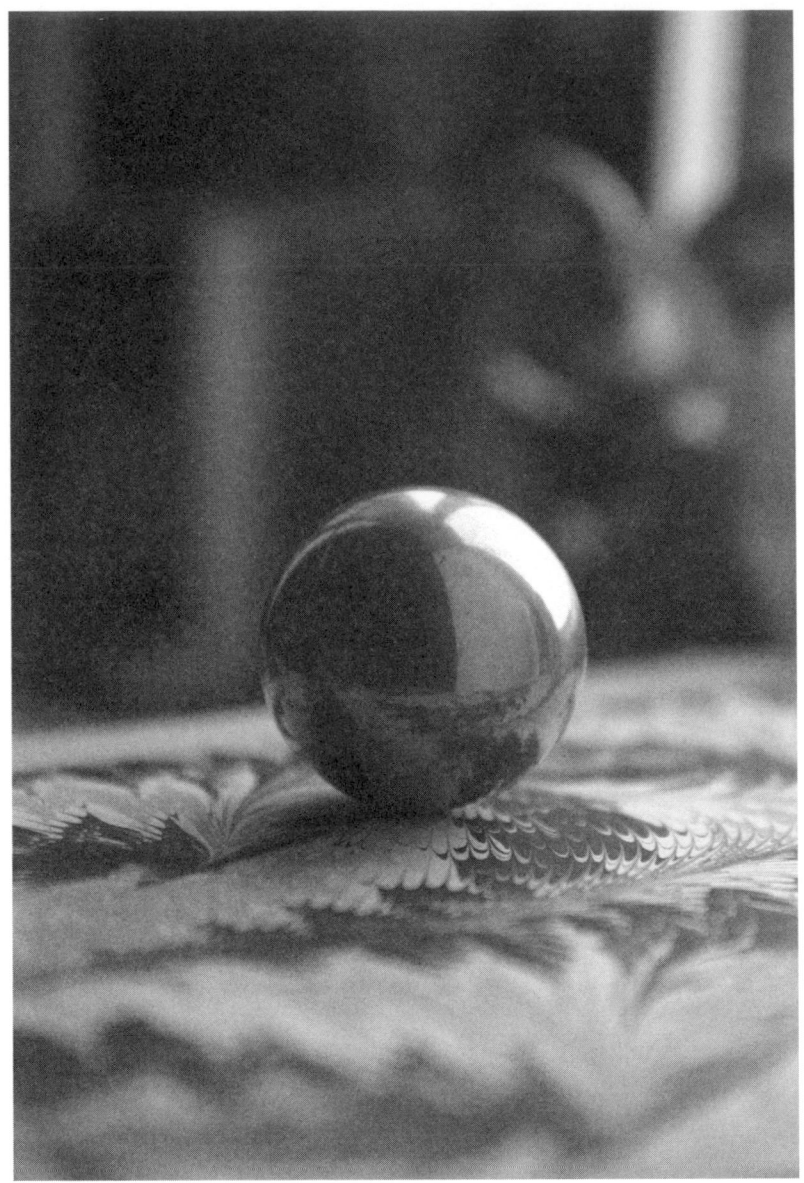

The music of the sphere

W e never grow up – only older, then old – and our need for toys does not abate. I still remember with awful clarity the bitter, angry tears I shed as a little boy when, on a family outing one Sunday afternoon to the Cistercian Abbey at Mount Melleray in County Waterford, my mother refused to buy for me in the gift shop there a miniature missal bound in white calfskin on which I had fixed a longing eye. Nowadays I write my novels in manuscript books handmade for me by one of the great contemporary master bookbinders, Tony Cains. These beautiful volumes, covered in Cockerell paper with vellum spines, are more than toys, of course, but at one of the many levels on which we engage with our possessions I am sure I see in them a consolation for that original, never to be forgotten, missed missal.

Another time, another desired bauble. It was in Arles, twenty-some years ago, that I spotted it, in one of those bijou knick-knack shops the French do so well, presided over by a handsome, melancholy lady *d'un certain âge*. To look at, it was nothing much, a seamless silver sphere the size of a 'steeler', as we used to call those jumbo ball bearings that trundled unstoppably through our games of marbles; when picked up, however, it made a delightful musical sound, a cross between the tinkling of a tiny harpsichord and a glass harmonica's ethereal whisperings.

I wanted it – oh, I did so want it. But I also wanted a music box with a prancing Pierrot on the lid, which played a tune from *The Magic Flute*, and since I could not make up my mind I chose neither.

My friends hung back, however, and ten minutes later appeared at the outdoor cafe where I was sipping a *petit blanc* and presented me with the musical ball; they knew me better than I knew myself, they said, and were sure I would never forgive myself if I were to leave Arles without at least one trophy. And they were right.

I loved that little silly thing, extravagantly, shamefacedly, superstitiously. I would make no journey without it, would board no train, embark on no boat, buckle myself into no aeroplane seat, if it was not in my pocket or my bag. Strangely, it never set off a single security alarm; I would walk through screening gates beltless, shoeless, walletless but with a metal object in my pocket the shape of a miniature anarchist's bomb, and no bell would shrill. On reading tours, how many lonely hotel rooms in how many anonymous cities have I crawled into at the end of another day spent impersonating myself, and picked up and listened to that ball, like a lost and landlocked South Sea Islander pressing a seashell against his ear to catch the sound of home.

And then, one day, it was gone. I had been to Australia and when I got home I searched in my bags but could not find it. Australia! That haystack, and my precious needle somewhere in it! I tried to track it down. I contacted hotels in Sydney, Melbourne, Adelaide; I called friends whose houses I had visited; I pleaded with airline representatives. No good, no trace. In one of Nabokov's works – this is another of my lost trouvailles – a character tells of someone losing something, a ring, I think it was, in a rock pool somewhere on the Riviera and returning a year later to the day and finding it again in exactly the spot where it was lost, but that kind of thing only happens in the Russian enchanter's magical version of our sullenly acquisitive world.

Elizabeth Bishop did her best to comfort me, when in her wonderful and jauntily melancholy poem 'One Art' she assures that the art of losing is one that is not hard to master, and that so many things 'seem filled with the intent / to be lost that their loss is no disaster'. And she is right, I know she is, this sensible and practical poet – 'Lose something every day' – for anything as doted on as my musical talisman was bound to make a break for freedom. I only hoped it was happy, playing its little tune for the wallabies and the platypuses out there in the Outback.

I found a source on the Internet and got a new one; it was bigger, shinier, and played what to my ear was a coarser music. It was better than nothing, but just about. And then, a year ago, preparing for another trip abroad, I took down the bag I had not used since coming back from Australia and heard something as I did so, a faint, far, plaintive little chime. I delved in an inner pouch, thinking of kangaroos, and there it was, in its scuffed old velvet bag, my original and best-loved Arlesienne. Some toys, it seems, do return from the attic. ■

TWO TIDES

Eleanor Catton

ILLUSTRATION BY GEORGE BUTLER

The harbour at Mana was a converted mudflat, tightly elbowed and unlovely at any tide but high. I had never been there when the tide was high. The birds were shags mostly. The fish were small. Low water showed the scabbed height of the yellow mooring posts, and the thick curded foam that shivered under the wharves, and the dirty bathtub ring on the rocks on the far side of the bay. The waves left a crust of sea lice and refuse and weed.

The marina was tucked into the crook of the elbow, facing back towards the shore. To make the hairpin journey from the shallow flats to open sea was dangerous, and so a central trench had been excavated in the seabed to create a channel deep enough for yachts to travel safely, even on the ugliest of tides.

'Bad luck to have a woman on board,' Craig said as I stepped down into the cockpit and took the tiller in my hand. 'That's the oldest in the book. But I'll tell you something else. There are grown men on this marina, educated men, who will never leave an anchor on a Friday. Grown men. Never leave on a Friday. It isn't just a quirk for them –

something runs deeper. And you know the reason why?'

I did: he'd told me this twice already, the first time at the yacht club with a gale wind thrashing at the door and the second time in the conical dry space beneath a fir tree on the Plimmerton domain, passing the last cigarette back and forth between us with our fingers cupped tight to keep it burning.

'No,' I said. I smiled at him. 'What's the reason?'

'*Vendredi* is French, that's Friday. Right? That's a word from way back when. And *Vendredi* means ruled by Venus. Right? And Venus is the ruler of women. And women are bad luck at sea. Right?' Craig sucked in the wind through his teeth. 'So never leave on a Friday.'

'Would you?' I said. 'Would you leave on a Friday?'

Craig thought for a moment.

'Say if the conditions were *perfect*,' I said. 'Say if the Strait was like *glass*.'

'Depends on the journey,' he said at last. 'If it was a day trip I would. But if it was some voyage – some huge beginning – I'd think twice. You don't want a curse on that.'

The limit was five knots inside the marina, impossibly slow. Even the speedboats seemed to drift. Once they passed the five-knot post you heard the grinding click and then the roar. The vessels ghosted by, passing close enough to whisper. I saw a seasick dog on a cabin roof and a charcoal smoker pouring steam and a scalloping basket hung like a flag from a boatswain's chair. It was still morning.

We left Mana with our faces turned back towards the harbour, watching the leading lights that showed the safe passage out of the bay. The leading lights comprised three colossal lengths of sewer pipe, diverging in three spokes and set into the hillside against the scrub. The central pipe was aligned with the excavated channel down the middle of the harbour, so if you were sailing safely you would be able to look cleanly up the length of the pipe and see the white light at the far end. If you strayed from your course you would no longer be looking down the unobstructed length of this middle pipe, and so the white light would disappear. Too far port and you would come into alignment with the left-hand pipe, which showed the warning red light; too far starboard and you would be aligned with the right-hand pipe, which showed a warning green.

There were two sets of leading lights in the harbour. The first was to guide you out of the marina and past the moored yachts, all shelved and slotted into the skeletal docks like a vast nautical library. Once these leading lights diminished in the distance and the light became difficult to see, you looked around to find the next set, fixed at an obtuse angle to the first and mounted on the shore above the motorway. The leading lights fascinated me. I drove the tiller to the right and left just to see over my shoulder the warning flash of green and then of red, leaping out from the hillside like a private flare.

Craig was smoking a cigarette and the ash was whipping off the butt and shredding whitely in the wind. The mainsail was up, but tightly reefed, and we hadn't yet switched off the diesel. He called the horsepower 'not quite enough to make a herd' and the description amused him so much that he had said it more than once, with minor variations. His foot was cocked, pinning a Primus stove upright against the hatch cover so it didn't fall and gutter as we bucked and rolled. The pale flame was invisible in the brightness of the day but I could see that the water in the billy was beading and ready to boil.

I was standing braced against the sides of the cockpit, half-turned and holding the tiller arm behind my back. 'Like backing a trailer,' Craig said. 'Just push the opposite to where you want to go.' I was not strong and my hand seemed to shiver on the tiller arm, the stout taper of teak wound around its length with a tight coil of waxed rope bleached grey by the salt and the sun. My awkwardness showed in the bunching lather of our wake. Craig's helming always left a crisp and minted streak; it conveyed a sense of purpose, a resolve. My wake was full of doubt. I looked back over my shoulder at the white spearhead stamp of our passing and watched the spume get sucked downward into the blue.

Craig flicked the end of his cigarette into the sea.

'That's what's missing,' I said. 'A dog.'

'You never met Snifter,' Craig said. 'Hell of a dog. He got so crook in the end, his skin just hung down. Kidneys. The boys said goodbye and I said I wanted to take him to the vet myself, in the truck, just him and me. But I took him out to our Foxton plot instead and we walked into the trees and I told him to sit, and I shot him. I bloody shot him. God, I cried that day. I cried. Could hardly see. That was a shit of a year. My dad died that year, and a bunch of other shitty stuff. Never found it in me to get another dog in place of Snifter. Buried him myself, under the trees.'

I'd seen the grave on his land at Foxton. There was a pine cross driven into the earth and a piece of aluminium was stapled to the upright spar like a plaque. With a shaky engraving tool Craig had written LOOK OUT, LOOK OUT, THERE'S A TERRIER ABOUT! and underneath, SNIFTER MᶜNICHOL and a pair of dates. I'd come across it on my own, ducking off to take a piss behind a blackberry while Craig lopped Christmas trees with pruning shears and dragged them by their stump ends to make a pile. My hands were sticky from the sap. Later we sat on collapsible chairs on the Foxton drag and drank a case of beer and sold the trees for ten dollars, five for the ugly ones.

I thought about him sobbing as he dug the slender grave.

'Christ, I loved that dog,' Craig said. 'It's stupid. It's stupid. Hell of a dog.'

He reached down and pinched out the Primus flame. With one hand wrapped in a gutting glove he picked up the billy and poured out the hot water into two plastic mugs jammed tight between a cleat and the steel frame of the windshield. He was alert to the pitch and roll of the boat and he poured in steady, deliberate gulps. Nothing spilled. He tipped in coffee grains and milk and used the saw blade of his pocketknife to stir.

'It's bloody primitive,' he said as he passed the mug to me. 'Bloody primitive, savage really. The milk – I steal those creamers, anywhere I can. I can't offer – savage really. Acid in your mouth.'

He was embarrassed. I said, 'It's exactly right. It's great.' My hair was whipped across my face from the wind.

'It's bloody primitive,' he said, scowling now, and then backed swiftly down the narrow hatch into the saloon. I heard him sliding the panels behind the engine where his tools were stowed. The tiller leaped against my hand and I flexed my arm to hold her firm. I listened to him rummage and over the noise I said, more loudly, 'It's exactly what I feel like.'

Craig was nervous when he showed me the marina for the first time. I think I'd expected something charming and toothsome, some old glamour gone to seed, but his boat was capable and wifely and broad.

The causeway between the berths had a central grip of chicken wire stapled flat to the planking and it was ridged every metre with a strip of dowelling that made our handcart ring out sharply as we walked. *Sea Lady, Gracie, Taranui, Stoke.* Craig pointed and said, 'Wanker – wanker – he's an alright bloke but the boat's just for show – wanker – *that* boat's been all around the world, would you believe it – she's just changed hands, haven't met the new owner – *he's* a wanker – look at that, isn't she a beauty? – see this one? That's the boat I'd want if I downgraded to a sloop. *Precision*, she's a piece of work. Owner's a right prick though. And *here*,' as we finally stopped, third from the end, beside the *Autumn Mist.*

She slotted snug between a pair of gin palaces, shining white bridge-deckers with tinted glass and squared-off cabins that sat high and proud in the water and bobbed brightly in the crosswind. The *Autumn Mist* didn't bob. There was a weight to her, a low-slung gravity, a guarded economy of pitch and roll that seemed quietly to undermine the jouncing of the boats on either side. She was mute-coloured and scabbed with rust, trimmed with sky blue and antifouled with grey. I saw the new wind vane, mounted above the dented gutting tray at the stern, but the clean whiteness of the fin threw the rest of the boat into poor relief. Her sail covers were patched and tatted and fringed with loose threads. The gaskets hung slack. The cockpit windshield was coming apart from its steel framing. There was a dinghy strapped upside down on the bow and the triple bones of its keel showed darkly silver where a thousand landings had worn the paint away.

I thought about dogs that come to resemble their owners and turned to Craig with the tease already in my mouth, but I was startled to see that he was looking downright anxious. He had turned red and he was flapping his hand strangely, turning his wrist over and over.

'What do you make of it?' he said.

I put my hand up to shield the sun. 'Didn't you say once? Man can only have one mistress. Didn't you say that?'

'That's the truth.' He looked pleased, and ceased his flapping. After a moment he said, 'Meet the mistress,' and we stood in silence and bucked on our heels against the wind.

'I'm looking for scratches on the hatch,' I said.

'Don't say that when we get to Furneaux.'

'Too soon, you reckon.'

'All the boys in the yard been calling me Scott, or Mr Watson.'

'Yeah.'

'That keel's an inch thick and she's been to Tonga and back.'

'Yeah.'

'The name is from "Puff the Magic Dragon". Silly really.'

'Lived by the sea...'

Craig said, 'I know she needs a paint job.'

'Sorry,' I said, repenting. 'I shouldn't have said about the scratches.'

'But antifoul is a fuck of a business. It's best to find some shallow bay, somewhere that gives you a big margin between the tides, low and high. Got to pop her on blocks and then paint like mad until the tide comes back. Or you can pay for the crane and lift, but you'd be looking at five hundred just for the privilege.'

'She's lovely, Craig,' I said. 'Really she is.'

'I been thinking, a dragon on the wind vane,' he said. 'Some cheeky dragon with a spade on the end of his tail. I reckon I might like that. Always in my head I called that dinghy *Puff*.'

He leaned out over the water to grab the stainless braid of the shroud and haul the vessel closer to the marina where we stood. For a second she didn't move. Craig's biceps stood out on his arm. Then the great weight rolled towards us, against the grain of her keel, and slowly the gap of water between the marina and the boat narrowed and then closed. The low side of the deck touched the buffered planking with a thud.

'Jen – my wife,' Craig said suddenly, as I stepped over the braided rail on to the *Autumn Mist* and felt the slow dip as she rolled under my weight, 'she'd be white-knuckled. Any time I tried to take her – she'd sit and clamp. White-knuckled. It's the way she always was.'

He stepped past me on to the cabin roof to unlock the deadbolt on the hatch and the blond wool of his forearm touched my hand. I was disgusted at myself suddenly and I said, 'But the badminton, and cycling, and the half-marathon. It isn't like – I mean, she's got the things she loves.'

Craig's keyring was a plastic buoy, to keep his keys afloat if they ever fell in.

'My marriage,' he said. 'You wouldn't – you don't – Francie – it's just—' and then he shook his head and rattled his keys and breathed hard through his nose and said, 'Cunt-struck. I was cunt-struck when I married her. That's all.'

I watched a gannet make a free-fall dive. Craig reappeared, holding a spherical compass that rolled around like a weighted eyeball in his palm. I watched as he climbed one-handed out of the hatch and fitted the compass into a socket in the centre of the boom. It was about the size of an infant skull, heavy and wet-looking, and it sat just low enough to show the phosphorous degrees that spun around its equator beneath the glass. The red needle swung and hovered in its lolling underwater way.

'You got to have a compass above board,' he said as he dropped back into the cockpit and unwedged his coffee mug from beneath the windshield sill. 'If you got a steel hull you got to mount it up above. Makes the needle go funny below.'

We were flanking Mana Island now. I watched the red needle pitch back and forth and tried to hold her at twenty degrees. The northern fingers of the Sounds were still pale and fogged and flattened by the distance. I saw now that the surface of the sea had a pattern to it, a weave, and I could feel it through my arm and the arches of my feet as a push or a pull. The wind gusts showed a long way off before they struck; they approached like a little burnished patch of silver where the water was disturbed. You could predict exactly the moment when the flat hand of the wind would strike your face.

I said, 'How long would they have lasted, the bodies of those kids? If he pitched them over and weighed them down.'

They had made an arrest for the murders, Hope and Smart. We saw it on the news. There were fingernail scratches on the inside cover of the hatch, and a slender female hair on a swab in the saloon. The evidence was small. But the man was sour and dirty and he had a bad family like a killer ought. The story was he'd pitched them over, both of them, somewhere deep. He might have raped the girl. What were we doing that night, we all asked – that New Year's Eve, a few dark hours past the midnight toll, while somewhere north of Picton two lovers were stabbed, or brained, or strangled, while the boats all around them trembled back and forth on some dark sheet of oily calm? Lovers. It was too awful. The worst thing was that no one knew – no one knew the method of the kill.

Craig said, 'They'd disappear. Flesh like that. Fish would eat them away in days, maybe a week. If he weighed them down all right. They'd disappear.'

Scott Watson's boat was called the *Blade*.

I said, 'The temptation would be to cover them in plastic. That's what I would want to do. Isn't that stupid? To want to preserve the bodies somehow. Like an instinct. To make them keep.'

Craig laughed and shot me a sly look. We didn't speak again for a long time. I finished my coffee and switched hands on the tiller and rolled my shoulder joint to feel it click. The cockpit floor was choked with empties, and mismatched sea boots, and the roped saltwater bucket, and a pair of life jackets that showed a fine spray of mould against the yellow. All of it shifted back and forth.

I watched him. Craig was short, five four. His hair had been reddish once but it was sandy now, white at the temples and the sides of his beard. He had a white scar above his left eye and a thick pink scar running down his left forearm like a vein. His hands were big. He was stocky and barrelled but his legs were slender and his calves were fine. I watched him watch the ocean and saw how his weathered squint had left the crinkles of his crow's feet untanned, so when his expression softened you could see two pale stars at the outer corners of his eyes. The tawny skin on the back of his neck was creased three times.

The first time I went to sea was as a child, when the replica of the *Endeavour* came to circumnavigate New Zealand and retrace Cook's voyage from the north. I sailed out to meet the great square-bellied ship in a restored yacht belonging to a friend of my father's. Lionel was a giant wrathful man who cursed at his children and ridiculed his wife, but from time to time he would lay his hands upon his boat with such a private, secret tenderness it was as if he believed himself to be alone on board.

Lionel kept the *Indigo* like a thoroughbred mare. A poor knot would turn him purple with fury. He screamed across the water at any vessel that flouted maritime law, and blacklisted any sailor who jammed the radio channels with ordinary talk. He would flare with a scarlet contempt if you said *rear* instead of *aft* or *back* instead of *stern*. He let nobody in the steering house when the *Indigo* was at sea, and he called for complete silence whenever he drove her glossy hips in or out of her marina berth, in case his concentration broke. We tucked ourselves against the mast on the aft cabin between his children and his wife and we tried to touch nothing, but he called us lubbers anyway. There was a brass plaque above the freshwater pump that read THE CAPTAIN'S WORD IS LAW.

Craig was generous with the *Autumn Mist*. He showed me every part of her. He watched while I fumbled with the tiller or dipped my hand down into the streaky black damp of the bilges or traced the fuel line to understand why the ignition wouldn't catch. He let me make the radio calls to the coastguard watch. He taught me to rope off the mooring line around the forward block and showed me how to cross the rope neatly over the top of the block so the knot could unravel with a single blow of an axe.

He said, 'Imagine if the boom clocked my temple and I went out cold. You have to know everything.'

When the *Endeavour* docked at Lyttelton we went aboard and marvelled at the five-foot ceilings and the swarming hammocks clustered tight and the giddy drop of the overboard latrines. They served limes. We touched the flayed catgut fingers of the cat-o'-nine-tails and learned how a single lash could shred a man. The crew were dressed in period costumes, rough linen for the seamen and covered buttons for the captain's men. Lionel hung back with his hands in his pockets and looked up the length of her mast. He said, 'Square-bottomed, now, and ship-rigged. Nothing much to look at. But what a life.'

The kauri shelves above the swabs in the *Autumn Mist*'s saloon were stuffed with faded thriller novels and food for the week ahead. In the morning before we left Mana I went below to stow my duffel bag in the V-shaped cabin underneath the bow and I saw that Craig had stuffed a box of Cadbury's chocolates into the stow hole beside the anchor chain. The box had been stowed so roughly: it was dented and a corner of the cellophane was pierced.

Craig was the full-time trucker and I worked weekends with the other girls in the store. The day that I came to work in hardware was the day that Craig became a kind of luminary in the timber yard. He shredded an order sheet in his customer's face, screamed, 'Don't you treat me like this shitty job is the only thing that makes my life worthwhile, you smug prick,' and then destroyed $600 worth of cement-board sheeting under the wheels of the delivery truck as he drove away with his middle finger out the driver's window of the cab. The ill fit of his leather working glove augmented the length of his finger by a withered inch where the glove sat thick and high on his hand.

This small detail, coupled with the fine Marxist flavour of his short speech, transformed the incident into an iconic protest, a movement on behalf of all the dirty timber boys who worked hard hours for a poor wage. He swiftly turned his celebrity to his advantage. He came to work blind drunk and slept through whole afternoons in the shade of the cab. He shaved each pallet-load of whatever he thought easiest to steal. He clocked false hours on his time card and often left inexplicably in the middle of the day, vaulting the fence and stuffing his red uniform into the scrubby tussock behind the gate. I think he only stayed on as a trucker to steal the diesel. Every morning he drove the truck home to his garage to siphon it into his own van, and when the van was full he filled whatever vessel was closest until the truck's tank ran close to dry. Every possible container in his garage was brimful of stolen diesel. There were drums and cans and barrels and buckets and jam jars lined up along his worktop bench. I even saw a sardine can – tiny, holding less than quarter of a cup.

The timber boys saw all of this and didn't rat on him once, even when they had to pick up the slack, or mop his sick, or cover for a lie. This was partly in recognition of Craig's heroic act of retail justice: he was a rebel darling now, and stood apart. But it was mostly from compassion, because everyone had heard the whisper that Craig was having trouble at home.

I was working weekends while I finished up with film school at the Newtown Polytech. When I took the job I'd just lost a lover for the first time. I was bitter. I drank a lot and cut my hair. I found in Craig a sympathetic streak of rawness, a muted anger, a grieving nostalgia that I thought I shared.

Craig said, 'I see a woman with a tattoo and I think, she's walked a little to the wild side. She's got spirit. I see a sense of adventure there.'

I said, 'It was stupid and now it's there for good.'

He turned my arm over to look at the bird again. 'All adventures are stupid,' he said. 'Anyone with any sense, they stay at home.'

Later, when I had spent more time at the yacht club, I came to understand that he spoke like a sailor. He talked often about mystery, and belief, and the deep and hallowed cradle of the sea. We were drunks together. I listened while he talked about his life, all the things he wanted and all the things he didn't have. He talked about the solo journeys he was planning, ten days to Fiji, three months to the bottom of Cape Horn. The parachute sail he wanted to buy, the anchor he couldn't afford. His depth sounder was broken. His mainmast needed to be stripped. His voice was always wistful. He talked about death by drowning, his brothers, his boys.

On the mainmast, each shackle was stamped with a stainless-steel tag that identified the lines: spinnaker, mainsail, jib. The stays and the halyards ran underneath the windshield and tied off on the two cleats behind the plastic sheeting, the main halyard on the starboard cleat and the jib halyards on port, so if the weather was foul and Craig was manning the boat on his own he could haul the sails without leaving the tiller. That was the first thing I noticed: the *Autumn Mist* was rigged for a solo crew.

I didn't meet Craig right away. One morning I was filling in at dispatch and the truck walkie fizzed and his voice came through saying, 'Top pair of tits in the trade office, get out here quick.' I buzzed back and said, 'Patrick's on lunch sorry Craig.' The handset fizzed again and Craig said, 'What's the use having a girl on the walkie line? That's a fine pair of tits wasted,' and then the light went out.

The hardware girls were doubtful.

Izzie said, 'Craig's drunk all the time.'

Gina said, 'He talks about sex.'

Laura said, 'He's gross. Patrick says he sleeps in the truck.'

In fact he slept on the *Autumn Mist* most nights, cuddled up on the swabs between a pair of sails. When I first stepped down into the saloon I saw the hollow that his body made between the sail sacks, one marked MIZZEN, the other MAIN. At nights he sat by the kerosene lamp that hung from a pivoted collar so it moved in rhythm with the swell. He filled the bilges with beer and the paper labels on the stubbies went soft in the water and peeled away. There was an extra fee for liveaboards so he left the marina early in the morning, before the yacht club opened and the fishers arrived. Showers were free.

After a while I asked about his wife.

'You'd be surprised,' he said. 'I lucked out with Jen. You wouldn't know to look at me but my wife is a very attractive woman. You wouldn't pick her from a line-up. You'd guess too low, I'd make a bet on that. She's a very attractive woman. I've had four affairs. Four affairs in thirty years. Christ, Francie, I'm a shit of a man.'

I asked about the women and he sucked on his lager and gazed up at the mounted row of trophy hoofs behind the bar, crooked downwards like tub faucets. He said, 'You would have liked the first one. Pat. She had a hell of a laugh. But I'll always remember: one night near the end I climbed up to her balcony to look in her bedroom window. She was there, with her husband, on her hands and knees. He was at her from behind and I'll never forget it, he had a blue magazine, a porno, open on her back. He was *turning the pages*. I remember it. As if she wasn't even there. God, she wasn't a beauty or anything. But *turning the pages*. And she just knelt there, rocking, hands and knees. Course I just crept away. But the image stayed. She got a job in Sydney after that.'

Craig liked to introduce me as his mid-life crisis to the salts at the yacht club. If anyone looked sceptical he'd just laugh and say I was actually his niece. That sounded worse, and he knew it.

At the yacht club there were lengths of waxed rope to practise knot work and Craig watched as I laid out the lengths on the tabletop and tried to copy the half-hitch and the Turk's head and the shroud.

'Pig's ear,' he said. 'Look at it! Jesus, do you have six thumbs? Remind me never to ask you for a handjob.'

He laughed and I laughed but the salts were quiet and they looked out the window or up at the television over the bar. Somebody coughed.

We both liked it, that nobody was sure.

At our Christmas party the store manager cocked his head at me and said, 'You and Craig are friends, I guess.'

I said, 'It's someone to share a drink with.'

He said, 'You're too young to be a cynic, Francie,' and handed me a beer. He must have kept watching from across the bar though, while I laughed at Craig's five-second pint, no hands (he dipped his nose into the glass and gripped the rim between his teeth, then lifted the glass with his jaw and threw his head back, and the pint disappeared in three open-throated slugs), because after a while he came back to me and said, 'What I mean to say is this. This is only a phase for you. This shitty job. Working weekends to earn a few bucks for a beer. But Craig is full-time. And he's a father. His kids—'

'His kids are grown up and they both live in Australia.'

'You got to understand. This isn't your *life*. Being a student is your life. Working here is just a phase for you. You don't—'

'It's a phase for him too.'

'Don't be a tourist. That's all I'm saying. It's not fair on him.'

I got to be mad at that, which was pleasant in its own way.

The fine-stemmed coral spray of the Sounds reached north as if it once had touched the other island, only to be knocked westward, out of true. Tory Channel, where the containers and the passenger ferries ran back and forth between the islands, was many miles to the east and from where I stood at the tiller I couldn't see a single craft in any direction. Even the fishing boats at Mana were out of sight now, hidden behind the island or melted flat against the diminishing coast. Wellington Harbour was invisible from this far west and there were no houses on the peninsula at all, just a dirty thread of a road that ran around the shoreline, long since swallowed by the distance and the mist of the sea. There was nothing. I couldn't even see any birds.

'I'm going to turn off the diesel,' Craig said. 'Turn those horses out to pasture for a spell.' He ducked back down the hatch and after a moment I heard a shuddering splat and then the sudden dead roar of the sea. I realized we'd been shouting. All at once the tiller lurched out of my hand and the boom swung right out over the water and the *Autumn Mist* pitched so violently that the edge of the starboard deck lapped under. A sheet of spray slammed into the windshield and hit my face. We spun like a coin and I saw the open mouth of Mana and the drunken whip of our wake, and then the sail snapped fatly and we spun back again. Craig lost his footing and fell back against the cockpit ladder. He laughed.

Craig had explained to me the concept of the sail ('You know how a plane lifts off? How a vacuum is created underneath the wing?') and the concept of the compression engine ('You know how a bike pump heats up if you pump it really fast?') but I simply couldn't hold the physics in my head. In practice I was utterly inept and growing hot with frustration as I hauled at the tiller and ducked under the boom again and again. The compass spun.

'See that?' Craig said every now and again. 'See? That's yawing, what we're doing now. And see that – how we're changing direction now? This is gybing. See how it swings? We're gybing now.' He didn't ask for the tiller. He kept low under the boom and turned his face to the sea.

Cook Strait is one of the most treacherous passages of open water in the world. The tropical bulk of the Tasman rushes in to meet head-on the fierce Antarctic rush of the Pacific, and in the narrow space between two islands the oceans vie for tidal supremacy, like two armies at a front. At French Pass, the narrow channel between d'Urville Island and the long arm of the outer Sounds, the seam between the two seas is so distinct that the water flows visibly downhill. Craig had seen it.

'Think of the whole of the Tasman trying to squeeze through that little gap. The water drops, clear as anything. I've seen boats on full throttle that can't make one bit of headway against the tide. It's amazing. It's bloody amazing. Never believed it until I saw it with my own eyes.'

He pointed out how the rat-tail threads on the mainsail showed the direction of the wind from the way they hung. Our course was about sixty degrees out and still weaving. My arm was sore.

'Tell you what,' he said. 'Sailing around d'Urville one time, just me on my own. I've got a mainsail up and that's all. Right? There I am nosing along, less than five knots probably, and then all of a sudden

Autumn Mist spun right around, like the minute hand on a clock coming round a full hour. She spins three hundred and sixty degrees, just like that, and then the wind picks her up again and she continues on. Looking back, there was only the tiniest of depressions in the water, like a fingerprint, to give any sort of clue. It was a whirlpool that spun me round.'

'Can you take the tiller?' I said. 'I think I'm going to be sick.'

'Bucket and chuck it,' Craig said. 'Get the wind on your face.'

On New Year's Eve Craig and I drove up to the dark hill above Wellington with a parcel of fish and chips and a crate of beer. We sat under the still blades of the wind turbine and as the sun went down we watched a tiny yacht tack its way right around the coast. The sky emptied over the narrow throat of the harbour. Even from the hilltop we could see whitecaps, which meant the sea was rough. The yacht blew back and forth. The slip of its sail stood out against the dark rumple of the sea.

'Hell's teeth. But still. They'll have a hell of a story if they make it,' Craig said.

'They're headed for Chaffers, anyway,' I said. 'They must be rich.'

'Too right,' Craig said.

He drank another six or seven beers and then he said, 'I'm not trying to get in your pants. That's the truth. It's just someone to talk to. Jen's got her sister. And her mum.'

There was a foam mattress in the back of his van. He slept there on the nights he was too tired to make it to the *Autumn Mist*. Behind the driver's seat was a twelve-pack of canned spaghetti, and a bulk stack of cigarette packets purchased duty-free, and a duffel bag full of underwear and socks. There were tools everywhere. It smelled of oil.

Sometime long after the faraway pop of the midnight fireworks we were both afflicted by a sudden flash of conscience and agreed that it was much too dangerous for him to drive. He always drove drunk. He'd driven drunk for years.

I remember Craig mumbling, 'I can sleep sitting up, the driver's seat is fine, it's fine,' but we just kept looking out over the ocean and he didn't move.

In the end we slept under the rough wool of his Swannie on the foam, tucked together so my head was on his shoulder and one leg was crooked up over his knee. In the morning I saw that the teeth of the Swannie zipper had left a bite mark along the bone of my arm.

The next morning was a Saturday and we were both rostered to work. My vision was bright and grainy and the skin on my face felt like sand. Craig's eyes were bloodshot and his breath was sour. He dropped me off three blocks from the store and then drove around for a while. I wasn't sober until after lunch. At afternoon smoko he waited for the other girls to stab out their cigarettes and walk away, and then when we were alone he asked me if I would like to take a trip to Mana where his boat was moored.

Olivia Hope and Ben Smart went to a New Year's party at Furneaux Lodge in Queen Charlotte Sound. The only access to the lodge is by water or over the walking tracks to the bays on either side. Sometime after midnight, they found that their accommodation plans had fallen through. It was too far, and too late, to get a water taxi back to Picton. They had been drinking. A local man offered them lodging on his yacht. (A sloop? A ketch? The detail would be crucial when both of them were dead.) When the police seized the *Blade* several weeks later the nail scratches seemed to clinch it: there had been a struggle, and someone had tried to escape. But Olivia Hope played the piano and her fingernails were always trimmed to the quick.

Furneaux Lodge is gorgeous. The cabins are weatherboard and stone and the lawns are lush. The bush comes right down to the water. It's a place for weddings. There's a pebbled beach and a wharf and the water is clear and warm.

The store manager in hardware said, 'Francie, don't you think it's bad taste? Going to Queen Charlotte, and everything. The very place. You know?'

I said, 'Come on. You can't think like that.'

'I'm just talking about respect,' he said.

The Watson counter-story was that the police had pounced too early. Their story was: Scott Watson was a dirty loner, but he was not a bad man.

Craig's patience with my helming had leached the afternoon away. With the diesel and the sail together we might have made the passage to Queen Charlotte in five hours, but without the diesel it could take as long as twelve. I realized that the light had paled. Sundown was at nine.

'See those islands?' Craig said now, pointing. 'Those two little teeth standing up out of the water there? We'll have a better view soon. They're called the Brothers.'

The Brothers were like dark chips of stone against the burnished blue of the Strait. One was taller and prouder: the elder and the heir. As we made our slow and arcing journey around them I marvelled at the deception of distance and space: the two rocks seemed to be constantly changing shape, revealing shoulders, elbows, knuckles, fusing together and then apart. The outermost fingers of the Queen Charlotte Sound slowly took a clearer shape before us. The hills were blue.

'You saw the *Endeavour* replica?' Craig said.

'Yeah. At Lyttelton though.'

'The place we're dropping anchor tonight is where Cook suffered the greatest disappointment of his lifetime,' Craig said. 'It was only when he climbed to the lookout on Arapawa Island that he saw how the Strait cleaved the two islands right through. Then he really knew the voyage was a failure. They were looking for the great southern continent. Right? The unknown southern land. It didn't exist.'

'I thought he came to record the transit of Venus.'

'Cover story,' Craig said. 'The official purpose was to look for the unknown southern continent, and claim it for the Brits.'

'Australia?'

'No. Something bigger,' Craig said. 'Some enormous land mass to balance out the top-heavy north. Something to give the world a symmetry. A kind of weight. In the beginning they thought the west coast of New Zealand was the edge of it. Not an island or a pair of islands. An edge.'

'And that's where we're headed.'

'Ship Cove,' Craig said. 'How's your stomach?'

'Empty,' I said.

The hills were darkest at the ridge. Their rims were sharp. The vivid purple faded into lightness where the hillside met the shore, so the still water seemed to give off a kind of luminosity, a haze. The winds died as the sun set and the Sound shimmered with perfect calm. Once we left the open water and entered the Sound we had to furl the mainsail and turn on the motor again.

Craig said, 'Six horses now. Not quite enough to make a herd.'

On that New Year's night above the bright lights of the city I asked him, 'Have you ever thought you might leave your wife?' I didn't mean for me. My bottle was beaded with moisture, and cold. We could no longer see the small white streak of the yacht below.

Craig said, 'My wife – my wife doesn't want an adventure. She draws a blank. Me, I'm restless. I'd rather quit a job and start again. I'd rather give the finger. And I can strike up anywhere. And – God. She's an attractive woman. You wouldn't think, to look at me. You wouldn't pick her for my wife.'

He fell silent. A bird called in the dark. Craig said, 'I don't know, Francie. How can I answer that? I left her before I even married her. There's nothing there to leave.'

'What's she doing now probably?' I said. 'Tonight, for New Year's Eve.'

'Waiting,' Craig said, and then he didn't speak again for a long time.

Night fell before we found our mooring. Like the leading lights at Mana, safe passage around the Sounds was navigable by another system of lights. Craig showed me how the nautical map of the outer

Sounds was studded with small lanterns, and beside each was a bracketed numeral in a tiny script. 'We wait for the flash and then count out the seconds,' he said. When we saw the white flare leap out of the darkness he began to count aloud until he saw the flash again. 'Thirteen,' Craig said, and consulted the map. There, on the outer edge of the slivered Arapawa Island, was a tiny lantern and the number thirteen. This meant that we could be sure that the light that we were seeing was indeed the Arapawa light, and so our position was confirmed; it also meant that the water between us and the island was clear, so if we sailed directly towards the flash we could be sure that we would not run aground.

'Think if we were *here*, and we had angled into this cove by mistake, thinking we were one bay over,' Craig said, stabbing at the map with his finger. 'We'd see the light flash, but then it wouldn't flash again because the lantern light would be obstructed by this flank here, and we wouldn't see it. Right? So we'd know we'd gone wrong somewhere. We'd retrace.'

The lights flashed, Craig said, so they could be distinguished from anchor lights, which were a constant white, and nav lights, which were a constant red and green. As we crept into Ship Cove I looked across the oily black of the water and saw a dull point of white shining out of the dark, and then another, and then a third.

'Oh, bad luck,' Craig said. 'That's bad luck. The moorings are taken. See here? Those three crosses? Show where the moorings are.'

'I definitely see three lights,' I said.

'So do I.' Craig looked back at the map at that moment and chewed his lip. He appeared older in the dark. 'Didn't think they'd be taken,' he said. 'But it's school holidays I guess. Damn.'

'Can't we share a mooring?' I said. I was holding the torch over the map for him but when I lifted it the yellow beam picked out the shrouds and they shone.

'You mean raft up,' Craig said. 'The way it's done, you shove a couple of buoys over the railing to keep from bashing together, and then you rope together tight, flank to flank.'

'Can't we do that?'

'You're only a metre apart then,' Craig said. 'With conversation and everything. It's worse than a hotel room.'

'But just to be safe.'

He rubbed at his chin with his forefinger as if he hadn't heard me. 'Plus, it's late,' he said. 'Be rude. We'd have to shout out over the water and they'd have to get up and help us motor up, to raft. No.'

'Should we go back?' I said uselessly.

'We'll motor close to the shore and drop an anchor. Hope she'll catch.'

She didn't catch. The seabed was rocky and too hard. Craig dropped thirty feet of chain and then another fifty. He said he hoped the weight of the chain would be enough. But he looked unhappy. We were thirty feet from the shore and if she dragged in the night the *Autumn Mist* would list on to the rocks.

He made stew from a can on the galley stove and scowled when I said it was good. After dinner we lit the kerosene lamp and played cribbage in the yellow light. Craig rummaged in the forward stow hole for the box of Cadbury's chocolates. He thrust it at me with a jerk and looked at the panelling above my head.

'May as well do a thing properly,' he said, which was funny, in the neglected seedy hole of the saloon, under the broken light fitting, in front of the unpainted stow holes, sitting on swabs that were stale and discoloured and patched. I didn't laugh. He watched me rip the cellophane and lift the lid.

'Turkish delight goes first in our family,' Craig said.

'With us it's the mint one,' I said.

'But we've got boys,' Craig said. 'That's a factor. Scrabble for the feed.'

I went topside to take a piss in the bucket and spit my toothpaste into the sea. When I came back down below, Craig was spreading a sleeping bag on the starboard swab. He said, 'This is for you. I'm going to watch the chain for a spell. Makes me uneasy. Thought of dragging. Couldn't sleep even if I tried.'

I fell asleep in my clothes against the sail bags and I think he must have tucked the sleeping bag around me where I was lying.

Craig was sitting in the cockpit boiling water for coffee when I woke up in the first gauze of dawn. The tide was high and the water was dull and flat. The *Autumn Mist* was hardly moving, but she rolled lazily under my weight when I climbed up the ladder out of the saloon. The ochre rocks at the water's edge showed like the rind of a fruit.

Craig moved his knees to let me past but I had to put my hand on his shoulder, for balance.

'We should have done a rolling watch,' I said. 'I feel bad.'

'You slept like a kitten. Your eyes.'

'Did the chain hold?'

'Hasn't dragged an inch. This is for coffee, if you want one.'

'Yeah. Have you slept?'

'No. Didn't mind,' Craig said. 'The stars were out. Wasn't cold.'

He was happy. He whistled a short little burst of something and then he said, 'This is what I wanted to show you. This – anyway. Here it is. Here it is. Dawn over the fiord.'

I sat down on the slats and drew my knees up to my chest and looked out over Ship Cove to the James Cook memorial and the mounted brass cannon on the shore. I could see the three moored yachts now, in the light, over the far side of the anchorage. They were all gin palaces, rich and smart, with swimming costumes pegged along the rails.

'Nothing stirred all night,' Craig said. 'They must be sleeping.'

IN THE CROSSFIRE

Ha Jin

ILLUSTRATION BY TILMAN FAELKER

The employees could tell that the company was floundering and that some of them would lose their jobs soon. For a whole morning Tian Chu stayed in his cubicle, processing invoices without a break. Even at lunchtime he avoided chatting with others at length, because the topic of layoffs unnerved him. He had worked here for only two years and might be among the first to go. Fortunately, he was already a US citizen and wouldn't be ashamed of collecting unemployment benefits, which the INS regards as something like discredit against one who applies for a green card or citizenship.

Around mid-afternoon, as he was typing, his cellphone chimed. Startled, he pulled it out of his pants pocket.

'Hello,' he said in an undertone.

'Tian, how's your day there?' came his mother's scratchy voice.

'It's all right. I told you not to call me at work. People can hear me on the phone.'

'I want to know what you'd like for dinner.'

'Don't bother about that, Mom. You don't know how to use the stove and oven and might set off the alarm again. I'll pick up something on my way home.'

'What happened to Connie? Why can't she do the shopping and cooking? You shouldn't spoil her like this.'

'She's busy, all right? I can't talk more now. See you soon.' He shut the phone and stood to see if his colleagues in the neighbouring cubicles had been listening in. Nobody seemed interested.

He sat down and massaged his eyebrows to relieve the fatigue from peering at the monitor screen. He yawned and knew his mother must feel lonely at home. She often complained that she had no friends here and there wasn't much to watch on TV. True, most of the shows were reruns and some were in Cantonese or Taiwanese, neither of which she could understand. The books Tian had checked out of the library for her were boring too. If only she could go out and chit-chat with someone. But their neighbours all went to work in the daytime, and she dared not venture out on her own, unable to read the street signs in English. This neighbourhood was too quiet, she often grumbled. It looked as if there were more houses than people. Chimneys were here and there, but none of them puffed smoke. The whole place was deserted after nine a.m., and not until mid-afternoon would she see traces of others – and then only kids getting off the school buses and padding along the sidewalks. If only she could have had a grandchild to look after, to play with. But that was out of the question, since Connie Liu, her daughter-in-law, was still attending nursing school and wanted to wait until she had finished.

It was already dark when Tian left work. The wind was tossing pedestrians' clothes and hair and stirring the surfaces of slush puddles that shimmered in the neon and the streetlights. The remaining snowbanks along the kerbs were black from auto exhaust and had begun encrusting again. Tian stopped at a supermarket in the basement of a mall and picked up a stout eggplant, a bag of spinach and a flounder. He knew that his wife would avoid going home to cook dinner because she couldn't make anything her mother-in-law would not grouch about. So these days he cooked. Sometimes his mother offered to help, but he wouldn't let her, afraid she might make something Connie couldn't eat – she was allergic to most bean products, especially to soy sauce and tofu.

The moment he got home, he went into the kitchen. He was going to cook a spinach soup, steam the eggplant and fry the flounder. As he was gouging out the gills of the fish, his mother stepped in.

'Let me give you a hand,' she said.

'I can manage. This is easy.' He smiled, cutting the fish's fins and tail with a large pair of scissors.

'You never cooked back home.' She stared at him, her eyes glinting. Ever since her arrival a week earlier, she'd been nagging him about his being henpecked. 'What's the good of standing six feet tall if you can't handle a small woman like Connie?' she often said. In fact, he was five feet ten.

He nudged the side of his bulky nose with his knuckle. 'Mom, in America, husband and wife both cook – whoever has the time. Connie is swamped with schoolwork these days, so I do more household chores. This is natural.'

'No, it's not. You were never like this before. Why did you marry her in the first place if she wouldn't take care of you?'

'You're talking like a fuddy-duddy.' He patted the flatfish on a paper towel to make it splutter less in the hot corn oil.

She went on, 'Both your dad and I told you not to rush to marry her, but you were too bewitched to listen. We thought you must've got her in trouble and had to give her a wedding band. Look, now you're trapped and have to work both inside and outside the house.'

He didn't reply; his longish face stiffened. He disliked the way she spoke about his wife. In fact, prior to his mother's arrival, Connie had always come home early to make dinner. She would also wrap lunch for him early in the morning. These days, however, she'd leave the moment she finished breakfast and wouldn't return until evening. Both of them had agreed that she should avoid staying home alone with his mother, who was lecturing her at every possible opportunity.

Around six-thirty his wife came back. She hung her parka in the closet; stepping into the kitchen, she said to Tian, 'Can I help?'

'I'm almost done.'

She kissed his nape and whispered, 'Thanks for doing this.' Then she took some plates and bowls out of the cupboard and carried them to the dining table. She glanced into the living room, where Meifen, her mother-in-law, lounged on a sofa, smoking a cigarette and watching the news aired by New Tang Dynasty TV, a remote control in her leathery hand. How many times Connie and Tian had told her not to smoke in here, but the old woman had ignored them. They dared not confront her. This was just her second week here. Imagine, she was going to stay half a year!

'Mother, come and eat,' Connie said pleasantly when the table was set.

'Sure.' Meifen clicked off the TV, got to her feet and stubbed out her cigarette in a saucer serving as an ashtray.

The family sat down to dinner. The two women seldom spoke to each other at the table, so it was up to Tian to make conversation. He mentioned that people in his company had been talking about layoffs. That didn't interest his mother or his wife; probably they both believed his job was secure because of his degree in accountancy.

His mother grunted, 'I don't like this fish, flavourless like egg white.' She often complained that nothing here tasted right.

'It takes a while to get used to American food,' Tian told her. 'When I came, I couldn't eat vegetables in the first week, so I ate mainly bananas and oranges.' That was long ago, twelve years exactly.

'True,' Connie agreed. 'I remember how rubbery bell peppers tasted to me in the beginning. I was amazed—'

'I mean this fish needs soy sauce, and so does the soup,' Meifen interrupted.

'Mom, Connie's allergic to that, I told you.'

'Just spoiled,' Meifen muttered. 'You have a bottle of Golden Orchid soy sauce in the cabinet. That's a brand-name product and I can't see how on earth it can hurt anyone's health.'

Connie's oval face fell, her eyes glaring at the old woman and then at Tian. He said, 'Mom, you don't understand. Connie has a medical condition that—'

'Of course I know. I used to teach chemistry in a middle school. Don't treat me like an ignorant crone. Ours is an intellectual family.'

'You're talking like an old fogey again. In America people don't think much of an intellectual family and most kids here can go to college if they want to.'

'She's hinting at my family,' Connie broke in, and turned to face her mother-in-law. 'True enough, neither of my parents went to college, but they're honest and hard-working. I'm proud of them.'

'That explains why you're such an irresponsible wife,' Meifen said matter-of-factly.

'Do you imply I'm not good enough for your son?'

'Please, let's have a peaceful dinner,' Tian pleaded.

Meifen went on speaking to Connie. 'So far you've been awful. I don't know how your parents raised you. Maybe they were too lazy or too ignorant to teach you anything.'

'Watch it – you mustn't bad-mouth my parents!'

'I can say whatever I want to in my son's home. You married Tian but refuse to give him children, won't cook or do household work. What kind of wife are you? Worse yet, you even make him do your laundry.'

'Mom,' Tian said again, 'I told you we'll have kids after Connie gets her degree.'

'Believe me, she'll never finish school. She just wants to use you, giving you one excuse after another.'

'I can't take this any more.' Connie stood and carried her bowl of soup upstairs to the master bedroom.

Tian sighed, again rattled by the exchange between the two women. If only he could make them shut up, but neither of them would give ground. His mother went on, 'I told you not to break with Mansu, but you wouldn't listen. Look what a millstone you've got on your back.'

Mansu was Tian's ex-girlfriend and they'd broken up many years before, but somehow the woman had kept visiting his parents back in Harbin.

'Mom, don't bring that up again,' he begged.

'You don't have to listen to me if you don't like it.'

'Do you mean to destroy my marriage?'

At last Meifen fell silent. Tian heard his wife sniffling upstairs. He wasn't sure whether he should remain at the dining table or go join Connie. If he stayed with his mother, his wife would take him to task later on. But if he went to Connie, Meifen would berate him, saying he was spineless and daft. She used to teach him that a man could divorce his wife and marry another woman any time whereas he could never disown his mother. In Meifen's words, 'You can always trust me, because you're part of my flesh and blood and I'll never betray you.'

Tian took his plate, half-loaded with rice and eggplant and a chunk of the fish, and went into the kitchen, where he perched on a stool and resumed eating. If only he'd thought twice before writing his mother the invitation letter needed for her visa. The old woman must still bear a grudge against him and Connie for not agreeing to sponsor his nephew, his sister's son, who was eager to go to Toronto for college. Perhaps that was another reason Meifen wanted to wreak havoc here.

Since his mother's arrival, Tian and his wife had slept in different rooms. That night he again stayed in the study, sleeping on a pull-out couch. He didn't go upstairs to say goodnight to Connie, afraid she'd demand that he send the old woman back to China right away. Also, if he shared the bed with Connie, Meifen would lecture him the next day, saying he must be careful about his health and mustn't indulge in sex. He'd heard her litany too often: some women were vampires determined to suck their men dry; this world had gone to seed – nowadays fewer and fewer young people were willing to become parents, and all avoided responsibilities; it was capitalism that corrupted people's souls and made them greedier and more selfish. Oh, how long-winded she could become! Just the thought of her prattling would set Tian's head reeling.

Before leaving for work the next morning, he drew a map of the nearby streets for his mother and urged her to go out some so that she might feel less lonesome – 'stir-crazy' was actually the expression that came to his mouth, but he didn't let it out. She might like some of the shops downtown and could buy something with the eighty dollars he'd just given her. 'Don't be afraid of getting lost,' he assured her. She should be able to find her way back as long as she had the address he'd written down for her – someone could give her directions.

At work Tian drank a lot of coffee to keep himself awake. His scalp was numb and his eyes heavy and throbbing a little as he was crunching numbers. If only he could have slept two or three more hours a day. Ever since his mother had come, he'd suffered from sleep deprivation. He'd wake up before daybreak, missing the warmth of Connie's smooth skin and their wide bed, but he dared not enter the master bedroom. He was certain she wouldn't let him snuggle under the comforter or touch her. She always gave the excuse that her head would go numb and muddled in class if they had sex early in the morning. That day at work, despite the strong coffee he'd been drinking, Tian couldn't help yawning and had to take care not to drop off.

Towards mid-morning Bill Nangy, the manager of the company, stepped into the large, low-ceilinged room and went up to Tracy Malloy, whose cubicle was next to Tian's. 'Tracy,' Bill said, 'can I speak to you in my office a minute?'

All eyes turned to plump Tracy as she walked away with their boss, her head bowed a little. The second she disappeared past the door, half a dozen people stood up in their cubicles, some grinning while others shook their heads. Tracy had started working here long before Tian. He liked her, a good-natured thirty-something, though she talked too much. Others had warned her to keep her mouth shut at work, but she'd never mended her ways.

A few minutes later Tracy came out, scratching the back of her ear, and forced a smile. 'Got the axe,' she told her colleagues, her eyes red and watery. She slouched into her cubicle to gather her belongings.

'It's a shame,' Tian said to her, and rested his elbow on top of the chest-high wall, making one of his sloping shoulders higher than the other.

'I knew this was coming,' she muttered. 'Bill allowed me to stay another week, but I won't. Just sick of it.'

'Don't be too upset. I'm sure more of us will go.'

'Probably. Bill said there'll be more layoffs.'

'I'll be the next, I guess.'

'Don't jinx yourself, Tian.'

Tracy put her eyeglass case beside her coffee cup. She didn't have much stuff – a few photos of her niece and nephews and of a Himalayan cat named Daffie, a half-used pack of chewing gum, a pocket hairbrush, a compact, a romance novel, a small Ziploc bag containing rubber bands, ballpoints, Post-its, dental floss, a chap stick. Tian turned his eyes away as though the pile of her belongings, not enough to fill her tote bag, upset him more than her dismissal.

As Tracy was leaving, more people got up and some spoke to her. 'Terribly sorry, Tracy.' 'Take care.' 'Good luck.' 'Keep in touch, Tracy.' Some of the voices actually sounded relieved and even cheerful. Tracy shook hands with a few and waved at the rest while mouthing 'Thank you.'

The second she went out the door, George, an orange-haired man who always wore a necktie at work, said, 'This is it,' as if to assure everyone that they were all safe.

'I don't think so. More of us will get canned,' Tian said gloomily.

Someone cackled, as if Tian had cracked a joke. He didn't laugh or say another word. He sat down and tapped the space bar on the keyboard to bring the monitor back to life.

'Oh, I never thought Flushing was such a convenient place, like a big county seat back home,' his mother said to him that evening. She had gone downtown in the morning and had a wonderful time there. She tried some beef and lamb kebabs at a street corner and ate a tiny steamer of buns stuffed with chives, lean pork and crabmeat at a Shanghai restaurant. She also bought a bag of mung bean noodles for only a dollar twenty. 'Really cheap,' she said. 'Now I believe it's true that all China's best stuff is in the US.'

Tian smiled without speaking. He stowed her purchase in the cabinet under the sink because Connie couldn't eat bean noodles. He put a pot of water on the stove and was going to make rice porridge for dinner.

From that day on, Meifen often went out during the day and reported to Tian on her adventures. Before he left for work in the morning, he'd make sure she had enough pocket money. Gradually Meifen got to know people. Some of them were also from the northeast of China and were happy to converse with her, especially those who frequented the eateries that specialized in Mandarin cuisine – pies, pancakes, sauerkraut, sausages, grilled meats, moo shu, noodles and dumplings. In a small park she ran into some old women pushing their grandchildren in strollers. She chatted with them, and one woman had lived here for more than a decade and wouldn't go back to Wuhan City any more because all her children and grandchildren were in North America now. How Meifen envied those old grandmas, she told Tian, especially the one who had twin grandkids. If only she could live a life such as theirs.

'You'll need a green card to stay here long enough to see my babies,' Tian once told his mother jokingly.

'You'll get me a green card, won't you?' she asked.

Well, that was not easy, and he wouldn't promise her. She hadn't been here for three weeks yet, but already his family was kind of dysfunctional. How simple-minded he and Connie had been when they encouraged Meifen to apply for a half-year visa. They should have limited her visit to two months or even less. That way, if she became too much of a pain in the ass, they could say it was impossible to get her visa extended and she'd have no choice but to go back. Now there'd be twenty-three more weeks for them to endure. How awful!

The other day Tian and Connie had talked between themselves about the situation. She said, 'Well, I'll take these months as a penal term. After half a year, when the old deity has left, I hope I'll have survived the time undamaged and our union will remain unbroken.' She gave a hysterical laugh, which unsettled Tian, and he wouldn't joke with her about their predicament any more. All he could say was, 'I'm sorry, really sorry.' Yet he wouldn't speak ill of his mother in front of his wife.

As Connie spent more time away from home, Tian often wondered what his wife was doing during the day. Judging from her appearance, she seemed at ease and just meant to avoid rubbing elbows with his mother. In a way, Tian appreciated that. Connie used to be a good helpmate by all accounts, but the old woman's presence here had transformed her. Then, who wouldn't have changed, given the circumstances? So he ought to feel for his wife.

One evening, as he was clearing the table while Connie was doing the dishes in the kitchen, his mother said, 'I ran into a fellow townswoman today and we had a wonderful chat. I invited her to dinner tomorrow.'

'Where are you going to take her?' Tian asked.

'Here. I told her you'd pick her up with your car.'

Connie, having overheard their conversation, came in holding a dishtowel and grinning at Tian. Her bell cheeks were pink while her eyes twinkled naughtily. Again Tian was amazed by her charming face. She was a looker, six years younger than he. He was unhappy about Meifen's inviting a guest without telling him in advance, but before he could speak Connie began, 'Mother, there'll be a snowstorm tomorrow – Tian can't drive in the bad weather.'

'I saw it on TV,' Meifen said. 'It will be just six or seven inches, no big deal. People even bike in snow back home.'

Tian told her, 'It's not whether I can pick up your friend or not, Mom. You should've spoken to me before you invited anyone. I'm busy all the time and must make sure my calendar allows it.'

'You don't need to do anything,' Meifen said. 'Leave it to me. I'll do the shopping and cooking tomorrow.'

'Mom, you don't get it. This is my home and you shouldn't interfere with my schedule.'

'What did you say? Sure, this is your home, but who are you? You're my son, aren't you!'

Seeing a smirk cross his wife's face, Tian asked his mother, 'You mean you own me and my home?'

'How can I ever disown you? Your home should also be mine, no? Oh heavens, I never thought my son could be so selfish. Once he has his bride, he wants to disown his mother!'

'You're unreasonable,' he said.

'And you're heartless.'

'This is ridiculous!' He turned and ambled out of the dining room.

Connie put in, 'Mother, just think about it, what if Tian already has another engagement tomorrow?'

'Like I said, he won't have to be around if he has something else to do. Besides, he doesn't work on Saturdays.'

'Still, he'll have to drive to pick up your friend.'

'How about you? Can't you do that?'

'I don't have a driver's licence yet.'

'Why not? You cannot let Tian do everything in this household. You must do your share.'

Seeing this was getting nowhere, Connie dropped the dishtowel on the dining table and went to the living room to talk with Tian.

However, Tian wouldn't discuss the invitation with Connie, knowing his mother was eavesdropping on them. Meifen, already sixty-four, still had sharp ears and eyesight. Tian grimaced at his wife and sighed. 'I guess we'll have to do the party tomorrow.'

She nodded. 'I'll stay home and give you a hand.'

It snowed on and off for a whole day. The roofs in the neighbourhood blurred and lost their unkempt features, and the snow rendered all the trees and hedges fluffy. It looked clean everywhere and even the air smelled fresher. Trucks passed by, giving out warning signals while ploughing snow or spraying salt. A bunch of children were sledding on a slope, whooping lustily, and some lay supine on the sleds as they dashed down. Another pack of them were hurling snowballs at each other and shouting war cries. Tian, amused, watched them through a window. He had dissuaded his mother from giving a multiple-course dinner, saying that here food was plentiful and one could eat fish and meat quite often. Most times it was for conversation and a warm atmosphere that people went to dinner. His mother agreed to make dumplings in addition to a few cold dishes. Actually, they didn't start wrapping the dumplings when the stuffing and the dough were ready, because Meifen wanted to have her friend participate in preparing the dinner, to make the occasion somewhat like a family gathering.

Towards evening it resumed snowing. Tian drove to Corona to fetch the guest, Shulan, and his mother went with him, sitting in the passenger seat. The heat was on full blast while the wipers were busy sweeping the windshield; even so, the glass frosted in spots from outside and fogged from inside. Time and again Tian mopped the moisture off the glass with a pair of felt gloves, but the visibility didn't improve much. 'See what I mean?' he said to his mother. 'It's dangerous to drive in such weather.'

She made no reply, staring ahead, her beaky face as rigid as if frozen and the skin under her chin hanging in wattles. Fortunately Shulan's place was easy to find. The woman lived in an ugly tenement, about a dozen storeys high and with narrow windows. She was waiting for them in the footworn lobby when they arrived. She looked familiar to Tian. Then he recognized her – this scrawny person in a dark blue overcoat was nobody but a saleswoman at the nameless snack joint on Main Street, near the subway station. He had encountered her numerous times when he went there to buy scallion pancakes or sautéed rice noodles or pork buns for lunch. He vividly remembered her red face bathed in perspiration during the dog days when she wore a white hat, busy selling food to passers-by. That place was nothing but a flimsy lean-to, open to waves of heat and gusts of wind. In winter there was no need for a heater in the room because the stoves were hot and the pots sent up steam all the time, but in summer only a small fan whirred back and forth overhead. When customers were few, the salespeople would participate in making snacks, so everybody in there was a cook of sorts. Whenever Tian chanced on this middle-aged Shulan, he'd wonder what kind of tough life she must have been living.

What vitality, what endurance and what sacrifice must have suffused her personal story? How often he'd been amazed by her rustic but energetic face furrowed by lines that curved from the wings of her nose to the corners of her broad mouth. Now he was moved, eager to know more about this fellow townswoman. He was glad that his mother had invited her.

'Where's your daughter, Shulan?' Meifen asked, still holding her friend's chapped hand.

'She's upstairs doing a school project.'

'Go get her. Let her come with us. Too much brainwork will spoil the girl's looks.'

Tian said, 'Please bring her along, Aunt.'

'All right, I'll be back in a minute.' Shulan went over to the elevator. From the rear she looked smaller than when she stood behind the food stand.

Tian and Meifen sat down on the lone bench in the lobby. She explained that Shulan's husband had come to the States seven years before, but had disappeared a year later. Nobody was sure of his whereabouts, though rumour had it that he was in Houston, manning a gift shop and living with a young woman. By now Shulan was no longer troubled by his absence from home. She felt he had merely used her as his cook and bed warmer, so she could manage without him.

'Mom, you were right to invite her,' Tian said sincerely.

Meifen smiled without comment.

A few minutes later Shulan came down with her daughter, a reedy, anaemic fifteen-year-old wearing circular glasses and a chequered mackinaw that was too big on her. The girl looked unhappy and climbed into the car silently. As Tian drove away, he reminded the guests in the back to buckle up. Meanwhile, the snow abated some, but the flakes were still swirling around the street lights and fluttering outside glowing windows. An ambulance howled, its strobe slashing the darkness. Tian pulled aside to let the white van pass, then resumed driving.

Tian and Connie's home impressed Shulan as Meifen gave her a tour through the two floors and the finished basement. The woman kept saying in a sing-song voice, 'This is a real piece of property, so close to downtown.' Her daughter, Ching, didn't follow the grown-ups but stayed in the living room fingering the piano, a Steinway, which Tian had bought for Connie at a clearance sale. The girl had learned how to play the instrument before coming to the United Sates, though she could tickle out only a few simple tunes, such as 'Jingle Bells', 'Yankee Doodle Dandy', and 'The Newspaper Boy Song'. Even those sounded hesitant and disjointed. She stopped when her mother came back and told her not to embarrass both of them with her 'clumsy fingers' any more. The girl then sat before the TV, watching a well-known historian speaking about the recent Orange Revolution in Ukraine and its impact on the last few Communist countries. Soon the four grown-ups began wrapping dumplings. Tian used a beer bottle to press the dough, having no rolling pin in the house. He was skilled but couldn't make wrappers fast enough for the three women, so Connie found a lean hot-sauce bottle and helped him with the dough from time to time. Meifen was unhappy about the lack of a real rolling pin and grumbled, 'What kind of life you two have been living! You have no plan for a decent home.'

Connie wouldn't talk back, just picked up a wrapper and filled it with a dollop of the stuffing seasoned with sesame oil and five-spice powder.

Shulan said, 'If I lived so close to downtown, I wouldn't cook at all and would have no need for a rolling pin either.' She kept smiling, her front teeth propping up her top lip a bit.

'Your place's pot stickers are delicious,' Tian said to her to change the subject.

'I prepare the filling every day. Meifen, next time you stop by, you should try it. It tastes real good.'

'Sure thing,' Meifen said. 'Did you already know how to make those snacks back home?'

'No way, I learned how to do that here. My boss used to be a hotel chef in Hangzhou.'

'You must've gone through lots of hardships.'

'I wouldn't complain. Life here is no picnic and most people work very hard.'

Tian smiled quizzically, then said, 'My dad retired at fifty-eight with a full pension. Every morning he carries a pair of goldfinches in a cage to the banks of the Songhua. Old people are having an easy time back home.'

'Not every one of them,' his mother corrected him. 'Your father enjoys some leisure only because he joined the Revolution early in his youth. He's entitled to his pension and free medical care.'

'Matter of fact,' Shulan said, 'most folks are as poor as before in my old neighbourhood. I have to send my parents money every two months.'

'They don't have a pension?' Meifen asked.

'They do, but my mother suffers from gout and high blood pressure. My father lost most of his teeth and needed new dentures. Nowadays folks can't afford to be sick any more.'

'That's true,' Tian agreed. 'Most people are the have-nots.'

The stout kettle whistled in the kitchen and it was time to boil the dumplings. Connie left to set the pot on, her waist-length hair swaying a little as she walked away.

'You have a nice and pretty daughter-in-law,' Shulan said to Meifen. 'You're a lucky woman, Elder Sister.'

'You don't know what a devil of a temper she has.'

'Mom, don't start again,' Tian begged.

'See, Shulan,' Meifen whispered, 'my son always sides with his bride. The little fox spirit really knows how to charm her man.'

'This is unfair, Mom,' her son objected.

Both women laughed and turned away to wash their hands.

Ten minutes later Tian went into the living room and called Ching to come over to the table, on which, besides the steaming dumplings, were plates of smoked mackerel, roast duck, cucumber and tomato salad, and spiced bamboo shoots. When they were all seated with Meifen at the head of the rectangular table, Tian poured plum wine for Shulan and his mother. He and Connie and Ching would drink beer.

The two older women continued reminiscing about the people they both knew. To Tian's amazement, the girl swigged her glass of beer as if it were a soft drink. Then he remembered she had spent her childhood in Harbin, where even children were beer drinkers. He spoke English with her and asked her what classes she'd been taking at school. The girl seemed too introverted to volunteer any information and just answered each question in two or three words. She confessed that she hated the Sunday class, in which she had to copy the Chinese characters and memorize them.

Shulan mentioned a man nicknamed Turtle Baron, the owner of a fishery outside Harbin.

'Oh, I knew of him,' Meifen said. 'He used to drive a fancy car to the shopping district every day, but he lost his fortune.'

'What happened?' Shulan asked.

'He fed drugs to crayfish so they grew big and fierce. But some Hong Kong tourists got food-poisoned and took him to court.'

'He was a wild man, but a filial son, blowing big money on his mother's birthdays. Where's he now?'

'In jail,' Meifen said.

'Obviously that was where he was headed. The other day I met a fellow who had just come out of the mainland. He said he wouldn't eat street food back home any more, because he couldn't tell what he was actually eating. Some people even make fake eggs and fake salt. It's mind-boggling. How can anyone turn a profit by doing that, considering the labour?'

They all cracked up except for the girl.

Sprinkling a spoonful of vinegar on the three dumplings on her plate, Shulan continued, 'People ought to believe in Jesus Christ. That'll make them behave better, less like animals.'

'Do you often go to church?' Meifen asked, chewing the tip of a duck wing.

'Yes, every Sunday. It makes me feel calm and hopeful. I used to hate my husband's bone marrow, but now I don't hate him any more. God will deal with him on my behalf.'

Ching listened to her mother without showing any emotion, as if Shulan were speaking about a stranger.

Meifen said, 'Maybe I should visit your church one of these days.'

'Please do. Let me know when you want to come. I'll introduce you to Brother Zhou, our pastor. He's a true gentleman. I've never met a man so kind. He used to be a doctor in Chengdu and still gives medical advice. He cured my stomach ulcer.'

Connie, eating focaccia bread instead of the dumplings that contained soy sauce, said under her breath, 'Ching, do you have a boyfriend?'

Before the girl could answer, her mother cut in, pointing her chopsticks at her daughter, 'I won't let her. It's just a waste of time to have a boyfriend so early. She'd better concentrate on her schoolwork.'

Ching said to Connie in English, 'See what a bitch my mom is? She's afraid I'll go boy-crazy like her when she was young.' The girl's eyes flashed behind the lenses of her black-framed glasses.

Both Connie and Tian giggled while the two older women were bewildered, looking at them enquiringly.

Tian told them, 'Ching's so funny.'

'Also tricky and headstrong,' added her mother.

When dinner was over, Shulan was eager to leave without having tea. She said she'd forgotten to sprinkle water on the bean sprouts in her apartment, where the radiators were too hot and might shrivel the young vegetables, which she raised and would sell to a grocery store. Before they left, Connie gave the girl a book and assured her, 'This is a very funny novel. I've just finished it and you'll like it.'

Tian glanced at the title – *The Catcher in the Rye* – as Meifen asked, 'What's it about?'

'A boy left school and goofed around in New York,' Connie answered.

'So he's a dropout?'

'Kind of.'

'Why give Ching such a book? It can be a bad influence. Do you mean to teach her to rebel against her mother?'

'It's a good book!' Connie spat out.

Tian said to the guests, 'Let's go.'

The moment they stepped out the door, he overheard his mother growl at Connie, 'Don't play the scholar with me! Don't ever talk back to me in front of others!'

'You were wrong about the book,' Connie countered.

Their exchange unsettled Tian, who knew they would bicker more when he was away. It got windy, the road iced over. He drove slowly. Before every lighted intersection he placed his foot on the brake pedal to make sure he could stop the car fully if the light turned red. Ching was in the back dozing away while her mother in the passenger seat chatted to Tian without pause. She praised Meifen as an educated woman who gave no airs. How fortunate Tian must feel to have such a clear-headed and warm-hearted mother, in addition to a beautiful, well-educated wife. Her words made Tian's molars itch and he wanted to tell her to shut her trap, but he checked himself. He still felt for this woman. Somehow he couldn't drive from his mind her image behind the food stand, her face steaming with sweat and her eyes downcast in front of customers while her knotted hands were packing snacks into Styrofoam boxes.

He dropped Shulan and Ching at their building and turned back. After he exited the highway and as he was entering College Point Boulevard, a police cruiser suddenly rushed out of a narrow street and slid towards him from the side. Tian slammed on the brakes, but the heads of the two cars collided with a bang; his Volkswagen, much lighter than the bulky Ford, was thrown aside and fishtailed a few times before it stopped. Tian's head had hit the door window, his ears buzzing, though he was still alert.

A black policeman hopped out of the cruiser and hurried over. 'Hey, man, are you okay?' he cried, and knocked on Tian's windshield.

Tian opened his door and nodded. 'I didn't see you, sorry about this, Officer.' He clambered out.

'I'm sorry, man.' Somehow the squarish cop chuckled. 'I hit you. I couldn't stop my car – the road is too damned slippery.'

Tian walked around and looked at the head of his sedan. The glass covers of the headlight and the blinker were smashed, but somehow all the lights were still on. A dent the size of a football warped the fender. 'Well, what should I do?' he wondered aloud.

The man grinned. 'It's my fault. My car slid into the traffic. How about this – I give you a hundred bucks and you won't file a report?'

Tian peered at the officer's cat-like face and realized that the man was actually quite anxious – maybe he was new here. 'Okay,' Tian said, despite knowing that the amount might not cover the repairs.

'You're a good guy.' The policeman pulled five twenties out of his billfold. 'Here you are. I appreciate it.'

Tian took the money and stepped into his car. The officer shouted, 'God bless you!' as Tian drove away. He listened closely to his car, which sounded noisier than before. He hoped there was no inner damage. On the other hand, this was an old car, worth less than a thousand dollars. He shouldn't worry too much about the dent.

The instant he stepped into his house, he heard his mother yell, 'Oh yeah? How much have you paid for this house? This is my son's home and you should be grateful that Tian has let you live here.'

'This is my home too,' Connie fired back. 'You're merely our guest, a visitor.'

Heavens, they'd never stop fighting! Tian rushed into the living room and shouted, 'You two be quiet!'

But Connie turned to him and said sharply, 'Tell your mother, I'm a co-owner of this house.'

That was true, yet his mother also knew that Connie hadn't paid a cent for it. Tian had added her name as a co-buyer because he wanted her to keep the home if something fatal happened to him.

His mother snarled at Connie, 'Shameless, a typical ingrate from un upstart's family!'

'Don't you dare run down my dad! He makes an honest living.'

Indeed, her father in Tianjin City was just scraping by with his used-furniture business.

'Knock it off, both of you!' Tian roared again. 'I just had an accident. Our car was damaged, hit by a cop.'

Even that didn't impress the women. Connie cried at Meifen, 'See, I told you there'd be a snowstorm, but you were too vain to cancel the dinner. Did you mean to have your son killed?'

'It was all my fault, huh? Why didn't you learn how to drive? What have you been doing all these years?'

'I've never met someone so irrational.'

'I don't know anyone as rude and as brazen as you.'

'Damn it, I just had an accident!' Tian shouted again.

His wife looked him up and down. 'I can see you're all right. It's an old car anyway. Let's face the real issue here: I cannot live under the same roof with this woman. If she doesn't leave, I will and I'll never come back.' She marched away to her own room upstairs.

As Tian was wondering whether he should follow her, his mother said, 'If you're still my son, you must divorce her. Do it next week. She's a sick, finicky woman and will give you weak kids.'

'You're crazy too!' he growled.

He stomped away and shut the door of the study, in which he was to spend that night trying to figure out how to prevent Connie from leaving him. He would lose his mind if that happened, he was sure.

On Monday morning Tian went to Bill Nangy's office. The manager looked puzzled when Tian sat down in front of him. 'Well, what can I do for you, Tian?' Bill asked in an amiable voice. He waved his large hand over the steaming coffee his secretary, Jackie, had just put on the desk. His florid face relaxed some as he saw Tian still in a gentle mood.

Tian said, 'I know our company has been laying off people. Can you let me go, like Tracy Malloy?' He looked his boss full in the face.

'Are you telling me you got an offer from elsewhere?'

'No. In fact, I will appreciate it if you can write me a good recommendation. I'll have to look for a job soon.'

'Then why do you want to leave us?'

'For family reasons.'

'Well, what can I say, Tian? You've done a crack job here, but if that's what you want, we can let you go. Keep in mind, you're not among those we plan to discharge. We'll pay you an extra month's salary and I hope that will tide you over until you find something.'

'Thanks very much.'

Tian liked his job but never felt attached to the company. He was pretty sure that he could find similar work elsewhere but might not get paid as much as he made now. Yet this was a step he must take. Before the noon break Jackie put a letter of recommendation on Tian's desk, together with a card from his boss that wished him good luck.

Tian's departure was a quiet affair, unnoticed by others. He was reluctant to talk about it, afraid he might have to explain why he had quit. He ate lunch and crunched some potato chips in the lounge with his colleagues as though he'd resume working in the afternoon, but before the break was over, he walked out with his stuffed bag and without saying goodbye to anyone.

He didn't go home directly. Instead, he went to a KTV joint and had a few drinks – a lager, a martini, a rye whiskey on the rocks. A young woman, heavily made up and with her hair bleached blonde, slid her hips on to the bar stool beside him. He ordered her a daiquiri but was too glum to converse with her. Meanwhile, two other men were chattering about Uncle Benshan, the most popular comedian in China, who was coming to visit New York, but the tickets for his show were too expensive for the local immigrants – as a result, his sponsors had been calling around to drum up an audience for him. When the woman placed her thin hand on Tian's forearm and suggested they spend some time in a private room where she could cheer him up, he declined, saying he had to attend a meeting.

Afterwards, he roamed downtown for a while, then went to a pedicure place to have his feet bathed and scraped. Not until the streets turned noisier and the sky darkened to indigo did he head home. But today he returned without any groceries. He went to bed directly and drew the comforter up to his chin. When his mother came in and asked what he'd like for dinner, he merely grunted, 'Whatever.'

'Are you ill?' She felt his forehead.

'Leave me alone,' he groaned.

'You're burning hot. What happened?'

Without answering, he pulled the comforter over his head. If only he could sleep a few days in a row. He felt sorry for himself and sick of everything.

Around six his wife came back. The two women talked in the living room. Tian overheard the words 'drunk', 'so gruff', 'terrible'. Then his mother whined, 'Something is wrong. He looks like he's in a daze.'

A few moments later Connie came in and patted his chest. He sat up slowly. 'What happened?' she asked.

'I got fired.'

'What? They didn't tell you anything beforehand?'

'No. They've been issuing pink slips right and left.'

'But they should've given you a warning or something, shouldn't they?'

'Come on, this is America. People lose jobs all the time.'

'What are you going to do?'

'I've no clue, I'm so tired.'

They continued talking for a while. Then he got out of bed and together they went up to Meifen in the living room. His mother started weeping after hearing the bad news, while he sprawled on a sofa, his face vacant. She asked, 'So you have no job any more?' He grimaced without answering. She went on, 'What does this mean? You won't have any income from now on?'

'No. We might lose the house, the car, the TV, everything. I might not even have the money for the plane fare for your return trip.'

His mother shuffled away to the bathroom, wiping her eyes. Connie observed him as if in disbelief. Then she smiled, showing her tiny, well-kept teeth, and asked in an undertone, 'Do you think I should look for a job?'

'Sure,' he whispered. 'But I shouldn't work for the time being. You know what I mean?' He winked at her, thin rays fanning out at the corners of his eyes.

She nodded and took the hint. Then she went into the kitchen to cook dinner. She treated her mother-in-law politely at the table that evening and kept sighing, saying this disaster would ruin their life. It looked like Tian and she might have to file for Chapter Eleven if neither of them could land a job soon.

Meifen was shaken and could hardly eat anything. After dinner, they didn't leave the table. Connie brewed tea and they resumed talking. Tian complained that he hadn't been able to stay on top of his job because his wife and his mother quarrelled all the time. That was the root of his trouble and made him too frazzled to focus on anything. In fact, he had felt the disaster befalling him and mentioned it to them several times, but they'd paid no attention.

'Can you find another job?' his mother asked.

'Unlikely. There're more accountants than pets in New York – this is the world's financial centre. Probably Connie can find work before I can.'

'I won't do that until I finish my training,' his wife said, poker-faced.

'Please, do it as a favour for me,' Meifen begged her.

'No, I want to finish nursing school first. I still have two months to go.'

'You'll just let this family go to pieces without lifting a finger to help?' her mother-in-law asked.

'Don't question me like that. You've been damaging this family ever since you came.' Connie glanced at Tian, who showed no response. She went on, 'Now your son's career is headed for a dead end. Who's to blame but yourself?'

'Is that true, Tian?' his mother asked. 'I mean, your career's over?'

'Sort of. I'll have to figure out how to restart.'

Meifen heaved a deep sigh. 'I told your sister I shouldn't come to America, but she was greedy and wanted me to get you to finance her son's college in Canada. She even managed to have the boy's last name changed to Chu so he could appear as your son on the papers. Now it's over. I'll call her and your father tomorrow morning and let them know I'm heading back.'

Connie peered at Tian's face, which remained wooden. He stood and said, 'I'm dog tired.' He left for the study.

Meifen wrapped Connie's hand in both of hers and begged, 'Please help him survive this crisis! Don't you love him? Believe me, he'll do everything to make you happy if you help him get on his feet again. Connie, you're my good daughter-in-law, please do something to save your family!'

'Well, I can't promise anything. I've never been on the job market before.'

Tian smiled and shook his head as he was listening in on them from the study. He was sure that his wife knew how to seize this opportunity to send his mother home.

For a whole week Tian stayed in while Connie called around and went out job hunting. She had several interviews. It wasn't hard for her to find work since she was already a capable nurse. The following Wednesday a hospital in Manhattan offered her a position that paid well, plus full benefits, and she persuaded the manager to postpone her start for a week. She showed the letter of the job offer to her husband and mother-in-law.

'Gosh,' Tian said, 'you'll make more than I ever can.'

Meifen perused the sheet of paper. Despite not understanding a word, she saw the figure $36. She asked in amazement, 'Connie, does this mean they'll pay you thirty-six dollars an hours?'

'Yes, but I'm not sure if I should take the job.'

'Don't you want to save this home?'

'This house doesn't feel like a home to me any more.'

'How can you be so cold-hearted while your husband is in hot water?'

'You made me and Tian always takes your side. So this house is no longer my home. Let the bank repossess it – I could care less.'

Tian said nothing and just gazed at the off-white wall where a painting of a cloudy landscape dotted with fishing boats and flying cranes hung. His mother started sobbing again. He sighed and glanced at his wife. He knew Connie must have accepted the job. 'Mom,' he said, 'you came at a bad time. See, I can't make you live comfortably here any more. Who knows what will happen to me if things don't improve. I might jump in front of a train or drive into the ocean.'

'Please don't think like that! You two must join hands and survive this blow.'

'I've lost heart after going through so much. This blow finished me off and I may never recover.'

'Son, please pull yourself together and put up a fight.'

'I'm just too heartsick to give a damn.'

Connie butted in, 'Mother, how about this? You go back to China next week and let Tian and me concentrate on the trouble here.'

'So I'm your big distraction, huh?'

'Yes, Mom,' Tian said. 'You two fought and fought and fought, and that made my life unbearable. I was completely stupefied and couldn't perform well at work. That's why they terminated me.'

'All right, I'll go next week, leave you two alone, but you must give me some money. I can't go back empty-handed, or our neighbours will laugh at me.' Her lips quivered as she spoke, her mouth as sunken as if she were toothless.

'I'll give you two thousand dollars,' Connie said. 'Once I start working, I'll send you more. Don't worry about the gifts for the relatives and your friends. We'll buy you some small pieces of jewellery and a couple packs of Wisconsin ginseng.'

'How about a pound of vegetable caterpillars? That will help Tian's father's bad kidneys.'

'That costs five thousand dollars! You can get them a lot cheaper in China. Tell you what, I can buy you five pounds of dried sea cucumbers, the Japanese type. That will help improve my father-in-law's health too.'

Mcifcn agreed, reluctantly – the sea cucumbers were at most three hundred dollars a pound. Yet her son's situation terrified her. If he declared bankruptcy, she might get nothing from the young couple, so she'd better take the money and leave. Worse, she could see that Tian might lose his mind if Connie left him at this moment. Meifen used to brag about him as a paragon of success to her neighbours and friends, and had never imagined that his life could be so fragile that it would crumble in just one day. No wonder people always talked about stress and insecurity in America.

Connie said pleasantly, 'Mother, I won't be able to take the job until I see you off at the airport. In the meantime, I'll have to help Tian get back on his feet.'

'I appreciate that,' Meifen said.

That night Connie asked Tian to share the master bedroom with her, but he wouldn't, saying they mustn't nettle his mother from now on. He felt sad, afraid that Meifen might change her mind. He remembered that when he was taking the entrance exam fourteen years back, his parents had stood in the rain under a shared umbrella, waiting for him with a lunch tin, sodas and tangerines wrapped in a handkerchief. They each had half a shoulder soaked through. Oh never could he forget their anxious faces. A surge of gratitude drove him to the brink of tears. If only he could speak freely to them again.

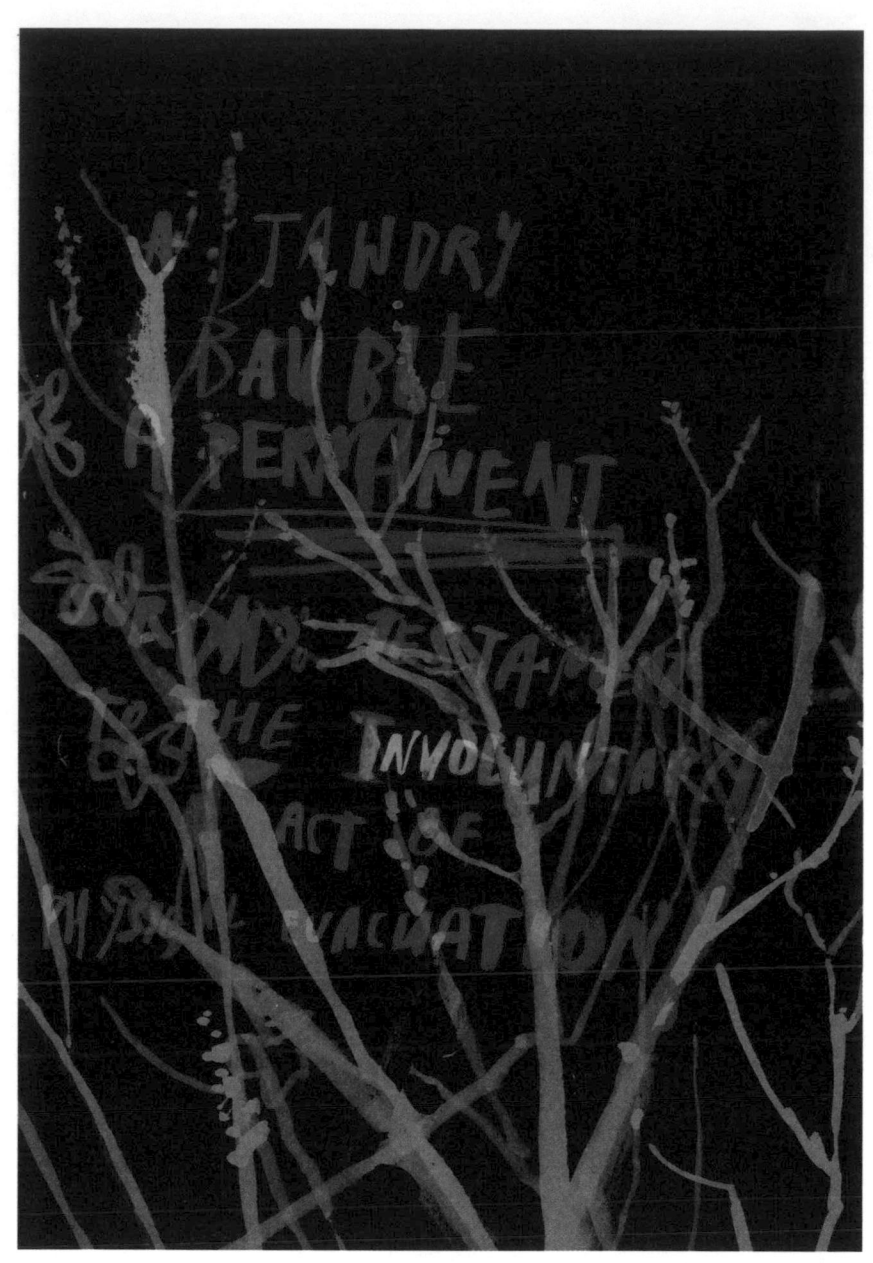

ILLUSTRATION BY CERI AMPHLETT

FOR THE EXCLUSIVE ATTN OF MS LINDA WITHYCOMBE

Nicola Barker

For the exclusive attn of
Ms Linda Withycombe –
Environmental Health Technician
Wharfedale District Council

> The Retreat
> Saxonby Manor
> Burley Cross
>
> 21.12.2006

Dear Ms Withycombe,[1]

Here is the information as requested by yourself on Friday, December 19, during our brief conversation after the public meeting re. 'the proposal for the erection of *at least* [my itals] two new mobile phone

---

1. Are you one of the Cirencester-based Withycombes? If so, then I was extremely privileged to serve with the Royal Air Force in Burma (1961–63) alongside your late, maternal grandfather, Major Cyril Withycombe (although – on further reflection – Cyril may well have been a Withyc<u>oo</u>mbe).

masts in the vicinity of Wharfedale...' (I don't think it would be needlessly optimistic of me to say that the 'nay's definitely seemed to have the best of things that day[2] – so let's just hope those foolish mules[3] at the phone company finally have the basic, common sense to sit down and rethink what is patently a reckless, environmentally destructive and fundamentally ill-conceived strategy, eh?)

Might I just add (while we're on the subject of the meeting itself) that I sincerely hope you did not take to heart any of the unhelpful – and in some cases extremely offensive – comments and observations made by the deranged and – quite frankly – tragic subject of this letter: Mrs Tirza Parry, widow (as she persists in signing herself in all of our correspondence; although on one occasion she signed herself Mrs Tirza Parry, window,[4] by mistake, which certainly provided we long-suffering residents of The Retreat with no small measure of innocent amusement, I can tell you).

Because of her petite stature, advanced years and charmingly 'bohemian' appearance (I use the word bohemian not only in the sense of 'unconventional' – the white plastic cowboy boots, the heavy, sometimes rather coarse-seeming,[5] pagan-style jewellery, clumsily moulded from what looks like unfired clay,[6] the popsocks, the paisley headscarves – but also with a tacit nod towards Mrs Parry's famously 'exotic' roots, although – as a point of accuracy – I believe her parents were Turks or Greeks rather than Slovaks; Tirza being a derivation of 'Theresa', commonly celebrated as the Catholic saint of information which, under the circumstances, strikes me – and may well strike you

2. Hurrah!
3. *Sic.*
4. Transparency is definitely *not* one of Mrs Parry's main characteristics!
5. I'll make no bones about it, dear: *phallic.*
6. Norma Spoot works part-time at the local butcher's, and told me – in between hysterical gales of laughter – of how she overheard Mrs Parry boasting (while she was having a chicken deboned last Tuesday) that her jewellery 'sells like hot cakes' on the Internet.

– as remarkably ironic. *NB I am just about to close this scandalously long bracket, and apologize, in advance, for the rambling – possibly even inconsequential – nature of this lengthy aside. Pressure of time – as I'm sure you'll understand – prohibits me from rewriting/restructuring the previous paragraph, so it may well behove you to reread the first half of the original sentence in order to make sense of the second. Thanks).* Mrs Parry has it within her reach to create, if not a favourable, then at least a diverting first impression during fledgling social encounters (I remember falling prey to such an impression myself, and would by no means blame you if such had been your own). There is no denying the woman's extraordinary dynamism (it's only a shame, I suppose, that all this highly laudable energy and enthusiasm is being so horribly – one might almost say *dangerously* – misdirected in this particular instance).

I've often remarked on how wonderfully blue and piercing Tirza Parry's eyes are – my dear wife, Shoshana, calls them 'lavender eyes', which I think describes them most excellently (although – as she has also remarked, and very tellingly, I think, a 'blueing' of the eyes can often signify the onset of Alzheimer's, dementia and other sundry ailments related to the loss of memory/reason in old age – I mean nothing derogatory by this statement – none of us are getting any younger, after all![7]).

You will doubtless remember Shoshana (from the aforementioned meeting) as that fearless, flame-haired dominatrix (with the tightly bound arm – more of which, *anon*) who was acting as temporary secretary that day[8] – Wallace Simms, who usually fills this role,[9] having been bedridden by yet another severe bout of his recurrent sciatica.

---

7. I do not mean to include you in this sweeping statement. That would obviously be ridiculous.
8. People refuse to believe that she actually became eligible for a free bus pass last February.
9. And then some! The poor chap's tall as a doorhandle but weighs in at over seventeen stone!

It briefly occurs to me – by the by – that it may prove helpful at this point (especially in light of some of the wild accusations being thrown around by TP[10] herself in the course of said meeting) if I provide you with a short *précis* of some of the complex, logistical issues currently being employed by that cunning creature as a pathetic smokescreen to obfuscate the real – the critical – subject at the dark heart of this letter. If you – like Mandy Williamson, your charming predecessor[11] – are already fully convinced of my impartiality as a witness/informant on this delicate – and rather distasteful – matter then feel free to skip the next section of this letter and rejoin the narrative in two pages' time (I have taken the trouble to mark the exact spot with a tiny sticker of a Bolivian tree frog).

The Retreat (please see first document enclosed, labelled Doc. 1) is a charming – although rather Lilliputian – residence situated just inside the extensive grounds of Saxonby Manor (I have circled the residence – and its small garden – on the map provided with a fluorescent yellow marker).

My dear, late wife (Emily Baverstock, *née* Morrison) inherited said property over seventeen years ago from her great aunt – the esteemed Lady Beatrix Morrison – who was then resident full-time at Saxonby (although she generally preferred to overwinter in the South of France, where she kept an immaculate, art deco-style penthouse flat in the heart of Biarritz).

When The Retreat was initially built (in the late 1920s) the property's principal use was as a summer house/changing room (situated – as it was – directly adjacent to a fabulous, heated, Olympic-sized swimming pool – now long gone, alas). It was constructed with all mod cons (i.e. toilet, shower etc.; see second document – Doc. 2 – a photocopy of the original architectural plans) and although undisputedly *bijou*, The Retreat was always intended to be more than

---

10. I'll abbreviate Mrs Parry from this point onwards, if it's all the same to you.
11. Did she have it yet? Was it – as I predicted – a bonny little chap with a bright tuft of ginger hair on top?

a mere 'adjunct'. As early as 1933 they added a small kitchen and a bedroom to allow guests to stay there overnight in greater luxury, and it was eventually inhabited – full-time – by a displaced family (the Pringles, I believe[12]) for the duration of WWII.

After the war it became the home of Saxonby's gardener, the infamous Samuel Tuggs (he sang and played the washboard with local folk sensations The Thrupenny Bits[13]) who was subsequently implicated in the mysterious disappearance of his wife's fifteen-year-old niece, Moira (1974) and – rather sadly for Lady Morrison[14] – while he was never formally tried for the crime,[15] an atmosphere of intense social pressure eventually obliged him to flee the area.

The Retreat's already fascinating history[16] was consolidated further when it was rented out (1981–90) to a writer of books about the science of code-breaking (a fascinating old chap called John Hinty Crew – 'Hinty' to his pals – a promiscuous homosexual whose real claim to fame was his inflammatory adolescent correspondence with Anthony Blunt[17]).

---

12. The youngest child's initials are still scratched into the bark of our old apple tree.
13. His voice ranged over several octaves – although my late wife used to say that while he might *reach* a note with all apparent ease, he could never actually succeed in *holding* one for any extended period. I used to tell her that this was simply 'the rustic style' (I'm fairly well informed on the subject), but she refused to be convinced.
14. The topiary was never as good after he left.
15. I call it 'a crime' although a corpse was never discovered (there were signs of a struggle and several suspicious spots of blood, however).
16. Bertrand Russell, the famous philosopher and coward, apparently stayed there on several occasions.
17. In the early 1990s these letters were adapted into a play called *My Dear Hinty*... I can't remember, off-hand, who starred in it – possibly that game young lad who used to ride his bicycle up and down those steep, cobbled streets in the old Hovis adverts. Either way, a dear schoolfriend of mine – Hortensia Sandle, an RE teacher, charming lass – who lived in the Smoke and had a penchant for the theatre – was persuaded to attend the opening

Up until this point the cottage possessed no formal/legal rights as an 'independent dwelling'. Lady Morrison had – quite naturally – never felt the need to apply for any, and my late wife's ownership of the property was only ever made explicit by dint of a short caveat in the old lady's will which forbade the sale of the Manor at any future date without a prior agreement that The Retreat (and its tiny garden) were to remain exclusively in the hands of the Morrison family. Rights of access were, of course, a necessary part of this simple arrangement.

It is, I'm afraid, this worryingly fluid and vague 'rights of access' issue that is the source of all our current heartache.

As you will no doubt have already observed on the map provided, The Retreat was actually constructed within a short walking distance of an arched, medieval gate in the outer wall of the larger estate, and this gate has always been used as an entrance/exit (into the village of Burley Cross beyond) by the inhabitants of said dwelling (rather than the main entrance to the Manor, which lies approximately 500 yards – again, see Doc. 1 – to its right[18]).

It goes without saying that many times over the years my wife(s) and I have applied for some kind of permanent, formal, *legal* right of way, if only to establish the property as an independent dwelling (so that we might pay rates, raise a mortgage, or even consider selling[19] at some future date, perhaps).

---

night (I'd been given free tickets by Hinty himself, but was a martyr to chronic piles at the time so found it difficult to remain seated for extended periods). I still don't know for sure what she actually made of the production (one review I read said the direction was 'all over the shop'), because – for some inexplicable reason – she refused to ever speak to me again afterwards. *Very* odd.

18. To use the main entrance would actually involve cutting through a yew hedge and then swimming across a large, Japanese pond full of ornamental carp.

19. The Morrison line ended with Emily. We had no children of our own – 'though certainly not through want of trying! Rumour has it that an inappropriate liaison between two first cousins in 1810 caused a genetic

Unfortunately, the current owners of the Manor (the Jonty Weiss-Quinns[20]) have never been keen to support this application. The chief plank in their Crusoe-esque style raft of objections[21] is that the land which lies between The Retreat and the gate was once the site of an old monastery (see Doc. 1 – I have used a pink pencil to shade in the area) which is considered by – among others – the National Trust[22] and English Nature to be 'an important heritage site'.[23]

Were you to come along – in person – and take a good look at what actually remains of this 'Old Monastery', I think you would be

weakness in the Morrison gene pool which rendered all subsequent issue physically and reproductively flawed. Aside from her infecundity, Emily had the added distinction of a third nipple. In poor light it could be mistaken for a large mole, but she was very self-conscious about it and always wore a robe whilst lounging by the pool. Once, on holiday in Kenya, she allowed her guard (and the robe) to fall and the mark was spotted by a sharp-eyed cocktail waiter. We were subsequently evicted, unceremoniously, from the hotel. To protect Emily's feelings I determined to keep the real reason for our eviction hidden from her (and was relatively successful, to boot). She always naively believed that we were turfed out because I queried the bar bill (and gave me no end of stick about it, too!).

20. Who have always been extremely genial landlords and have never sought to interfere with our ready access to the property – although they did kick up quite a stink two years ago when we built our conservatory or 'sunroom'. Apparently the light reflects quite sharply off its glass roof and can be seen very clearly from the window of their dining room (an added complication is that this small but precious 'space' was added to the property with the intention of creating a safe/therapeutic environment for Shoshana to sunbathe, au naturel. The poor creature is prone to seasonal attacks of chronic eczema and constant exposure to gentle sunlight really is the best possible cure).

21. Which I won't bore you with here.

22. Little Hitlers. It beggars belief that these people actually have the right to claim 'charitable status'.

23. I am considering trying to claim this same status myself – I'll be seventy-three in February!

astonished (as, indeed, are we[24]) that so much fuss could be generated by what basically amounts to a scruffy pile of broken stones (approx. three feet in diameter – aka the 'Old Cloister') and a slight dip or indentation in the ground (just to the left of the gate) which is apparently all that's now left of the 'Old Monk's Latrine' (!).

As I'm sure you can imagine, Shoshana and I have grown rather depressed and frustrated by this unsatisfactory legal situation, not least because our non-payment of council tax has allowed less sympathetic/imaginative members of the Burley Cross community[25] to accuse us of tight-fistedness and a lack of social/fiscal responsibility.[26] Much of this unnecessary hostility (as you are probably no doubt already fully aware) centres around the disposal/collection of rubbish.

The situation has recently developed to such a pitch of silliness and pettiness[27] that the local binmen have been persuaded[28] to ignore the black bin bags deposited outside our gate. This means that we are now obliged to skulk around like criminals at dawn on collection day, furtively distributing our bags among those piles belonging to other – marginally more sympathetic – properties in the local vicinity. Worse still, many of these sympathetic individuals – while perfectly happy to help us out – must live in constant terror of incurring the (not inconsiderable) wrath of TP, who has tried her utmost to transform this mundane issue into what she loves to call a 'point of principle'.

24. And you could hardly call us philistines – Shoshana is actually treasurer of our local History Club!
25. A marvellous, generous, open-minded bunch of individuals (with the odd, notable exception).
26. Last April Shoshana single-handedly staged and organized a charitable quiz night (in conjunction with Radio Wharfedale DJ Mark Sweet) to raise money for repairs to the church organ (which she plays – very competently – whenever the resident organist is away on holiday).
27. Encouraged, in no minor part, by the poison tongue of you know who.
28. Money changed hands. It definitely changed hands. I'm almost one hundred per cent sure of it.

As I'm sure you can now understand more fully, this complex situation re. the disposal/collection of our rubbish feeds directly into the severe problems the village is currently experiencing with TP and her borderline obsessive interest in matters surrounding dog fouling.

You mentioned (during our brief exchange after the meeting) that I might benefit from reading the latest pamphlet on this subject published by EnCams: *Dog Fouling and the Law: a guide for the public*) which your department usually distributes free to interested parties (although due to a temporary snarl-up with the council's acquisitions budget you regretted that you had yet to acquire any for general distribution – or even, you confessed, to become better acquainted with the finer details of said document yourself). I didn't get a chance to tell you at the time that I already possess several copies of this useful booklet (and have – as you will doubtless have already noticed[29] – taken the liberty of enclosing one for your own, personal use[30]).

Among the more fascinating details contained therein are the extraordinary statistics that (pg 2) the UK's population of approximately 7.4 million dogs produces, on average, around 1,000 tonnes of excrement/day.

Burley Cross (human population: 210; dog population: 33; cat population: 47)[31] certainly produces its fair share of the above, but,

---

29. The cover photo of a booted foot suspended above a huge pile of steaming excrement is certainly eye-catching. Shoshana is very squeamish and will not allow me to keep my copies in the house (even wrong-side-up!) so I have been obliged to resort to storing them – and all correspondence relating to this issue – on a shallow back shelf inside our tiny garden shed.
30. No need to return it. The yellow marks on the back cover are nothing more sinister than grass stains (from where it accidentally fell into my lawnmower's clippings bin on retrieval).
31. Although felines – very helpfully, but with the odd exception – bury their own.

thanks to a – by and large – very responsible, slightly older[32] population, the provision of two, special poop-scoop bins within the heart of the village and the wonderful, wide expanses of surrounding heath and moorland lying beyond, the matter had never – until TP's sudden arrival in our midst[33] – become an issue of serious public concern.[34]

I confess that I have walked[35] Shoshana's pedigree spitz, Samson,[36] morning and evening, regular as clockwork, for almost five years now,[37] and during that time have rarely – if ever – had my excursions sullied by the unwelcome apprehension of a superfluity of dog mess. If Samson – in common with most other sensible dogs I know – feels the urge to 'do his business', then he is usually more than happy to 'perform' some short distance off the path (his modesty happily preserved by delicate fronds of feathery bracken) on the wild expanses of our local moor. Here, dog faeces – along with other animal faeces, including those of the moorland sheep, fox and badger – are able to decompose naturally (usually within – on average – a ten-day period, depending – of course – on the specific climatic conditions). If Samson is 'caught short' and needs to 'go' in a less convenient location then I automatically pick up his 'business' and dispose of it accordingly.

Further to a series of in-depth discussions with a significant number of the dog owners in this village (and its local environs), I think

32. The average age of your Burley Cross resident is fifty-nine (this is a quotable statistic – feel free to use it – I researched it myself).
33. Approximately eighteen months ago.
34. That said, I was utterly appalled by the filth I encountered on a day trip to Haworth in 'Brontë country' recently.
35. And not without occasional resistance – especially on icy winter mornings!
36. Shoshana's family have a tradition of naming their dogs after Biblical characters.
37. Samson actually turns eight this year – he was a rescue dog and three years old when we got him. But before Samson I regularly walked Shoshana's beloved Highland terrier, Hezekiah (or 'Zeke') – although we were not resident full-time in Burley Cross at that stage.

it would be fair to say that the model I follow with Samson is the model that most other reasonable people also adhere to *i.e.* the collection of dog mess is <u>only</u> appropriate within an 'urban/residential' setting, in public parks (where people are liable to picnic, stroll, relax, and children play) and finally — under very special circumstances — where your animal might be perceived to have 'despoiled' a well-used moorland path to the detriment of other walkers' enjoyment of it (although this last requirement is not legally binding but simply a question of community spirit).

I believe I am correct in saying that all of the above criteria tally perfectly with the procedures formally established by local government, and that — up until TP chanced to throw her very large (very filthy!) spanner into the works — these procedures were generally held to be not only just, but successful, necessary and universally beneficial.

With the arrival of TP, however, this fragile consensus was attacked, savagely mauled and rent asunder.[38] TP, as you may well know, owns four large German shepherds and prefers — rather eccentrically — to take them on long walks on the moor in the moonlight (I say 'them', although so far as I am aware she only ever walks one dog at any given time[39]). These four, large dogs are usually kept confined inside a concrete 'compound'[40] in the back garden of Hursley End — her dilapidated bungalow on Lamb's Green.

It was initially — she insists — due to the difficulties she experienced in negotiating/avoiding random dog faeces during these night-time

---

38. Like an innocent, young rabbit cruelly disembowelled by a savage fox (and this is an entirely pointless killing — the cruel fox is not hungry — it does not pause to eat the rabbit — it has already killed and consumed the mother — so attacks the young one purely for 'sport').

39. Pathetic creature. *Hugely* overweight. And I'm pretty convinced that it's always the *same* dog she walks — it seems to be lame in one of its back legs — although I've never had the chance to meet it — and so identify it — in daylight.

40. No judgement whatsoever is involved in my use of this word.

hikes that her bizarre habit of bagging other people's dogs' faeces and leaving them deposited on branches, walls and fence posts – apparently as a warning/ admonishment to others less responsible than herself – commenced.[41] This activity continued for upwards of six months before anyone either commented on it publicly or felt the urge to root out/apprehend the strange individual in our midst who had inexplicably chosen to enact this 'special service' on our behalf.[42]

Given the idiosyncratic nature of the bags employed (TP prefers a small, pink-tinged, transparent bag[43] – probably better adapted for household use i.e. freezing meat[44] – instead of the usual, custom-made, matt-black kind[45]) it was easy – from very early on – to understand that the person bagging up and 'displaying' these faeces was not only happy, but almost *keen* to leave some kind of 'signature' behind.

When the bags were eventually identified as belonging to none other than TP (and she was calmly – very *sensitively* – confronted with her crimes), rather than apologizing, quietly retreating, or putting a summary halt to her bizarre activities, she responded – somewhat perversely – by actively *redoubling* her poop-gathering efforts! In fact she went *still one stage further*! She began to present herself in public[46] as a wronged party, as a necessary – if chronically undervalued – environmental watchdog, as a doughty, cruelly misunderstood moral crusader, standing alone and defenceless – clutching her trademark, transparent poo-bag to her heaving chest – against the freely defecating heathen marauder!

41. Although one really has to wonder at her facility to locate these random faeces in order to bag them up when it's apparently so difficult for her to avoid stepping in them in the first place!
42. I'm guessing that this is because the habit took a while to become properly established and then suddenly snowballed after the first few months.
43. The contents are, therefore, always fully visible.
44. Chops, perhaps, or liver/kidney/tongue and other smaller cuts.
45. To be purchased at any large supermarket or pet shop.
46. Quite belligerently.

And it gets worse! She then went on the offensive (see Docs. 3+4 – copies of letters sent to the local press), angrily accusing the general body of responsible dog owners in Burley Cross of actively destroying the picturesque and historic moor by encouraging our animals to 'evacuate'[47] there.

One occasion, in particular, stands out in my mind. I met her – quite by chance – on a sunny afternoon, overburdened by shopping from the village store.[48] I offered to take her bags for her and during the walk back to her home took some pains to explain to her that there was *no actual legal requirement* for dog owners to collect their dog's faeces from the surrounding farm and moorland (The Dogs Fouling of Land Act, 1996). Her reaction to this news was to blush to the roots of her hair, spit out the word 'justifier!', roughly snatch her bags from me[49] and then quote, at length, like a thing possessed (as if reciting some ancient, biblical proverb[50]) from the (aforementioned) EnCams publication on the subject.[51]

To return to this useful document for just a moment, in *Dog Fouling and the Law*, EnCams provide an invaluable 'profile of a dog fouler' (page 4 – when you read it for yourself you will discover that it is an extremely thorough and thought-provoking piece of analysis). Apparently the average 'fouler' enjoys watching TV and attending the cinema but has a profound mistrust of soap opera, around half of them have Internet access – mainly at home – but 'are not particularly confident in its usage', and they are most likely to read the *Sun* and *Mirror* (but very rarely the *Daily Mail* or the *Financial Times*).[52]

---

47. *Her* word.
48. God only knows what she had in those damn bags – they weighed a tonne!
49. Lucky for TP we were only fifty or so yards from her front door at this stage.
50. And quite incorrectly, it later transpired.
51. I had yet to come across this valuable little booklet and so was, as you can imagine, somewhat confused and nonplussed by this attack.
52. We get the *Sunday Express* at The Retreat, but only for the sudoku.

EnCams have invented their own broad label to describe these irresponsible individuals: they call them 'justifiers' i.e. they justify their behaviour on the grounds of a) *Ignorance* ('I didn't realize it was a problem...' 'But nobody has ever mentioned this to me before...' etc.) and b) *Laziness* ('But nobody else ever picks it up, so why should I?').

EnCams insist that these 'justifiers' will only ever openly admit that they allow their dog to foul in public when placed under extreme duress. Their fundamental instinct is to simply pretend it hasn't happened or to lie about it.

Although I cannot deny that this profile is both interesting and – I don't doubt – perfectly valid in many – if not *most* – instances, TP was nevertheless entirely wrong to try and label me – of all people – with this wildly inappropriate nomenclature: I am neither ignorant, lazy nor in denial. Quite the opposite, in fact. I am informed, proactive and socially aware. And although I do dislike soaps,[53] I very rarely go to the cinema,[54] and my computer skills are – as this letter itself, I hope, will attest – universally acknowledged to be tip-top.

Since my acquisition of the EnCams document I have tried – countless times – to explain to TP (see Doc. 5 + Doc. 6: some valuable examples of our early correspondence) that not only am I a keen advocate of poop-scooping in residential areas and public parks, but that it shows *absolutely no moral or intellectual inconsistency on my part* to hold that allowing excrement to decompose naturally on the moor is infinitely more environmental than bagging it up and adding it, quite unthinkingly, to this small island's already chronically over-extended quantities of landfill. I have also told her that by simply bagging up the faeces she finds and then dumping them, willy-nilly, she is only serving to exacerbate the 'problem'[55] because the excrement cannot be

---

53. Shoshana, I must confess, is an avid *Corrie* fan.
54. The last film I saw was *The Full Monty*, and I only went to that because my late wife convinced me it was all about El Alamein.
55. Although – as I've already emphasized – there *wasn't* a problem before TP arrived on the scene – TP *is* the problem!

expected to decompose inside its plastic skin. Rather than helping matters she is actually making them infinitely worse – once bagged, the excrement is there forever: a tawdry bauble – a permanent, sordid testament to the involuntary act of physical evacuation!

As you will no doubt be aware, around two months ago Wharfedale's Dog Warden – the 'criminally over-subscribed'[56] Trevor Horsmith – was persuaded[57] to start to take an interest in the problems being generated by TP's activities on the moor. It will probably strike you as intensely ironic that *TP herself* was one of the main instigators in finally involving Trevor in this little, local 'mess' of ours.[58]

After familiarizing himself with the consequences of TP's 'work' (on the moor and beyond[59]) Horsmith announced (I'm paraphrasing here[60]) that while he fully condoned – even admired![61] –TP's desire to keep the moor clean, it was still perfectly legitimate for dog owners to allow their pets to defecate there, and that while excrement could not, in all conscience, be calibrated as 'litter' (it decomposes for heaven's sake! Same as an apple core!) once it has been placed inside plastic (no

---

56. I won't bore you with the details here as I am sure Mr Horsmith will already have bored you with them himself.

57. His words, not mine. Shoshana once observed – very wittily – that Mr Horsmith makes *Alice in Wonderland*'s Dormouse seem hyperactive!

58. By a flurry of phone calls, emails and at least half a dozen letters to the local press (two of which mentioned him by name).

59. Three of her bags were recently discovered in Lowsley Edge – over *seven miles* away as the crow flies!

60. His letter was full of the most appalling grammatical errors.

61. This struck me as an astonishingly irresponsible thing to say given the deranged nature of the character we are dealing with here. As I said to Horsmith myself (on one of the rare occasions he actually made a visit to the village), by encouraging TP to think that she's got moral right on her side he's only sharpening a stick for her to beat him (and the rest of us) up with.

matter how laudable the motivation[62]) then it *must necessarily* be considered so.[63]

Horsmith's pronouncement on this issue was obviously the most devastating blow for TP (and her cause), yet it by no means prompted her to desist from her antisocial behaviour. By way of an excuse for (partial explanation of/attempt to distract attention from) her strange, nocturnal activities, she suddenly changed tack and began claiming (see Doc. 6 again – last three paras) that – for the most part – whenever she goes on walks she generally bags up the vast majority of the faeces she finds and disposes of them herself ('double-wrapped', she writes – somewhat primly – inside her dustbin, at home[64]) and that on the rare occasions when she leaves the bags behind it is either because a) the 'problem' (as she perceives it) is so severe that she feels a strong, public statement needs to be made to other dog owners, b) the sheer volume of excrement is such that it is simply too much for her to carry home all in one go (while managing a large dog at the same time), and c) that she is sometimes prey to the sudden onset of acute arthritic 'spasms' in her fingers, which mean that she is unable to grip the bags properly and so is compelled to leave them *in situ*, while harbouring 'every earthly intention' of returning to collect them at a later date.

I am not – of course – in any way convinced by this pathetic, half-cocked hodge-podge of explanations. In answer to a) I say that other dog owners are <u>completely within their rights</u> to allow their dogs to defecate responsibly on the moor. They have the <u>law</u> on their side. It is a perfectly <u>legitimate</u> and <u>natural</u> way to proceed. In answer to b) I say that the <u>volume</u> of excrement on the moor is rarely, if ever – in my extensive experience of these matters – excessive (especially given the general rate of decomposition etc.). In answer to c) I say that it strikes me as rather <u>odd</u> that the same person who can apparently manage to

---

62. Ye gads!
63. A point I made myself to Mr Horsmith – but to no avail – over six long months before!
64. I will return to this important detail a little later!

'bag up' huge quantities of excrement when their fingers are – *ahem* – 'spasming'[65] is somehow unable to perform that superficially <u>much less arduous</u> act of transporting it back home with them![66]

Many of TP's bags lie around on the moor for months on end and no visible attempt is made to move them. Last Thursday, for example, I counted over forty-two bags of excrement dotted randomly about the place on my morning stroll.

Sometimes I come across a bag displayed in the most extraordinary of places. Yesterday I found one dangling up high in the midst of a thorny bush. It was very obvious that not only would the person who hung the bag there have been forced to sustain some kind of injury in its display (unless they wore a thick pair of protective gloves), but that so would the poor soul (and *here's* the rub!) who felt duty-bound to retrieve it and dispose of it.[67] This was – in effect – a piece of purely spiteful behaviour – little less, in fact, than an act of social/ environmental terrorism.

Shoshana and I have both become so sickened, angered and dismayed by the awful mess TP has made of our local area (I mean who is to judge when an activity such as this passes from being 'in the public interest'[68] to a plain and simple public nuisance?[69]) that, in sheer desperation, we have begun to gather up the rotten bags ourselves.

On Friday, two weeks back,[70] Shoshana gathered up over thirty-six

---

65. A fiddly process at the best of times!
66. Let alone manufacture fashionable clay jewellery in such prodigious quantities!
67. I.e. Yours truly!
68. Which it never was, quite frankly.
69. This is intended as a purely rhetorical question – although, on further consideration, I suppose the person who might possibly be expected to make that vital judgement could very well turn out to be you, Linda.
70. There was a large convention of Girl Guides from Manchester and Leeds travelling to the moor for an orienteering weekend. Shoshana couldn't bear the idea of these lovely creatures being exposed to TP's vile 'handiwork'.

bags. On her way home – exhausted – from the village's poop-scoop bins[71] she tripped on a crack in the pavement, fell heavily, sprained her wrist and dislocated her collarbone.[72] I will not say that we blame TP *entirely* for this calamity, but we do hold her at least partially responsible.[73]

After Shoshana's 'accident' I marched over to TP's bungalow, fully intent on having it out with her,[74] but TP (rather fortuitously) was nowhere to be found. It was then – as I stood impotently in her front garden, seething with frustration – that I resolved[75] to take the opportunity to do a little private investigation of my own. If you remember,[76] TP had claimed that many – if not most – of the bags of excrement she retrieved from the moor, she automatically carried back home with her (only leaving the unmanageable excess behind) and placed them, double-wrapped, into her dustbin (alongside what I imagine would be the considerable quantities of excrement collected from her *own* four, chronically obese dogs which – as you know – she keeps penned up, 24/7,[77] inside that criminally small and claustrophobic, purpose-built concrete compound[78]).

71. Which could barely contain the sheer volume involved – amounting to almost 3,000 grams. If you have some difficulty imagining this weight in real terms, then it would be comparable to around twelve pats of best butter.
72. I have sent another letter to your colleague – Giles Monson – on this subject, along with directions from our lawyer.
73. Shoshana an angry seventy per cent, me, a more reasoned fifty-nine per cent (a broad, general majority, in other words).
74. Uncharacteristically hot-headed behaviour on my part.
75. Quite spontaneously. This was *in no way* premeditated.
76. But of course you do!
77. As the Yanks are wont to say.
78. Once again, I emphasize that *absolutely no judgement* is implied by my use of these words.

The day I visited Hursley End was a Monday, which is the day directly *before* refuse is collected in the village. I decided – God only knows why, it was just a random urge, I suppose – to peek inside her dustbin (literally deafened as I did so by the hysterical barks and howls of her four frantic German shepherds). By my calculation, I estimated that there would need to be *at least* forty-two dog faeces – from her own four animals – stored away inside there.[79] In addition to these I also envisaged a *considerable* number of stools collected from her nightly hikes on the 'filthy' moor.[80]

Once I'd made these quick calculations I steeled myself, drew a deep breath, grabbed the lid, lifted it high and peered querulously inside. Imagine my great surprise when I found *not a single trace of excrement within!* The bin was all but empty! I say again: the bin – *TP's* bin – was all but empty!! I quickly pulled on a pair of disposable gloves[81] and then gingerly withdrew the bin's other contents, piece by piece (just so as to be absolutely certain of my facts). I removed two large, empty Johnnie Walker bottles,[82] four family-size Marks and Spencer coleslaw containers, three packets of mint and one packet of hazelnut-flavoured Cadbury's Snaps biscuit wrappers, and the stinking remnants of two boil-in-the-bag fish dinners (Iceland) and one, ready-made, prawn biryani meal (from Tesco's excellent Finest range).

I stared blankly into that bin for several minutes, utterly confounded, struggling to make any sense of what I'd discovered. It then slowly dawned on me that TP might actually have *two* bins – one of which was specifically to be used for the storing of excrement. Bearing this in mind, I set about searching the untended grounds of

---

79. This figure was reached by estimating that, on average, each of TP's four dogs would be expected to defecate 1.5 times on any given day (an extremely conservative estimate, in actual fact).
80. Her word, obviously.
81. Which I just happened to have with me.
82. Not much of a recycler, then, our TP?!

her property[83] with a fine-tooth comb,[84] even going so far as to climb on to an upturned bucket and peer, trepidatiously, into the tiny concrete compound to the rear, where TP's four German shepherds barked and raced around – like a group of hairy, overweight banshees – frantic with what seemed to be a poignant combination of terror and excitement.[85]

No matter how hard I hunted, a second bin could not be found. I eventually abandoned my search on realizing how late it had grown[86] – Shoshana would definitely be worried, I thought, and if I tarried any longer I could be in serious danger of missing *Countdown*.[87] I left Hursley End, depressed and confused, only turning – with a helpless half-shrug – to peer back over towards the property once I'd reached the relative safety of the road beyond. It was then, in a blinding flash, that I had what I now refer to – somewhat vaingloriously, I'll admit – as my 'Moment of Epiphany'.[88]

83. TP is currently in the midst of having some major renovation work done to the external walls of her bungalow. If the rumours I hear about town are correct, she is trying to sue the former owners, Louise and Timothy Hamm, for some unspecified kind of 'negligence' – even though Timothy, an ex-GP and a truly inspirational human being, is in the final stages of Parkinson's and now lives in full-time residential care.

84. So to speak.

85. Probably thinking I was an animal-rights activist intent on releasing them from their hellish penury.

86. I'd been there for almost an hour!

87. I *didn't* miss it, which was most fortuitous as it was an especially good episode. One of the contestants came up with the high-scoring word 'toxocara', a term which refers to a type of roundworm which is responsible for generating the dangerous infection/disease called toxocariasis. This disease is produced when the toxocara roundworm's eggs are left to fester in the excrement of a dog for a period of two/three weeks after the faeces have been deposited. I was absolutely stunned when this word came up, and honestly believe it was some kind of message from 'The Beyond'!

88. Although Shoshana will insist on calling it my 'episcopy', the silly moo!

As I looked back at TP's property from a greater distance, I was able – with the benefit of perspective – to observe that recent renovation works to the bungalow had resulted in the temporary removal of large sections of the external fascia,[89] so that all that now remained of the property's original structure was the roof, the window frames and a series of basic, internal walls and supports, many of which had been copiously wrapped in thick layers of protective plastic (to safeguard the property against the worst of the weather, I suppose). By dint of this expedient – I suddenly realized, with a sharp gasp – TP's home had lately been transformed (voluntarily or otherwise) into a giant simulacrum of a *monstrous, semi-transparent poo-bag!*[90]

As this – admittedly strange and somewhat hysterical – thought[91] caught ahold of me, a second thought – running almost in tandem with it – quickly overtook my mind: if no evidence of excrement could be found in TP's garden – not even faeces from her *own four dogs* – then where on God's earth might she actually be...?

What?!

I suddenly froze.

'MARY, MOTHER OF JESUS!' I bellowed, then quickly covered my mouth with my hand.[92] But wasn't it *obvious*?! Hadn't the simple answer to this most perplexing of questions been staring me in the face *all along*?!

89. Many of the more modest properties in this village – built within a particular time frame – were constructed out of a special, aluminium-based concrete which, while it poses only limited health risks to the residents, can, in certain instances, make it extremely difficult to raise a mortgage.
90. With TP – I hate to have to say it, but say it I *must* – representing the steaming turd of festering excrement within.
91. Remember that – in my own defence – I was still in somewhat of a state after Shoshana's tragic fall.
92. For fear of attracting the unwanted attentions of TP's neighbours – one of whom, a Mrs Janine Loose, has grown extraordinarily jumpy and paranoid of late, since a canny gang of local schoolchildren appropriated

The moor!

Our beautiful, unbesmirched, virgin moor!

TP had *not* – as she'd always emphatically maintained – been piously and dutifully collecting/bagging excrement left by other, irresponsible dog owners, during those long, dark, nightly hikes of hers. Oh no! Quite the opposite, in fact! TP had actually been carefully bagging prodigious quantities of HER OWN FOUR DOGS' EXCREMENT and then CHEERFULLY FESTOONING THE LOCAL FOOTPATHS WITH IT!!!

'Good *Lord*!' I can almost hear you howl, your smooth, firm cheeks flushed pink with rage and indignation.' But...but *why*?'

I'm afraid that this is a question which – for all of my age and experience – I cannot answer. I can only imagine that TP must derive some sick and perverse feeling of excitement/gratification from performing this debased act. Perhaps it is an entirely <u>sexual</u> impulse, or maybe she has some deep yet inexplicable <u>grudge</u> against the people of Burley Cross which she is '<u>acting out</u>' through this strange and depraved pastime. Or perhaps the good people of this village have unwittingly come to '<u>represent</u>' something (or someone) to TP from her <u>tragic past</u> and she feels the uncontrollable urge to punish/ insult/degrade us all as a consequence of that. Or maybe – just maybe – a whole host of entirely *different* impulses are at play here. Shoshana had the fascinating idea that as a small child TP might've developed '<u>issues</u>' during her <u>anal phase</u>[93] brought on by an overly strict and prohibitive <u>potty-training regimen</u>. She discussed this idea with a neighbour of ours who might properly be called an 'expert' in the field,

---

the disused greenhouse at the bottom of her garden and secretly cultivated marijuana plants in it. Their illegal activities were only brought to light after Mrs Loose discovered two boys spreadeagled on her lawn, 'completely monged', when she went to hang out her washing one blustery, autumn afternoon.

93. Who started – but never completed – a child psychology correspondence course a few years back (then swapped to aromatherapy).

and they explained to her – at some length – how as children we have an innocent, perfectly natural conception of our own faeces as a kind of 'gift'[94] which we generously share with our parents.

Shoshana wondered whether TP's emotional/psychological development as a child was halted/blocked at this critical stage, leading to an unusual fixation with faeces in adult life, which, many decades later, still gives TP the childlike compulsion to 'share' this 'precious' substance with all of her friends and neighbours.[95]

Whatever the real reasons for TP's extraordinary behaviour, the hard fact remains that she is currently posing a serious threat to the health and safety of the general public and must be stopped as a matter of some urgency. To this end I sent a lengthy email to Trevor Horsmith, insisting that he take some kind of positive action to deter TP from her foul and aberrant path.

Horsmith,[96] while professing himself to be 'very interested' in my theories, calmly informed me that unless he was able to catch TP red-handed (transporting faeces from her home and depositing them on the moor) then he would be unable to take any kind of prohibitive action against her. Given that TP prefers to walk only after dark and Trevor Horsmith's working hours finish promptly at five, the likelihood of this ever happening is – at best, I feel – extremely limited. Horsmith also went on to discourage me – and in no uncertain terms,[97] either –

94. Apparently – according to Ms Sissy Logan, an old Bluebell dancing girl turned colonic irrigation practitioner – Carl Gustav Jung has written quite extensively on this peculiar subject.
95. Lucky old us, eh?!
96. As he will no doubt have informed you.
97. I found his insinuations extremely hurtful. As I told you after the meeting, nine out of the ten charges were dropped through lack of evidence, and in the tenth instance a credible witness was able to verify that I had merely asked the girl for directions to the nearest Tesco Metro. I have visited Leeds for many years and know the town well, but the rejuvenation of the riverside area and recent changes to the one-way system are liable to catch even a seasoned old pro like myself on the hop.

from taking any kind of independent action myself, claiming that a matter this sensitive was – I quote – 'always better left in the hands of qualified professionals'.[98]

So there you have it, Ms Withycombe; a detailed summary of the complex web of problems our small – but perfectly formed – village is currently struggling to grapple with. Call me a foolish, old optimist (if you must!), but I have a strong presentiment that your input in this matter will prove most beneficial, and am keenly looking forward to bashing out some kind of joint plan of action with you at the start of the New Year.

Yours, in eager anticipation,

Jeremy – aka *Jez* – Baverstock

PS Merry Christmas! (I almost forgot!!)
PPS You will probably have noticed that I have taken the great liberty of enclosing a small, festive gift for your private enjoyment over the holiday season: an – as yet – unpublished book[99] I once wrote about my nefarious activities as a reconnoiter, black hat and mole inside the Royal Horticultural Society of Great Britain.[100]

XXJ

98. Although I remain a little confused as to what his 'professional' status might actually be.
99. This edition is limited to only thirty copies. Shoshana is wholly responsible for the wonderful, colourful, internal artwork.
100. An organization that has – over recent years – fallen prey to rank corruption, chronic inefficiency and levels of bovine complacency the like of which you can hardly dare to imagine. My lack of an independent publisher is, I believe, at least partly down to the fact that members of this powerful institution are currently rife within all – and I *mean* all – areas of the national media. It may shock you to discover that the Duchess of Windsor, Peter Sissons, and that queer little chap who owns Sainsbury's – or possibly ASDA – were former members and dabbled, quite seriously, in the organization for a while.

SORRY?

Helen Simpson

ILLUSTRATION BY MICHAEL KIRKHAM

'Sorry?' said Patrick. 'I didn't quite catch that.'

'SOUP OF THE DAY IS WILD MUSHROOM,' bellowed the waiter.

'No need to shout,' said Patrick, putting his hand to his troublesome ear.

The new gadget shrieked in protest.

'They take a bit of getting used to,' grimaced Matthew Herring, the deaf chap he'd been fixed up with for a morale-boosting lunch.

'You don't say,' he replied.

Some weeks ago Patrick had woken up to find he had gone deaf in his right ear – not just a bit deaf but profoundly deaf. There was nothing to be done, it seemed. It had probably been caused by a tiny flake of matter dislodged by wear-and-tear change in the vertebrac, the doctor had said, shrugging. He had turned his head on his pillow, in all likelihood, sometimes that was all it took. This neck movement would have shifted a minuscule scrap of detritus into the river of blood running towards the brain, a fragment which must have finished by blocking the very narrowest bit of the entire arterial system, the ultra-fine pipe leading to the inner ear. Bad luck.

'I don't hear perfectly,' said Matthew Herring now. 'It's not magic, a digital hearing aid, it doesn't turn your hearing into perfect hearing.'

'Mine's not working properly yet,' said Patrick. 'I've got an appointment after lunch to get it seen to.'

'Mind you, it's better than the old one,' continued Matthew Herring comfortably. 'You used to be able to hear me wherever I went with the analogue one, it used to go before me, screeching like a steam train.'

He chuckled at the memory.

Patrick did not smile at this cosy reference to engine whistles. He had been astonished at the storm of head noise which had arrived with deafness, the whistles and screeches over a powerful cloud of hissing just like the noise from his wife Elizabeth's old pressure cooker. His brain was generating sound to compensate for the loss of hearing, he had been told. Apparently that was part and parcel of the deafness, as well as dizzy episodes. Ha! Thanks to the vertigo which had sent him arse over tip several times since the start of all this, he was having to stay with his daughter Rachel for a while.

'Two girls,' he said tersely in answer to a question from his tedious lunch companion. He and Elizabeth had wished for boys, but there you were. Rachel was the only one so far to have provided him with grandchildren. The other daughter, Ruth, had decamped to Australia some time ago. Who knew what she was up to but she was still out there so presumably she had managed to make a go of it, something which she had signally failed to do in England.

'I used to love music,' Matthew Herring was saying, nothing daunted. 'But it's not the same now I'm so deaf. Now it tires me out; in fact, I don't listen any more. I deliberately avoid it. The loss of it is a grief, I must admit.'

'Oh well, music means nothing to me,' said Patrick. 'Never has. So I shan't miss *that*.'

He wasn't about to confide in Matthew Herring, but of all his symptoms it had been the auditory hallucinations produced by the hearing aid that had been the most disturbing for him. The low violent stream of nonsense issuing from the general direction of his firstborn had become insupportable in the last week, and he had had to turn the damned thing off.

At his after-lunch appointment with the audiologist, he found himself curiously unable to describe the hallucinatory problem.

'I seem to be picking up extra noise,' he said eventually. 'It's difficult to describe.'

'Sounds go into your hearing aid where they are processed electronically,' she intoned, 'then played back to you over a tiny loudspeaker.'

'Yes, I know that,' he snapped. 'I am aware of that, thank you. What I'm asking is, might one of the various settings you programmed be capable of, er, amplifying sounds that would normally remain unheard?'

'Let's see, shall we?' she said, still talking to him as though he were a child or a halfwit. 'I wonder whether you've been picking up extra stuff on the Loop.'

'The Loop?'

'It works a bit like Wi-Fi,' she said. 'Electromagnetic fields. If you're in an area that's on the Loop, you can pick up on it with your hearing aid when you turn on the T-setting.'

'The T-setting?'

'That little extra bit of kit there,' she said, pointing at it. 'I didn't mention it before. I didn't want to confuse you while you were getting used to the basics. You must have turned it on by mistake from what you're saying.'

'But what *sort* of extra sounds does it pick up?' he persisted.

Rachel's lips had not been moving during that initial weird diatribe a week ago, he was sure of it, nor during the battery of bitter little remarks he'd had to endure since then.

'Well it can be quite embarrassing,' she said, laughing merrily. 'Walls don't block the magnetic waves from a Loop signal, so you might well be able to listen in to confidential conversations if neighbouring rooms are also on it.'

'Hmm,' he said. 'I'm not sure that quite explains this particular problem. But I suppose it might have something to do with it.'

'Look, I've turned off the T-setting,' she said. 'If you want to test what it does, simply turn it on again and see what happens.'

'Or hear,' he said. 'Hear what happens.'

'You're right!' she declared, with more merry laughter.

He really couldn't see what was so amusing, and said so.

B ack at Rachel's, he made his way to the armchair in the little bay window and whiled away the minutes until six o'clock by rereading the *Telegraph*. The trouble with this house was that it had been knocked through, so you were all in it hugger-mugger together. He could not himself see the advantage of being forced to witness every domestic detail. Frankly, it was bedlam, with the spin cycle going and Rachel's twins squawking and Rachel washing her hands at the kitchen sink yet again like Lady Macbeth. Now she was doing that thing she did with the brown paper bag, blowing into it and goggling her eyes, which seemed to amuse the twins at least.

Small children were undoubtedly tiresome, but the way she indulged hers made them ten times worse. Like so many of her generation she seemed to be making a huge song and dance about the whole business. She was ridiculous with them, ludicrously over-indulgent and lacking in any sort of authority. It was when he had commented on this in passing that the auditory hallucinations had begun.

'I don't want to do to them what you did to me, you old beast,' the voice had growled, guttural and shocking, although her lips had not been moving. 'I don't want to hand on the misery, I don't want that horrible Larkin poem to be true.'

He had glared at her, amazed, and yet it had been quite obvious she was blissfully unaware of what he had heard. Or thought he had heard.

He must have been hearing things.

Now he held up his wrist and tapped his watch at her. She waved back at him, giving one last puff into the paper bag before scurrying to the fridge for the ice and lemon. As he watched her prepare his first drink of the evening, he decided to test out the audiologist's theory.

'Sit with me,' he ordered, taking the clinking glass.

'I'd love to, Dad, but the twins...' she said.

'Nonsense,' he said. 'Look at them, you can see them from here, they're all right for now.'

She perched on the arm of the chair opposite his and started twisting a strand of her lank brown hair.

'Tell me about your day,' he commanded.

'My day?' she said. 'Are you sure? Nothing very much happened. I took the twins to Rainbow, then we went round Asda...'

'Keep talking,' he said, fiddling with his hearing aid. 'I want to test this gadget out.'

'...then I had to queue at the post office and I wasn't very popular with the double buggy,' she droned on.

He flicked the switch to the T-setting.

'...never good enough for you, you old beast, you never had any time for me, you never listened to anything I said,' came the low growling voice he remembered from before. 'You cold old beast, Ruth says you're emotionally autistic, definitely somewhere on the autistic spectrum anyway, that's why she went to the other side of the world but she says she still can't get away from it there, your lack of interest, you blanked us, you blotted us out, you don't even know the names of your grandchildren let alone their birthdays...'

He flicked the switch back.

'...after their nap, then I put the washing on and peeled some potatoes for tonight's dinner while they watched CBeebies...' she continued in her toneless, everyday voice.

'That's enough for now, thanks,' he said crisply. He took a big gulp of his drink, and then another. 'Scarlett and, er, Mia. You'd better see what they're up to.'

'Are you okay, Dad?'

'Fine,' he snapped. 'You go off and do whatever it is you want to do.'

He closed his eyes. He needed Elizabeth now. She'd taken no nonsense from the girls. He had left them to her, which was the way she'd wanted it. All this hysteria! Elizabeth had known how to deal with them.

H e sensed he was in for another bad night, and he was right. He lay rigid as a stone knight on a tomb, claustrophobic in his partially closed-down head and its frantic brain noise. The deafer he got the louder it became; that was how it was, that was the deal. He grimaced at the future, his other ear gone, reduced to the company of Matthew Herring and his like, a shoal of old boys mouthing at each other.

The thing was, he had been the breadwinner. Children needed their mothers. It was true he hadn't been very interested in them, but then, frankly, they hadn't been very interesting. Was he supposed to pretend? Neither of them had amounted to much. And he had had his own life to get on with.

He'd seen the way they were with their children these days – 'Oh that's wonderful darling! You *are* clever' and 'Love you!' at the end of every exchange, with the young fathers behaving like old women, cooing and planting big sloppy kisses on their babies as if they were in a Disney film. The whole culture had gone soft; it gave him the creeps. Opening up to your feminine side! He shuddered in his pyjamas.

Elizabeth was dead. That was what he really couldn't bear.

The noise inside his head was going wild: hooting and zooming and pressure-cooker hiss; he needed to distract his brain with – what had the doctor called it? – 'sound enrichment'. Give it some competition, fight fire with fire; that was the idea. Fiddling with the radio's tuning wheel in the dark, he swore viciously and wondered why it was you could never find the World Service when you needed it. He wanted talk but there was only music, which would have to do. Nothing but a meaningless racket to him, though at least it was a different *sort* of racket; that was the theory.

No, that was no better. If anything, it was worse.

Wasn't the hearing aid supposed to help cancel tinnitus? So the doctor had suggested. Maybe the T-setting would come into its own in this sort of situation. He turned on the tiny gadget, made the necessary adjustments, and poked it into his ear.

It was like blood returning to a dead leg, but in his head and chest. What an extraordinary sensation! It was completely new to him. Music was stealing hotly, pleasurably through his veins for the first time in his life, unspeakably delicious: at the same time it gave cruel pain, transporting inklings of what he had not known, intimations of things lovely beyond imagination which would never now be his as death was next. A tear crept down his face. He hadn't cried since he was a baby. Appalling! At this rate he'd be wetting himself. But it was so astonishingly beautiful, the music. Waves of entrancing sound were threatening to breach the sea wall. Now he was coughing dry sobs.

This was not on. Frankly he preferred any combination of troublesome symptoms to getting into this state. He fumbled with the hearing aid and at last managed to turn the damned thing *off*. Half-unhinged, he tottered to the bathroom and ran a basin of water over it, submerged the beastly little gadget, drowned it. Then he fished it out and flushed it down the lavatory. Best place for it.

No more funny business, he vowed. *That was that.* From now on he would put up and shut up, he swore it on Elizabeth's grave.

Back in bed, he once again lowered his head on to the pillow. Straight away the infernal noise factory started up; he was staggering along beat by beat in a heavy shower of noise and howling.

'It's not real,' he whispered to himself in the dark. 'Compensatory brain activity, that's what this is.'

Inside his skull all hell had broken loose. He had never heard anything like it.

Mavis Gallant at the Village Voice Bookshop, Paris, February 19, 2009

'USELESS CHAOS IS WHAT FICTION IS ABOUT'

Jhumpa Lahiri interviews Mavis Gallant

In 1997, I picked up a copy of Mavis Gallant's *Home Truths*, a collection of sixteen stories published in 1981, from a library book sale in the small New England town where I was raised. The first story I read, 'The Ice Wagon Going Down the Street', broke something in me – something about my prior understanding of what a story can do, and how. The story was a masterful chiaroscuro at once dense and nimble, urgent and orderly, light-hearted and dark; about experiences both pedestrian and profound. It was virtuosic without fuss, compassionate without sentimentality. It seemed to have been written in a radically different way than any story I'd read before, a live wire that crackled from start to finish on the page.

When my parents asked what I wanted for Christmas that year, I told them to get me *The Collected Stories of Mavis Gallant*, published in 1996. They honoured my request, and for the remainder of the winter I read little else but that volume, a total of 887 pages. The stories were mostly about North Americans and Europeans, many of them rootless either by circumstance or design. They were about uncovering the truth, about enduring disappointment and loss, about the recurrent shock of being alive. I was thirty years old that winter, a time when I was beginning to take the writing of stories seriously, but still lacked the conviction to regard myself as a writer. Reading those stories put an end to the questions, put the summit before me and put me on my path.

In November 2005, I met Mavis Gallant in person for the first time. The occasion was a celebration of her work held at Symphony Space in New York, in which I, along with Michael Ondaatje, Russell Banks and Edward Hirsch, took part. She had come from Paris, where she lives, to hear our tributes and then to give a reading. Mavis moved to Paris in 1950, when she was twenty-eight years old, in order to write fiction exclusively. Before that she worked as a journalist in Montreal, the city where she was born on August 11, 1922. She lost her father when she was ten years old, and was educated in a total of seventeen different convent, public and boarding schools. She married at the age of twenty and divorced five years later. In September 1951, her story, 'Madeline's Birthday', was published in *The New Yorker*. Since then, she has published more than one hundred short stories in the pages of that magazine. She has also published over a dozen collections of stories, two novels, a volume of non-fiction and a play. She is a Foreign Honorary Member of the American Academy of Arts and Letters, and among her numerous awards is the Rea Award for the Short Story, the Governor General's Award and the Order of Canada, which is the country's highest civilian honour.

By the time of our meeting at Symphony Space, Mavis was a writer I felt intimately connected to, whose work I'd read frequently and repeatedly and devotedly for close to a decade. I had never met a writer who has inspired me so greatly, and towards whom I felt such enormous debt. I was introduced to her backstage, sat with her along with the others and eventually mustered up the courage to ask her to sign one of her books. After the event there was a dinner, but because we were seated at separate tables, there had been no opportunity to talk.

The opportunity came in February 2009, when I travelled from

New York to Paris to conduct the following interview over three consecutive days. In preparing for our conversation, I decided to concentrate on three of her works. The first, *Green Water, Green Sky*, is her debut novel, published in 1959. Written in four parts, it centres on an American mother and daughter living in Europe. It is the first of many examples of the way Mavis has created a hybrid genre of complex narratives that are neither conventional chapters nor isolated stories, that are at once independent and connected and travel back and forth in time. She explores subjects that have remained preoccupations throughout her writing: foreigners in France, parents in absentia, the vicissitudes of marriage and the physical and emotional reality – as contradictory as any of her characters – of Paris itself. Each section unfolds from layered points of view, alighting, without the reader often being aware of it, from one character to the next. The result is a narrative that refuses to sit still, and the reward is the broad psychological perspective of many novels, concentrated in a relative handful of pages.

The second work I wanted to discuss, a long story called 'The Remission', published in 1979, is about an English family living in the south of France. A mature, unforgettable portrait of a dying man, 'The Remission' is thematically comparable, in my mind, to Tolstoy's 'The Death of Ivan Ilych'. The third work we discussed is a quartet of linked stories called 'The Carette Sisters', published in the mid-Eighties. Though similiar, structurally, to *Green Water, Green Sky*, the four sections of 'The Carette Sisters' do not constitute a novel. The grouping takes place, for the most part, in Montreal, and spans the lives of a widow and her two daughters over the course of half a century. My choice of the three texts was somewhat arbitrary, given that Mavis has written so many stories that may be considered paradigms of the form. Reading them together, I noted in each case, the bond – sometimes volatile, sometimes desperate, sometimes missing – between mothers and children. Representing, roughly, early, middle and late periods in Mavis's long-ranging body of work, they are three I happen to turn to again and again.

At eighty-six, Mavis remains an elegant woman. Each day she was impeccably dressed in a woollen skirt, sweater, scarf, stockings and square-heeled pumps. A medium-length coat of black wool protected her from the Paris chill and beautiful rings, an opal one among them, adorned her fingers. Her accent, soft but proper in the English manner, evoked, to my ear, the graceful and sophisticated speech of 1940s cinema. Her laughter, less formal, erupts frequently as a hearty expulsion of breath. French, the language that has surrounded her for over half a lifetime, occasionally adorns and accompanies her English. She is a spirited and agile interlocuter who tells stories as she writes them: bristling with drama, thick with dialogue, vividly rendered and studded with astringent aperçus.

We began talking at the Village Voice Bookshop, an English-language bookstore on rue Princesse in the neighbourhood of Saint-Germain-des-Prés. The shop, brightly lit and cheerfully utilitarian, has a winding metal staircase to one side, and is filled on two levels with books organized on black shelves. The owner, Odile Hellier, knows Mavis well, and warmly welcomed us both. Although Mavis suffers from osteoporosis and moves about, these days, with considerable difficulty, she ascended the metal staircase steadily on her own. Upstairs, the two of us sat by a window overlooking the dim, narrow street, on chairs wedged behind two square display tables piled with books. The view through the window was of a building covered with cloudy plastic and scaffolding. A folding table was set up between us, just large enough to hold a microcassette recorder and two glasses of water; a radiator affixed to the wall below the window kept us warm. While we were speaking, customers occasionally wandered upstairs to browse, but the atmosphere in the bookstore was tranquil, enough for us to agree to meet there the following day.

The third conversation was held at Le Dôme, a brasserie on the boulevard du Montparnasse, which is located in the neighbourhood where Mavis lives. She was greeted as a familiar when we arrived, and we were ushered to a yellow marble table set between two banquettes, where we sat beneath the glow of a hanging lamp. The atmosphere of the brasserie is old-fashioned and luxurious, with varnished wood-panelled walls, gold and amber-toned stained glass and wine-coloured velvet curtains. Mavis asked for a large cafe au lait and pointed out a cosy semi-circular banquette on the upper level, close to the bar, where Picasso liked to sit. Most of the other tables inside the restaurant were empty at that time of day and at one point a vacuum cleaner ran over the carpets. The head waiter, coming on for the night shift, also stopped by our table to say hello.

On Thursday, the day before my journey back to New York, Mavis and I read together at the Village Voice Bookshop. This time we sat side by side. Around her neck was a turquoise and dark blue silk scarf, a gift made in Brooklyn that I had presented to her at the beginning of our interview. Mavis read the story 'In Transit', followed by a scene from her play, *What is to be Done?* The crowd filled both levels of the store and each step of the staircase. As I told them before reading, that evening was the most thrilling moment of my life as a writer.

After answering questions and signing books, a small group of us walked a few doors down to have dinner at a Vietnamese restaurant. The wine was poured and conversation began to flow. I was seated directly across from Mavis, and though the interview was officially over, I kept asking her questions, about her travels, about certain scenes in her stories, about books we'd both read. When we parted, we promised to meet again one day at Le Dôme, this time for lunch, and sit at Picasso's table.

Jhumpa Lahiri, March 2009

JHUMPA LAHIRI: Was it winter when you first came to Paris?

MAVIS GALLANT: I arrived in October. I went to a hotel recommended to me by a musician I knew in Canada. It was just around the corner from here. This is only five years after the war, you see. So I lived there. The room was all red velvet. Not very clean, but I knew I had to get over that feeling. It was Paris, and I knew it was dirty. Let's see, what did I do? I unpacked, and I went for— oh yes, I went for a walk. I was coming from England, which, I have to tell you, I didn't like at all. Talk about illusion shattered.

JL: What didn't you like?

MG: I didn't like anything. I am more English than anything. I had an English father. My mother, being Canadian, was English, with, I think, some French mixed in. And I admired English writers very much, but I admired French painting more. I went for a walk, that's right, and it was still daylight. I had a large map of Paris in my apartment in Montreal, and had pasted this on my wall and studied it. I studied the Metro stops and all that. I knew them better than I know them now, because I don't take the train any more. I set out from my hotel down to the Seine and I reached the Ministry of Defence. A French sailor came over and asked for a direction in French, and I was able to give it to him. I said, '*Vous retraversez la pont, et vous verez le station Métro*', as if I'd lived here forever. I was so proud. And then I decided to have supper in a restaurant called Raffi. It wasn't recommended to me, I just looked at it. You had to go up some steps. I watched to see what people were eating. And I saw people eating radishes with butter on them, so I ordered that. For the first time in my life I tasted sweet butter, because we only had salted butter in Canada – it was called Jewish butter, and it was sold in the Jewish part of Montreal. I'd never tasted sweet butter. It was delicious! And I remember the radish didn't taste like our radishes, which were really just used for decoration. The bread was delicious, just lovely with sweet butter. And I had a pork chop.

JL: You remember.

MG: Oh, I do. And French fries. I think I had apple tart, but I'm not sure about that. I just looked at what people were eating. That I remember. Raffi's is now a Korean barbecue, and I recognize it only because there's still the steps. I've looked in – I've never eaten anything there – but the general skeleton of the place is still what it was in October 1950.

JL: Did anything disappoint you when you came here?

MG: I wouldn't say disappoint. I was very disappointed in London. I didn't like the people. I thought they were rude. They had a reputation for being polite, but they weren't. I didn't really understand. They were still rationed. They were bitter. They thought that we people from across the Atlantic were very well off, very spoiled; that we didn't know what a war was. And I became something I'm not really, which was nationalist. I don't like nationalism, and I thought, my God, every Canadian buried in a Commonwealth cemetery in the Second World War was a volunteer. There was no conscription in Canada for fighting. About halfway through the war, conscription was established for desk jobs, but service overseas was filled by volunteers. So there were all these people buried in France and Italy and Libya, taken at Hong Kong, taken at Singapore. I felt defensive of them because they were my generation. I didn't argue, but I didn't like it. They didn't like us. They took me for an American. I don't consider it an insult, and I was not looking to say, 'I'm one of these sweet Canadians everybody likes.'

JL: But Paris?

MG: To me it was literary.

JL: More than England?

MG: More than London. I'd read a great deal of French writers. I'd read a lot of Colette. François Mauriac. I'd always read French all my life, but I didn't prefer it to English, and I still don't. Not for writing, anyway. Oh, there were things I had to adjust to. I had been working on a newspaper, the *Standard* in Montreal, and suddenly I was in a large city. I had no more salary; I had no relatives here. I had introductions to people, but I didn't know anybody. I had all the expats somehow between me and France. It was a great time for expatriates. Five years after the war, everyone was dying to get to Europe. But what I loved in Paris itself – how can I explain it? Montreal at that time was a very cosmopolitan city because of the émigrés and refugees, which I liked, but there was hardly a bookstore you could rely on in English, and in Quebec there was a political oppression that I thought would never change. I had lived in New York so I didn't want to go back to New York. I wanted Europe. But here, there was a bookstore – many more, they're closing like mad – on every corner. There was something on every corner that was pleasing to me. I never made a move to meet anyone, to meet a writer. Whereas, when I came back from New York at eighteen, I found Montreal small, but as I lived in it and became a newspaper reporter I began to know the city and it was very complex; the French, the English, the Catholic, the Protestant. I made great efforts between eighteen and twenty-eight to meet every poet, every artist, every musician, because I seemed to need it. Once I got here I didn't need it. It was just there. I went to concerts, I went to the opera, sitting way up high in cheap seats. But I had no desire to meet them, to meet singers. It was the atmosphere.

JL: You had it.

MG: I had it here. So I got the feeling that Paris was like someone saying, 'You can have the run of the house, you can wander all over my house, you can open drawers and take books off the shelves, but we are apart.'

JL: 'We' being the French?

MG: Yes. But it was like a house where you could do anything you like.

JL: How long after you came here did you begin writing about it?

MG: I don't keep records, but I wrote a story called 'The Other Paris' [published in 1953], one of my first stories, and I wrote it that winter in Paris. It took me a long time to write. I left the hotel after a month because I realized I was seeing too many expatriates. I went to the Canadian Embassy and they had a book there of French people who wanted to rent rooms in their apartments. This was the hard-up French after the war. And they wanted – they didn't say this – but they wanted Canadians or Swedes or Swiss. Nice clean people. And I found a room that looked all right. The first man I talked to said, 'If this is a room, it's for you only, not *les copains, les copines'* because people would try to rent a room and squeeze all their friends in. I didn't like his tone, so I tried another phone number. I wanted a good bourgeois family who had roots in France – in Paris – so I could study them. I sound as if I was collecting butterflies, and I did. They lived on la rue de Monceau on the Right Bank, a very respectable street, infinitely respectable. It horrified the people I knew. 'You're going to live over there?' 'Yes, I am!' It was a youngish couple. They had two little boys. All of them became very fond of me. He was a civil servant and they were titled, but they were hard-up. They had beautiful furniture that they had inherited and they were very, very right wing, and if you wonder what I did, I kept my trap shut. I had no desire to argue. They were in their country, and I was friendly with them until they both died. Years and years and years.

JL: How long did you stay with them?

MG: In the spring I went for three months to the south, but I kept in touch with them, and they said, 'We always have a bed for you.' I rented something in the south of France because *The New Yorker* paid me for something.

JL: Were you here when you sold your first story to them?

MG: No, I sold one story when I was in Montreal. I gave my newspaper six months' leave – six months, what do you call it?

JL: Notice.

MG: Notice, thank you. It was funny, the men at the *Standard* were friendly in a brother-sister knockabout way, you know. But they just didn't want to work with women. One of them said to me, 'You're going over there? What are you going to do? What are you going to live on?' I said, 'Writing. I'm going to write.' He said, 'Write what?' I said, 'Stories'. He said, 'You know, you're like an architect who's never designed a garage.' That was his view of what I was going to do. But I had a lot of stories I'd never shown anyone, so I fished one out, typed it and sent it to *The New Yorker*. I didn't tell anyone. There was no note. There was my name and the address of my newspaper on the first page of the manuscript. It was up in the corner: St James Street West. And that came back, but with a letter, a very nice letter, saying we can't use this – they told me later why they couldn't – but is there anything else you can show us? So I sent a second one and they took it. They paid me six hundred dollars, which was more than I had ever had in the bank. I couldn't believe it. And I made the great mistake of showing my colleagues at the newspaper my letter of acceptance. It was a great mistake.

JL: Why?

MG: Because they were men.

JL: And they were upset?

MG: They were stupefied, first of all. And then, wishing they had the freedom to go away as I was going to go. They all had a mortgage and three kids. In a suburb.

JL: They were stuck.

MG: Stuck, yes. I had prepared three stories to show *The New Yorker*. They had rejected one and taken one. The third story, which was also accepted, I sent from Paris. At the beginning I wrote about foreigners, not understanding the French, or looking at them and getting it all wrong.

JL: And what interested you in that? Was it partly that you were going through it?

MG: Well, I'm a writer. That was the way I saw it, and I couldn't very well write about how the French looked at us. I couldn't get inside their skin. You have to be here for a long time, in a certain way. There was a story about the Americans in France called 'The Picnic'. Did you ever read that story?

JL: Yes. The picnic is concocted by an American magazine, an event to symbolize the unity between America and France. But there's no unity between the French and the American characters in the story. There's suspicion on both sides. The American woman worries that her children are being corrupted by French waywardness. And the French woman is appalled when the American throws out a wilting cauliflower. Which the French cook retrieves from the garbage.

MG: Those were situations I saw and felt and listened to, but I wanted to get into the French way of looking at us. So it began with 'The Other Paris' – the young woman expects so much from Paris and settles for something else. There's a story called 'Virus X' you may have come across. There are two Canadian girls. One of them has a fiancé in Canada. I've forgotten what she's doing here, but she's doing something.

JL: I believe she's writing a thesis about immigrants.

MG: The first wave of Asian flu was winter of 1952–53. And I caught it. I was in Strasbourg.

JL: Is that what the characters in 'The Cost of Living' also have, living in that hotel? Asian flu? You describe illness in a foreign place so effectively. I love the bit about the sister going out to get soup for everyone in a Thermos. 'Our grippe smelled of oranges, and of leek-and-potato soup.'

MG: Everybody got flu every winter. There was no vaccination in those days. First of all, the symptoms were like pneumonia, but nobody knew what it was. I mean, none of the doctors in the world knew what the first wave was about. That was why in France it was called Virus X. They were treating for pneumonia, which it turns out it wasn't at all, and there were a lot of deaths. I was in Strasbourg in a little hotel and at that point I had complicated my life with a dog. I was very very sick, had a very high temperature. There was a man in the next room, an elderly French man who lived there, and I was delirious. I thought I saw him walking through the wall. He used to say, *'Ma voisine, ma voisine!'* and he'd take my dog out. But in the story there's a girl – not me – and her boyfriend finally comes over to get her. And she is afraid that if she doesn't go back with him, she will be adrift. She's, on the contrary, very pleased to see him, and ready to go into a very restricted life because she's had a bad time with Virus X. *The New Yorker* ran that story. They would take a chance on things that others wouldn't.

JL: I asked you about the winter because I thought in many of those early stories, 'The Cost of Living' and 'The Other Paris', there's a very vivid experience of the season.

MG: The winters are rather dreadful.

JL: Differently from Montreal?

MG: In Montreal you're cold. You have sun on snow there.

JL: So it's the lack of sun.

MG: Lack of sun. That's why the first spring, I went for three months to Menton. I had never seen light in the south – I'd never been south of New York. I'd never seen the light that you get in the southern climate.

JL: And this made a big impression on you?

MG: I took a bus so that I could see a lot of France. Through Grenoble. We spent the night in Grenoble. Very interesting. Down, down, down to Nice. It was night when I arrived. I just asked in the bus station where I could find a hotel. I went to this hotel and my bed was facing a mirror, one of these big armoires with mirrored doors where you put your clothes, and the window was behind my head. And when I woke up in the morning, there was this fantastic sun in the window. I'd never seen that kind of light. Then I got a train and continued to Menton which was where my house was rented, my flat. And I carried my things and asked for directions and I found myself in the first old town I'd ever seen. It was medieval. In fact the old Roman road was the main street.

JL: Was that town partly inspiration for the setting of 'The Remission'?

MG: Much later. 'The Remission' is much later.

JL: But was it the same sort of place?

MG: No. I was in the old town. They collected the garbage with a horse and wagon. And the garbage man wore boots and stood in the middle of this unwrapped garbage. Just stood in the middle and people threw it out the window. It was really something. I loved it. I was very thrilled with it. Then I came back to Paris. I always came back to Paris. I spent ten years coming and going. I spent ten years, really, wandering through Western Europe.

JL: Your characters seem always to be comparing two ways of life in their minds. It's something I've grown up with, because my parents came from India and raised me in a place that was foreign to them.

MG: They didn't go home to live?

JL: No. They go to visit, but they've stayed in America. So I've been brought up with people who have that exchange rate going on in their brains, always converting and comparing.

MG: I don't compare.

JL: But your characters?

MG: I don't know. It depends.

JL: A lot of them have an idea of Paris, say, and then they come, and they're here, and it's not matching the image or the ideal, and they struggle with that.

MG: I remember one of the people around in that winter of 1950–51, and who I moved to the Right Bank to get away from, was Mordecai Richler. He was a bit of a brat. He was much younger. I'd met him in Montreal. The person who introduced me to him was the brother of the actor, Donald Sutherland. Anyway, he said, 'As you're going over to Europe, Mordecai Richler is going over and I'll have you meet him. He's very difficult, I warn you.' That winter everyone in the world was around Paris that I knew, practically. And I realized he didn't like it at all. For one thing, he couldn't speak any French. Though he came from Montreal, he couldn't say, 'Pass the salt.' He couldn't say anything.

JL: That's difficult for people, if they don't have the language. It affects you at every point.

MG: Well, it's a language you're able to learn. I mean, I didn't learn Finnish, I didn't even try, because it's not an Indo-European language, not anything I could cope with. I did speak English there, but I didn't live there. I rented a car, was just travelling along. But I didn't feel frustrated. It was their country, their language. But Mordecai resented having to speak French. He said, 'Anyway, what can you do in a country that's old and rotten and falling down?' Those were his words. Well at that time, it was burgeoning with writers, French writers. It was really the great period of the twentieth century. Colette was still alive, all these people were still alive, writing, producing. Gide had only just died that year. You breathed the air, the same air as these people I so admired. One day I was sitting reading in a cafe. And Mordecai came drifting over and he sat down and he grabbed the book out of my hand that I was reading. It was *The House in Paris*, Elizabeth Bowen's great novel.

JL: Which I just read.

MG: Oh it's wonderful. And he read some in a mocking voice. A mocking English voice which he didn't do very well. And he said, 'You know, if you go on reading this crap you're never going to get anywhere.' So I just took the book back.

* * *

JL: I want to talk about your first novel, *Green Water, Green Sky*, which consists of four parts. How did it begin?

MG: I had it pretty well in mind. It was my idea of a novel. *The New Yorker* published the first three parts. They didn't publish the fourth because you couldn't understand the fourth if you hadn't read the other three.

JL: It moves from Venice to Paris to Cannes, and then returns to Paris. Chronologically, it goes back and forth. Why did you decide to do that?

MG: I can't tell you. That's what I wanted.

JL: I find it so much more poignant because it's out of sequence. We know how things are going to turn out, and that they don't turn out well. Bob and Flor's marriage, for example. The first time I read this, I remembered being so haunted by the description, in the second section, of Flor staying alone in the apartment in August, when everybody in Paris famously goes away.

MG: This was someone with schizophrenia.

JL: When I reread it a few months ago, I remembered the moment she's wandering in the kitchen, looking for something to eat, and finds a sticky packet of dates. As I was reading that section, I suddenly remembered that that detail was approaching, and I dreaded it, because I knew how much it would unsettle me. That happens to me a lot when I read your stories. The smallest details are so incredibly resonant. And so memorable.

MG: Eating with her fingers.

JL: Yes, eating with her fingers. Eating mushrooms out of a tin.

MG: Well you see, that part of it is very dated, because now she would be cured with pills. Then there was no cure.

JL: Even with medication, people still suffer from schizophrenia these days. Flor's suffering is acute in the second part. She sees a psychiatrist, a relationship that threatens her family.

MG: Well, she has a mental argument with a psychiatrist, who is a woman – *you old frump, trying to tell me...* – and unaware of the way people will react to her. Completely unaware. She speaks to people and they don't know who she is. Being frightened by a stuffed horse in a window. That actually existed. There was a stuffed horse in a window at an antique store. I don't think anyone was meant to buy it. It was just there. She slides away.

JL: Did you know that this would be her mental state when you began the novel?

MG: I had roomed at school with a girl with schizophrenia. Her reaction was very different. Though she didn't like her mother, either. I remember she scribbled all over her mother's picture. I read Proust later on, and you get the thing about the lesbian making the other lesbian scribble all over her parents' picture. So I thought, 'That's true, that can happen, Mr Proust.' She ran around the room screaming. She had asked her mother for some money to buy a bathing suit. And her mother had written – I remember the letter – 'Buy a simple, modest number.' And she ran around the room.

JL: How old were you when you knew this girl?

MG: I was about fifteen. And I felt I should never tell anyone. I never told anyone about this rampage. I didn't think I should.

JL: But eventually, this girl inspired Flor's character.

MG: It was a determined ending. There was no other way out. I didn't know of any way out but going deeper and deeper. In her case, silence.

JL: The third section, which was published as a story called 'Travellers Must be Content', takes place in Cannes. Can you talk a little about the character of Wishart, a bachelor who comes to visit Flor and her mother, Bonnie? He's so horrible. A snob, a liar, an operator, a misogynist.

MG: I don't think people try so hard to shed their background now. In fact, they'll say, my father drove a bus, look where I've got. Wishart works to be accepted in America as an okay Englishman, and accepted in England as an okay American.

JL: So much dissimulation.

MG: I don't know if you've ever been with anyone like that. They abound. Then they'll make some mistake.

JL: He reminded me of a less benign version of someone like Jay Gatsby or Holly Golightly, one of those American characters who try fully to conceal who they are, and where they're from.

MG: His mistake is when he thinks that Flor's mother is offering her daughter. That's his social mistake.

JL: And he has such a terrible impression of the world of women. To him it's 'an area dimly lighted and faintly disgusting, like a kitchen in a slum…a world of migraines, miscarriages, disorder and tears'.

MG: Well, he's gay.

JL: I don't think being gay has anything to do with that.

MG: There are men like that, who have the depths of horror about what happens to women.

JL: Yet Wishart's also dependent on women, a parasite. He seeks them out.

MG: A leech, socially.

JL: But we can't fully condemn him. I can't. He's vulnerable in his own way, standing on his skinny legs. The story opens and ends with dreams. I like that you write about dreams. I was warned when I was just starting out writing, by a wonderful writer and teacher, never to write about people dreaming. He was against characters having dreams in stories.

MG: Well they're the people who think dreams are boring. I think they're fascinating.

JL: Have you kept a journal since childhood?

MG: I've stopped, except now and then. Up to 2000, I wrote regularly.

JL: When did you begin it?

MG: I had one when I was still in Canada, but I destroyed it when I left. I was going to a new life.

JL: So you wanted to destroy the evidence. Did you start it as a child? A teenager?

MG: I did as a teenager, sporadically. I had to be very careful, living with my mother. She went through my things like a beaver.

JL: But you always wrote in it honestly?

MG: At fourteen I wrote a poem called 'Why I am a Socialist'. It began, 'You ask?' Of course, no one had ever asked me if I even knew what socialism was. I had got hold of *A New Anthology of Modern Poetry*, published in 1938. I was fifteen and that was the Depression. Left-wing poetry I admired enormously. I liked the marching rhythm. There was Auden and company. There was Ezra Pound, so they weren't all left wing. I read this stuff over and over, knew it by heart. Muriel Rukeyser; the gang. And this inspired 'Why I am a Socialist'. It was a better world. And my mother found this. She wanted to know who I was mixed up with. Mothers then were very interested in preserving their daughters' sexual purity.

JL: Some mothers now, too.

MG: For the marriage market. She drove me cuckoo. She read everything. I never could keep anything to myself.

JL: So you destroyed the journal when you left Canada.

MG: In the building where I was living, in Montreal, you could burn garbage. People just threw things down a slot and there was a fire smouldering. I don't know why we weren't all asphyxiated.

JL: You've published some parts of your journal. I keep a journal as well, but it's never seen the light of day. It's hard for me to imagine having a part of it published. How does that feel?

MG: It feels – nothing. They're authentic. They sound different because it's where I am when I'm writing.

JL: One usually writes a journal with a different sensibility. You don't think of anyone reading it.

MG: But I think some things are interesting to read.

JL: You published a section of your journal in 1988 in the literary magazine *Antaeus* which I came across. On April 25, 1987 you wrote,

'I am thankful I do not have to live in a village, anywhere.'

MG: Oh, I would hate it.

JL: I was struck by that.

MG: I remember going to a dreary village outside Paris. They're very ugly. There's one street and everything is battleship grey. Awful colour. But that's the Ile de France. You go in to buy a newspaper and they all stop talking, to look at you. I love cities.

JL: Me too. But I wasn't raised in one. I was raised in pretty much a village. It's difficult as an adult, because I wasn't brought up in any other place, so all my memories of childhood are connected to a place I feel deeply ambivalent about. It wasn't until I got to a city, in my case New York, that I felt I could breathe properly and things were normal, even though it was a place that I didn't know at all. Until that moment, I really did feel that I was holding my breath.

MG: What I have noticed is how much you redo places and houses you've lived in when you were young. I think it was James Thurber who wrote a very funny essay called 'Mind's Eye Trouble', because you unconsciously take some house you lived in as a child and you redo it in your mind and there are these other characters, but it's not where you lived at all. It could be in a different city. Have you ever noticed that?

JL: I haven't lived in very many houses, but the ones I remember, I remember fairly well.

MG: To me the Chateauguay river, which is outside Montreal, has been everything. Even the Nile.

JL: It stands in for other things.

MG: They stand in. Whereas the characters don't do that. They come up – I don't know where they come from. They're just – they're there.

JL: In your journals and essays, you're such a shrewd observer of the world, and of world events. That section of your journal we were just discussing follows the Klaus Barbie trial.

MG: Don't forget, I was a journalist from age twenty-one to twenty-eight. That's a big chunk of your life.

JL: And you've maintained a journalistic connection with the world.

MG: Less now, because I'm physically hobbled. For example, in that journal – 'Paris '68' – I get up in the middle of the night, I get dressed, I go out to see somebody throwing stones. But now I stay home because I'm physically fragile. I could be knocked over. I could break all my bones.

JL: And yet some of your characters are so shamefully ignorant. I'm thinking of Marie and her mother, Madame Carette, in 'The Chosen Husband', who have never heard of Korea while a war is taking place there.

MG: 'There's a war on. Where? Not there, in Korea.'

JL: Do you think it's easier or harder to be a foreigner in France these days?

MG: It's hard for me to say. I'm not often taken for a foreigner.

JL: But in your observations?

MG: I wouldn't want to be a foreigner in the US, I can tell you.

JL: Even now?

MG: No.

JL: I actually think it's somewhat easier to be a foreigner there now. For some groups it's harder. But for the most part, I think America has gotten more accustomed to the idea of foreign populations arriving and settling and working their way into the culture. When I was growing up, most Americans had no real sense of India. But now, there's a relatively more informed sense of India, and of other parts of the world as well. And there's more of an effort, on the whole, to be inclusive. Obama is an obvious symbol for all this.

MG: We were all cuckoo for Obama.

JL: But have attitudes toward foreign populations in France changed or intensified? I was in Italy last summer, and the Italians seem really to be struggling in terms of what's happening to the identity of their country. There seems to be a real fear of the culture being watered down, tarnished somehow.

MG: In France there will be many, many foreign-born people who can carry on the culture. Which is declining, by the way. It's not declining because of foreigners. It's declining because the French school system is declining. I hear the French spoken around me and I say, no! The vocabulary is shrinking. With foreigners in Canada, they were left alone. They were there and they were working and paying taxes, and that's all. I was writer in residence for a year in Toronto.

JL: When was this?

MG: 1983–84.

JL: Did you enjoy that experience?

MG: I would never do it again. I think it's a dead loss. I'm opposed to it. You can't teach writing.

JL: Given that you were there, what did you teach them?

MG: They should know their language and read. Read, read, read.

JL: What did you have your students read?

MG: I was considered staff, so I had a markdown in the campus bookstore. I bought a lot of paperbacks, Penguins, with twenty per cent off. I had them on my desk. They'd say, 'Well I don't have any money on me.' And I said, 'No, I'm not selling them. If you like it, keep it. If you don't like it, give it to a friend or bring it back and I'll give it to someone else.' I gave them books I myself don't care for. I gave them Raymond Carver.

JL: Why did you give them books you didn't care for?

MG: I thought it my duty to open them up to different things. Otherwise I was there for nothing.

JL: Who was the person who first read your writing and told you that you should keep going?

MG: Just, 'Have you anything else you can show me?' Her name was Mildred Wood. She read the first story I sent to *The New Yorker*. I saw her twice, at *The New Yorker*, before I went to Europe.

JL: And she was the first person you ever showed your work to? Had you shown your writing to anyone else along the way? Any friend?

MG: Very seldom. I didn't want them to talk to me about it. There was one friend at the newspaper, Barbara. She wanted to be a poet, so we talked together and showed each other things, but that was it. I don't think anyone can help, you know. Now *Green Water* I showed – I had the proofs, and I was in hospital in Switzerland because of my back. I'd gone there instead of France, because in France they didn't know much about spines at the time. The owner of this clinic had studied psychiatry, this Swiss gentleman, but then he felt that most things are physical and he got interested in the brain, so he worked on brains and spines. And the proofs arrived in that clinic that I had to read and correct. And I still wasn't sure about the last story. I gave him just the last story to read.

JL: What were you unsure of?

MG: I wasn't sure if it was clinically correct. I didn't want something imaginative and poetic where she goes off into a dream. I asked, 'Do people like that commit suicide?' and he said, 'No, it's another thing altogether.' So that was really helpful. And I left it as I had it, where she goes into silence. He said she wouldn't have the initiative to pick up a gun or throw herself out the window. It's not despair – it's something up here [points to her head] – but she would have been unable to come to a decision.

JL: There's a real intimacy to the scenes. I would love for the novel to be reissued so that people could buy it and read it. I'd like to talk about the way you write about children.

MG: I like children. I had no desire to bring up children, that was a different thing. But I like them and I often feel sorry for them. The first time I ever saw children being hit in the face was when I came to France. I couldn't stand it. You'd go to a park and the mother's first gesture was to... I'd never seen that. The face slap.

JL: You often write about children who are profoundly neglected. Their parents are off doing things, living their lives. I think a degree of that is healthy, but so many children in your stories are just passing the time, wandering around, while difficult, grown-up things are happening, and the grown-ups are oblivious to their needs. The children in 'The Remission', for example.

MG: They're culturally dropped. I see it often happen with writers and artists who take their children to a village in Provence. They put them in the ordinary school, and they're culturally deprived, because they don't read what their parents read, and then it's too late.

JL: I didn't read what my parents read.

MG: But you had books around you. I can't remember not seeing books. And my books were separated from the grown-up books because my father had a lot of books of art and reproductions. I thought they were stories, illustrations for something I hadn't read. One book he was very careful of, an out-of-print book about Egyptian art. The colour pages had white behind them, that's how old a book it was. And then there were sepia photographs of different things, which were very interesting to me. What interested me was that you could colour this book, and I took it into my room and with wax crayons I coloured all the white sheets and made drawings. Then I tackled the black-and-white engravings and then I tackled the sepia photos and I put the book back. And once he had a friend in for something and he said, 'I'll just show you what I mean' and he pulled out the book, and it was ruined. So from that day on... I wasn't punished, but I was struck by his distress. 'You can do what you like, but don't touch anything else, ever!'

JL: I find children a particular challenge to write about. Do you feel the same way?

MG: In my house in the south of France I had a spare room for friends, and I sometimes had a child or two thrust into my care just so the parents could have a few days if they were travelling; nip down to Florence without them screaming in the back seat. I never had a problem with a child. I would say, 'Would you like to eat this, or not?' and they always said yes. We went up to an Italian place on the frontier and they had a choice of spaghetti or pizza, and then ice cream.

JL: I think children just like to be taken seriously. When I read your stories, I think you take them seriously, and that's the key. Because the parents don't.

MG: I had one little boy, Olivier. I was very fond of him. He would come up with the most astonishing things. One day – he was a very talkative little boy – I was trying to think of something. And I said, 'Olivier, sit down, don't talk, and don't talk for at least two minutes.' He didn't know if he should call me *vous* or *toi*. I left it up to him, and he'd say *vous-toi*. He said, '*Vous-toi*, you're not nice. *Tu n'est pas gentille*', and I said, 'I'm very nice indeed.' And he said, 'You're not as nice as you think you are.' Remarkable. And you think, I wonder if that's true? If they see clearly.

JL: My children teach me a lot. They'll say something and I really have to stop and look at things differently. The sense of childhood in your stories is really one of being in a prison. The children have no freedom. I felt that growing up.

MG: The prison of childhood used to come into my mind sometimes. Not when I was a child. Later.

JL: It's a phrase of yours, in the story 'In Youth is Pleasure'. Nabokov is an example of a writer who looks back on his childhood with such pure fondness.

MG: They had a high life.

JL: But many people, my own mother included, look back on their childhood and think of it as a liberating, dreamy, ideal period. My mother grew up and everything landed on her shoulders. I feel exactly the opposite way.

MG: Oh, me too.

★ ★ ★

JL: I'd like to ask you some questions about 'The Remission'. This is a story you wrote in the Seventies but that takes place in the Fifties. Can you talk about what inspired the story?

MG: I don't know. I just had an image of them getting down from the train, which I didn't use in the story, with the children.

JL: Can you talk about the experience of going back in time to write a story?

MG: They come with their clothes on, and he's going to die on National Health. No one would say that any more. Meaning social security. I've written a lot about the British on the Riviera after the war. I found them highly comic.

JL: In what way?

MG: Nylon skirts came in during that period. You could hang them up to dry and there was no ironing. Miraculous! I had a Black Watch tartan skirt with pleats. I'd wash it and dry it on a line and my British neighbour, whom I was renting my darling cottage from, came up when I was hanging it and she said, 'My dear, are you a Scot?' Actually there's a trace of Scot on my father's side, but I didn't go into that. And I said, 'No' and she said, 'You should not be wearing that kind of tartan you're putting up.' And I said, 'Why?' 'Well it's an insult to the family.' I said, 'I don't know much about Scots, we don't have them in Canada.' My dear, we have the largest number of Robbie Burns statues in the whole world! She said, 'It's just that the Scots take great objection to the wrong people wearing their tartans.'

JL: You talked yesterday about experiencing the light for the first time in the south of France. When I read this story, I'm always struck by the husband's and wife's separate relationships to the sun. Alec initially seeks the sun, moving from England to the south of France for it, but ends up hiding in the shadows. While Barbara is sunbathing nude, like something out of Greek mythology.

MG: She imagines the gardener looking up at her. But you know, she's not unkind to her husband. I don't think she's an unkind woman at all. She sits beside him as he's dying, she takes his hand. She talks about their future together. The fact that she has a lover doesn't come into it. She keeps that in another compartment.

JL: This is one of many examples in your stories where at some point or another we're in every character's head. It's an amalgam of points of view. It's what Tolstoy does in his novels, but you do it in the confines of a story. For me, it was very hard to get to that point. When I first started writing, I always wrote from a single person's point of view. But in your work, even in something early like *Green Water, Green Sky*, you're already dipping in and out of various characters' minds. Was this something that came easily?

MG: It must have, or I wouldn't have done it.

JL: I felt that I couldn't do it. I read your stories and other people's stories to learn. I didn't know how to go about it. But for you it felt natural?

MG. I never questioned it. The problem is getting it right.

JL: You're very funny, in this story, describing assiduous tourists. They struggle up steep hills to look at early Renaissance frescoes. Meanwhile, to Barbara's eyes, they're just 'some patches of peach-coloured smudge'. This must have been a time in Europe when a lot of tourists were arriving?

MG: I've never known it without tourists. Not like now, not like these mechanized hordes.

JL: One of the reasons Barbara seems pathetic to me is that she's so dependent on other people, other family members, for money. Things have changed so much since then, for women of my generation, certainly, in terms of more women being part of the workforce and being able to stand on their own.

MG: The sister-in-law is the pathetic one to me. She gives up part of her capital, which is tiny, so that her brother can go rest in the south of France. I don't think she's ever adequately thanked.

JL: Do you remember how long it took you to write this story?

MG: It took a very long time. I'm a very slow writer. There are things I've taken out, put away, taken out, put away. Other things, 'Across the Bridge', I wrote at great speed.

JL: Your writing is remarkable across the board, but I find 'The Remission' particularly first-rate. Do you have a sense of how strong it is?

MG: I don't compare stories. They're like the beads on this [fingers her necklace].

JL: But looking back, is there a point when you think, 'This was my earlier effort?' Are you aware of a progression?

MG: It's just a straight line to me.

JL: It's all connected, one off the next?

MG: I suppose so. There were years when I was doing nothing else. In the south of France I just wrote the whole time.

JL: Where did you work on this story? In Paris?

MG: Mostly in Paris.

JL: It ran in *The New Yorker*. Was it edited by Bill Maxwell?

MG: Yes. Then he had to leave because he was sixty-five. There's never been as good an editor. He was prudish, and I had trouble with his prudishness, not to speak of William Shawn's. They would say to me,

'Maybe those things go on in Canada, but they don't go on here.' The slightest hint of anything. I don't like pornography. But I'm very conscious of sexual tension. I think that's the most interesting thing to write about, the tension.

JL: There's a moment in this story that's so powerful. The children have come to see their father in the hospital, and he's about to die. After the visit, there's a description of them skipping down the stairway now that the obligation is over with, 'taking the hospital stairs headlong, at a gallop'. To me it's an example of why I love short stories. You can compress such enormous emotion and human experience into just a handful of words. It happens very seldom in novels. Novels have a more cumulative effect.

MG: There are novels sent to me by publishers to read. And I do try. And I can see where they had to fill a gap. I see it! I think, why did they need that? Take it out and tighten it.

JL: I'm working on a novel now, but I'm always conscious of that, of putting in something to fill the space between point A and point B. I just want to go, AB, not A, A-and-a-half, B.

MG: Exactly. Absolutely.

JL: I think that's the difference between stories and novels.

MG: Well, in the short story you can't fiddle around and wander. There are writers who do it, but I don't like it.

JL: Did you watch the Coronation on television the way the characters do in the story?

MG: Oh yes. I was living in the south. And the man who gets up to watch, the father… I realized years later that was my father. He didn't live beyond thirty-four. I don't mean he was crazy about the royal family: I never heard him talk about them – he died some twenty years before the Queen's coronation – but I recognized that he was that man.

JL: Does that happen often when you look back at things? You see something you didn't at the time of writing?

MG: Later. When I read, I think, my God. That's so deep in me.

JL: Do you look at your writing if you don't have to?

MG: If I have to give a reading I read a lot of things.

JL: How is that experience?

MG: It's completely mechanical, looking at the clock. I time them and I read them. There's a difference between speaking your work and reading. It's meant to be read silently, of course. So while I'm reading I'll change just a few words.

JL: Have you read 'The Remission' aloud?

MG: No. It's very long.

JL: Not even a part of it?

MG: I don't read parts of stories. Unless it's an evening where everything is in bits. Then I might. I don't prefer it, but if that's what they ask me to do.

JL: 'They'. The authorities.

MG: The police.

JL: I can't say I've read everything you've written, I haven't.

MG: Of course not. You're not writing a PhD, for God's sake.

JL: But every time I go back to one of your stories, it's absolutely fresh. It never tires. There's something so alive about your work. I can never just say, 'Oh, I've read that one.' No matter how many times I've read it. That experience is very rare.

MG: That's very good to hear for my age. My point in life. It's good to hear that you feel that.

JL: That's why I've read some of your stories literally a dozen or fifteen times. I keep turning to them. I can never fully take them in. I mean that in a good way.

MG: I had that experience with Elizabeth Bowen's 'Mysterious Kôr'.

I knew it almost by heart. It's one of her wartime London stories. It's a couple in the blackout with a bright moon. He's leaving, he's got one day's leave. They go hand in hand, they look at a park. They have nowhere to sleep together is what I'm trying to say. She starts to recite Andrew Lang's 'Mysterious Kôr' by moonlight. He's probably someone who's never heard a poem in his life, but he listens. And she is living in London with another young woman whose apartment it is and who is very – I can't say prudish because that was the period. So this girl is trying to get the girl who owns this apartment to go to a hotel for a night. And she says, 'Oh my dear, I don't think your mother would want me to do that. I don't mind playing gooseberry.' You know what a gooseberry was? The chaperone.

JL: What do you admire in particular about Bowen?

MG: Oh, I loved her stories.

JL: Did you ever meet her?

MG: I never tried to. But there's a book of her love letters to Charles Ritchie, and I did know him very well. He was Canadian. I knew his whole family. I was married from his aunt's house in Ottawa. Bowen was married to the head of the BBC and it was an unconsummated marriage. I don't know what happened. She wouldn't leave him to go marry Ritchie, the love of her life and her lover for years. And he got fed up with the situation. In the long run he may have felt it was humiliating for him to hang around.

JL: Have you kept count of how many stories you've written?

MG: There are over one hundred in *The New Yorker*. My files were always a big mess. When did we find out how many stories there were? Oh yes, when they were putting together what I call The Big Book [the *Collected Stories*, also called the *Selected Stories* in Britain and Canada]. There were over one hundred published in *The New Yorker* and then those that were published elsewhere. At the beginning they didn't take everything I sent so they appeared in other magazines like *Glamour* and *Esquire*. There weren't many outlets for fiction.

JL: Now even less so.

MG: I don't understand why they train students to write short stories when there's so little outlet for them.

JL: I think they're easier to respond to. My sense is that it's easier to tell a student what's working and not working in ten pages than in two hundred and fifty. When I first started writing, my efforts were just two or four pages. I didn't write more because I wanted to make sure those two or four pages were okay. I've crept incrementally toward longer work.

MG: I don't approve of writing classes for people with no talent.

JL: I don't know if I would ever have written fiction if I hadn't been in a class where someone encouraged me.

MG: Encouragement is different. But to teach them, how can you do that? And your teacher's only one person. There might be ten other people who read your work in ten different ways. I had a student in Toronto with talent and I had made her swear she wouldn't go to writing class after I'd gone back to Paris. I said, 'Above all don't go to one of those writing classes where other students criticize your work, because they're only going to look for things to pick on. Just read and read and go your own way.' It's not called a class, it's a writing—

JL: Programme?

MG: No, that's easy. Some junkie word.

JL: Workshop.

MG: Yes.

JL: Do you work on more than one thing at the same time?

MG: Yes, I've done that. Unless there's a point with the story when I can't do anything else. And at that point the flowers die because I don't change the water, dishes are in the sink. But that's when the story is almost ready and I stay with it.

★ ★ ★

JL: Last summer I visited the home of Marguerite Yourcenar, the Belgian-born French novelist who spent the latter part of her life in the United States. She had a house on Mount Desert Island, in Maine. It's called Petite Plaisance.

MG: Is it kept as a shrine?

JL: It's a sort of museum. They have everything preserved. Her rooms, her things, her books, her kitchen. She kept her refrigerator in a closet. It's a tiny little house, tiny rooms you walk in and out of. Her office is very lovely. She and Grace Frick sat at a single desk, facing one another.

MG: You mean she was able to work with someone else in the room?

JL: Apparently.

MG: What was Grace Frick working on?

JL: She was translating. When I came back from Maine, I read your essay on Yourcenar, 'Limpid Pessimist', in the *New York Review of Books*. You quote a phrase of hers: 'useless chaos'. And then you write that 'useless chaos is what fiction is about'. I keep turning that over in my head. I love her work, though I haven't read her in French.

MG: The translations are uniformly terrible. She would not accept anything that was not a word-for-word translation.

JL: And she collaborated on her own translations.

MG: Yes, but that was a tragedy. I don't think Yourcenar had a sense of English. Apparently Grace Frick didn't, either. If you translate French to English word for word, it goes on and on like a dead old spider web in the dust. I think that's one of the reasons she didn't have the Nobel. The committee only reads in Swedish translations or English. They probably got lost halfway through every book. Her lovely work was really her autobiographical work. They rang true and were wonderfully written.

JL: You grew up with your two distinct realities, privy to two languages, two ways of life, two sets of attitudes. It reminds me of my own upbringing. When I was growing up with that double life, I felt a lot of anxiety. Did you feel that?

MG: No. I spoke English at home and French when I was going to French schools.

JL: And you accepted it.

MG: I accepted most things like that. I don't look back at anything being very hard except the death of my father and my mother's remarriage and her abandonment of me. I found it very hard to be in the world without a father. I had no one to stick up for me. My one desire was to grow up and get away.

JL: Did you feel that you had a certain advantage, being able to speak the two languages?

MG: I remember we spent summers in a house in a town called Chateauguay, outside Montreal. I played with French-Canadian children on the farm where we bought eggs and chickens. Their name was Dansereau. I had English-speaking friends too, but I couldn't mix them. I remember my best friend was called Dottie Hill. She was so fair she looked albino: blue eyes and little stubby white lashes, flaxen hair. I remember a sister and brother from the farm came, peering through the vines that surrounded the gallery, and I said, 'Come on.' They didn't want to come because we were speaking English, and Dottie said, very prudently, 'Do you play with them?' And I said, 'Yes'.

JL: That's admirable of you. When I was a child I only wanted life to be a single way. I didn't appreciate knowing a second language. I wanted to hide the things that marked me as different.

MG: For me it was *comme ça*. There were things I didn't want to do. I didn't want to play the piano, I don't know why. I came from a family where everybody played instruments. My father, as a young man, played cello. He brought it with him from England as a young man. It was behind the sofa *chez nous*. You'd see the case lying on its side.

JL: Did he keep it up?

MG: By the time I became conscious of it, no, but before, apparently yes. My mother played the violin and my grandmother played the piano. They played together. When my mother was in a good mood and wanted to amuse me, she'd make it speak.

JL: The violin?

MG: I'd say, 'What is it saying?' And she'd say, 'It's saying it's time for Mavis to go to bed.' 'No it isn't!' That was when she was in a good mood.

JL: You were adamant about not wanting to play piano, but you love music.

MG: I love music. It's been part of my life. When I hear something on the radio in the middle of something, I'm a step ahead of them. I know the notes that are coming, I know the pauses. I just did not want, myself, to do it, and I don't know why. I was very stubborn about it and I would sit and cry. I married a musician, and he wanted to teach me the piano, but the moment he said, 'This is middle C,' I said, 'Don't do it! Please, no!' It seemed to me a lot of fiddling. It wasn't what I wanted to learn.

JL: What did you want to learn?

MG: I liked to read a lot. I painted with paintboxes. I had lovely paintboxes.

JL: When you were able to get around more easily, did you like going to museums here in Paris?

MG: One of the things I miss now is going to art galleries. Walking and standing – it's too difficult.

JL: Who are some of the painters you love?

MG: I love Goya. I'm not crazy about all the Impressionists, but I like Manet. I react to certain painters. De Staël I love. There's not much I turn away from. I don't like Dalí. It's fake. To me, anyway.

JL: Do you reread a lot?

MG: I was hospitalized for two months last year, and I was just thinking this morning, I wouldn't want to be back there, but I missed the time I had to read. Marilyn Hacker, the American poet, told me that every time she came to see me I was either reading or writing. She came two or three times a week. And I thought this morning, I wish I had that time again. My life – I'm not grumbling, I'm just telling you – is not quite in my hands, it's in the hands of visiting nurses, doctors and all that. It's chopped up. In the hospital, for hours, I just sat and read. Or I walked in the corridor for exercise, hanging on to something on the wall. I reread Tolstoy. My friends all bought me different kinds of books. As soon as I finished one, I'd take another. I hadn't read that way since I was an adolescent.

JL: I can't do that any more myself. I remember, a few months ago, I was on the subway in New York. I had a book in my hands. And I saw a young woman across the aisle with a book in her hands, but she was pouring her whole body into it.

MG: She was living it.

JL: It was incredible. I looked at her and for a moment I felt intense envy, because I can't attain that degree of connection with books in my life now. It's too difficult. What are you reading now?

MG: Different things. There's a pile on my kitchen table. But I can't just finish a book and pick up another one. I don't have that kind of time. For one thing, I'm slower physically.

★ ★ ★

JL: In a television interview you did in 2005 with the Canadian journalist, Stéphan Bureau, you said, 'One can't become something.' You were talking about one's origins.

MG: I'm not patriotic. Certainly not nationalist. You can't turn into something. I could have had an American passport. I could also have had a British one.

JL: I feel in my life that I'm always becoming something, because I never felt I was any one thing to begin with. I was born in London, and when my parents moved to the United States we had green cards, and I was appended to my mother's Indian passport.

MG: How old were you when you moved?

JL: I was two when we left London. My Indian passport always bothered me as a child, because I hadn't been born there. Then it was time to go to college, and for practical reasons, in terms of what it meant to be a resident alien versus a citizen, I was naturalized and received an American passport. Then eventually it began to bother me that I didn't have my English passport, because I was born there. So in my late twenties I applied, and the next thing I knew, the maroon thing embossed with a lion and a unicorn arrived.

MG: What do you use when going over a border?

JL: It depends on where I'm going. I always bring my UK passport when I'm in Europe now, since it's part of the European Union.

MG: In other words, the passport has no meaning any more.

JL: No. Mine never has. Though it does to other people, and I can understand that. I remember when my mother became a US citizen, it was a traumatic experience for her.

MG: She didn't have both?

JL: No.

MG: They let Canadians have both.

JL: America is full of people who feel they are becoming something. Because it's such a relatively young country, there's a process of becoming American. There's the possibility of it. I don't know if it happens in the same way in other countries. When I was growing up in the United States, I never felt American because I never felt I could get away with calling myself an American. People would question it, because of my name and appearance, and some still do. It's taken me about forty years to feel I can say that, and now I do feel more

American than I used to, but still with caveats.

MG: Are you married to an American?

JL: An American citizen, yes. My husband grew up in various parts of the world.

MG: I didn't feel I needed an extra passport. I can go anywhere in the world with a Canadian passport.

JL: You've lived here for so many years. How do the French regard you? Does it matter to you, how they regard you?

MG: Canadian. If they ask me I tell them, '*Je suis Canadienne.*' It is what I am, it's just a fact of life. It could have been another fact. I could have been something else. It's part of the deal, one of the cards they gave me when I was born. Then you don't think about it. That's that, that's settled.

JL: It never felt settled to me. I still sometimes wish I had the ability to say I'm from one place. That 'I'm X.' I always have to say, 'I'm XYZ.'

MG: I haven't any desire to get a French passport. I'm not French. I'm not British. You would have had to reject where you were born, and I didn't want to.

JL: I sometimes wonder what would have happened if my parents had never left India, or never left London. I think I might not have become a writer. Do you ever think about what would have happened if you hadn't come to Paris?

MG: I would not have stayed in Canada. The government in Quebec at that time was very right wing, under the heel of a particularly repressive Catholic Church. I told you about the Padlock Law, didn't I? There was a law passed while I was there, working for the *Standard*, that if anyone had left-wing literature, even private correspondence in their home, the police could enter – they didn't have to have a search warrant – and they could put you out of your home and padlock the door behind you. I couldn't get the English Canadians worried about this because it seldom happened to them. No one would come into an

'I would not have been happy if I had not tried.' Mavis Gallant in Paris in the 1960s.

English Canadian's home unless he was poor or unless he was left wing and Jewish. The majority of the French Canadians thought if you were in any way left wing there was something wrong with you. I covered a number of strikes as a reporter. I had very fixed ideas on the subject. And I thought, 'I can't go on living here, I'm going to end up with no soul, just me waving my hat or shutting up.' So I would not have stayed. But it seemed natural. I thought about living in France from the time I was fourteen or fifteen. But it came from films, pre-war films, and books.

JL: The idea to come to France?

MG: *La vie en France.* I would not have been happy if I had not tried. I had to try and I had to do it before I was thirty. I didn't want to marry again. I travelled alone most of the time. I liked it. When you're young you meet people very easily. You stand on a street corner and you have to beat them off with a baseball bat.

* * *

JL: How did you feel about John Updike's recent death? Did you like his work?

MG: I liked a lot of it. He didn't like me as a person. I don't know why. He once reviewed me nicely. He said I wrote nicely about men. I loved his first book, *The Poorhouse Fair*, and his short stories. He was a real writer – I mean that he could not have been anything else. I didn't like *Couples.* I thought he was a puritan in territory where he didn't belong.

JL: I liked him for always writing stories along with novels. For not abandoning them.

MG: And he wrote poetry, and he wrote criticism, and wrote about art.

JL: I agree with him that you write well about men. I admire Richard Yates, but when I read *Revolutionary Road* I thought to myself, 'This could only have been written by a man.' Do you ever think that about something you've read?

MG: Oh yes. One thing is, men don't know how women talk when they're together, just as we really don't know how men talk among themselves. You have to rather intuit it from something the man will let drop. And you'll think, 'Oh, so they do gossip.'

JL: People often ask me a question I find ridiculous. They ask why the main character of my novel is male. They think it's something radical I've done. And I want to say, 'Well have you ever read any Mavis Gallant? Every other story is from the point of view of a man.' Or, 'Have you read Chekhov, where every other story is from the point of view of a woman?'

MG: Not to speak of Flaubert.

JL: People seem to have no context about the history of writing and what writers have done all along.

MG: But you have to be careful. When I wasn't sure about something I'd written about a man I'd show it to a man friend, but never an intellectual.

JL: And did they ever say anything?

MG: Once. I had one scientific friend I'd ask to be a reader. Someone who didn't want to write himself. It was a story called 'Potter'. I wanted to make absolutely sure I wouldn't fall flat on my face because that was a tricky one. He was not only a man but he was another nationality.

JL: Polish?

MG: Polish, right. And it was set at the period of the Wall. I was very close to the Polish diaspora in Paris, the intellectuals who'd fled the communists. So I knew how they thought, but how to express their thoughts? So I gave it to this fellow who's actually German. And I said, 'If there's anything there that a man wouldn't say or do, in your opinion, tell me.' And there was one thing: it was a man who burst into tears on the street. And he said, 'I've never seen a guy do that.'

JL: What did you do? Did you take it out?

MG: I took it out. I just cut it out with scissors and pasted the page together with Scotch tape. It was just a sentence. I thought, I can't take a chance with this. But then, imagine what happened. I was in the post office here in Paris, and there was a fellow getting his mail from the Poste Restante. I went over, there was a ledge where you could put stamps on letters, and I was there stamping with stamps I'd just bought. And he was there next to me, and there fell out of an envelope a picture of a very young woman with a baby, and he burst into tears. And his tears were falling, and he didn't care if I was there or if anybody was there. And I thought, this is somebody looking for a job in France. I don't know where they come from. Tears were falling and I thought, 'I should have left it in, maybe.' On the other hand, many men reading might have said, 'What kind of person is this?' We have very little weeping in the streets. I'd never actually seen that myself, but I could imagine it. In 'Potter' he sees something that reminds him of her in the street, some oranges marked 'Venice'. I didn't mean he was standing there sobbing, just that he brimmed over. I've seen men wipe their eyes at funerals.

JL: Once I showed a story to my husband. I don't think we were married yet. I'd written a story from a male point of view and I wasn't sure about it. He said one thing. The story is about a husband and a wife, told from the husband's point of view. At one point the husband is looking at his wife's shoe. And my husband said, 'He wouldn't think of the shoe in such detail.'

MG: I don't agree with that.

JL: He said there was something too technical about my description of the shoe, something a man wouldn't know. That he would perceive it in other terms.

MG: So you took it out.

JL: I altered it. I made it less specific. Did you ever work in cafes?

MG: As a waitress?

JL: I meant to write in.

MG: No. People worked in cafes when their homes weren't heated.

Particularly in the war. That's when you had Simone de Beauvoir and all those people working in cafes, because they had a modicum of heat. There was a cafe near where I lived, on the corner of my street, but now, unfortunately, it's a restaurant. I used to be able to go in there at any hour and ask if there was something to eat. I could go in at three o'clock in the afternoon and say, 'Whatever you have, heat it up.' As long as it wasn't spinach, which I don't like. They would save it for me and they would let me have a marble-topped table for four next to a window. I'd bring proofs to correct. I was never bothered by the noise of people talking. But it's a restaurant now. And I miss it.

JL: I thought we could talk today about 'The Carette Sisters'. Here's a case where you group a few stories together, something you've done a number of times, something I like very much and tried doing myself in my last book. When was the first time you decided to do that?

MG: My dear, I don't know. You'd have to ask a *universitaire* for that. I have absolutely no idea when I thought of this. Usually I thought of a novel. And then I would not do the novel because, as we discussed, there are only certain points in a life that are turning points.

JL: And you wanted to stick to the turning points?

MG: Yes. Those are the important ones.

JL: In this case, did you write the sections as sections?

MG: I didn't write a whole novel, no. Some of it was already written. And the curve of the thing, I knew who they were, I knew what it was about. There's space between them, time between them, because sometimes I'd work on something else and come back to it.

JL: These were published in the 1980s. Was there any reason, when you were working on these stories, why you were going back to Montreal in your mind?

MG: I couldn't tell you. If I knew that I'd stop writing.

JL: Why?

MG: Because it has to come from something unknown in you. If I knew that I wouldn't bother writing. I'd be something else. I'd be a champion cricket player. Maybe I am a champion cricket player, in another life.

JL: The first story begins with an ending, with a husband dying. Madame Carette is twenty-seven years old and left with two young daughters. Yesterday we talked about 'The Remission', which is a story about a husband dying, and a soon-to-be widow with children. Madame Carette's life takes such a different path after her husband dies. She remains a widow and dresses in half-mourning, whereas Barbara, in 'The Remission', takes a lover before her husband is in the grave. Not knowing either of those times personally, and granting that they are very different characters, I wonder, how did society change for women between those periods? Specifically, for women who had lost their husbands?

MG: The circumstances are already different because the Carette girls were meant to work. They grew up with the idea of having jobs.

JL: And there's also the expectation for them to get married.

MG: That was universal in those days. I had it, not the same way, but I saw it. When I was seventeen I had a girlfriend, we were in school together. One day she told me a dreadful secret. She'd 'gone all the way', as we used to hear, with an older boy. And this was very secret. I said, 'You're not pregnant, are you?' She said, 'No'. And I said, 'You mustn't imagine your life is over.' But secretly I thought, 'Who ever will marry her?'

JL: That was the way it was.

MG: In the first place there was no birth control. There was a terrible risk all the time. To us condoms were for whores and sailors. Or soldiers. And so there was a terrible fear, I mean the fear of pregnancy was very real. There was no question of abortion, it wouldn't cross your mind. And you were cast out of society, the society you knew. We lived in fear. And it was up to women, girls, to prevent it going that far. If you didn't say hands off, they wouldn't be hands off. It was completely unnatural, but the consequences were dire. You can't imagine now. Babies being born and being given immediately up for adoption, back-street abortions. A girl who had a baby could be sent away, far from her family. So you have to put yourself back in that time.

JL: It's true that these stories are set in a time I haven't known. And yet 'The Chosen Husband', which is about finding Madame Carette's daughter, Marie, a suitable husband – arranging the match and chaperoning their meetings – reminds me of some of the old-fashioned expectations with which I was raised.

MG: Because of India?

JL: Because of the culture my parents came from, yes.

MG: But you came into a culture with birth control.

JL: I did. But throughout my adolescence the expectation in my family was for a young woman to remain sexually pure and then to get married, even though I was raised in a time and place when that was no longer the norm, and not at all how most of my peers were raised. The fact that I didn't get married until I was thirty-three was considered very old and unconventional by much of my parents' crowd.

MG: And they were worried about that?

JL: I think my parents tried not to worry, but it was there. My relatives in India were distressed when I would visit at the age of twenty-seven, twenty-eight, twenty-nine… 'Find her a husband, time's running out', etc. So my parents had to decide to trust me.

MG: Did they push you?

JL: There was some pressure, yes. I could never fully ignore it. When I was a teenager the idea of being married off to someone I didn't know or like was a real terror to me. But that's why, when I read these stories, I understand some of that attitude. The way the minute Madame Carette sees Louis Driscoll, Marie's suitor, and notes his ultramarine eyes, she immediately thinks ahead and hopes her grandchildren will inherit that colour. It's something I recognize.

MG: I can't imagine writing something that doesn't have a time attached and I don't like reading something that could happen anytime, anywhere. For example, in *Green Water*, the story when they're on the beach. It's early morning and the Vespas are starting. A translator who wanted to translate this into French said she wanted to take out any mention that it is the Fifties. And I said, 'No, I'm not making these changes.'

JL: What was her point?

MG: To bring it up to date.

JL: That's something I don't understand.

MG: She thought readers would not understand what a Vespa was. But one of the things I remember from that period is when they would start up in the morning. They'd rush along the roads. The Lambrettas too. When I'm reading, I like it if there's a mention of something that doesn't exist any more.

JL: I agree.

MG: Like a man giving a lady a light for her cigarette. It was very complex [leans over, imitating the gesture]. That was part of the seduction of the period, which I particularly noticed when I came to Europe. I'd been at a newspaper where they'd bang you on the back with the flat of the hand and say 'Hi, Mavis!' Then I came here where they were kissing my hand up to the elbow.

JL: The first of these stories begins in 1933, in Montreal. You would have been eleven years old that year.

MG: In 1936 I moved to New York, and when I came back at eighteen, I stayed with my old nurse. No one in Montreal knew I was coming. I got out at the railway station called Bonaventure, which doesn't exist any more, in Montreal, and I looked her up in the phone book. When I didn't find her, I searched the 'Red Book', a directory of Montreal addresses. I remembered her name and I took it for granted she would take me in. It never dawned on me that she might not even remember me. I had my last five dollars and I got into the taxi. It would have been sixty cents in the taxi. So I took a taxi to that address. It was the east end of Montreal. I went up some steep indoor stairs. Her house was very old and I trudged up those stairs. I was carrying two things: a suitcase and a typewriter that someone had given me. If you wanted to get any job at all, even as a hairdresser, as a woman, you had to learn to type, and I'd done that. I had left a trunk at the station. And she opened the door and she was smaller than I was! In my memory of her in my early childhood, I was always looking up. She didn't understand who I was, and I told her, and she said, '*Tu vis?*' 'You're alive?' And she let me in. At that point she did have a phone – I don't know why she wasn't in the phone book – and she called her daughter and she called her son and they came rushing to see me. They had been told I was dead. They'd been having a Mass said for me every birthday every year. They thought I was very tall: '*Tu est belle, tu est grande!*' I was five foot three.

JL: You write about this return to Montreal in the Linnet Muir stories.

MG: In disguise.

JL: But as you tell the story, I remember reading the fictional version, and Linnet going up the steep staircase.

MG: We had tea. She brought out a big pot of honey with pictures of bees on the outside. I remember picking up the honey pot to help her, and it was sticky and I said, '*C'est collant.*' I was speaking minimal French, but it began to come back. She asked what my plans were, and I said I was going to get a job. The very next day I looked for jobs. She gave me a room on the other side of the kitchen. It was a real room with a radiator, a dresser. It was clean as a whistle – she had a passion for cleaning. I think my rent was two dollars a week. When I started to get my pay we raised it to five. I was perfectly happy with her. We went over the past. I filled in what she didn't know and she filled in what I didn't know. They had adored me when I was a baby. Her son said, 'My mother and sister were so crazy about you that they used to watch you sleeping.'

JL: Those are the moments I feel the strongest love for my children, when I watch them sleeping. It all comes together then.

MG: I'm sure.

JL: Of course, they can't bother you in those moments.

MG: She was a widow, my nurse. She was a seamstress. In those days, bourgeois people had a seamstress come to the house who did the curtains, shortened the lengths on the winter coats or made one from scratch, worked a certain number of hours. She did work for my grandmother.

JL: Did she inspire the character of Madame Carette at all, a woman who takes in sewing after her husband dies?

MG: No, Madame Carette is something else altogether.

JL: The bond between Marie and Berthe, the sisters in these stories, is very strong. They protect each other all their lives. You were an only child. Did you ever feel the lack of a sibling?

MG: I thought it would be nice to have a brother. My father and mother both encouraged me to be friends with children from other families, go to their birthday parties, this and that. I was horrified because they were always quarrelling. I was bewildered by this.

JL: The relationship between Marie and Berthe is one of the most loving relationships, I think, in all your work.

MG: Wouldn't it be natural?

JL: It's not always the case. Marie and Berthe remain so devoted to each other. They almost have their own sort of marriage.

MG: They hold hands behind the groom's back.

JL: Berthe never marries. She earns her own money and buys her own fur coats.

MG: That was just beginning. Just the beginning of the change in Quebec.

JL: Raymond, Marie's son, loses his father as well. Not at such a young age as his mother loses her father, but still fairly young. And then he's raised by women. I saw a little of myself in Raymond.

MG: Why?

JL: The part in Florida, when his mother comes and he points out all the Canadian things in Florida. It's the sort of thing I would say to my mother if she came to visit me. I would go out of my way to find things in the US to remind her of Calcutta. I thought it would console her, to see signs of the place she missed. Also, the way they communicate. The coexistence of two languages, the separate but simultaneous conversations taking place. Raymond wants to tune out his mother speaking French, but he can't. He's a hybrid, like me.

MG: He's a high-school dropout.

JL: He goes to fight for the Americans in Vietnam, and meanwhile the Americans who didn't want to fight in that war were running to Canada.

MG: Did you think of that?

JL: At the end of the story, Marie and her daughter-in-law, Mimi, who is pregnant, have a surprising moment of connection. One minute Marie is suffering through Mimi's shrimp and rice, but then, when Raymond and Mimi fight and Raymond storms out, Marie physically enfolds Mimi and says, 'count on me'. It seemed very much a cycle of stories of the various bonds between women. Mothers, daughters, sisters. I found it very beautiful, looking at those connections.

MG: Well, I believe in that. There's a different kind of bond with men. It's a different thing altogether.

JL: I missed Madame Carette after she died. You don't mention her death, but I felt her absence. In those scenes when Louis comes to visit, there's something of the writer in her, the way she scrutinizes and sizes up a potential son-in-law. No detail escapes her.

MG: You think so? It wasn't meant to be. She would never write books. She would read newspapers.

JL: But she shares a certain trait with writers.

MG: You know, children have it. They lose it. They can come into a room and feel every tension between the adults. And not have the vocabulary for it, but they notice.

JL: Where did you come up with the idea of Marie being electric? Her thinking she's picking up a current?

MG: In Montreal there were all sorts of rumours about electricity, because when you came in out of the cold you could strike sparks. The doors in houses in Montreal had that brass letter drop where the postman puts the mail. It's brass all round, and there's a little flap that comes down. Children were always calling through the mailbox, 'I have to go to the bathroom, Mummy!' Otherwise they wouldn't let you in. They were having tea with cinnamon toast indoors, and we were out there freezing under grey skies. And they'd say, 'Don't put your tongue on the metal. It sticks.' But if you rubbed the metal, you might see a spark.

JL: I remember my mother telling me once that my grandmother was afraid of getting a shock from a light switch, and so she would protect her finger with the material of her sari when she turned the switch on and off. When I read this story, I remembered that detail my mother had told me about my grandmother.

MG: It depended on how cold your hands were, how cold it was outside, what it was like when you came in. And your feet shuffling on certain carpets.

JL: Did you ever know anybody like Marie, who was convinced she was electric?

MG: No, I just meant she was a bit dumb.

JL: It's idiotic, but it's also profound. 'We've got to make sure we're grounded,' she says at the end of the story. There's a meaning to that, even though she may not know what it is.

MG: I like '1933', the one where they're little girls. And the dog.

JL: The bilingual dog. There's a lot in this story about the specificity of origin. There's no such thing as simply Canadian. That really comes across.

MG: There's no such thing as a Canadian childhood. I've written about that in the introduction in The Big Book. You're Protestant or Catholic. You're East or West.

JL: Do you have any stories that you feel haven't been properly understood? Or do you not think about that?

MG: There's bound to be things that aren't understood. But you can still read a story. There's one, 'The Pegnitz Junction'.

JL: The characters in that story are German. What drew you to those characters?

MG: One of the things I wanted to know more about when I came to Europe was what really happened in Germany in the war. Because I could not understand how people so cultured – they have such extraordinary culture there – could do the things they let be done. And that came to me as a way of doing it. A great deal of it is satire on already published things. Kafka's *The Castle*. Wilhelm Busch. I used Busch names for the boys watching the train go by at a level crossing. Actually, only a German who had been given Busch as a child would spot that.

JL: Did you ever take a train journey like that?

MG: I took a very long journey. I've forgotten which year. On the German side – this was a long, long, long time ago – they changed to an old steam train. I started going to Germany in the Fifties but not right away. I didn't want to go there because I was distressed by what had happened. Did I tell you about my first seeing photographs?

JL: No.

MG: We really didn't know what was happening, that's the God's truth. I was working at the newspaper. I thought the Germans shot Jews by firing squad. That's what I believed. That any Jew who got out of handcuffs got shot. It was an enormous shock, and I had to write about it. The editor had the pictures face down on his desk. He turned them over very quickly and I didn't understand what I was seeing. I had to write eight hundred words and all the photo captions. I asked if I could take them home. He said, 'You can't show them to anybody,' because there was a fixed, international date for publication. But I had a friend, a young doctor in the army who was home on leave, and I showed him the pictures. 'What's wrong with these people?' I asked him. He said he thought they must be prisoners suffering from untreated tuberculosis. Actually, they had been systematically starved, but we couldn't imagine that. We couldn't take it in. Once I got on the subject, I wanted to go to the very end of it. The shorter stories in the collection *The Pegnitz Junction* are post-war. The book was published in 1973. I still think the title story is perhaps my best work. Everything is involved.

JL: Did you feel that as you were writing it?

MG: No. A lot of people didn't understand it but mostly they could read it for some sort of magic realism. I don't like magic realism at all. Like the girl on the train hearing this information. I didn't do anything else along that line. That is the book that's had the most written about it. MAs, that kind of thing. At least, the most who have come to me for help.

JL: Was the story too long for *The New Yorker*?

MG: It was returned to me because it was too long. William Maxwell said we can run the last sixteen pages and I said I wouldn't do it, because I knew this book was coming out anyway a year later. Years later, in the Nineties, not long before he died, he reread all my work and he wrote me a letter of apology. He said, 'I don't know what was wrong with me. My mind must have been out to lunch.' Imagine an editor saying that. He said also that he had felt bound by *The New Yorker*'s policy that fiction had to be linear. And this wasn't, it went all over the place.

JL: Do you still read *The New Yorker*?

MG: It's the one thing in life I've ever had free. I probably don't read every word now. Sometimes I come across a story that I think is marvellous. With some I read the beginning, the end, a bit in the middle, and I think, 'That to get to that?'

JL: It was a different magazine when you started appearing in it.

MG: You opened on to a story. It was a literary journal.

JL: How does your writing life change as you grow older?

MG: It changes in the sense that I have no hands any more.

JL: Holding a pen is difficult?

MG: I find it harder and harder.

JL: And the things you've been compelled to write about, to think about, to express – how does that evolve over the years?

MG: I'll tell you what happens when you get older. Things seem inevitable.

JL: In the writing?

MG: No, in life. They seem inevitable in some way. You feel less— I don't know what it is. You don't lose compassion. You know, *Men have died and worms have eaten but never I think for love.* Shakespeare had it.

JL: What are you working on now?

MG: I'm working on a story about my imaginary writer, Henri Grippes. And I do want to finish that. But it's massive, unreadable at the moment. I should have a clear mind, but ever since I came out of hospital everything seems a burden sometimes.

JL: Does the writing feel like a burden?

MG: Not the writing, but finding the time. I got to the point the other day, I said to myself, 'Are you sad because you left the hospital?'

JL: You were writing in the hospital, you said.

MG: I took up a journal because I didn't want to forget.

JL: What was happening to you?

MG: Not to me, but around me. Because I was eighty-five I was taken to a geriatric hospital. Some patients had gallstones, some chronic bronchitis and some had Alzheimer's. I'd never seen Alzheimer patients before. So I took notes. Rereading this set of notebooks, I found that I gave everybody a nickname because I was afraid the nurses or someone could read English and would recognize themselves.

JL: Do your journals ever give you ideas for writing stories?

MG: No, but they give me ideas of how things were. What was going on around that time. Sometimes descriptions of cities take you back. Not really people. Or they're people I've just had a glimpse of. I find them stuck back there in the brain. Like the Englishwoman I told you about yesterday, about the skirt. The one who said, 'My dear, are you a Scot?' I would not have remembered that if I hadn't written it. ∎

AMERICAN SUBSIDIARY

William Pierce

ILLUSTRATION BY ADAM SIMPSON

One spring morning – it was early May, and sunlight had just reached the ivy at his shoulder – Joseph Stone leaped up at his boss's call, then slowly, so as not to remind himself of Pavlov's dog, tucked his chair back under the shelf that held his keyboard.

He did not have far to go: three steps, four at most, took him from his cubicle to Peter Halsa's pale, wood door.

'*Entschuldigung?*' he asked, pronouncing the German word slackly, as any American would. 'Excuse me?'

Herr Halsa was drying the inside of his ear with a white hand towel. This was nothing strange. It had seemed unusual at first, months ago, but then Joseph had asked himself why certain behaviours should be off-limits at work, especially to the boss. He tugged at his nose, waiting for Herr Halsa's answer.

He felt only mildly ridiculous thinking of his boss as Herr Halsa. Everyone else was required to use formal German address, and it seemed right, though he'd explicitly been asked to call him Peter, that Joseph not call too much attention to what was already unpleasantly obvious: the gratifying fact that his boss relied on him utterly.

Herr Halsa lifted his head, looked up – he was now drying the nape of his neck, having apparently rushed from home with his head still wet – and grunted in a German way that pleased Joseph, because it meant again that Joseph worked at a German company, among Germans, who might at any time release deep, Bavarian grunts.

'Nothing, no, you can return to your work. I was just saying good morning. Good morning.' Herr Halsa nodded, still rubbing his hair with his head aslant, and closed the office door. He preferred to give orders in his own good time, when he'd chanced across things that needed doing, and in the meantime he expected his employees to stay busy on their own.

Joseph returned to what he'd been doing. He was typing up another proposal for robots that would replace human workers in an engine factory.

No one else in the building, only Joseph Stone, could say that his cubicle opened on to the boss's door. The other cubicles, their short walls panelled in grey carpeting, were strung together to form two separate mazes, each of which closed in on itself and had a single entrance at the printers and copy machine, not far from the kitchen door. Herr Halsa's office took up the corner diagonally opposite.

To the gear-hobbing maze belonged seasoned American salesmen who were unable to sell machines, though not for want of escorting potential buyers to golf courses and strip clubs. For whatever reason, probably some sort of native laxness, the Americans were unsuccessful – and with them one German who was so good at selling gantries that he'd been transferred to raise the *Amerikaner* out of their slump, and had instead fallen into one himself. To the gantry maze belonged newcomers who had not sold anything before their arrival from Germany. They were young and hungry and German and knew how to browbeat their former colleagues at the *Automationsfabrik* to give them extremely large discounts. Why shouldn't the parent division sell its robots at a loss if it meant gaining a toehold in the prestigious American car market? These good *Kerle* had rubbed elbows in company showers with the very men they now called on for favours. The Americans in gear hobbing had visited Germany too, but only to try the Wiener schnitzel and spend a few days in seminar rooms.

Joe Stone was the exception. He was American and the company hadn't even sent him to Europe yet, but his was the cubicle that opened like a secret on to the boss's door. Despite various drawbacks, the arrangement suited him well. He preferred to be visible to no one, and at midday Herr Halsa would close his door and tighten the slats on the narrow shade covering the long, tall window beside it and (Joseph was fairly sure) nap. Herr Halsa idolized the chief of the Volkswagen company, and the chief of Volkswagen held as his guiding principle that nothing must remain on his desk overnight. So, to ensure that nothing violated this adopted dictum, Herr Halsa forbade everyone from putting papers or objects on his desk during the day also. Which left him with extraordinarily little to do.

Herr Halsa opened his door with the fresh snap of someone about to take the air and disappeared into the matrix of grey-walled cubicles. Joseph pasted another block of boilerplate just where it belonged, then plucked the lemon out of his iced tea to resqueeze it. The rind of a lemon, with its regular dimples and high yellow complexion, cheered him so extraordinarily that he plucked and resqueezed several times as he drank each glass. The sun warmed his back, the sky had receded higher than ever, it was an uncontainably beautiful day.

The silence broke.

'I don't care if the file is on your hard drive!' Herr Halsa cried. He was straining to yell as loudly as possible, no doubt to make an example for everyone in the building. 'I expect to see it in the next ten minutes, or your job will appear in tomorrow's classifieds!'

Whatever else one could say – such as 'Joseph Stone was badly paid' or 'Joe Stone the PhD was out of place here' – he did not forget to enjoy the small pleasures of his job.

Joseph held up his cutting and pasting and listened. He heard, of course, the soft scrapings made by the German receptionist, Roswitha, as she wiped each office plant's leaves with a handkerchief. But the dust-up seemed to be over.

It was no fault of the boss's that he knew nothing about computers. He'd never been shown how to use one, and his book learning, which pre-dated the era of workplace computers, was more in the nature of a technical apprenticeship.

Joseph considered the factory layout the company was proposing this time, but the German sales engineers, as they were called, knew plenty that he could not assess. It was a small marvel that the gantries could carry engine blocks not only high over the aisles but also through the women's room. Joseph's friend the mechanical draughtsman, an American, took great pleasure in formalizing the Germans' mistakes. 'I do *exactly* what I'm asked to,' he said. He liked to be challenged so he could repeat it.

'You might get a bigger raise if you—'

'I do exactly what I'm asked to.'

A few minutes later, the American salesman Alan Freedman – his name was spelled wrong according to Herr Halsa, who thought it should be *Friedmann* – ambled into the boss's office with his naked, silver hard drive and the large, sideburned service manager, Helmut Schall, who waved a screwdriver as he explained in German that he'd removed the hard drive at Freedman's insistence. Naturally anyone in Herr Halsa's position who had once been a service mechanic would hesitate before spending too much work time in the presence of a man who might, just by his rough familiarity, remind people where the boss had started out, so, pulling his suit jacket from the back of his chair, Herr Halsa excused Alan Freedman – 'All right, all right, go back to your phone calls!' – and closed the door on his friend Helmut Schall.

Joseph could easily sympathize with the boss on this occasion, for Herr Halsa's duke, his overlord, the very stylish Herr Doktor Hühne, who might as well have come from Berlin between the wars rather than any part of coarse *gemütlich* Bavaria, was scheduled to enter in the middle of this scene and, after half an hour, exit with nearly every German speaker to a gala welcoming lunch. Following this, Herr Doktor Hühne, without Joseph's boss, was to call on customers in the afternoon. Herr Halsa had spent days revising a very smart, thoroughgoing agenda for the kick-off meeting.

When Hans Hühne arrived, he shook the beefy hand of his prime underling in the United States, Herr Halsa – who had in the meantime calmed himself and reopened his office for the grand arrival – accepted Roswitha's requisite offer of *Kaffee*, and promptly left the office to shake Joseph's hand and enter into private negotiations.

Joseph felt courted. Here was perhaps the most stylish suit-wearing man he had ever met – Herr Doktor Hans Friedrich Hühne crossed his legs even while standing, and turned his head gently to the side, not with any hint of arrogance but nevertheless with the suggestion of a long cigarette holder and a thin black tie – and, very consciously no doubt, he chose to address Joseph before anyone else. At this formal moment, the occasion of receiving a well-regarded superior who has just disembarked from a transatlantic flight, Peter Halsa could not very well emerge from his office. Herr Doktor Hühne had chosen to leave it and would return in his own time. But Herr Halsa clattered about – chairs, his empty outbox – to express impatience to Joseph in a language that Herr Doktor Hühne would not recognize.

'You translated the gantry catalogue, isn't it?' Hühne said. He spoke English with a smooth accent.

'*Das habe ich, ja,*' Joseph answered, wondering if he'd made any kind of mistake in his German.

'We have a new project in need of the highest-quality translation, and I'd like us to work on it together, you and me,' he went on, speaking German now.

Herr Halsa went so far as to clear his throat, but Joseph heard the softness in it, a touching womanliness that would mean to Herr Doktor Hühne, if he happened to hear, that Halsa intended nothing peremptory. On the contrary, it brimmed with comic lightness, the kind of mild rebuke that one might direct towards an old woman, perhaps a receptionist who had chosen this inopportune moment to dust the plants.

Joseph nodded with grave interest – he enjoyed being important;

who doesn't? – and stood up to match Herr Doktor Hühne's height, making certain in his American way to advance this relationship by allowing his arm to bump a few times against Herr Doktor Hühne's while they reviewed the as-yet-unreleased German prospectus for a new overhead-railcar system.

Herr Halsa appeared briefly at his door, then pulled back. Joseph saw his image there, the faintest double exposure, wearing the fine Italian jacket that usually hung behind the door.

Once Herr Doktor Hühne returned to Halsa's office, where the German salesmen were now gathered around the conference table, Herr Halsa grew expansive and host-like. At these times his bearing made Joseph proudest to have this unexpected opportunity, which had come up almost by accident six months before, to be the translator here instead of a mere secretarial temp. Joseph sat off to the side, his favourite fountain pen poised for note-taking. The Americans on staff were excluded from these meetings for the simple reason that the conversations were conducted in German, and for the complex reason that the Americans were American.

Not much happened during the meeting in terms of company business. But several important psychological or interpersonal things took place, and Joseph marvelled at how curious they were, and how lucky he was to be here to witness these intimate workings of an executive office – without having to suffer from any very significant attachment to the questions being discussed. First, the railcar system went unmentioned. Joseph felt fairly deep loyalty on this point and scratched out a reminder to tell Herr Halsa about the project as soon as the überboss left. Second, he noticed the obvious: the disappointment that caused Herr Halsa's eyes to shift nervously just ten minutes into the meeting, after the anecdotes and jokes and hellos. Charismatic Herr Doktor Hühne began to ask questions and guide the conversation – no guest-playing for him – and it became only too obvious that the written agenda would go unfollowed. Herr Doktor Hühne would have no chance to see, though tomorrow was another day, how tightly his next-in-command ran this important subsidiary.

Joseph, meantime, was smiling and nodding. He couldn't understand half of what was being said, the quick Bavarian retorts, the irony-drenched allusions to who knows what. But no matter. Joseph was the company translator and, with that credential, a fully vested German speaker. Even his mother said he wasn't a very good listener – how could anyone expect one hundred per cent comprehension here, where the salesmen were discussing technical matters foreign to Joseph even in English? Why should he squint or shrug or ask the others to repeat themselves when silence and a few well-timed laughs would carry him through?

Herr Doktor Hühne had worked himself into a bluster over the notion of *Handwerk*. Joseph took a few disjointed notes, hoping to record this fascinating paradox without scrambling it. *No matter how many 'machines' assemble our robots,* Herr Doktor Hühne seemed to be saying, *everything that the factory produces is 'handmade'.* Hühne was the kind of urbane man you might find in a pale linen suit smoking thin, stinking cigars, so his bluster did not throw him forward on to the points of his elbows, anxious and combative, but took him deeper into the chair, his fingers tepeed and restless and occasionally pressed against his lips. 'Customized production, gentlemen,' he said in English.

'Ah, customized production,' Herr Halsa joked. He didn't switch to English unless he had to. '*Kundenspezifische Fertigung.* I thought you wanted Reinhold to use handsaws and toilet plungers.'

Herr Halsa leaned back, trying to work himself as low in his chair as Herr Doktor Hühne, but of course it was impossible. Herr Halsa spent too many of his evenings in steakhouses.

'Let's leave American work to the Americans,' the highest-grossing salesman said.

Herr Hühne laughed. 'Yes, *Handwerk* in the manner of watchmakers, not plumbers.'

Joseph pulled at his upper lip and immediately read his own gesture. It was hardly-to-be-restrained pride. These men could tell their jokes about 'American work', their rather offensive jokes in which

'American' replaced what must have been 'Turk' back home, and altogether forget that Joseph was, in some ways – well, in every way – an American.

He liked to manoeuvre towards near-paradoxes, to insinuate himself into scenes that most could never hope to be part of.

At lunchtime, when the meeting broke up – Herr Doktor Hühne abruptly rose, declaring his hunger – the line of salesmen, and among them Herr Halsa, strolled towards the building's front door in twos and threes behind the visiting executive, who was a personal friend of the family that owned the company. Herr Doktor Hühne had walked ahead with the highest-grossing salesman, a curly-topped redhead far thinner than the rest and willing to make any kind of joke, transgress in any way, even to the point of yanking Hühne's tie, beeping like the Roadrunner, and calling the regent *Dingsbums.*

Joseph, too, proceeded to the front door. But this was where his deficiency cut him off. He could ride all of the other rides, but here at last he came upon a minimum height for the Tilt-a-Whirl, the requirement of actual Germanness, which he missed by a finger or two. It was his secret goal to grow into it, to convince Halsa next year or the year after, by silent competence – it would take just once to change the expectation permanently – and then he could board one of the cars departing for an inner-sanctum lunch.

Along behind the *Automationsabteilung,* as the only American invited to the restaurant, the sales rep Jack Wilson paddled out. He'd been talking all this while to Ted and Alan and the other non-German speakers in the hobbing area. Maybe he'd even done the rounds of the service department, the warehouse that occupied the back two-thirds of the building and marked the hunting grounds of the only birds lower than Americans in this peculiar aviary: the *Bauern,* Helmut Schall and his staff of Bavarian farmers who'd never had their moles removed. Joseph liked them, in fact they were some of the best men in the company, but the defensive jokes about their moles and so on – Herr Halsa's repertoire – any employee would have found funny, and Joseph felt justified in leaning back from his note-taking and giving a full-on laugh. Just the same, as he directed a quick salute to the sales rep Wilson, a slightly pleasant superciliousness washed over him, a feeling of gratitude to the fate that had given him cafes and saved him from the America of sports bars and chewing tobacco. Why shouldn't he enjoy some of the privileges conferred on him here and consider himself every bit as superior as the true Germans felt?

Joseph watched through the kitchen window and, like a basketball player who could dribble without looking, engineered a second iced tea blind. It did make sense, despite a tensing in his shoulders, that this man, Jack Wilson, would go to the restaurant. He was the one scheduled to escort Herr Doktor Hühne to the customer's plant that afternoon. Wilson and Hühne would tour the No. 3 Engine Plant in Cleveland, which had accepted the very first proposal that Joseph had written – an eleven-million-dollar project, the German factory's largest yet. And Herr Halsa was right to consider Hühne's impression of things. The previous executive vice-president had been recalled for capitulating too quickly to the American way of doing business – particularly by replacing German components with much cheaper substitutes.

In inviting Wilson to lunch there was no awkwardness, because Wilson did not work for the company. He was a kind of mercenary who agreed to play golf on the company's behalf exclusively and get drunk on the company's behalf exclusively and frequently with people who might or might not have purchasing clout at whatever plant Wilson had led the Germans to target. He was a go-between. A middleman. The aesthetics of the thing were less germane than the logic: it made sense for Wilson to liaise over popcorn shrimp. Nevertheless, when Alan Freedman walked into the lunch room, his hair full and proud, unlike all the monk-topped Germans, Joseph couldn't resist saying something conspiratorial.

'Look at Wilson out there laughing. Do you think he's drunk?'

Wilson soft-shoed into his son's minivan, the star of his own silent movie.

Freedman was forever in good spirits – he was a man of the highest, proudest, most natural spirits Joseph had ever known – and he pulled a Sam's Choice lemon-lime soda from the refrigerator along with his brown sack of lunch, and laughed with a gentle calm that put Wilson's bluster to shame. 'He deserves to be happy, no? A million and a half for the Cleveland plant, I'd be handing out tulips and Swiss chocolates.'

The pulp of Joseph's lemon went on spinning in his glass even after he'd stopped stirring, the swirls of dissolved sugar warping and turning like heatwaves coming up from a car. He often felt blessed by small things and now, with the young sun glinting off windshields and beckoning him outside with his lunch, he felt deeply fortunate to have this packet of sugar in his hand, to be already rolling the torn-off piece of it between his fingers, to be here in this job, a translator instead of a temp, twenty dollars an hour instead of eight-fifty.

A million and a half.

'And – do you get commissions when you sell?' he asked, expecting the worst. Every one of them must have been making too much money to care about anything. He was halfway back to his cubicle – a little-used door next to Herr Halsa's office led to the lawn behind the building – and Freedman was about to disappear into the gear-hobbing maze.

'Nope. I guess commissions are an American thing,' Freedman said wistfully. He was still smiling. He was almost laughing, and his hands were plunged so far into his pockets that his elbows were straight. Joseph thought he'd like to have him as an older brother or confidant who could advise on all the stages to come. 'It makes me think I should go out on my own. But damn, a drought's a drought when you're repping, and it doesn't matter how many daughters you have in school.'

What, Joseph asked himself as he sat on the cool May grass and looked out over the pond, is a million and a half dollars but an abstraction on a beautiful day like this, with a fresh iced tea, an egg salad sandwich with big pebbly capers, a slightly crunchy pear? The pond was a fire reservoir, man-made according to some code that required a certain-sized body of water for every so-and-so many feet of manufacturing space: the neighbouring company made baseballs, softballs, soccer balls, basketballs, volleyballs, all of inexpensive design and quality, for the use of small children. But even if their pond was square and covered across half its surface with algae, the jets that aerated the other half caught the light magnificently, scattering it like chips of glass, and the tiny green circles that undulated on the near side resembled stitches in a beautiful knitted shawl that the pond wore garishly in the sunlight. Joseph thought of his wife of less than a year, back in their apartment, studying by the window; his parents gardening five hundred miles away; his grandparents outside too, no doubt, mowing their tiny lawns just to walk under this magnificent sun.

When Joseph was back inside, Herr Doktor Hühne returned to pick up his briefcase, which he'd left in the middle of Herr Halsa's empty desk.

'Why didn't you join us for lunch?' he asked in German. 'That was unexpected. We arrived at the restaurant and I looked around myself, wanting to ask you a question, and what's this? He doesn't eat?'

Hühne left again with Wilson and the top-grossing salesman, and an hour passed by in welcome silence. Joseph worked steadily, with his usual dedication, no one but Roswitha interrupting. She sprayed Herr Halsa's window, his silk plants, his brass lamp, wiped and rubbed, a water spritzer in one hand, an ammonia bottle in the other, wiping, rubbing and spraying, holding the plant handkerchief between her cheek and shoulder and a roll of paper towel under her wing.

'I'm saying nothing, I'm saying nothing,' she said. 'Keep on with your work.' She spoke in heavily accented English and switched to German only when someone spoke in German to her. She was eighty or so, extremely short, with grey skirts that wrapped not far below her breasts. 'He keeps you busy too, I know that. With his whims,' she whispered, and shushed herself.

Joseph liked having a mercurial boss. *Mercurial* was a good word for him. He was pleased to have thought of it.

When Herr Halsa returned, it was clear where he'd gone after lunch – to the gym, as he often did. The advantages of a workout, not just for Herr Halsa's health but for the whole organization's well-being, so far outweighed any cause for criticism that Joseph wondered at his own momentary derision, the thought skittering into his head that these workouts seemed to follow on occasions of secret, carefully hidden stress. Who else was privy to Herr Halsa's fears and thoughts? Aside maybe from Frau Halsa and a few personal friends, no one but Joseph could have guessed at what was happening in the boss's mind.

On occasional weekend nights, with little notice, everyone at the company was invited to a German hall for drinks and music and laughing repetitions of the chicken dance. Herr Halsa would wrap his arm around every shoulder he came to and lift his beer *Krug* in a toast. *What? You have no beer?* He'd hesitate just long enough to show he regretted spending the company's money, then raise his finger to signal for another. By Monday, no one dared to remind or even to thank him.

Without exception, he returned from the gym with his face the deepest red, as if he were holding his breath through a heart attack. But in exchange, he was calm. His hair, as usual, remained wet, and he rubbed at it with the same towel that had started the day, bending his neck left and right, arching his back, and moving in other cat-like ways that would have seemed impossible an hour before. Joseph envied him his midday showers.

Then that was it for a while. Halsa retreated behind the closed door of his office and drew the shades of his tall, narrow windows – presumably so that others, instead of watching him eat an apple, might mistake this for his most productive hour. He would emerge afterwards, either confirmed in his good opinion of the day or reminded of some fresh inconvenience that needed a scapegoat.

Today, by the magic of endorphins, he was confirmed – his arms behind his back showed it immediately – and he took his flat expression from desk to desk and watched his employees' computer screens over their shoulders, occasionally nodding at what was for him the mystery of how things appeared and disappeared, moved, grew, changed and scrolled on the various monitors. Witnessing the growth of a letter on screen might have occupied him for hours if he hadn't realized, perhaps more acutely than anyone, that this rapt staring resembled ignorance.

'Come in here. Come in, come in,' Herr Halsa called from his office. Joseph had no idea who he was talking to. With the door open Joseph had a view into the room, but Herr Halsa was looking down at the things on his desk, reordering them according to some new, afternoon priority – name plate, lamp, telephone, pen stand. And Joseph could not see as far as Herr Halsa could along the hallway formed by the cubicle walls. Maybe someone was standing there: a petitioner. What's more, the boss was speaking not in German but in English. 'This is something you need to finish for the end of the day, so we must sit together. Quickly I think. Joe!'

Joseph hurried into the office with a notebook, two pens and some papers he'd finished the day before but not yet presented to Herr Halsa. 'Excuse me, I—'

'We're ready to send out a letter just now and offer this very good job. Inventory manager for the new production area,' Herr Halsa added, as if he'd forgotten that Joseph had sat in on every one of the interviews. The new 'production area' was an assembly room where this new employee would take robotic cranes out of their boxes, count the screws, assemble everything, test the completed system, then transfer it to a flatbed truck for shipment to the customer's plant. Joseph's attempt at a job description had muddled everything, though – no one asked if he'd ever written one before – so that several applicants showed up expecting to run an automated inventory system and a couple of others wanted a division reporting to them. But no matter. His influence held. After each interview, Herr Halsa would ask Joseph what the man (he couldn't help it that no women had been included) had meant by this and that, and very often what Herr Halsa wanted to know had nothing to do with the delta between languages at all.

The American salesmen liked to say that Peter Halsa was aptly named. He had risen beyond his competence and didn't know what to do with his time: the Peter Principle. Had anyone dared to repeat this to Herr Halsa, he would have said that he didn't need to understand his job – it was Joseph's responsibility to explain it to him.

Joseph sat while Herr Halsa paced, and here came a tremendous mistake that changed the course of the day. Even after five p.m., Joseph would resist thinking he'd made a mistake. But it was a mistake, and he knew it was a mistake, because a competent employee reads his boss's signs and does not transgress against the boss's most deeply held expectations.

Joseph believed he knew exactly what they'd be doing. They'd be writing to the candidate far more experienced than the others. And because it was a beautiful day and the sun was making use of each passing car's windshield to launch itself at the office walls, where long, overlapping triangles played across motivational posters framed in gold and black, Joseph nodded, looked Herr Halsa in the eye – calm Herr Halsa, for whom Herr Doktor Hühne's visit had been sweated out in the gym – and said, 'I'm happy to help.'

At first, nothing happened. And nothing seemed likely to happen. Why would it? Perhaps no one – least of all Joseph – would have expected anything to come of such innocuous or even friendly words on such a life-affirming day, where beyond the recirculating air of this boxy metal building the trillionth generation of bumblebees was unfurling from its hidden combs.

Herr Halsa smoothed a résumé like an angry mother pressing a shirt. 'This is the one we're hiring. Fred Wagner,' he said, still speaking in English.

Herr Halsa respected his translator, Joseph knew that. He felt the boss's admiration every day. There was the unusual latitude that Herr Halsa afforded him, and one day, when Joseph was off sick, Halsa had moved him into that cubicle by the door – the other Americans he pushed to the periphery and spied on. Of all the employees in the American subsidiary, German and English, Joseph Stone was the only person allowed to keep a real plant. All other plants were required to be silk or plastic. So when Herr Halsa tickled a file into his hand and sat down with a tired sigh, Joseph at some level did not hear the words he had just spoken. Frederick Lebeaux Wagner? Herr Halsa pronounced the name 'Vagna', the German way – though the underqualified good ol' boy with bobbing eyebrows and a love of dirty jokes was as American as Joseph himself.

Halsa placed his hand on Joseph's shoulder, then patted it. He leaned forward with whatever he had to say. 'Do you know why Hühne is a doctor?' he asked. Joseph couldn't get over how unusual this was: Herr Halsa speaking English to him in private. 'Hühne's a doctor because the owner's son, the old man's son, who went to *Gymnasium* with Hans, has a younger brother who became – chancellor, is it? – at the University Köpfingen. But a chancellor at the University Köpfingen doesn't give away free doctorates so easily, without work, so they arranged it in this way, that Hans Hühne, who couldn't rise so high on the technical side without a doctor's degree, would take his doctorate in insects, in *bugs*, and the university would confirm, yes, he's a doctor, with no diploma printed. He's a specialist in the dung beetle with his shit degree. I have only a certificate, but Doktor Schwanz Hühne has not even that much.' His face, which had cooled off since the gym, veered back towards plum as he spoke.

Joseph laughed because he thought Herr Halsa expected and even demanded a laugh from him – a good, strong, close-lipped laugh that said, *Wow, is that true? I won't ever tell anyone.* But on the table in front of him, Halsa's folder named the wrong man for inventory manager, very clearly and prejudicially wrong.

'What about Gary Jackson? For this job,' he said, tapping on the file. 'The applicant who did the same job before.' Also the applicant Joseph had recommended. Herr Halsa had nodded, and the other person in the room had nodded, and Joseph had in fact written the offer letter already, and it was in his hand here, behind the other papers for which he'd already, while Herr Halsa was talking about the shit doctorate, gotten his trusting signature, and he'd been planning to go up front after this meeting and drop it in the mail.

'Gary Jackson?' Herr Halsa said. 'The black one? I didn't know you wore white make-up to work.'

'You said on the phone with the lawyer that you need more minorities.'

'Do not refer to private conversations between me and my lawyer,' Halsa said, abruptly switching to German. 'You're in the room to explain his meaning when I'm lost in garbagey lawyer words. You're not supposed to remember any of it.'

'I'm just trying to help.'

Herr Halsa leaned in and pushed his chest hard against the table. He was speaking English again. 'I don't ask for your help,' he said, looking into Joseph's eyes but pressing his thumb against the table's high shine. 'I don't need your help ever, do you understand? I pay you!'

A truck flashed a stutter of sunlight across the posters again.

Joseph tried to think how to react like a German. Most of his German friends would have quit. The good, decent, strong-willed Germans would have argued, then quit. But what about the businessy Germans? The *Nieten in Nadelstreifen*, idiots in pinstripes? Or come to think of it, this bitter subversive feeling most closely matched his friend who drafted all the factory drawings here, that's who he felt most like. It was maybe pure American bitterness that welled up and spat a calculating line back at Herr Halsa in Joseph's most cordial tone of voice: something that would stab the boss without giving him grounds for firing.

'Herr Doktor Hühne just wants me to translate a new catalogue.'

This manoeuvre, once he'd completed it, did seem German to him – after all, his American friend, the draughtsman, had lived in Darmstadt for fifteen years. And Peter Halsa proved more adept at it.

'You're not the company translator waiting for everyone's work,' he said. 'You take your jobs from me. If anyone needs your time, tell them to ask first, they can knock on my door. But I won't give up my secretary's time for everybody's pet project.'

Without quite knowing how, Joseph retired from Herr Halsa's office to his own cubicle, where he could at least drink the melted ice at the bottom of his long-finished iced tea. He didn't buck forward or run. He walked upright, and he remembered squaring the signed papers on the boss's table in a very casual way before excusing himself. Halsa had already said, too, that there wasn't enough time to write to Fred Wagner before five and they should do it first thing in the morning. Joseph slipped his signed letter to Gary Johnson into a company envelope, affixed one of the personal stamps he kept in his top drawer and licked the envelope shut, exultant to have the last word. Sooner than face a lawsuit, they'd keep Johnson on – the most qualified man, a balm or salt to their racism, salutary either way.

The afternoon had lengthened the building's shadow more than halfway to the ball factory, nearly there, where the five o'clock shift had just arrived, bringing with it a fleet of cars vetted and certified to meet the arcane union rules for what it meant to be 'Made in the USA'.

Herr Halsa was hiring an inventory manager for one reason. He had fired two lawyers and with Joseph's help retained a third who'd given him the legal opinion that putting in the last few bolts in the production area would allow the company to pitch its robots as 'Assembled in the USA'. The lawyer before this latest had sent a long description in quotation marks, with his signature below: 'Final assembly done partially in the United States from some parts manufactured from metals mined and smelted partially in the USA.' And now, as Joseph squeezed another lemon into a fresh iced tea and breathed in the spray of lemon oil, he felt with decreasing urgency the embarrassment of having helped Herr Halsa turn away from the truth. Herr Halsa didn't want the truth of anything. He wanted whatever would seem to raise him up, well past his competence.

Meandering past Helmut Schall's test gantries, which flung an engine block back and forth ten, fifteen, twenty thousand times to prove their stamina, Joseph kept himself safe with an extra-wide margin, in case the many-worlds theory proved to be true and a few random quantums of difference in some conceivable world, leading to a stumble or a careless turn, put him fatally close. Whenever he approached a precipitous edge, or a car passed near enough to unsettle him, he wondered if in some other universe his mother would have cause to grieve now, and the thought of hurting her in that way, somewhere, saddened him.

He didn't pace for long. The company was paying. But he could feel how little that mattered now. He needed to finish the proposal by tomorrow and despite everything he couldn't help wanting it to be perfect, down to the indentations and centrings. Thirty pages' worth. But none of that was the main reason he sat at his desk again, resqueezing his lemon, dusting a few leaves of his ivy plant – a final act of defiance, since Herr Halsa's 'permission' was unspoken and grudging – and pasted in more blocks of pre-written text. These cubicles of words: he'd worried over them, like a boss getting a new job description right, and then, without testing it overmuch, he'd called the cut-and-paste system finished, suitable for all occasions, never to be questioned again. The main reason he dropped his disgust, gave up pacing and returned to his privileged corner was that he was bored.

At five o'clock Herr Halsa came out of his office and Joseph's pulse quickened. Towards or away? He glanced over: towards, and it was clear that Herr Halsa had forgotten everything, put it all behind him. He was wearing his smart suit jacket, finely tailored – Joseph took particular note of it. And he looked confident now. You couldn't think about the Peter Principle when Herr Halsa wore that suit jacket. Maybe Joseph should spend some of his paycheque on a hand-tailored suit. He didn't know what occasion he'd have to wear such a thing, but it seemed the perfect antidote to moulded rubber balls, a factory pond, the grey rugs climbing up the walls of his cubicle.

Herr Halsa laughed. He had a deep, hearty laugh when the day was done. And he told Joseph to go play a little.

Joseph chuckled and nodded. 'Good advice,' he said.

'*Das ist kein Ratschlag, das ist ein Befehl*,' Herr Halsa said. 'It's not advice. It's an order.'

Almost drunk now, Joseph gave a casual evening salute. '*Jawohl. Tschüß!*' he said familiarly. Swatting the envelope against his wrist, back and forth, he watched Herr Halsa swagger away, and noticed with a certain amount of unbecoming pleasure that even as the boss passed a trio of underperforming American salesmen he said nothing to them, lost in his pre-dinner whistling.

That was it. Without considering what was inside, or rather, thinking of it sidelong, as evidence of his importance here, Joseph raised the sealed envelope in a toast and shredded it, along with a few sensitive documents that Herr Halsa didn't want the others to see. He stood up and, with the last moments of the day – because Herr Halsa had left twenty-five seconds early – he wetted a square of paper towel in his melted ice and wiped the leaves of the ivy until they glowed.

'*A Country in the Moon* is literary travel writing at its best: elegiac, informative and profound. It's probably the best travel book I will read this year'
Jim Blackburn, *Wanderlust* 'Book of the Month'

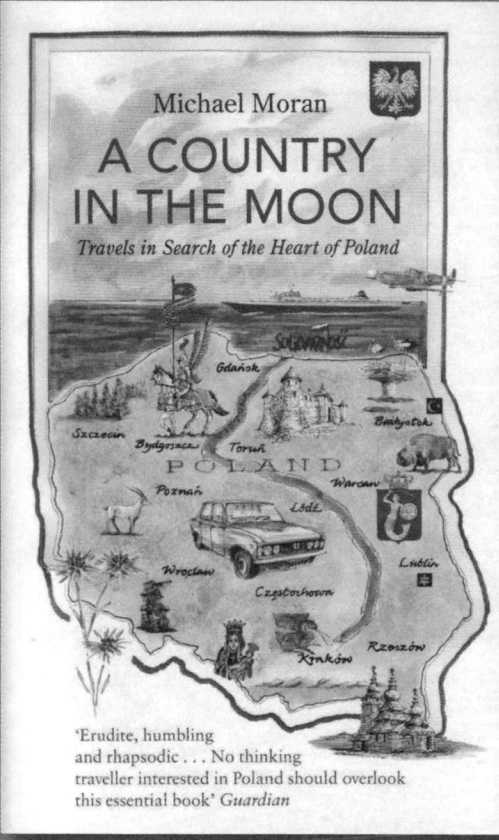

ISBN 9781847081049 • Paperback

'As much cultural history as conventional travel narrative . . . This lively and intelligent book is stuffed with original material that is both fascinating and quite new to most people in the West'
Robert Carver, *Times Literary Supplement*

'Wonderful' Giles Foden, *Condé Nast Traveller*

www.granta.com

UNTITLED

Chris Ware

THE TOP OF HIS HEAD

PINK FROM THE SUN.

A KISS GOODBYE

FOR ME ON THE WAY TO WORK

EVERY DAY.

HIS COUGH: A GRINDING RASP, STIFLED UNTIL HE'D RETRIEVED HIS HANDKERCHIEF

koff kooff koff kf

THE SMELL OF LEATHER AND WOOL... A MASCULINE, MUCOUSY WOODINESS

STILL

FROM THE FOLDS OF HIS COAT.

MOTHER, RUNNING THE ELECTRIC CARPET SWEEPER

JUST TO ANNOY ME.

WHY DID SHE HAVE TO BOB HER HAIR LIKE MINE, ANYWAY?

TRYING TO LOOK YOUNG

WHILE I DO EVERYTHING I CAN

TO LOOK GROWN UP.

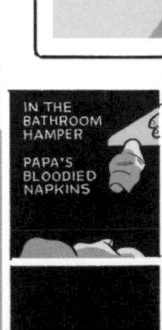

IN THE BATHROOM HAMPER

PAPA'S BLOODIED NAPKINS

MIXED IN WITH MINE.

HAFFNER

Adam Thirlwell

ILLUSTRATION BY RACHEL TUDOR BEST

1

And so the century ended: with Haffner watching a man caress a woman's breasts.

It was an imbroglio. He would admit that much. But at least it was an imbroglio of Haffner's making.

He might have been seventy-eight, but in Haffner's opinion he counted as young. He counted, in the words of the young, as hip. Or as close to hip as anyone else. Only Haffner, after all, would have been found in this position.

What position?

Concealed in a wardrobe, the doors darkly ajar, watching a woman be nakedly playful to her boyfriend.

This was why I admired him. Haffner Unbound! But there were other Haffners, too – Haffner Pensive, Haffner Abandoned. He tended to see himself like this; as in a dream, in poses: the Loves of Haffner. Like the panels of a classical frieze.

A tzigani pop album – disco drumbeats, accordions, sporadic

trumpets – was being broadcast by a compact-disc player above the minibar. This weakened his squinting concentration. He disliked the modern combination of sex and music. It was better, thought Haffner, for bodies to undress themselves in the quiet of the everyday background hum. In Naples once, in what, he had to say, could only be described as a dive, in the liberated city, the lights went suddenly out, and so the piano stopped, and in the ensuing silent twilight Haffner watched a woman undress so slowly, so awkwardly, so peacefully – accompanied only by the accidental chime of wine glasses, the brief struck fizz of matches – that she had, until this moment more than fifty years later, remained his ideal of beauty.

Now, however, Haffner was unsure of his ideals.

He continued looking at Zinka. It wasn't a difficult task. Her hair was dark; her nipples were long, and almost black, with stained pools of areolae; her stomach curved gently towards her hips, where the bone then steeply rose; her legs were slender. Her breasts and nose were cute. If Haffner had a type, then this was it: the feminine unfeminine. The word for her, in his heyday, would have been gamine. She was a *garçonne*. If those words were, he mused, at the end of his century, still used for girls at all.

They were not.

A suckling noise emerged from Niko, who was now tugging at Zinka's nipples with the pursed O of his mouth.

Haffner was lustful, selfish, vain – an entirely commonplace man. It was the unavoidable conclusion. He had to admit it. In London and New York he had practised as a banker. His life had been unremarkable. It was the twentieth century's idea of the bourgeois: the grey Atlantic Ocean. The horizontal placid waves of the grey Atlantic Ocean. With Liberty at one extreme, and the Bank of England at the other. But Haffner wasn't straddling the Atlantic any more. A hotel in a spa town was now Haffner's temporary home. He was landlocked – adrift in the centre of Europe, aloft in the Alps.

And now he was hidden in a wardrobe.

He was not, however, the usual voyeur. It was true that Niko was unaware of his presence. But Zinka, Zinka knew all about this spectral form in the wardrobe. Somehow, in a way that had seemed natural at the time, Zinka and Haffner had developed this idea of Haffner's unnatural pleasure. The causes were obscure, occasioned by some random confluence of Haffner's charm and the odd mixture Zinka felt of tenderness for Haffner and mischief towards her boyfriend. But however obscure its causes, the conclusion was obvious.

So, ladies and gentlemen, maybe Haffner was grand, in a way. Maybe Haffner was an epic hero. And if Haffner was a hero, then his wallet, with its creased photographs, was his mute mausoleum. Take a look! Haffner in Rome, wonkily crowned by the curve of the Coliseum, a Medusan pile of spaghetti in front of him; Haffner and Livia at a garden party in Buckingham Palace, trying to smile while hoping that Livia's hat – a plate on which lay a pile of flowers – would not erupt and blow away; Haffner's grandson Benjamin, aged four, in a Yankees baseball cap, pissing with cherubic abandon – a live renaissance fountain – in the gardens of a country house.

All photo albums are unhappy, in the words of the old master, in their own particular way.

2

And me? I was born sixty years after Haffner. I was just a friend. I went to see him, in a hospital on the outskirts of London. His finale in the centre of Europe was a decade ago. Now, Haffner was dying. But then Haffner had been dying for so long.

—The thing is, he said, —I just need to plan for the next forty-eight hours. We just need to organize the next few days of the new era.

And when I asked him what new era he meant, he replied that this was exactly what we had to find out.

Everything was ending. On the television, a panel was discussing the crisis. The money was disappearing. The banks were disappearing. The end, as usual, was continuing. I wasn't sorry for the money, however. I was sorry for Haffner. There was a miniature rose in bud on the table. Haffner was trying to explain.

Something, he said, had gone very very wrong. Perhaps, he said, we just needed to get this closed – pointing to a bedside cabinet, whose lock was gone.

He was lower than the dust, he told me. Lower than the dust. After an hour, he wanted to go to the bathroom. He started trying to undress himself, there in his armchair. And so I called a nurse and then I left him, as he was ushered into the women's bathroom, because that bathroom was closer to the room in which Haffner was busily dying.

Standing in the hospital's elliptical concrete drive, as the electric doors opened and closed behind me, I waited for the taxi to take me to the trains – back to the city. Across the silver fields the mauve fir trees kept themselves to themselves. It was neither the country nor the city. It was nowhere.

And as I listened to the boring sirens, I contemplated my memories of Haffner.

With my vision of Haffner – his trousers round his ankles, his hands nervous at his cream underwear – I began my project for his resurrection. Like that historian looking down at the ruins of Rome, in the twilight – with the tourists sketching their souvenirs, and the bells beginning, and the pestering guides, and the water sellers, and the sun above them shrinking: the endless and mortal sun.

3

His career had been the usual success story. After the war Haffner had joined Warburg's. He had distinguished himself with the money he made on the exchange crisis. But his true moment had arrived some years later, when it was Haffner who had realized, as the Fifties wore on, the American crisis with dollars. Only Haffner had quite understood the obviousness of it all. The obtuseness of Regulation Q! Naturally, more and more dollars would leave, stranded as they were in the vaults of the United States, and come to Europe. This was what he had explained to an executive in Bankers Trust, who was over in London to encourage men like Haffner to move to New York. In 1963, therefore, Haffner left Warburg's for America, where he stayed as a general manager for eight years. He was the expert in currency exchange: doyen of the international. Then, in 1974, he returned as Chief General Manager in the London office of Chase Manhattan. Just in time for the birth of his grandson – who had promised so much, thought Haffner, as another version of Haffner, and yet delivered so little. Then, finally, there came Haffner's final promotion to the board of directors. His banishment, joked Haffner.

Haffner, I have to admit, didn't practise the usual art of being a grandfather. Cowardice, obscenity, charm, moral turpitude: these were the qualities Haffner preferred. He had bravado. And so it was that, a decade ago, in the spa town, when everything seemed happier, he avoided the letters from his daughter, the telephone calls from his grandson, the metaphysical lamentation from his exasperated family. Instead, he continued staring at Zinka's breasts, as Niko clumsily caressed them.

Since Zinka was the other hero of Haffner's finale, it may be useful to understand her history.

To some people, Zinka said she was from Bukovina. This was where she had been born, at the eastern edge of Europe – on a night, her mother said, when everything had frozen, even the sweat on her forehead. Her mother, as Zinka knew, was given to hyperbole. To other people, Zinka said she was from Bucharest; and this was true too. It was where she had grown up, in an apartment block out to the north of the city: near the park. But to Haffner, she had simply said she was from Zagreb. In Zagreb, she had trained in the corps de ballet. Until History, that arrogant personification, decided to interrupt. So now she worked here, in this hotel in a spa town, in the unfashionable unfrequented Alps, north of the border with Italy – as a health assistant to the European rich.

This was where Haffner had discovered her – on the second day of his escape. Sipping a coffee he had seen her – the cute yoga teacher – squatting and shimmying her shoulders behind her knees, while the hotel guests comically mimicked her. She was in a grey T-shirt and grey tracksuit trousers: a T-shirt and trousers that could not conceal the twin small swelling of her breasts, borrowed from an even younger girl, and their reflection, the twin swelling of her buttocks, borrowed from an even younger boy. Then she clasped her hands above her back, in a pose that Haffner could only imagine implied such infinite dexterity that his body began to throb, and he felt the old illness return. The familiar, peristaltic illness of the women.

Concealed in a bedroom wardrobe, he looked up at what he could see of the ceiling: where the electric bulb's white light was converted by a dusty trapezoid lampshade into a peachy, emollient glow.

He really didn't want anything else. The women were the only means of Haffner's triumph – his ageing body still a pincushion for the multicoloured plastic arrows of the victorious kid-god: Cupid.

4

Reproductions of these arrows could now be found disporting on Niko's forearms, directing the observer's gaze up to his biceps, where two colourful dragons were eating their own tails – dragons which, if he could have seen them in detail, would have reminded Haffner of the lurid mythical beasts tattooed on the arms of his CO in the war. But Haffner could not see these dragons in detail. Gold bracelets tightly gilded Niko's other wrist. Another more abstract tattoo spread over the indented muscles of his stomach – a background, now, to his erect penis, to which Zinka – dressed only in the smallest turquoise panties – was attending.

Situations like these were Haffner's habitat – he lived for the women, ever since he had taken out his first ever girl, to the Ionic Picture Theatre on the Finchley Road. Her name was Hazel. She let him touch her hand all through the feature. The erotic determined him. The film they had seen had been chosen by Hazel: a romance involving fairies, and the spirits of the wood. None of the effects – the billowing cloths, the wind machines, the fuzzy light at the edges of each frame, the doleful music – convinced sarcastic Haffner of their reality. Afterwards, he had bought her two slices of chocolate cake in a Lyons tea house, and they looked at each other, softly – while in a pattern that would menace Haffner all his life he began to wonder when he might acceptably, politely, try to kiss her.

He was mediocre, he was unoriginal. He admitted this freely. With only one thing had Haffner been blessed – with the looks. There was no denying, Haffner used to say, mock-ruefully, that Haffner was old – especially if you took a look at him. In the words of his favourite comedian. But Haffner knew this wasn't true. He was unoriginal – but the looks were something else. It was not just his friends who said this; his colleagues acknowledged it too. At seventy-eight, Haffner possessed more hair than was his natural right. This hair was blond. His eyes were blue, his cheeks were sculpted. Beneath the silk weave of his polo necks, his stomach described the gentlest of inclinations.

Now, however, Haffner's colleagues would have been surprised.

Haffner was dressed in waterproof sky-blue tracksuit trousers, a sky-blue T-shirt, and a pistachio sweatshirt. These clothes did not express his inner man. This much, he hoped, was obvious. His inner man was *soigné*, elegant. His mother had praised him for this. In the time when his mother praised him at all.

—Darling, she used to say to him, —you are your mother's man. You make her proud. Let nobody forget this.

She dressed him in white sailor suits, with navy stripes curtailing each cuff. At the children's parties, Haffner tried to forget this. As soon as he could, he preferred the look of the gangster: the Bowery cool, the Whitechapel raciness. Elegance gone to seed. His first trilby was bought at James Lock, off Pall Mall; his umbrellas came from James Smith & Sons, at the top of Covent Garden. The royal patent could seduce him. He had a thing for glamour, for the mysteries of lineage. He could talk to you for a long time about Haffner's lineage. The problem was that now, at the end of the twentieth century, his suitcase had gone missing. It had vanished, two weeks ago, on his arrival at the airport in Trieste. It had still not been returned. It was imminent, the airline promised him. Absolutely. His eyesight, therefore, had been forced to rely on itself – without his spectacles. And he had been corralled into odd collages of clothes, bought from the outdoor clothes shops in this town. He walked round the square, around the lake, up small lanes, and wondered where anyone bought their indoor clothes. Was the indoors so beyond them? Was everyone always outdoors?

He was a long way, thought Haffner, sadly, from the bright lights of the West End.

Zinka leaned back, grinned up at Niko, who pushed strands of her hair away from her forehead: an idyll. He began to kiss her, softly. He talked to her in a language that Haffner did not know. But Haffner knew what they were saying. They were saying they loved each other.

It was midsummer. He was in the centre of Europe, as high as Haffner could go. As far away as Haffner could get. Through the slats on the window he could see the blurred and Alpine mountains, the vague sky and its clouds, backlit by the setting sun. The view was pricked by conifers.

And Haffner, as he watched, was sad.

He lived for the women, true. And Haffner would learn nothing. He would learn nothing and leave everyone. That was what Barbra had said of him, when she patiently shouted at him and explained his lack of moral courage, his pitiful inadequacy as a husband, as a father, as a man. He would remain inexperienced. It seemed an accurate description.

But as Zinka performed for her invisible audience, Haffner still felt sad. He thought he would feel exultant, but he did not. And the only explanation he could think of was that, once again, Haffner was in love. But this time there was a difference. This, thought Haffner, was the real thing. As he had always thought before, and then had always convinced himself that he was wrong.

5

The mute pain of it perturbed him. To this pain, he also acknowledged, there was added the more obvious pain in his legs. He had now been standing for nearly an hour. The difficulty of this had been increased by the tension of avoiding the stray coat hangers Haffner had not removed. It was ridiculous, he thought. He was starting to panic. So calm yourself, thought Haffner. He tried to concentrate on the naked facts – like the smallness of Zinka's breasts, but their smallness simply increased his panic, since they only added to the erotic charge with which Haffner was now pulsing. They were so little to do with function, so much to do with form – as they hung there, unsupported. The nipple completed them, the nipple exhausted them. They were dark with areola. Their proportions all tended to the sexual, away from the neatly maternal.

Haffner wasn't into sex, after all, for the family. The children were the mistake. He was in it for all the exorbitant extras.

No, not for Haffner – the normal curves, the pedestrian features. His desire was seduced by an imperfectly shaved armpit, or a tanning forearm with its swatch of sweat. That was the principle of Haffner's mythology. Haffner, an admirer of the classics. So what if this now made him laughable, or ridiculous, or – in the newly moralistic vocabulary of Benji, his orthodox and religious grandson – sleazy. As if there should be closure on dirtiness. As if there should ever be, thought Haffner, any shame in one's lust. Or any more shame than anyone else's. If he could have extended the epic of Haffner's lust for another lifetime, then he would have done it.

In this, he would confess, he differed from Goldfaden. Goldfaden would have preferred a happy ending. He was into the One, not the Many. In New York once, in a place below Houston, Goldfaden had told him that some woman – Haffner couldn't remember her name, some secretary he'd been dealing with in Princeton, or Cambridge – was the kind of woman you'd take by force when the world fell apart.

Not like his wife, said Goldfaden: nothing like Cynthia. Then had downed his single malt and ordered another.

At the time, helpful Haffner's contribution to the list of such ultimate women was Evelyn Laye, the star of stage and screen. The most beautiful woman he had ever laid eyes on, when she accompanied her husband to his training camp in Hampshire, in 1939 – the year of Haffner's manhood. They arrived in a silver Wolseley 14/16. Goldfaden, however, had contradicted Haffner's choice of Evelyn Laye. As he contradicted so many of Haffner's opinions. She was passable, Goldfaden argued, but it wasn't what he had in mind.

And Haffner wondered – as now, so many years later, he watched while Niko stretched Zinka's slim legs apart, displaying the indented hollows inside her thighs, the tattooed mermaid's head protruding from her panties – whether Goldfaden would have agreed that in Zinka he had finally found this kind of woman: the unattainable, the one who would be worth any kind of immorality. If Goldfaden was still alive. He didn't know. He didn't, to be honest, really care. Why, after all, would you want anyone when the world fell apart? It was typical of Goldfaden: this macho exaggeration.

But Haffner no longer had Goldfaden. Which was a story in itself. He no longer had anyone to use as his mute audience.

This solitude made Haffner melancholy.

The ethos of Raphael Haffner – as businessman, raconteur, wit, jazzman, reader – was simple: no experience could be more pleasurable than its telling. The description was always to be preferred to the reality. Yet here it was: his finale – and there was no one there to listen. In the absence of this audience, in Haffner's history, anything had been known to take its place; anything could be spoken to in Haffner's intimate yell: himself, his ghosts, his absent mentors, even – why not? – the more neutral and natural spectators, like the roses in his garden, or the bright impassive sun.

He looked at Zinka, who suddenly crouched in front of Niko, with her back to Haffner, and allowed her hand to be elaborate on Niko's penis.

As defeats went, thought Haffner, it was pretty comprehensive. Even Papa never got himself as messed up as this.

Was it too late for him to change? To undergo one final metamorphosis? I am not what I am! That was Haffner's constant wish, his mantra. He was a man replete with mantras. He would not act his age, or his Age. He would not be what others made of him.

And yet; and yet.

The thing was, said a friend of Livia's once, thirty years ago, in the green room of a theatre on St Martin's Lane, making smoke rings dissolve in the smoky air – a habit that always reminded Livia of her father. The thing was, he was always saying that he wanted to disappear.

She was an actress. He wanted this actress, very much. Once, in their bedroom with Livia before a party, he had seen her undress; and although asked to turn away had still fleetingly seen the lavish shapeless bush between her legs. With such memories was Haffner continually oppressed. It wasn't new. With such memories did Haffner distress himelf. But he couldn't prevent the thought that if she'd undressed in front of him like that then it was unlikely that she looked on him with any erotic interest – only a calm and uninterested friendliness.

Yes, she continued, he was always saying how he'd prefer to live his life unnoticed, free from the demands of other people.

But let me tell you something, Raphael, said Livia's friend. You don't need to disappear.

Then she paused; blew out a final smoke ring; scribbled her cigarette out in an ashtray celebrating the natural beauty of Normandy; looked at Livia.

—Because no one, she said, —is ever looking for you.

How Haffner had tried to smile, as if he didn't care about her jibe! How Haffner continued to try to smile, whenever this conversation returned to him.

Maybe, he thought, she was right: maybe that was the story of his life, of his century.

And now it was ending – Haffner's twentieth century. What had Haffner done with the twentieth century? He enjoyed measuring himself like this, against the grand categories. But that depended, perhaps, on another question. What had the twentieth century done with him?

6

The era in which Haffner's finale took place was an interregnum: a pause. The British Empire was over. The Hapsburg Empire was over. Over, too, was the Communist Empire. All the ideologies were over. But it was not yet the time of full aromatherapy, the era of celebrity: of chakras, and pressure points. It was after the era of the spa as a path to health, and before the era of the spa as a path to beauty. It was not an era at all.

Everything was almost over. And maybe that was how it should be. The more over things were, the better. You no longer needed to be troubled by the constant conjuring with tenses.

In this hiatus, in the final year of the previous century, occurred Haffner's finale.

The hotel where Haffner was staying defined itself as a mountain escape. It had the normal look. It was all white – with a roof that rose in waves of red tile and green louvred shutters on all three floors, each storey narrower than the one below. The top storey resembled a little summerhouse with a tiny structure made of iron shutters on the roof, like an observation post or a weather station with instruments inside and barometers outside. On top of it all, at the very peak, a red weathercock turned in the wind. Every window on every floor had a balcony entered through a set of French doors. Behind it rose the traces of conifered paths, ascending to a distant summit; in front of it pooled the lake, with its reflections. Beside this lake, on the edge of the town, there was a park, with gravel diagonals, and a view of a distant factory.

Once, the town had been the main location for the holidays of the central European rich. This was where Livia's family had spent their summers, out of Trieste. They had gone so far, in 1936, as to purchase a villa, with hot and cold water, on the outskirts of the town. In this town, said Livia's father, he felt happy. It had style. The restaurants were replete with waiters – replete, in their turn, with eyebrow. Then, in the summer of 1939, when she was seventeen, Livia and her younger brother Cesare had not come to the mountains, but instead had made their way to London. And they had never come back. Seven years later, in a hotel dining room in Honfleur, where Haffner had taken her for the honeymoon that the war had prevented, she described to Haffner – entranced by the glamour – the dining rooms of her past: the spa's sophisticated restaurants. Crisp mitres of napkins sat in state on the tables. The guests were served the classics of their heritage: schnitzel Holstein, and minestrone. The Béarnaise sauce was served in a silver boat, its lip warped into a moue. There was the clearest chicken soup with the lightest dumplings.

And now, when this place belonged to another country, here was Haffner, her husband: alone – to claim the villa, to claim an inheritance which was not his.

The hotel still served the food of Livia's memory. This place was timeless: it was the end of history. The customer could still order steak Diane, beef Wellington – arranged on vast circles of china, with a thin gold ring inscribing its circumference. Even Haffner knew this wasn't chic, but he wasn't after the chic. He just wanted an escape. An escape from what, however, Haffner could not say.

No, Haffner could never disappear.

In 1974, in the last year of his New York life, when Barbra – who was twenty-nine, worked in the Wall Street office as his secretary and smoked Dunhills which she kept in a cigarette holder, triple facts that made her desirable to Haffner as he passed middle age – asked him why it was he still went faithfully back every night to his wife, he could not answer. It didn't have to be like that, she said. With irritation, as he looked at Barbra, the steep curve between her breasts, he remembered his snooker table in the annexe at home, its blue baize built over by Livia's castles of unread books. He knew that the next morning he would be there, at home: with his breakfast of Corn Chex, morosely reading the Peanuts cartoons. He knew this, and did not want to know it. So often, he wanted to give up, and elope from his history. The problem was in finding the right elopee. He only had Haffner. And Haffner wasn't enough.

Zinka turned in the direction of the wardrobe. Usually, she wore her hair sternly in a ponytail. But now she let it drift out, on to her shoulders. And Haffner looked away. Because, he thought, he loved her. He looked back again. Because, he thought, he loved her.

No, there was no escape. And because this is true, then maybe in my turn I should not always allow Haffner the luxury of language. He was burdened by what he thought was love. But therefore he did not express it in this way. No, trapped by his temptations, Haffner simply sighed.

—Ouf, he exhaled, in his wardrobe. —Ouf: ouf: ouf. ∎

COMPASSION AND MERCY

Amy Bloom

ILLUSTRATION BY LAURA CARLIN

N o power.
The roads were thick with pine branches and whole birch trees, the heavy boughs breaking off and landing on top of houses and cars and in front of driveways. The low, looping power lines coiled on to the road and even from their bedroom window, Clare could see silver branches dangling in the icy wires. Highways were closed. Classes were cancelled. The phone didn't work. The front steps were slippery as hell.

William kept a fire going in the living room and Clare toasted rye bread on the end of fondue forks for breakfast, and in the early afternoon they wrapped grilled cheese sandwiches in tinfoil and threw them into the embers for fifteen minutes. William was in charge of dinner and making hot water for Thai Ginger Soup-in-a-Bowl. They used the snowbank at the kitchen door to chill the Chardonnay.

They read and played Scrabble and at four o'clock, when daylight dropped to a deep indigo, Clare lit two dozen candles and they got into their pile of quilts and pillows.

'All right,' William said. 'Let's have it. You're shipwrecked on a desert island. Who do you want to be with – me or Nelson Slater?'

'Oh my God,' Clare says. 'Nelson. Of course.'

'Good choice. He did a great job with the firewood.'

William kept the fire going all night. Every hour, he had to roll sideways and crouch and then steady himself and then pull himself up with his cane and then balance himself, and because Clare was watching and worried, he had to do it all with the appearance of ease. Clare lay in the dark and tried to move the blankets far to one side so they wouldn't tangle William's feet.

'You're not actually helping,' he said. 'I know where the blankets are, so I can easily step over them. And then, of course, you move them.'

'I feel bad,' Clare said.

'I'm going to break something if you keep this up.'

'Let me help,' Clare said.

When the cold woke them, Clare handed William the logs. They talked about whether or not it was worth it to use the turkey carcass for soup and if they could really make a decent soup in the fireplace. William said that people had cooked primarily in hearths until the late eighteenth century. William told Clare about his visit to his cardiologist and the possible levels of fitness William could achieve ('A lot of men your age walk five miles a day,' the doctor said. 'My father-in-law got himself a personal trainer, and he's eighty.'). Clare said maybe they could walk to the diner on weekends. They talked about Clare's sons Adam and Danny and their wives and the two grandchildren and they talked about William's daughter Emily and her pregnancy and the awful man she'd married ('I'd rather she'd taken the veil,' William said. 'Little Sisters of Gehenna.'). When the subject came up, William and Clare said nice things about the people they used to be married to.

It had taken William and Clare five years to end their marriages. William's divorce lawyer was the sister of one of his old friends. She was William's age, in a sharp black suit with improbably black hair and blood-red nails. Her only concession to age was black patent flats, and

William was sure that for most of her life this woman had been stalking and killing wild game, in stiletto heels.

'So,' she said. 'You've been married thirty-five years. Well, look, Dr Langford—'

'Mister is fine,' William said. 'William is fine.'

'Bill?' the woman said, and William shook his head no and she smiled and made a note.

'Just kidding. It's like this. Unless your wife is doing crack cocaine or having sex with young girls and barnyard animals, what little you have will be split fifty/fifty.'

'That's fine, Mrs Merrill,' William said.

'Not really,' the woman said. 'Call me Louise. Your wife obviously got a lawyer long before you did. I got a fax today, a list of personal property your wife believes she's entitled to. Oil paintings, a little jewellery, silverware.'

'That's fine. Whatever it is.'

'It's not fine. But let's say you have no personal attachment to any of these items. And let's say it's all worth about twenty thousand dollars. Let's have her give you twenty thousand dollars and you give her the stuff. There's no reason for us to just roll over and put our paws up in the air.'

'Whatever she wants,' William said. 'You should know, I'm not having sex with a graduate student. Or with porn stars.'

'I believe you,' Mrs Merrill said. 'You may as well tell me, as it'll all come out in the wash. Who are you having sex with?'

'Her name is Clare Wexler. She teaches. She's a very fine teacher. She makes me laugh. She can be a difficult person,' he said, beaming as if he was detailing her beauty. 'You'd like her.' William wiped his eyes.

'All right,' said Louise Merrill. 'Let's get you hitched, before we're all too old to enjoy it.'

A year later, when they could finally marry, Clare called her sons.

Her oldest said, 'You might want a prenup. I'm just saying.'

Her youngest said, 'Jeez, I thought Isabel was your friend.'

William called his daughter Emily and she said 'How can you do this to me? I'm trying to get pregnant' and her husband Kurt had to take the phone because she was crying so hard. He said 'We're trying not to take sides, you know.'

Three days after the storm had passed, classes resumed, grimy cars filled slushy roads and Clare called both of her sons to say they were essentially unharmed.

'What do you mean, essentially?' Danny said, and Clare said, 'I mean my hair's a mess and I lost at Scrabble seventeen times and William's back hurts from sleeping near the fireplace. I mean, I'm absolutely and completely fine. I shouldn't have said "essentially".'

William laughed and shook his head when she hung up.

'They must know me by now,' Clare said.

'I'm sure they do,' William said, 'but knowing and understanding are two different things. *Verstehen und erklären.*'

'Fancy talk,' Clare said and she kissed his neck and the bald top of his head and the little red dents behind his ears, which came from sixty-five years of wearing glasses. 'I have to go to Baltimore tomorrow. Remember?'

'Of course,' William said.

Clare knew he'd call her the next day to ask about dinner, about Thai food or Cuban or would she prefer scrambled eggs and salami and then when she said she was on her way to Baltimore, William would be, for just a quick minute, crushed and then crisp and English.

They spoke while Clare was on the train. William had unpacked his low-salt, low-fat lunch. ('Disgusting,' he'd said. 'Punitive.') Clare had gone over her notes for her talk on *Jane Eyre* ('In which I will reveal my awful, retrograde underpinnings') and they made their night-time phone date for ten p.m., when William would still be at his desk at home and Clare would be in her bed at the University Club.

Clare called William every half-hour from ten until midnight and then she told herself that he must have fallen asleep early. She called him at his university office on his cellphone and at home. She called him every fifteen minutes from seven a.m. until her talk and she began calling him again, at eleven, as soon as her talk was over. She begged off the faculty lunch and said that her husband wasn't well and that she was needed at home; her voice shook and no one doubted her.

On the train, Clare wondered who to call. She couldn't ask Emily, even though she lived six blocks away; she couldn't ask the pregnant woman to go see if her father was all right. By the time she'd gotten Emily to understand what was required, and where the house key was hidden and that there was no real cause for alarm, Emily would be sobbing and Clare would be trying not to scream at her to calm the fuck down. Isabel was the person to call but Clare couldn't call her. She could imagine Isabel saying, 'Of course, Clare, leave it to me,' and driving down from Boston to sort things out; she'd make the beds, she'd straighten the pictures, she'd gather all the overdue library books into a pile and stack them near the front door. She'd scold William for making them worry and then she would call Clare back to say that all broken things had been put right.

Clare couldn't picture what might have happened to William. His face floated before her, his large, lovely face, his face when he was reading the paper, his face when he'd said to her, 'I *am* sorry,' and she'd thought, 'Oh, Christ, we're breaking up again, I figured we'd go until April at least,' and he'd said, 'You are everything to me, I'm afraid we have to marry,' and they cried so hard, they had to sit down on the bench outside the diner and wipe each other's faces with napkins.

Clare saw that the man in the seat across from her was smiling uncertainly; she'd been saying William's name. Clare walked to the little juncture between cars and called Margaret Slater, her former cleaning lady. There was no answer. Margaret's grandson Nelson didn't get home until three so Margaret might be running errands for another two hours. They pulled into Penn Station. If Margaret had a cellphone, Clare didn't know the number. Clare called every half-hour, home and then Margaret's number, leaving messages and timing herself, reading a few pages of the paper between calls. 'Goddammit, Margaret,' she thought, 'you're retired. Pick up the fucking phone.'

Clare pulled into their driveway just as the sun was setting and Margaret pulled in right after her. Water still dripped from her gutters and the corners of the house and it would all freeze again at night.

'Oh, Clare,' Margaret said, 'I just got your messages. I was out of the house all day. I'm so sorry.'

'It's all right,' Clare said, and they both looked up at the light in William's window. 'He probably unplugged the phone.'

'They live to drive us crazy,' Margaret said.

Clare scrabbled in the bottom of her bag for the house key, furiously tossing tissues and pens and chap sticks and quarters on to the walk, and thinking with every toss, 'What's your hurry? This is your last moment of not knowing, stupid, slow down.' But her hands moved fast, tearing the silk lining of the bag until she saw, out of the corner of her eye, a brass house key sitting in Margaret's flat, lined palm. Clare wanted to sit down on the porch and wait for someone else to come. She opened the door and wished she could turn around and close it behind her.

They should call his name, she thought, it's what you do when you come into your house and you haven't been able to reach your husband, you go, *William, William, darling, I'm home*, and then he pulls himself out of his green-leather desk chair and comes to the top of the stairs, his hair standing straight up and his glasses on the end of his nose. He says, relief and annoyance clearly mixed together, *Oh, darling, you didn't call, I waited for your call*. And then you say, *I did call, I called all night, but the phone was off the hook, you had the phone off*, and he says that he certainly did not and Margaret watches, bemused. She disapproved of the divorce (she all but said, I always thought Charles would leave you, not the other way around) but gave herself over on the wedding day when she'd brought platters of devilled eggs and put Nelson in a navy blue suit, and cried, shyly.

'Fulgent,' William said after the ceremony, and he said it several times, a little drunk on champagne. 'Absolutely *fulgent*.' It wouldn't have mattered if no one had been there, but everyone except William's sister had been, and they got in one elegant foxtrot before William's ankle acted up. William will call down, 'I'm so sorry we inconvenienced you, Mrs Slater,' and Margaret will shake her head fondly and go, and you drop your coat and bag in the hall and he comes down the stairs, slowly, careful with his ankle, and he makes tea to apologize for having scared the shit out of you.

Margaret waited. As much as she wanted to help, it wasn't her house or her husband and Clare had been in charge of their relationship for the last twenty years; this was not the moment to take the lead. Clare walked up the stairs and right into their bedroom, as if William had phoned ahead and told her what to expect. He was lying on the bed, shoes off and fully dressed, his hand on *Jane Eyre*, his eyes closed and his reading glasses on his chest. ('He is not to them what he is to me,' Jane thought. 'While I breathe and think, I must love him.') Clare lay down next to him, murmuring, until Margaret put her hand on Clare's shoulder and asked if she should call the hospital or someone.

'I have no idea,' Clare said, lying on the bed beside William, staring at the ceiling. These things get done, Clare thought, whether you know what you're doing or not. The hospital is called, the funeral home is contacted, the body is removed, with some difficulty, because he was a big man and the stairs are old and narrow. Your sons and daughters-in-law call everyone who needs to be called, including the terrible sister in England who sent William one note, explaining that she could not bring herself to attend a wedding that so clearly should not be taking place.

Margaret comes back the next day and makes up one of the boys' bedrooms for you, just in case, but when your best friend flies in from Cleveland, you are lying in your own room, wrapped in William's bathrobe, and you wear his robe and his undershirt while she sits across from you, her sensible shoes right beside William's wingtips, and she helps you decide chapel or funeral home, lunch or brunch, booze or wine, and who will speak. Your sons and their wives and the babies come and it's no more or less terrible to have them in the house. You move slowly and carefully, swimming through a deep but traversable river of shit. You must not inhale, you must not stop, you must not stop for anything at all. Destroyed, untouchable, you can lie down on the other side when they've all gone home.

Clare was careful during the funeral. She didn't listen to anything that was said. She saw Isabel sitting with Emily and Kurt, a little cluster of Langfords; Isabel wore a grey suit and held Emily's hand and she left as soon as the service ended. At the house, Clare imagined Isabel beside her; she imagined herself encased in Isabel. Even in pyjamas, suffering a bad cold, Isabel moved like a woman in beautiful silk. Clare made an effort to move that way. She thanked people in Isabel's pleasant, governessy voice. Clare straightened Danny's tie with Isabel's hand and then wiped chocolate fingerprints off the back of a chair. Clare used Isabel to answer every question and to make plans to get together with people she had no intention of seeing. She hugged Emily the way Isabel would have, with a perfect degree of appreciation for Emily's pregnant and furious state.

Clare went upstairs and lay down on the big bed and cried into the big, tailored pillows William used for reading. Clare held his glasses like a rosary. Clare walked over to the dresser and took out one of William's big Irish linen handkerchiefs and blotted her face with it. (Clare and Isabel did their dressers the same way, William said: odds and ends in the top drawer, then underwear, then sweaters, then jeans and T-shirts and white socks. Clare put William's almost empty bottle of Tabac in her underwear drawer.) She rearranged their two, unlikely stuffed animals.

'Oh, rhino and peckerbird,' William had said. That's how he saw them and two years ago Clare had found herself in front of a fancy toy store in Guilford on a spring afternoon buying a very expensive plush grey rhino and a velvety little brown and white bird and putting the pair on their bed that night.

'You're not so tough,' William had said.

'I was,' Clare said. 'You've ruined me.'

★

Clare wanted to talk with Isabel about Emily; they used to talk about her all the time. Once, after William's second heart attack, when he was still Isabel's husband, Isabel and Clare were playing cards in William's hospital room and Emily and Kurt had just gone off to get sandwiches and Clare had stumbled over something nice to say about Kurt and Isabel slapped down her cards and said, 'Say what you want. He's dumb in that awful preppy way and a Republican and if he says "no disrespect intended" one more time, I'm going to set him on fire.' William said, '*De gustibus non disputandum est*', which he said about many things, and Isabel said, 'That doesn't help, darling.'

Clare looked at William's lapis cufflinks and at the watch she'd given him when they were in the third act of their affair. 'You can't give me a watch,' he'd said. 'I already have a perfectly good one.' Clare took his watch off his wrist, laid it on the asphalt and drove over it, twice. 'There,' she'd said. 'Terrible accident, you were so careless. You had to replace it.' William took that beautiful watch she'd bought him out of the box and kissed her in the parking lot of a Marriott halfway between his home and hers. He'd worn it every day until last Thursday. Clare walked downstairs holding William's jewellery and when she passed her sons pouring wine for people, she dropped the watch into Danny's pocket. Adam turned to her and said, 'Mom, do you want a few minutes alone?' and Clare realized that the time upstairs had done her no good at all. She laid the lapis cufflinks in Adam's free hand. 'William particularly wanted you to have these,' she said, and Adam looked surprised, as well he might, Clare thought.

Clare took the semester off. She spent weeks in the public library, crying and wandering up and down the mystery section, looking for something she hadn't read. A woman she didn't know popped out from behind the stacks and handed her a little ivory pamphlet, the pages held together with a dark blue silk ribbon. On the front it said: GOD NEVER GIVES US MORE THAN WE CAN BEAR. The woman ran off and Clare caught the eye of the librarian, who mouthed the words 'ovarian cancer'. Clare carried it with her to the parking lot and looked over her shoulder to make sure the woman was gone and then she tossed it in the trash.

After the library, Clare went to the coffeehouse or to the Turkish restaurant where they knew how to treat widows. Every evening at six, men would spill out of the church across the street from the coffeehouse. A few would smoke in the vestibule and a few more would come in and order coffee and a couple of cookies and sit down to play chess. They were not like the chess players Clare had known.

One evening, one of the older men, with a tidy silver crew cut and pants yanked up a little too high, approached Clare. (William dressed beautifully. Clare and Isabel used to talk about how beautifully he dressed; Clare said he dressed the way the Duke of Windsor would have if he'd been a hundred pounds heavier and not such a weenie and Isabel said, 'That's wonderful. May I tell him?')

The man said, gently, 'Are you waiting for the meeting?'

Clare said, in her Isabel voice, that it was very kind of him to ask, but there was no meeting she was waiting for.

He said, 'Well, I see you here a lot. I thought maybe you were trying to decide whether or not to go to the next meeting.'

Clare said that she hadn't made up her mind, which could have been true. She could just as soon have gone to an AA meeting as to a No Rest for the Weary meeting or a People Sick of Life meeting. And Clare did know something about drinking, she thought. Sometime after she and William had decided, for the thousandth time, that their affair was a terrible thing, that their love for their spouses was much greater than their love for each other, that William and Isabel were *suited*, just like Charles and Clare were suited, and that the William and Clare thing was nothing more than some odd summer lightning that would pass as soon as the season changed, Clare found herself having three glasses of wine every night. Her goal, every night, was to climb into bed early, exhausted and tipsy, and fall deeply asleep before she could say anything to Charles about William. It was her version of One Day at a Time and it worked for two years until she woke up one night, crying in her sleep and saying William's name into her pillow over and over again. Clare didn't think that that was the kind of reckless behaviour that interested the people across the street.

The man put *AA for the Older Alcoholic* in front of Clare and said, 'You're not alone.'

Clare said, 'That is *so* not true.'

She kept the orange and grey pamphlet on her kitchen table for a few weeks, in case anyone dropped in, because it made her laugh, the whole idea. Her favourite part (she had several, especially the stoic recitation of ruined marriages, dead children, estranged children, alcoholic children, multiple car accidents (pedestrian and vehicular), forced resignations, outright firings, embezzlements, failed suicides, diabetic comas), her absolute favourite in the category of the telling detail, was an old woman carrying a fifth of vodka hidden in a skein of yarn. She finally put the pamphlet away so it wouldn't worry Nelson Slater when he came for Friday-night dinner. Margaret dropped him off at six and picked him up at eight-thirty, which gave her time for Bingo and Nelson and Clare time to eat and play checkers or cribbage or Risk.

Nelson Slater didn't know that William's Sulka pyjamas were still under Clare's pillow, that the bedroom still smelled like his cologne (and that Clare bought two large *flacons* of it and sprayed the room with it, every Sunday), that his wingtips and his homely black sneakers were in the bottom of the bedroom closet. He knew that William's canes were still in the umbrella stand next to the front door and that the refrigerator was filled with William's favourite foods (chicken liver pâté, cornichons, pickled beets, orange marmalade and Zingerman's bacon bread) and there were always two or three large Tupperware containers of William's favourite dinners, which Clare made on Friday, when Nelson came over, and then divided in half or quarters for the rest of the week. Nelson didn't mind. He had known and loved Clare most of his young life and he understood old-people craziness. His great-aunt believed that every event in the Bible actually happened and left behind physical evidence you could buy, like the splinter from Noah's Ark she kept by her bed. His Cousin Chick sat on the back porch, shooting the heads off squirrels and chipmunks and reciting poetry. Nelson had known William Langford since he was five years old and Nelson had got used to him. Mr Langford was a big man with a big laugh and a big frown. He gave Nelson credit for who he was and what he did around the house and he paid Nelson, which Clare never remembered to do. ('A man has to make a living,' he said one time, and Nelson did like that.) Nelson liked the Friday-night dinners and until Clare started doing something really weird, like setting three places at the table, he'd keep coming over.

'Roast pork with apples and onions and a red-wine sauce. And braised red cabbage. And Austrian apple cake. How's that?'

Nelson shrugged. Clare was always a good cook, but almost no one knew it. When he was six years old and eating gingerbread in the Wexler kitchen one afternoon, Mr Wexler came home early. He reached for a piece of the warm gingerbread and Nelson told him that Clare had just baked it and Wexler looked at him in surprise. 'Mrs Wexler doesn't really cook,' he said, and Nelson had gone on eating and thought, 'She does for me, Mister.'

Clare put the pork and apples on Nelson's plate and poured them both apple cider. When Nelson lifted the fork to his mouth and chewed and then sighed and smiled, happy to be loved and fed, Clare left the kitchen for a minute.

After a year, everything was much the same. Clare fed Nelson on Friday nights, she taught half-time, she wept in the shower and at the end of every day, she put on one of William's button-down shirts and a pair of his socks and settled herself with a big book of William's or an English mystery. When the phone rang, Clare jumped.

'Clare, how are you?'

'Good, Lauren. How are you? How's Adam?'

Lauren would not be deflected. She tried to get her husband to call his mother every Sunday night but when he didn't (and Clare could just hear him, her sweet boy, passive as granite: 'She's okay, Lauren. What do you want me to do about it?') Lauren, who was properly brought up, made the call.

'We'd love for you to visit us, Clare.'

I bet, Clare thought. 'Oh, not until the semester ends, I can't. But you all could come out here. Any time.'

'It really wouldn't be suitable.'

Clare said nothing.

'I mean, it just wouldn't,' Lauren said, polite and stubborn.

Clare felt sorry for her. Clare wouldn't want herself for a mother-in-law, under the best of circumstances.

'I'd love to have you visit.' This wasn't exactly true but she would certainly rather have them in her house than be some place that had no William in it. 'The boys' room is all set, with the bunk beds, and your room, of course, for you and Adam. There's plenty of room and I hear Cirque du Soleil will be here in a few weeks.' Clare and Margaret will take Nelson, before he's too grown-up to be seen in public with two old ladies.

Lauren's voice dropped. Clare knew she was walking from the living room, where she was watching TV and folding laundry, into a part of the house where Adam couldn't hear her.

'It doesn't matter how much room there is. Your house is like a mausoleum. How am I supposed to explain that to the boys, Clare? Grandma loved Grandpa William so much she keeps every single thing he ever owned or read or *ate* all around her?'

'I don't mind if that's what you want to tell them.'

In fact, I'll tell them myself, Little Miss Let's-Call-a-Spade-a-Gardening-Implement, Clare thought, and she could hear William saying, 'Darling, you are as clear and bright as vinegar but not everyone wants their pipes cleaned.'

'I don't want to tell them that. I want, really, we all want, for you just to begin to, oh, you know, just to get on with your life, a little bit.'

Clare said, and she thought she never sounded more like Isabel, master of the even, elegant tone, 'I completely understand, Lauren, and it is very good of you to call.'

Lauren put the boys on and they said exactly what they should:

Hi, Grandma, thanks for the Lego. (Clare put Post-its next to the kitchen calendar and at the beginning of every month, she sent an educational toy to each grandchild, so no one could accuse her of neglecting them.) Lauren walked back into the kitchen and forced Adam to take the phone and Clare said to him, before he could speak, 'I'm all right, Adam. Not to worry,' and he said, 'I know, Mom,' and Clare asked about Adam and his work and Lauren's classes and she asked about Jason's karate and the baby's teeth and when she could do nothing more, she said, 'Oh, I'll let you go now, honey,' and she sat on the floor, with the phone still in her hand.

One Sunday, Danny called and said, 'Have you heard about Dad?' And Clare's heart clutched, just as people describe, and when she didn't say anything, Danny cleared his throat and said, 'I thought you might have heard. Dad's getting married,' and Clare was so relieved she was practically giddy. 'Oh, wonderful,' she said. 'That nice tall woman who golfs?' Danny laughed. Almost everything you could say about his future stepmother points directly to the ways she's not his mother – particularly nice, tall and golfs. Clare got off the phone and sent Charles and his bride – she doesn't remember her name, so she sends it to Mr and Mrs Charles Wexler, which has a nice old-fashioned ring to it – a big pretty Tiffany vase of the kind she'd wanted when she married Charles.

The only calls Clare makes are to Isabel. She calls in the early evening, before Isabel has turned in. (There's nothing she doesn't know about Isabel's habits. They shared a beach house three summers in a row and she'd slept in their guest room in Boston a dozen times. She knows Isabel's taste in linens, in kitchens, in moisturizer and make-up and movies. There's not a single place on earth that you could put Clare that she couldn't point out to you what would suit Isabel and what would not.) She dials her number, William's old number, and when Isabel answers she hangs up, of course.

Clare calls Isabel about once a week, after watching *Widow's Walk*, the most repulsive and irresistible show she's ever seen. Three, sometimes four women sit around and say things like, 'It's not an ending; it's a beginning.' What makes it bearable to Clare is that the women are all ardent Catholics and not like her, except the discussion leader, who is so obviously Jewish and from the Bronx that Clare has to google her and discovers that she has a PhD in philosophical something and converted to Catholicism after a personal tragedy. Clare gets to hear a woman who sounds a lot like her great-aunt Frieda say, 'I pray for all widows and we must all keep on with our faith and never forget that Jesus meets every need.' Clare waits for the punchline, for the woman to yank her cross off her neck and say, 'And if you believe that, bubbeleh, I've got a bridge I'd like to sell you,' but she never does. She does sometimes say, in the testing, poking tone of a good rabbi, 'Isn't it interesting that so many women saints came to their sainthood through being widows? They were poor and desperate, alone in the world with no protection, but the sisters took them in and even educated their children. Isn't it *interesting* that widowhood led them to become saints and extraordinary women, to know themselves and Jesus better?' The other widows, the real Catholics, don't look interested at all. The good-looking one, in a red suit and red high heels, keeps reminding everyone that she is very recently widowed (and young and pretty) and the other two, a garden gnome in baggy pants and black sneakers which don't touch the floor and a tall woman in a frilly blouse with her glasses taped together at the bridge, talk, in genuinely heartbroken tones, about their lives now that they are alone. They rarely mention their husbands, although the gnome does say, more than once, that if she can forgive her late husband, anyone can forgive anyone.

Clare dials, as soon as the organ music dies down, and Isabel picks up after one ring. Clare doesn't speak.

'Clare?'

Clare sighs. Hanging up was bad enough.

'Isabel.'

Isabel sighs as well.

'I saw Emily a few weeks ago. I dropped off a birthday present for the baby. She's beautiful. Emily seems very happy. I mean, not to see me, but in general.'

'Yes, she told me.'

'I shouldn't have gone.'

'Well. If you want to offer a relationship and generous gifts, it's up to Emily. Kurt's mother's dead. I guess it depends on how many grandmothers Emily wants Charlotte to have, regardless of who they are.' There was no one like Isabel.

'I guess it does. I mean, I'm not going to presume. I'm not going to drop in all the time with a box of rugelach and a hand-knit sweater.'

'I wouldn't think so. Clare—'

'Oh, Isabel, I miss you.'

'Goodnight, Clare.'

When Clare gets off the phone, there's a raccoon in her kitchen, on the counter. It, although Clare immediately thinks *he*, is eating a slice of bacon bread. He's holding it in his small, nimble and very human black hands. He looks at her over the edge of the bread, like a man peering over his glasses. A fat, bold, imperturbable man with a twinkle in his dark eyes.

Even though she knows better, even though William would have been very annoyed at her for doing so, Clare says softly, 'William.'

The raccoon doesn't answer and Clare smiles. She wouldn't have wanted the raccoon to say 'Clare' because then she would have had to call her boys and have herself committed, and although this is not the life she hoped to have, it's certainly better than being in a psychiatric hospital. The raccoon has started on his second slice of bacon bread. Clare would like to put out the orange marmalade and a little plate of honey. William never ate peanut butter, but Clare wants to open a jar for the raccoon. She's read that they love peanut butter and she doesn't want him to leave.

In an ideal world, the raccoon would give Clare advice. He would speak to her like Quan Yin, the Buddha of Compassion and Mercy. Or he would speak to her like St Paula, the patron saint of widows, about whom Clare has heard so much lately.

Clare says, without moving, 'And why is St Paula a saint? She dumps her four kids at a convent, after the youngest dies. She runs off to *hajira* with St Jerome. How is that a saint? You've got shitty mothers all over America who would love to dump their kids and travel.'

The raccoon nibbles at the crust.

'Oh, it's very hard,' Clare says, sitting down slowly and not too close. 'Oh, I miss him so much. I didn't know. I didn't know that I would be like this, that this is what happens when you love someone like that. I had no idea. No one says, there's no happy ending at all. No one says, if you could look ahead, you might want to stop now. I know, I know, I know I was lucky. I was luckier than anyone to have had what I had. I know now. I do, really.'

The raccoon picks up two large crumbs and tosses them into his mouth. He scans the counter and the canisters and looks closely at Clare. He hops down from the counter to the kitchen stool and on to the floor and strolls out the kitchen door.

Clare told Nelson about the raccoon and they encouraged him with heels of bread and plastic containers of peanut butter leading up the kitchen steps but he didn't come back. She told Margaret Slater who said she was lucky not to have gotten rabies and she told Adam and Danny, who said the same thing. She bought a stuffed animal raccoon with round black velvet paws much nicer than the actual raccoon's, and she put him on her bed with the rhino and the little bird and William's big pillows. She told little Charlotte about the raccoon when she came to babysit (how could Emily say no to a babysitter six blocks away and free and generous with her time?). She even told Emily who paused and said, with a little concern, that raccoons could be very dangerous.

'I don't know if you heard,' Emily said. 'My mother's getting married. A wonderful man.'

Clare bounced Charlotte on her knee. 'Oh, good. Then everyone is happy.' ∎

INVISIBLE

Paul Auster

ILLUSTRATION BY SAM MESSER

I shook his hand for the first time in the spring of 1967. I was a second-year student at Columbia then, a know-nothing boy with an appetite for books and a belief (or delusion) that one day I would become good enough to call myself a poet, and because I read poetry, I had already met his namesake in Dante's hell, a dead man shuffling through the final verses of the twenty-eighth canto of the *Inferno*. Bertran de Born, the twelfth-century Provençal poet, carrying his severed head by the hair as it sways back and forth like a lantern – surely one of the most grotesque images in that book-length catalogue of hallucinations and torments. Dante was a staunch defender of de Born's writing, but he condemned him to eternal damnation for having counselled Prince Henry to rebel against his father, King Henry II, and because de Born caused division between father and son and turned them into enemies, Dante's ingenious punishment was to divide de Born from himself. Hence the decapitated body wailing in the underworld, asking the Florentine traveller if any pain could be more terrible than his.

When he introduced himself as Rudolf Born, my thoughts immediately turned to the poet. Any relation to Bertran? I asked. Ah, he replied, that wretched creature who lost his head. Perhaps, but it doesn't seem likely, I'm afraid. No *de*. You need to be nobility for that, and the sad truth is I'm anything but noble.

I have no memory of why I was there. Someone must have asked me to go along, but who that person was has long since evaporated from my mind. I can't even recall where the party was held – uptown or downtown, in an apartment or a loft – nor my reason for accepting the invitation in the first place, since I tended to shun large gatherings at the time, put off by the din of chattering crowds, embarrassed by the shyness that would overcome me in the presence of people I didn't know. But that night, inexplicably, I said yes, and off I went with my forgotten friend to wherever it was he took me.

What I remember is this: at one point in the evening, I wound up standing alone in a corner of the room. I was smoking a cigarette and looking out at the people, dozens upon dozens of young bodies crammed into the confines of that space, listening to the mingled roar of words and laughter, wondering what on earth I was doing there, and thinking that perhaps it was time to leave. An ashtray was sitting on a radiator to my left, and as I turned to snuff out my cigarette, I saw that the butt-filled receptacle was rising toward me, cradled in the palm of a man's hand. Without my noticing them, two people had just sat down on the radiator, a man and a woman, both of them older than I was, no doubt older than anyone else in the room – he around thirty-five, she in her late twenties or early thirties.

They made an incongruous pair, I felt, Born in a rumpled, somewhat soiled white linen suit with an equally rumpled white shirt under the jacket and the woman (whose name turned out to be Margot) dressed all in black. When I thanked him for the ashtray, he gave me a brief, courteous nod and said *My pleasure* with the slightest hint of a foreign accent. French or German, I couldn't tell which, since his English was almost flawless. What else did I see in those first moments? Pale skin, unkempt reddish hair (cut shorter than the hair of most men at the time), a broad, handsome face with nothing particularly distinctive about it (a generic face, somehow, a face that would become invisible in any crowd), and steady brown eyes, the probing eyes of a man who seemed to be afraid of nothing. Neither thin nor heavy, neither tall nor short, but for all that an impression of physical strength, perhaps because of the thickness of his hands. As for Margot, she sat without stirring a muscle, staring into space as if her central mission in life was to look bored. But attractive, deeply attractive to my twenty-year-old self, with her black hair, black turtleneck sweater, black miniskirt, black leather boots, and heavy black make-up around her large green eyes. Not a beauty, perhaps, but a simulacrum of beauty, as if the style and sophistication of her appearance embodied some feminine ideal of the age.

Born said that he and Margot had been on the verge of leaving, but then they spotted me standing alone in the corner, and because I looked so unhappy, they decided to come over and cheer me up – just to make sure I didn't slit my throat before the night was out. I had no idea how to interpret his remark. Was this man insulting me, I wondered, or was he actually trying to show some kindness to a lost young stranger? The words themselves had a certain playful, disarming quality, but the look in Born's eyes when he delivered them was cold and detached, and I couldn't help feeling that he was testing me, taunting me, for reasons I utterly failed to understand.

I shrugged, gave him a little smile, and said: Believe it or not, I'm having the time of my life.

That was when he stood up, shook my hand, and told me his name. After my question about Bertran de Born, he introduced me to Margot, who smiled at me in silence and then returned to her job of staring blankly into space.

Judging by your age, Born said, and judging by your knowledge of obscure poets, I would guess you're a student. A student of literature, no doubt. NYU or Columbia?

Columbia.

Columbia, he sighed. Such a dreary place.

Do you know it?

I've been teaching at the School of International Affairs since September. A visiting professor with a one-year appointment. Thankfully, it's April now, and I'll be going back to Paris in two months.

So you're French.

By circumstance, inclination, and passport. But Swiss by birth.

French Swiss or German Swiss? I'm hearing a little of both in your voice.

Born made a little clucking noise with his tongue and then looked me closely in the eye. You have a sensitive ear, he said. As a matter of fact, I *am* both – the hybrid product of a German-speaking mother and a French-speaking father. I grew up switching back and forth between the two languages.

Unsure of what to say next, I paused for a moment and then asked an innocuous question: And what are you teaching at our dismal university?

Disaster.

That's a rather broad subject, wouldn't you say?

More specifically, the disasters of French colonialism. I teach one course on the loss of Algeria and another on the loss of Indochina.

That lovely war we've inherited from you.

Never underestimate the importance of war. War is the purest, most vivid expression of the human soul.

You're beginning to sound like our headless poet.

Oh?

I take it you haven't read him.

Not a word. I only know about him from that passage in Dante.

De Born was a good poet, maybe even an excellent poet – but deeply disturbing. He wrote some charming love poems and a moving lament after the death of Prince Henry, but his real subject, the one thing he seemed to care about with any genuine passion, was war. He absolutely revelled in it.

I see, Born said, giving me an ironic smile. A man after my own heart.

I'm talking about the pleasure of seeing men break each other's skulls open, of watching castles crumble and burn, of seeing the dead with lances protruding from their sides. It's gory stuff, believe me, and de Born doesn't flinch. The mere thought of a battlefield fills him with happiness.

I take it you have no interest in becoming a soldier.

None. I'd rather go to jail than fight in Vietnam.

And assuming you avoid both prison and the army, what plans?

No plans. Just to push on with what I'm doing and hope it works out.

Which is?

Penmanship. The fine art of scribbling.

I thought as much. When Margot saw you across the room, she said to me: Look at that boy with the sad eyes and the brooding face – I'll bet you he's a poet. Is that what you are, a poet?

I write poems, yes. And also some book reviews for the *Spectator*.

The undergraduate rag.

Everyone has to start somewhere.

Interesting…

Not terribly. Half the people I know want to be writers.

Why do you say *want*? If you're already doing it, then it's not about the future. It already exists in the present.

Because it's still too early to know if I'm good enough.

Do you get paid for your articles?

Of course not. It's a college paper.

Once they start paying you for your work, then you'll know you're good enough.

Before I could answer, Born suddenly turned to Margot and announced: You were right, my angel. Your young man is a poet.

Margot lifted her eyes towards me, and with a neutral, appraising look, she spoke for the first time, pronouncing her words with a foreign accent that proved to be much thicker than her companion's – an unmistakable French accent. I'm always right, she said. You should know that by now, Rudolf.

A poet, Born continued, still addressing Margot, a sometime reviewer of books, and a student at the dreary fortress on the heights, which means he's probably our neighbour. But he has no name. At least not one that I'm aware of.

It's Walker, I said, realizing that I had neglected to introduce myself when we shook hands. Adam Walker.

Adam Walker, Born repeated, turning from Margot and looking at me as he flashed another one of his enigmatic smiles. A good, solid American name. So strong, so bland, so dependable. Adam Walker. The lonely bounty hunter in a CinemaScope Western, prowling the desert with a shotgun and six-shooter on his chestnut-brown gelding. Or else the kind-hearted, straight-arrow surgeon in a daytime soap opera, tragically in love with two women at the same time.

It sounds solid, I replied, but nothing in America is solid. The name was given to my grandfather when he landed at Ellis Island in 1900. Apparently, the immigration authorities found Walshinksky too difficult to handle, so they dubbed him Walker.

What a country, Born said. Illiterate officials robbing a man of his identity with a simple stroke of the pen.

Not his identity, I said. Just his name. He worked as a kosher butcher on the Lower East Side for thirty years.

There was more, much more after that, a good hour's worth of talk that bounced around aimlessly from one subject to the next. Vietnam and the growing opposition to the war. The differences between New York and Paris. The Kennedy assassination. The American embargo on trade with Cuba. Impersonal topics, yes, but Born had strong opinions about everything, often wild, unorthodox opinions, and because he couched his words in a half-mocking, slyly condescending tone, I couldn't tell if he was serious or not. At certain moments, he sounded like a hawkish right-winger; at other moments, he advanced ideas that made him sound like a bomb-throwing anarchist. Was he trying to provoke me, I asked myself, or was this normal procedure for him, the way he went about entertaining himself on a Saturday night? Meanwhile, the inscrutable Margot had risen from her perch on the radiator to bum a cigarette from me, and after that she remained standing, contributing little to the conversation, next to nothing in fact, but studying me carefully every time I spoke, her eyes fixed on me with the unblinking curiosity of a child. I confess that I enjoyed being looked at by her, even if it made me squirm a little. There was something vaguely erotic about it, I found, but I wasn't experienced enough back then to know if she was trying to send me a signal or simply looking for the sake of looking. The truth was that I had never run across people like this before, and because the two of them were so alien to me, so unfamiliar in their affect, the longer I talked to them, the more unreal they seemed to become – as if they were imaginary characters in a story that was taking place in my head.

I can't recall whether we were drinking, but if the party was anything like the others I had gone to since landing in New York, there must have been jugs of cheap red wine and an abundant stock of paper cups, which means that we were probably growing drunker and drunker as we continued to talk. I wish I could dredge up more of what we said, but 1967 was a long time ago, and no matter how hard I struggle to find the words and gestures and fugitive overtones of that initial encounter with Born, I mostly draw blanks. Nevertheless, a few vivid moments stand out in the blur. Born reaching into the inside pocket of his linen jacket, for example, and withdrawing the butt of a half-smoked cigar, which he proceeded to light with a match while informing me that it was a Montecristo, the best of all Cuban cigars – banned in America then, as they still are now – which he had managed to obtain through *a personal connection* with someone who worked at the French embassy in Washington. He then went on to say a few kind words about Castro – this from the same man who just minutes earlier had defended Johnson, McNamara and Westmoreland for their heroic work in battling the menace of communism in Vietnam. I remember feeling amused at the sight of the dishevelled political scientist pulling out that half-smoked cigar and said he reminded me of the owner of a South American coffee plantation who had gone mad after spending too many years in the jungle. Born laughed at the remark, quickly adding that I wasn't far from the truth, since he had spent the bulk of his childhood in Guatemala. When I asked him to tell me more, however, he waved me off with the words *Another time.*

I'll give you the whole story, he said, but in quieter surroundings. The whole story of my incredible life so far. You'll see, Mr Walker. One day, you'll wind up writing my biography. I guarantee it.

Born's cigar, then, and my role as his future Boswell, but also an image of Margot touching my face with her right hand and whispering: Be good to yourself. That must have come towards the end, when we were about to leave or had already gone downstairs, but I have no memory of leaving and no memory of saying goodbye to them. All those things have been blotted out, erased by the work of forty years. They were two strangers I met at a noisy party one spring night in the New York of my youth, a New York that no longer exists, and that was that. I could be wrong, but I'm fairly certain that we didn't even bother to exchange phone numbers.

I assumed I would never see them again. Born had been teaching at Columbia for seven months, and since I hadn't crossed paths with him in all that time, it seemed unlikely that I would run into him now. But odds don't count when it comes to actual events, and just because a thing is unlikely to happen, that doesn't mean it won't. Two days after the party, I walked into the West End Bar following my final class of the afternoon, wondering if I might not find one of my friends there. The West End was a dingy, cavernous hole with more than a dozen booths and tables, a vast oval bar in the centre of the front room, and an area near the entrance where you could buy bad cafeteria-style lunches and dinners – my hang-out of choice, frequented by students, drunks, and neighbourhood regulars. It happened to be a warm, sunfilled afternoon, and consequently few people were present at that hour. As I made my tour around the bar in search of a familiar face, I saw Born sitting alone in a booth at the back. He was reading a German newsmagazine (*Der Spiegel,* I think), smoking another one of his Cuban cigars, and ignoring the half-empty glass of beer that stood on the table to his left. Once again, he was wearing his white suit – or perhaps a different one, since the jacket looked cleaner and less rumpled than the one he'd been wearing Saturday night – but the white shirt was gone, replaced by something red – a deep, solid red, midway between brick and crimson.

Curiously, my first impulse was to turn around and walk out without saying hello to him. There is much to be explored in this hesitation, I believe, for it seems to suggest that I already understood that I would do well to keep my distance from Born, that allowing myself to get involved with him could possibly lead to trouble. How did I know this? I had spent little more than an hour in his company, but even in that short time I had sensed there was something off about him, something vaguely repellent. That wasn't to deny his other qualities – his charm, his intelligence, his humour – but underneath it all he had emanated a darkness and a cynicism that had thrown me off balance, had left me feeling that he wasn't a man who could be trusted. Would I have formed a different impression of him if I hadn't despised his politics? Impossible to say. My father and I disagreed on nearly every political issue of the moment, but that didn't prevent me from thinking he was fundamentally a good person – or at least not a bad person. But Born wasn't good. He was witty and eccentric and unpredictable, but to contend that war is the purest expression of the human soul automatically excludes you from the realm of goodness. And if he had spoken those words in jest, as a way of challenging yet another anti-militaristic student to fight back and denounce his position, then he was simply perverse.

Mr Walker, he said, looking up from his magazine and gesturing for me to join him at his table. Just the man I've been looking for.

I could have invented an excuse and told him I was late for another appointment, but I didn't. That was the other half of the complex equation that represented my dealings with Born. Wary as I might have been, I was also fascinated by this peculiar, unreadable person, and the fact that he seemed genuinely glad to have stumbled into me stoked the fires of my vanity – that invisible cauldron of self-regard and ambition that simmers and burns in each one of us. Whatever reservations I had about him, whatever doubts I harboured about his dubious character, I couldn't stop myself from wanting him to like me, to think that I was something more than a plodding, run-of-the-mill American undergraduate, to see the promise I hoped I had in me but which I doubted nine out of every ten minutes of my waking life.

Once I had slid into the booth, Born looked at me across the table, disgorged a large puff of smoke from his cigar, and smiled. You made a favourable impression on Margot the other night, he said.

I was impressed by her too, I answered.

You might have noticed that she doesn't say much.

Her English isn't terribly good. It's hard to express yourself in a language that gives you trouble.

Her French is perfectly fluent, but she doesn't say much in French either.

Well, words aren't everything.

A strange comment from a man who fancies himself a writer.

I'm talking about Margot—

Yes, Margot. Exactly. Which brings me to my point. A woman prone to long silences, but she talked a blue streak on our way home from the party Saturday night.

Interesting, I said, not certain where the conversation was going. And what loosened her tongue?

You, my boy. She's taken a real liking to you, but you should also know that she's extremely worried.

Worried? Why on earth should she be worried? She doesn't even know me.

Perhaps not, but she's gotten it into her head that your future is at risk.

Everyone's future is at risk. Especially American males in their late teens and early twenties, as you well know. But as long as I don't flunk out of school, the draft can't touch me until after I graduate. I wouldn't want to bet on it, but it's possible the war will be over by then.

Don't bet on it, Mr Walker. This little skirmish is going to drag on for years.

I lit up a Chesterfield and nodded. For once I agree with you, I said.

Anyway, Margot wasn't talking about Vietnam. Yes, you might land in jail – or come home in a box two or three years from now – but she wasn't thinking about the war. She believes you're too good for this world, and because of that, the world will eventually crush you.

I don't follow her reasoning.

She thinks you need help. Margot might not possess the quickest brain in the Western world, but she meets a boy who says he's a poet, and the first word that comes to her is *starvation*.

That's absurd. She has no idea what she's talking about.

Forgive me for contradicting you, but when I asked you at the party what your plans were, you said you didn't have any. Other than your nebulous ambition to write poetry, of course. How much do poets earn, Mr Walker?

Most of the time nothing. If you get lucky, every now and then someone might throw you a few pennies.

Sounds like starvation to me.

I never said I planned to make my living as a writer. I'll have to find a job.

Such as?

It's difficult to say. I could work for a publishing house or a magazine. I could translate books. I could write articles and reviews. One of those things, or else several of them in combination. It's too early to know, and until I'm out in the world, there's no point in losing any sleep over it, is there?

Like it or not, you're in the world now, and the sooner you learn how to fend for yourself, the better off you'll be.

Why this sudden concern? We've only just met, and why should you care about what happens to me?

Because Margot asked me to help you, and since she rarely asks me for anything, I feel honour-bound to obey her wishes.

Tell her thank you, but there's no need for you to put yourself out. I can get by on my own.

Stubborn, aren't you? Born said, resting his nearly spent cigar on the rim of the ashtray and then leaning forward until his face was just a few inches from mine. If I offered you a job, are you telling me you'd turn it down?

It depends on what the job is.

That remains to be seen. I have several ideas, but I haven't made a decision yet. Maybe you can help me.

I'm not sure I understand.

My father died ten months ago, and it appears I've inherited a considerable amount of money. Not enough to buy a chateau or an airline company, but enough to make a small difference in the world. I could engage you to write my biography, of course, but I think it's a little too soon for that. I'm still only thirty-six, and I find it unseemly to talk about a man's life before he gets to fifty. What, then? I've considered starting a publishing house, but I'm not sure I have the stomach for all the long-range planning that would entail. A magazine, on the other hand, strikes me as much more fun. A monthly, or perhaps a quarterly, but something fresh and daring, a publication that would stir people up and cause controversy with every issue. What do you think of that, Mr Walker? Would working on a magazine be of any interest to you?

Of course it would. The only question is: why me? You're going back to France in a couple of months, so I assume you're talking about a French magazine. My French isn't bad, but it isn't good enough for what you'd need. And besides, I go to college here in New York. I can't just pick up and move.

Who said anything about moving? Who said anything about a French magazine? If I had a good American staff to run things here, I could pop over every once in a while to check up on them, but essentially I'd stay out of it. I have no interest in directing a magazine myself. I have my own work, my own career, and I wouldn't have the time for it. My sole responsibility would be to put up the money – and then hope to turn a profit.

You're a political scientist, and I'm a literature student. If you're thinking of starting a political magazine, then count me out. We're on opposite sides of the fence, and if I tried to work for you, it would turn into a fiasco. But if you're talking about a literary magazine, then yes, I'd be very interested.

Just because I teach international relations and write about government and public policy doesn't mean I'm a philistine. I care about art as much as you do, Mr Walker, and I wouldn't ask you to work on a magazine if it wasn't a literary magazine.

How do you know I can handle it?

I don't. But I have a hunch.

It doesn't make any sense. Here you are offering me a job and you haven't read a word I've written.

Not so. Just this morning I read four of your poems in the most recent number of the *Columbia Review* and six of your articles in the student paper. The piece on Melville was particularly good, I thought, and I was moved by your little poem about the graveyard. *How many more skies above me / Until this one vanishes as well?* Impressive.

I'm glad you think so. Even more impressive is that you acted so quickly.

That's the way I am. Life is too short for dawdling.

My third-grade teacher used to tell us the same thing – with exactly those words.

A wonderful place, this America of yours. You've had an excellent education, Mr Walker.

Born laughed at the inanity of his remark, took a sip of beer, and then leaned back to ponder the idea he had set in motion.

What I want you to do, he finally said, is draw up a plan, a prospectus. Tell me about the work that would appear in the magazine, the length of each issue, the cover art, the design, the frequency of publication, what name you'd want to give it, and so on. Leave it at my office when you're finished. I'll look it over, and if I like your ideas, we'll be in business.

Young as I might have been, I had enough understanding of the world to realize that Born could have been playing me for a dupe. How often did you wander into a bar, bump into a man you had met only once, and walk out with the chance to start a magazine – especially when the *you* in question was a twenty-year-old nothing who had yet to prove himself on any front? It was too outlandish to be believed. In all likelihood, Born had raised my hopes only in order to crush them, and I was fully expecting him to toss my prospectus into the garbage and tell me he wasn't interested. Still, on the off chance that he meant what he'd said, that he was honestly intending to keep his word, I felt I should give it a try. What did I have to lose? A day of thinking and writing at the most, and if Born wound up rejecting my proposal, then so be it.

Bracing myself against disappointment, I set to work that very night. Beyond listing half a dozen potential names for the magazine, however, I didn't make much headway. Not because I was confused, and not because I wasn't full of ideas, but for the simple reason that I had neglected to ask Born how much money he was willing to put into the project. Everything hinged on the size of his investment, and until I knew what his intentions were, how could I discuss any of the myriad points he had raised that afternoon: the quality of the paper, the length and frequency of the issues, the binding, the possible inclusion of art, and how much (if anything) he was prepared to pay the contributors? Literary magazines came in numerous shapes and guises, after all, from the mimeographed, stapled underground publications edited by young poets in the East Village to the stolid academic quarterlies to more commercial enterprises like the *Evergreen Review* to the sumptuous *objets* backed by well-heeled angels who lost thousands with every issue. I would have to talk to Born again, I realized, and so instead of drawing up a prospectus, I wrote him a letter explaining my problem. It was such a sad, pathetic document – *We have to talk about money* – that I decided to include something else in the envelope, just to convince him that I wasn't the out-and-out dullard I appeared to be. After our brief exchange about Bertran de Born on Saturday night, I thought it might amuse him to read one of the more savage works by the twelfth-century poet. I happened to own a paperback anthology of the troubadours – in English only – and my initial idea was simply to type up one of the poems from the book. When I began reading through the translation, however, it struck me as clumsy and inept, a rendering that failed to do justice to the strange and ugly power of the poem, and even though I didn't know a word of Provençal, I figured I could turn out something better working from a French translation. The next morning, I found what I was looking for in Butler Library: an edition of the complete de Born, with the original Provençal on the left and literal prose versions in French on the right. It took me several hours to complete the job (if I'm not mistaken, I missed a class because of it), and this is what I came up with:

> I love the jubilance of springtime
> When leaves and flowers burgeon forth,
> And I exult in the mirth of bird songs
> Resounding through the woods;
> And I relish seeing the meadows
> Adorned with tents and pavilions;
> And great is my happiness
> When the fields are packed
> With armoured knights and horses.
>
> And I thrill at the sight of scouts
> Forcing men and women to flee with their belongings;
> And gladness fills me when they are chased
> By a dense throng of armed men;
> And my heart soars
> When I behold mighty castles under siege
> As their ramparts crumble and collapse
> With troops massed at the edge of the moat
> And strong, solid barriers
> Hemming in the target on all sides.

And I am likewise overjoyed
When a baron leads the assault,
Mounted on his horse, armed and unafraid,
Thus giving strength to his men
Through his courage and valour.
And once the battle has begun
Each of them should be prepared
To follow him readily,
For no man can be a man
Until he has delivered and received
Blow upon blow.

In the thick of combat we will see
Maces, swords, shields, and many-coloured helmets
Split and shattered,
And hordes of vassals striking in all directions
As the horses of the dead and wounded
Wander aimlessly around the field.
And once the fighting starts
Let every well-born man think only of breaking
Heads and arms, for better to be dead
Than alive and defeated.

I tell you that eating, drinking, and sleeping
Give me less pleasure than hearing the shout
Of 'Charge!' from both sides, and hearing
Cries of 'Help! Help!,' and seeing
The great and the ungreat fall together
On the grass and in the ditches, and seeing
Corpses with the tips of broken, streamered lances
Jutting from their sides.

Barons, better to pawn
Your castles, towns, and cities
Than to give up making war.

Late that afternoon, I slipped the envelope with the letter and the poem under the door of Born's office at the School of International Affairs. I was expecting an immediate response, but several days went by before he contacted me, and his failure to call left me wondering if the magazine project was indeed just a spur-of-the-moment whim that had already played itself out – or, worse, if he had been offended by the poem, thinking that I was equating him with Bertran de Born and thereby indirectly accusing him of being a warmonger. As it turned out, I needn't have worried. When the telephone rang on Friday, he apologized for his silence, explaining that he had gone to Cambridge to deliver a lecture on Wednesday and hadn't set foot in his office until twenty minutes ago.

You're perfectly right, he continued, and I'm perfectly stupid for ignoring the question of money when we spoke the other day. How can you give me a prospectus if you don't know what the budget is? You must think I'm a moron.

Hardly, I said. I'm the one who feels stupid – for not asking you. But I couldn't tell how serious you were, and I didn't want to press.

I'm serious, Mr Walker. I admit that I have a penchant for telling jokes, but only about small, inconsequential things. I would never lead you along on a matter like this.

I'm happy to know that.

So, in answer to your question about money… I'm hoping we'll do well, of course, but as with every venture of this sort, there's a large element of risk, and so realistically I have to be prepared to lose every penny of my investment. What it comes down to is the following: How much can I afford to lose? How much of my inheritance can I squander away without causing problems for myself in the future? I've given it a good deal of thought since we talked on Monday, and the answer is twenty-five thousand dollars. That's my limit. The magazine will come out four times a year, and I'll put up five thousand per issue, plus another five thousand for your annual salary. If we break even at the end of the first year, I'll fund another year. If we come out in the black, I'll put the profits into the magazine, and that would keep us going for all or part of a third year. If we lose money, however, then the second year becomes problematical. Say we're ten thousand dollars in the red. I'll put up fifteen thousand, and that's it. Do you understand the principle? I have twenty-five thousand dollars to burn, but I won't spend a dollar more than that. What do you think? Is it a fair proposition or not?

Extremely fair, and extremely generous. At five thousand dollars an issue, we could put out a first-rate magazine, something to be proud of.

I could dump all the money in your lap tomorrow, of course, but that wouldn't really help you, would it? Margot is worried about your future, and if you can make this magazine work, then your future is settled. You'll have a decent job with a decent salary, and during your off-hours you can write all the poems you want, vast epic poems about the mysteries of the human heart, short lyric poems about daisies and buttercups, fiery tracts against cruelty and injustice. Unless you land in jail or get your head blown off, of course, but we won't dwell on those grim possibilities now.

I don't know how to thank you...

Don't thank me. Thank Margot, your guardian angel.

I hope I see her again soon.

I'm certain you will. As long as your prospectus satisfies me, you'll be seeing as much of her as you like.

I'll do my best. But if you're looking for a magazine that will cause controversy and stir people up, I doubt a literary journal is the answer. I hope you understand that.

I do, Mr Walker. We're talking about quality...about fine, rarefied things. Art for the happy few.

Or, as Stendhal must have pronounced it: *ze appy foo*.

Stendhal and Maurice Chevalier. Which reminds me... Speaking of chevaliers, thank you for the poem.

The poem. I forgot all about it—

The poem you translated for me.

What did you think of it?

I found it revolting and brilliant. My faux ancestor was a true samurai madman, wasn't he? But at least he had the courage of his convictions. At least he knew what he stood for. How little the world has changed since 1186, no matter how much we prefer to think otherwise. If the magazine gets off the ground, I think we should publish de Born's poem in the first issue.

I was both heartened and bewildered. In spite of my doleful predictions, Born had talked about the project as if it was already on the brink of happening, and at this point the prospectus seemed to be little more than an empty formality. No matter what plan I drew up, I felt he was prepared to give it his stamp of approval. And yet, pleased as I was by the thought of taking charge of a well-funded magazine, which on top of everything else would pay me a rather excessive salary, for the life of me I still couldn't fathom what Born was up to. Was Margot really the cause of this unexpected burst of altruism, this blind faith in a boy with no experience in editing or publishing or business who just one week earlier had been absolutely unknown to him? And even if that was the case, why would the question of my future be of any concern to her? We had barely talked to each other at the party, and although she had looked me over carefully and given me a pat on the cheek, she had come across as a cipher, an utter blank. I couldn't imagine what she had said to Born that would have made him willing to risk 25,000 dollars on my account. As far as I could tell, the prospect of publishing a magazine left him cold, and because he was indifferent, he was content to turn the whole matter over to me. When I thought back to our conversation at the West End on Monday, I realized that I had probably given him the idea in the first place. I had mentioned that I might look for work with a publisher or a magazine after I graduated from college, and a minute later he was telling me about his inheritance and how he was considering starting up a publishing house or a magazine with his newfound money. What if I had said I wanted to manufacture toasters? Would he have answered that he was thinking about investing in a toaster factory?

It took me longer to finish the prospectus than I'd imagined it would – four or five days, I think, but that was only because I did such a thorough job. I wanted to impress Born with my diligence, and therefore I not only worked out a plan for the contents of each issue (poetry, fiction, essays, interviews, translations, as well as a section at the back for reviews of books, films, music, and art) but provided an exhaustive financial report as well: printing costs, paper costs, binding costs, matters of distribution, print runs, contributors' fees, news-stand price, subscription rates, and the pros and cons of whether to include ads. All that demanded time and research, telephone calls to printers and binders, conversations with the editors of other magazines, and a new way of thinking on my part, since I had never bothered myself with questions of commerce before. As for the name of the magazine, I wrote down several possibilities, wanting to leave the choice to Born, but my own preference was *The Stylus* – in honour of Poe, who had tried to launch a magazine with that name not long before his death.

This time, Born responded within twenty-four hours. I took that as an encouraging sign when I picked up the phone and heard his voice, but true to form he didn't come right out and say what he thought of my plan. That would have been too easy, I suppose, too pedestrian, too straightforward for a man like him, and so he toyed with me for a couple of minutes in order to prolong the suspense, asking me a number of irrelevant and disjointed questions that convinced me he was stalling for time because he didn't want to hurt my feelings when he rejected my proposal.

I trust you're in good health, Mr Walker, he said.

I think so, I replied. Unless I've contracted a disease I'm not aware of.

But no symptoms yet.

No, I'm feeling fine.

What about your stomach? No discomfort there?

Not at the moment.

Your appetite is normal, then.

Yes, perfectly normal.

I seem to recall that your grandfather was a kosher butcher. Do you still follow those ancient laws, or have you given them up?

I never followed them in the first place.

No dietary restrictions, then.

No. I eat whatever I want to.

Fish or fowl? Beef or pork? Lamb or veal?

What about them?

Which one do you prefer?

I like them all.

In other words, you aren't difficult to please.

Not when it comes to food. With other things yes, but not with food.

Then you're open to anything Margot and I choose to prepare.

I'm not sure I understand.

Tomorrow night at seven o'clock. Are you busy?

No.

Good. Then you'll come to our apartment for dinner. A celebration is in order, don't you think?

I'm not sure. What are we celebrating?

The *Stylus*, my friend. The beginning of what I hope will turn out to be a long and fruitful partnership.

You want to go ahead with it?

Do I have to repeat myself?

You're saying you liked the prospectus?

Don't be so dense, boy. Why would I want to celebrate if I hadn't liked it?

I remember dithering over what present to give them – flowers or a bottle of wine – and opting in the end for flowers. I couldn't afford a good enough bottle to make a serious impression, and as I thought the matter through, I realized how presumptuous it would have been to offer wine to a couple of French people anyway. If I made the wrong choice – which was more than likely to happen – then I would only be exposing my ignorance, and I didn't want to start off the evening by embarrassing myself. Flowers on the other hand would be a more direct way of expressing my gratitude to Margot, since flowers were always given to the woman of the house, and if Margot was a woman who liked flowers (which was by no means certain), then she would understand that I was thanking her for having pushed Born to act on my behalf. My telephone conversation with him the previous afternoon had left me in a state of semi-shock, and even as I walked to their place on the night of the dinner, I was still feeling overwhelmed by the altogether improbable good luck that had fallen down on me. I remember putting on a jacket and tie for the occasion. It was the first time I had dressed up in months, and there I was, Mr Important himself, walking across the Columbia campus with an enormous bouquet of flowers in my right hand, on my way to eat and talk business with *my publisher.*

He had sublet an apartment from a professor on a year long sabbatical, a large but decidedly stuffy, over-furnished place in a building on Morningside Drive, just off 116th Street. I believe it was on the third floor, and from the French windows that lined the eastern wall of the living room there was a view of the full, downward expanse of Morningside Park and the lights of Spanish Harlem beyond. Margot answered the door when I knocked, and although I can still see her face and the smile that darted across her lips when I presented her with the flowers, I have no memory of what she was wearing. It could have been black again, but I tend to think not, since I have a vague recollection of surprise, which would suggest there was something different about her from the first time we had met. As we were standing on the threshold together, before she even invited me into the apartment, Margot announced in a low voice that Rudolf was in a foul temper. There was a crisis of some sort back home, and he was going to have to leave for Paris tomorrow and wouldn't return until next week at the earliest. He was in the bedroom now, she added, on the telephone with Air France arranging his flight, so he probably wouldn't be out for another few minutes.

As I entered the apartment, I was immediately hit by the smell of food cooking in the kitchen – a sublimely delicious smell, I found, as tempting and aromatic as any vapour I had ever breathed. The kitchen happened to be where we headed first – to hunt down a vase for the flowers – and when I glanced at the stove, I saw the large covered pot that was the source of that extraordinary fragrance.

I have no idea what's in there, I said, gesturing to the pot, but if my nose knows anything, three people are going to be very happy tonight.

Rudolf tells me you like lamb, Margot said, so I decided to make a *navarin* – a lamb stew with potatoes and *navets*.

Turnips.

I can never remember that word. It's an ugly word, I think, and it hurts my mouth to say it.

All right, then. We'll banish it from the English language.

Margot seemed to enjoy my little remark – enough to give me another brief smile, at any rate – and then she began to busy herself with the flowers: putting them in the sink, removing the white paper wrapper, taking down a vase from the cupboard, trimming the stems with a pair of scissors, putting the flowers in the vase, and then filling the vase with water. Neither one of us said a word as she went about these minimal tasks, but I watched her closely, marvelling at how slowly and methodically she worked, as if putting flowers in a vase of water were a highly delicate procedure that called for one's utmost care and concentration.

Eventually, we wound up in the living room with drinks in our hands, sitting side by side on the sofa as we smoked cigarettes and looked out at the sky through the French windows. Dusk ebbed into darkness, and Born was still nowhere to be seen, but the ever-placid Margot betrayed no concern over his absence. When we'd met at the party ten or twelve days earlier, I had been rather unnerved by her long silences and oddly disconnected manner, but now that I knew what to expect, and now that I knew she liked me and thought I was *too good for this world*, I felt a bit more at ease in her company. What did we talk about in the minutes before her man finally joined us? New York (which she found to be dirty and depressing); her ambition to become a painter (she was attending a class at the School of the Arts but thought she had no talent and was too lazy to improve); how long she had known Rudolf (all her life); and what she thought of the magazine (she was crossing her fingers). When I tried to thank her for her help, however, she merely shook her head and told me not to exaggerate: she'd had nothing to do with it.

Before I could ask her what that meant, Born entered the room. Again the rumpled white pants, again the unruly shock of hair, but no jacket this time, and yet another coloured shirt – pale green, if I remember correctly – and the stump of an extinguished cigar clamped between the thumb and index finger of his right hand, although he seemed not to be aware that he was holding it. My new benefactor was angry, seething with irritation over whatever crisis was forcing him to travel to Paris tomorrow, and without even bothering to say hello to me, utterly ignoring his duties as host of our little celebration, he flew into a tirade that wasn't addressed to Margot or myself so much as to the furniture in the room, the walls around him, the world at large.

Stupid bunglers, he said. Snivelling incompetents. Slow-witted functionaries with mashed potatoes for brains. The whole universe is on fire, and all they do is wring their hands and watch it burn.

Unruffled, perhaps even vaguely amused, Margot said: That's why they need you, my love. Because you're the king.

Rudolf the First, Born replied, the bright boy with the big dick. All I have to do is pull it out of my pants, piss on the fire, and the problem is solved.

Exactly, Margot said, cracking the largest smile I'd yet seen from her.

I'm getting sick of it, Born muttered, as he headed for the liquor cabinet, put down his cigar, and poured himself a full tumbler of straight gin. How many years have I given them? he asked, taking a sip of his drink. You do it because you believe in certain principles, but no one else seems to give a damn. We're losing the battle, my friends. The ship is going down.

This was a different Born from the one I had come to know so far – the brittle, mocking jester who exulted in his own witticisms, the displaced dandy who blithely went about founding magazines and asking twenty-year-old students to his house for dinner. Something was raging inside him, and now that this other person had been revealed to me, I felt myself recoil from him, understanding that he was the kind of man who could erupt at any moment, that he was someone who actually *enjoyed* his own anger. He swigged down a second belt of gin and then turned his eyes in my direction, acknowledging my presence for the first time. I don't know what he saw in my face – astonishment? confusion? distress? – but whatever it was, he was sufficiently alarmed by it to switch off the thermostat and immediately lower the temperature. Don't worry, Mr Walker, he said, doing his best to produce a smile. I'm just letting off a little steam.

He gradually willed himself out of his funk, and by the time we sat down to eat twenty minutes later, the storm seemed to have passed. Or so I thought when he complimented Margot on her superb cooking and praised the wine she had bought for the meal, but it proved to be no more than a temporary lull, and as the evening progressed, further squalls and gales came swooping down on us to spoil the festivities. I don't know if the gin and burgundy affected Born's mood, but there was no question that he packed away a good deal of alcohol – at least twice the amount that Margot and I downed together – or if he was simply out of sorts because of the bad news he had received earlier in the day. Perhaps it was both in combination, or perhaps it was something else, but there was scarcely a moment during that dinner when I didn't feel that the house was about to catch on fire.

It began when Born raised his glass to toast the birth of our magazine. It was a gracious little speech, I thought, but when I jumped in and started mentioning some of the writers I was planning to solicit work from for the first issue, Born cut me off in mid-sentence and told me never to discuss business while eating, that it was bad for the digestion and I should learn to start acting like an adult. It was a rude and unpleasant thing to say, but I hid my injured pride by pretending to agree with him and then took another bite of Margot's stew. A moment later, Born put down his fork and said to me: You like it, Mr Walker, don't you?

Like what? I asked.

The *navarin*. You seem to be eating it with relish.

It's probably the best meal I've had all year.

In other words, you're attracted to Margot's food.

Very much. I find it delicious.

And what about Margot herself? Are you attracted to her as well?

She's sitting right across the table from me. It seems wrong to talk about her as if she weren't here.

I'm sure she doesn't mind. Do you, Margot?

No, Margot said. Not in the least.

You see, Mr Walker? Not in the least.

All right, then, I answered. In my opinion, Margot is a highly attractive woman.

You're avoiding the question, Born said. I didn't ask if you found her attractive, I want to know if *you* are attracted to *her*.

She's your wife, Professor Born. You can't expect me to answer that. Not here, not now.

Ah, but Margot isn't my wife. She's my special friend, as it were, but we aren't married, and we have no plans to marry in the future.

You live together. As far as I'm concerned, that's as good as being married.

Come, come. Don't be such a prude. Forget that I have any connection to Margot, all right? We're talking in the abstract here, a hypothetical case.

Fine. Hypothetically speaking, I would hypothetically be attracted to Margot, yes.

Good, Born said, rubbing his hands together and smiling. Now we're getting somewhere. But attracted to what degree? Enough to want to kiss her? Enough to want to hold her naked body in your arms? Enough to want to sleep with her?

I can't answer those questions.

You're not telling me you're a virgin, are you?

No. I just don't want to answer your questions, that's all.

Am I to understand that if Margot threw herself at you and asked you to fuck her, you wouldn't be interested? Is that what you're saying? Poor Margot. You have no idea how much you've hurt her feelings.

What are you talking about?

Why don't you ask her?

Suddenly, Margot reached across the table and took hold of my hand. Don't be upset, she said. Rudolf is only trying to have some fun. You don't have to do anything you don't want to do.

Born's notion of fun had nothing to do with mine, alas, and at that stage of my life I was ill-equipped to play the sort of game he was trying to drag me into. No, I wasn't a virgin. I had slept with a number of girls by then, had fallen in and out of love several times, had suffered through a badly broken heart just two years earlier and, like most young men around the world, thought about sex almost constantly. The truth was that I would have been delighted to sleep with Margot, but I refused to allow Born to goad me into admitting it. This wasn't a hypothetical case. He actually seemed to be propositioning me on her behalf, and whatever sexual code they lived by, whatever romps and twisted dalliances they indulged in with other people, I found the whole business ugly, off-kilter, sick. Perhaps I should have spoken up and told him what I thought, but I was afraid – not of Born exactly, but of causing a rift that might lead him to change his mind about our project. I desperately wanted the magazine to work, and as long as he was willing to back it, I was prepared to put up with any amount of inconvenience and discomfort. So I did what I could to hold my ground and not lose my temper, to absorb *blow upon blow* without falling from my horse, to resist him and appease him at the same time.

I'm disappointed, Born said. Until now, I took you for an adventurer, a renegade, a man who enjoys thumbing his nose at convention, but at bottom you're just another stuffed shirt, another bourgeois simpleton. How sad. You strut around with your Provençal poets and your lofty ideals, with your draft-dodger cowardice and that ridiculous necktie of yours, and you think you're something exceptional, but what I see is a pampered middle-class boy living off daddy's money, a poseur.

Rudolf, Margot said. That's enough. Leave him alone.

I realize I'm being a bit harsh, Born said to her. But young Adam and I are partners now, and I need to know what he's made of. Can he stand up to an honest insult, or does he crumble to pieces when he's under attack?

You've had a lot to drink, I said, and from all I can gather you've had a rough day. Maybe it's time for me to be going. We can pick up the conversation when you're back from France.

Nonsense, Born replied, pounding the table with his fist. We're still working on the stew. Then there's the salad, and after the salad the cheese, and after the cheese, dessert. Margot has already been hurt enough for one night, and the least we can do is sit here and finish her remarkable dinner. In the meantime, maybe you can tell us something about Westfield, New Jersey.

Westfield? I said, surprised to discover that Born knew where I had grown up. How did you find out about Westfield?

It wasn't difficult, he said. As it happens, I've learned quite a bit about you in the past few days. Your father, for example, Joseph Walker, age fifty-four, better known as Bud, owns and operates the Shop-Rite supermarket on the main street in town. Your mother, Marjorie, aka Marge, is forty-six and has given birth to three children: your sister, Gwyn, in November 1945; you in March 1947; and your brother, Andrew, in July 1950. A tragic story. Little Andy drowned when he was seven, and it pains me to think how unbearable that loss must have been for all of you. I had a sister who died of cancer at roughly the same age, and I know what terrible things a death like that does to a family. Your father has coped with his sorrow by working fourteen hours a day, six days a week, while your mother has turned inward, battling the scourge of depression with heavy doses of prescription pharmaceuticals and twice-weekly sessions with a psychotherapist. The miracle, to my mind, is how well you and your sister have done for yourselves in the face of such calamity. Gwyn is a beautiful and talented girl in her last year at Vassar, planning to begin graduate work in English literature right here at Columbia this fall. And you, my young intellectual friend, my budding wordsmith and translator of obscure medieval poets, turn out to have been an outstanding baseball player in high school, co-captain of the varsity team, no less. *Mens sana in corpore sano.* More to the point, my sources tell me that you're a person of deep moral integrity, a pillar of moderation and sound judgement who, unlike the majority of his classmates, does not dabble in drugs. Alcohol yes, but no drugs whatsoever – not even an occasional puff of marijuana. Why is that, Mr Walker? With all the propaganda abroad these days about the liberating powers of hallucinogens and narcotics, why haven't you succumbed to the temptation of seeking new and stimulating experiences?

Why? I said, still reeling from the impact of Born's astounding recitation about my family. I'll tell you why, but first I'd like to know how you managed to dig up so much about us in such a short time.

Is there a problem? Were there any inaccuracies in what I said?

No. It's just that I'm a little stunned, that's all. You can't be a cop or an FBI agent, but a visiting professor at the School of International Affairs could certainly be involved with an intelligence organization of some kind. Is that what you are? A spy for the CIA?

Born cracked up laughing when I said that, treating my question as if he'd just heard the funniest joke of the century. The CIA! he roared. The CIA! Why on earth would a Frenchman work for the CIA? Forgive me for laughing, but the idea is so hilarious, I'm afraid I can't stop myself.

Well, how did you do it, then?

I'm a thorough man, Mr Walker, a man who doesn't act until he knows everything he needs to know, and since I'm about to invest twenty-five thousand dollars in a person who qualifies as little more than a stranger to me, I felt I should learn as much about him as I could. You'd be amazed how effective an instrument the telephone can be.

Margot stood up then and began clearing plates from the table in preparation for the next course. I made a move to help her, but Born gestured for me to sit back down in my chair.

Let's return to my question, shall we? he said.

What question? I asked, no longer able to keep track of the conversation.

About why no drugs. Even the lovely Margot has a joint now and then, and to be perfectly frank with you, I have a certain fondness for weed myself. But not you. I'm curious to know why.

Because drugs scare me. Two of my friends from high school are already dead from heroin overdoses. My freshman room-mate went off the rails from taking too much speed and had to drop out of college. Again and again, I've watched people climb the walls from bad LSD trips – screaming, shaking, ready to kill themselves. I don't want any part of it. Let the whole world get stoned on drugs for all I care, but I'm not interested.

And yet you drink.

Yes, I said, lifting my glass and taking another sip of wine. With immense pleasure, too, I might add. Especially with stuff as good as this to keep me company.

We moved on to the salad after that, followed by a plate of French cheeses and then a dessert baked by Margot that afternoon (apple tart? raspberry tart?), and for the next thirty minutes or so the drama that had flared up during the first part of the meal steadily diminished. Born was being nice to me again, and although he continued to drink glass after glass of wine, I was beginning to feel confident that we would get to the end of the dinner without another outburst or insult from my capricious, half-crocked host. Then he opened a bottle of brandy, lit up one of his Cuban cigars, and started talking about politics.

Fortunately, it wasn't as gruesome as it could have been. He was deep in his cups by the time he poured the cognac, and after an ounce or two of those burning, amber spirits, he was too far gone to engage in a coherent conversation. Yes, he called me a coward again for refusing to go to Vietnam, but mostly he talked to himself, lapsing into a long, meandering monologue on any number of disparate subjects as I sat there listening in silence and Margot washed pots and pans in the kitchen. Impossible to recapture more than a fraction of what he said, but the key points are still with me, particularly his memories of fighting in Algeria, where he spent two years with the French army interrogating *filthy Arab terrorists* and losing whatever faith he'd once had in the idea of justice. Bombastic pronouncements, wild generalizations, bitter declarations about the corruption of all governments – past, present, and future; left, right, and centre – and how our so-called civilization was no more than a thin screen masking a never-ending assault of barbarism and cruelty. Human beings were animals, he said, and soft-minded aesthetes like myself were no better than children, diverting ourselves with hair-splitting philosophies of art and literature to avoid confronting the essential truth of the world. Power was the only constant, and the law of life was kill or be killed, either dominate or fall victim to the savagery of monsters. He talked about Stalin and the millions of lives lost during the collectivization movement in the Thirties. He talked about the Nazis and the war, and then he advanced the startling theory that Hitler's admiration of the United States had inspired him to use American history as a model for his conquest of Europe. Look at the parallels, Born said, and it's not as far-fetched as you'd think: extermination of the Indians is turned into the extermination of the Jews; westward expansion to exploit natural resources is turned into eastward expansion for the same purpose; enslavement of the blacks for low-cost labour is turned into subjugation of the Slavs to produce a similar result. Long live America, Adam, he said, pouring another shot of cognac into both our glasses. Long live the darkness inside us.

As I listened to him rant on like this, I felt a growing pity for him. Horrible as his view of the world was, I couldn't help feeling sorry for a man who had descended into such pessimism, who so willfully shunned the possibility of finding any compassion, grace, or beauty in his fellow human beings. Born was just thirty-six, but already he was a burnt-out soul, a shattered wreck of a person, and at his core I imagined that he must have suffered terribly, living in constant pain, lacerated by the jabbing knives of despair, disgust, and self-contempt.

Margot re-entered the dining room, and when she saw the state Born was in – bloodshot eyes, slurred speech, body listing to the left as if he was about to fall off his chair – she put her hand on his back and gently told him in French that the evening was over and that he should toddle off to bed. Surprisingly, he didn't protest. Nodding his head and muttering the word *merde* several times in a flat, barely audible voice, he allowed Margot to help him to his feet, and a moment later she was guiding him out of the room towards the hall that led to the back of the apartment. Did he say goodnight to me? I can't remember. For several minutes, I remained in my chair, expecting Margot to return in order to show me out, but when she didn't come back after what seemed to be an inordinate length of time, I stood up and headed for the front door. That was when I saw her – emerging from a bedroom at the end of the hall. I waited as she walked towards me, and the first thing she did when we were standing next to each other was put her hand on my forearm and apologize for Rudolf's behaviour.

Is he always like that when he drinks? I asked.

No, almost never, she said. But he's very upset right now and has many things on his mind.

Well, at least it wasn't dull.

You comported yourself with great discretion.

So did you. And thank you for the dinner. I'll never forget the *navarin*.

Margot gave me one of her small, fleeting smiles and said: If you want me to cook for you again, let me know. I'll be happy to give you another meal while Rudolf is in Paris.

Sounds good, I said, knowing I would never find the courage to call her but at the same time feeling touched by the invitation.

Again, another flicker of a smile, and then two perfunctory kisses, one on each cheek. Goodnight, Adam, she said. You will be in my thoughts.

I didn't know if I was in her thoughts or not, but now that Born was out of the country, she had entered mine, and for the next two days I could barely stop thinking about her. From the first night at the party, when Margot had trained her eyes on me and studied my face with such intensity, to the disturbing conversation Born had provoked at the dinner about the degree of my attraction to her, a sexual current had been running between us, and even if she was ten years older than I was, that didn't prevent me from imagining myself in bed with her, from wanting to go to bed with her. Was the offer to give me another dinner a veiled proposition, or was it simply a matter of generosity, a desire to help out a young student who subsisted on the wretched fare of cheap diners and warmed-over cans of precooked spaghetti? I was too timid to find out. I wanted to call her, but every time I reached for the phone, I understood that it was impossible. Margot lived with Born, and even though he had insisted that marriage wasn't in their future, she was already claimed, and I didn't feel I had the right to go after her.

Then she called me. Three days after the dinner, at ten o'clock in the morning, the telephone rang in my apartment, and there she was on the other end of the line, sounding a little hurt, disappointed that I hadn't been in touch, in her own subdued way expressing more emotion than at any time since we'd met.

I'm sorry, I lied, but I was going to call you later today. You beat me to it by a couple of hours.

Funny boy, she said, seeing right through my fib. You don't have to come if you don't want to.

But I do, I answered, meaning every word of it. Very much.

Tonight?

Tonight would be perfect.

You don't have to worry about Rudolf, Adam. He's gone, and I'm free to do whatever I like. We all are. Nobody can own another person. Do you understand that?

I think so.

How do you feel about fish?

Fish in the sea or fish on a plate?

Grilled sole. With little boiled potatoes and *choux de Bruxelles* on the side. Does that appeal to you, or would you rather have something else?

No. I'm already dreaming about the sole.

Come at seven. And don't trouble yourself with flowers this time. I know you can't afford them.

After we hung up, I spent the next nine hours in a torment of anticipation, daydreaming through my afternoon classes, pondering the mysteries of carnal attraction, and trying to understand what it was about Margot that had worked me up to such a pitch of excitement. My first impression of her had not been particularly favourable. She had struck me as an odd and vapid creature, sympathetic at heart, perhaps, intriguing to look at, but with no electricity in her, a woman lost in some murky inner world that shut her off from true engagement with others, as if she were some silent visitor from another planet. Two days later, I had run into Born at the West End, and when he told me about her reaction to our meeting at the party, my feelings for her began to shift. Apparently she liked me and was concerned about my welfare, and when you're informed that a person likes you, your instinctive response is to like that person back. Then came the dinner. The languor and precision of her gestures as she cut the flowers and put them in the vase had stirred something in me, and the simple act of watching her move had suddenly become fascinating, hypnotic. There were depths of sensuality in her, I discovered, and the bland, uninteresting woman who seemed not to have a thought in her head turned out to be far more astute than I had imagined. She had defended me against Born at least twice during the dinner, intervening at the precise moments when things had threatened to fly out of control. Calm, always calm, barely speaking above a whisper, but each time her words had produced the desired effect. Thrown by Born's prodding insinuations, convinced that he was trying to lure me into some voyeuristic mania of his – watching me make love to Margot? – I'd assumed that she was in on it as well, and therefore I had held back and refused to play along. But now Born was on the other side of the Atlantic, and Margot still wanted to see me. It could only be for one thing. I understood now that it had always been that one thing, right from the moment she'd spotted me standing alone at the party. That was why Born had behaved so testily at the dinner – not because he wanted to instigate an evening of depraved sexual antics, but because he was angry at Margot for telling him she was attracted to me.

She cooked us dinner for five straight nights, and for five straight nights we slept together in the spare bedroom at the end of the hall. We could have used the other bedroom, which was larger and more comfortable, but neither one of us wanted to go in there. That was Born's room, the world of Born's bed, and for those five nights we made it our business to create a world of our own, sleeping in that tiny room with the single barred window and the narrow bed, which came to be known as the love bed, although love finally had nothing to do with what happened to us during those five days. We didn't fall for each other, as the saying goes, but rather we fell into each other, and in the deeply intimate space we inhabited for that short, short time, our sole preoccupation was pleasure. The pleasure of eating and drinking, the pleasure of sex, the pleasure of taking part in a wordless animal dialogue that was conducted in a language of looking and touching, of biting, tasting, and stroking. That doesn't mean we didn't talk, but talk was kept to a minimum, and what talk there was tended to focus on food – *What should we eat tomorrow night?* – and the words we exchanged over dinner were wispy and banal, of no real importance. Margot never asked me questions about myself. She wasn't curious about my past, she didn't care about my opinions on literature or politics, and she had no interest in what I was studying. She simply took me for what I represented in her own mind – her choice of the moment, the physical being she desired – and every time I looked at her, I sensed that she was drinking me in, as if just having me there within arm's reach was enough to satisfy her. What did I learn about Margot during those days? Very little, almost nothing at all. She had grown up in Paris, was the youngest of three children, and knew Born because they were second cousins. They had been together for two years now, but she didn't think it would last much longer. He seemed to be growing bored with her, she said, and she was growing bored with herself. She shrugged when she said that, and when I saw the distant expression on her face, I had the terrible intuition that she already considered herself to be half-dead. After that, I stopped pressing her to open up to me. It was enough that we were together, and I cringed at the thought of accidentally touching on something that might cause her pain.

Margot without make-up was softer and more earthbound than the striking female object she presented to the public. Margot without clothes proved to be slight, almost meagre, with small, pubescent-like breasts, slender hips, and sinewy arms and legs. A full-lipped mouth, a flat belly with a slightly protruding navel, tender hands, a nest of coarse pubic hair, firm buttocks, and extremely white skin that felt smoother than any skin I had ever touched. The particulars of a body, the irrelevant, precious details. I was tentative with her at first, not knowing what to expect, a bit awed to find myself with a woman so much more experienced than I was, a beginner in the arms of a veteran, a fumbler who had always felt shy and awkward in his nakedness, who until then had always made love in the dark, preferably under the blankets, coupling with girls who had been just as shy and awkward as he was, but Margot was so comfortable with herself, so knowledgeable in the arts of nibbling, licking, and kissing, so unreluctant to explore me with her hands and tongue, to attack, to swoon, to give herself without coyness or hesitation, that it wasn't long before I let myself go. If it feels good, it's good, Margot said at one point, and that was the gift she gave me over the course of those five nights. She taught me not to be afraid of myself any more.

I didn't want it to end. Living in that strange paradise with the strange, unfathomable Margot was one of the best, most unlikely things that had ever happened to me, but Born was due to return from Paris the next evening, and we had no choice but to cut it off. At the time, I imagined it was only a temporary ceasefire. When we said goodbye on the last morning, I told her not to worry, that sooner or later we'd figure out a way to continue, but for all my bluster and confidence Margot looked troubled, and just as I was about to leave the apartment, her eyes unexpectedly filled with tears.

I have a bad feeling, she said. I don't know why, but something tells me this is the end, that this is the last time I'll ever see you.

Don't say that, I answered. I live just a few blocks from here. You can come to my apartment anytime you want.

I'll try, Adam. I'll do my best, but don't expect too much from me. I'm not as strong as you think I am.

I don't understand.

Rudolf. Once he comes back, I think he's going to throw me out.

If he does, you can move in with me.

And live with two college boys in a dirty apartment? I'm too old for that.

My room-mate isn't so bad. And the place is fairly clean, all things considered.

I hate this country. I hate everything about it except you, and you aren't enough to keep me here. If Rudolf doesn't want me anymore, I'll pack up my things and go home to Paris.

You talk as if you want it to happen, as if you're already planning to break it off yourself.

I don't know. Maybe I am.

And what about me? Haven't these days meant anything to you?

Of course they have. I've loved being with you, but we've run out of time now, and the moment you walk out of here, you'll understand that you don't need me anymore.

That's not true.

Yes, it is. You just don't know it yet.

What are you talking about?

Poor Adam. I'm not the answer. Not for you – probably not for anyone.

It was a dismal end to what had been such a momentous time for me, and I left the apartment feeling shattered, perplexed, and perhaps a little angry as well. For days afterward, I kept going over that final conversation, and the more I analysed it, the less sense it made to me. On the one hand, Margot had teared up at the moment of my departure, confessing that she was afraid she would never see me again. That would suggest she wanted our fling to go on, but when I proposed that we begin meeting at my apartment, she had become hesitant, all but telling me it wouldn't be possible. Why not? For no reason – except that she wasn't as strong as I thought she was. I had no idea what that meant. Then she had started talking about Born, which quickly devolved into a muddle of contradictions and conflicting desires. She was worried that he was going to kick her out, but a second later that seemed to be exactly what she wanted. Even more, perhaps she was going to take the initiative and leave him herself. Nothing added up. She wanted me and didn't want me. She wanted Born and didn't want Born. Each word that came out of her mouth subverted what she had said a moment earlier, and in the end there was no way to know what she felt. Perhaps she didn't know herself. That struck me as the most plausible explanation – Margot in distress, Margot pulled apart by equal and opposite forces – but after spending those five nights with her, I couldn't help feeling hurt and abandoned. I tried to keep my spirits up – hoping she would call, hoping she would change her mind and come rushing back to me – but deep down I knew it was finished, that her fear of never seeing me again was in fact a prophecy, and that she was gone from my life for good.

CONTRIBUTORS

Paul Auster is the bestselling author of, among other titles, *Man in the Dark*, *The Brooklyn Follies* (part of which appeared in *Granta* 87) and *The Book of Illusions*. He has also appeared in the magazine with 'The Red Notebook' (*Granta* 44), 'Dizzy' (*Granta* 46), 'The Money Chronicles' (*Granta* 58) and 'It Don't Mean a Thing' (*Granta* 71). 'Invisible' is an extract from his new novel of the same title, which will be published in November 2009.

John Banville was awarded the Man Booker Prize in 2005 for *The Sea*. His new novel, *The Infinities*, will be published in the autumn. He last appeared in *Granta* 56 with 'The Enemy Within'.

Nicola Barker's most recent novel, *Darkmans*, was shortlisted for the Man Booker and Ondaatje prizes, and won the Hawthornden Prize. In 2003 she was named as one of *Granta*'s Best of Young British Novelists. 'For the Exclusive Attn of Ms Linda Withycombe' will be published in *Burley Cross Postbox Theft*, an epistolary novel to be published in 2010. She lives in London.

Amy Bloom is the author of one novel, *Away*, and two books of short stories. 'Compassion and Mercy' is taken from a new collection, *I Love to See You Coming, I Hate To See You Go*, to be published in 2010. She is at work on a new novel.

Eleanor Catton was born in 1985 in Ontario, Canada and raised in New Zealand. Her first novel, *The Rehearsal*, won the 2007 Adam Award from the International Institute of Modern Letters. It will be published in the UK in July 2009 and in the USA in 2010. She is currently a student at the Iowa Writers' Workshop.

Mavis Gallant was born in Montreal in 1922. When she was twenty-eight she gave up her job as a journalist, moved to Paris and devoted herself to writing fiction. In 1951 she published her first short story in *The New Yorker* and since then she has established an international following as one of the world's greatest short-story writers. She is the author of over twelve collections of stories, two novels, a volume of non-fiction, *Paris Notebooks: Essays and Reviews*, and a play. A selection of her work from

1951–71, *The Cost of Living*, will be published in autumn 2009.

Fanny Howe's poetry collections include *On the Ground*, shortlisted for the Griffin Poetry Prize, and *The Lyrics*. *The Winter Sun: Notes on a Vocation*, a book of essays, was published earlier this year.

Ha Jin was born in Liaoning, China, in 1956, and moved to America in 1984. His books include the novel *Waiting*, winner of the PEN/Faulkner Award and the National Book Award; *War Trash*, which won the PEN/Faulkner Award; *Under the Red Flag*, which won the Flannery O'Connor Award for Short Fiction; and *Ocean of Words*, which won the PEN/Hemingway Award. A new collection of stories, *A Good Fall*, will be published in November 2009. He is a professor of English at Boston University.

Jhumpa Lahiri is the author of *The Namesake*, a novel, and two collections of stories, *Interpreter of Maladies*, which won the Pulitzer Prize, the PEN/Hemingway Award and *The New Yorker* Debut of the Year, and *Unaccustomed Earth*,

winner of the Frank O'Connor International Short Story Award. She lives in Brooklyn, New York.

William Pierce is Senior Editor of the American literary and cultural magazine *AGNI*, and publishes a series of essays there called 'Crucibles'. He is currently at work on a novel, *A Man of Restraint.*

Helen Simpson is the author of five collections of short stories: *Four Bare Legs in a Bed, Dear George, Hey Yeah Right Get a Life* (*Getting a Life* in the US), *Constitutional* (*In the Driver's Seat* in the US) and *In-Flight Entertainment*, which will be published later this year. In 1993 she was chosen as one of *Granta*'s Best of Young British Novelists. 'In-Flight Entertainment' was published in *Granta* 100. She lives in London.

Adam Thirlwell was born in 1978 and named one of *Granta*'s Best of Young British Novelists in 2003. His story, 'The Cyrillic Alphabet', appeared in the issue of that title. His first novel, *Politics*, was followed by an essay on the art of fiction, *Miss Herbert*, published in 2007 and winner of The Somerset Maugham Award in 2008. His second novel,

The Escape (from which 'Haffner' is taken), will be published in 2010.

Chris Ware lives in Oak Park, Illinois, and is the author of *Jimmy Corrigan – The Smartest Kid on Earth*. He has guest-edited *Timothy McSweeney's Quarterly Concern* and Houghton-Mifflin's *The Best American Comics*, and was the first cartoonist chosen to regularly serialize an ongoing story in the *New York Times*. A contributor to *The New Yorker* and *The Virginia Quarterly Review*, his work was included in the 2002 Whitney Biennial and later enjoyed an exhibit of its own at the Museum of Contemporary Art Chicago.

Contributing Editors
Diana Athill, Jonathan Derbyshire, Sophie Harrison, Isabel Hilton, Blake Morrison, Philip Oltermann, John Ryle, Sukhdev Sandhu, Lucretia Stewart.

ILLUSTRATORS

Ceri Amphlett's commissions include the artwork for the album *Thunder, Lightning, Strike* by British band The Go! Team. She has also shown her work internationally, most recently as part of *The Art of Lost Words* exhibition.

Rachel Tudor Best draws on the rich and diverse experience of her home life and travels to provide the source and inspiration for her work, developing ideas through the playful use of art materials, photographs and books.

George Butler has been a freelance illustrator since 2007. The majority of his work could be described as reportage illustration but he has also undertaken commercial jobs for Descent ski holidays and has been named Illustrator in Residence at *The Globalista Travel Journal*.

Laura Carlin won a V&A Illustration Award for her contribution to Barbara Toner's piece 'Inside a Rape Trial' (*Guardian*). While at the Royal College of Art she twice received the Quentin Blake Award, and her recent clients include British Airways and the *New York Times*.

Tilman Faelker lives in Stuttgart, Germany, and has been a freelance illustrator since the beginning of 2009. His work has appeared in *Beef* – the magazine of the Art Directors Club of Germany – and the Italian cultural quarterly *Drome*.

Michael Kirkham won the D&AD 'Best New Blood' award in 2006 and the Association of Illustrators' 'New Talent' Gold award in 2007. His commissions have included work for the Folio Society, Random House and *The Times*.

Sam Messer is an artist and teacher whose work is exhibited and collected internationally. He has also collaborated with writers including Denis Johnson, Jonathan Safran Foer and Paul Auster, with whom he published *The Story of My Typewriter*.

Adam Simpson's clients include Conran and the *LA Times*. His work encompasses design, animation and illustration, but always with an emphasis on drawing. He has exhibited internationally and has lectured on art and design at the Universities of Derby and Plymouth.

AMERICAN ESSAYS IN LITURGY

SERIES EDITOR, EDWARD FOLEY

LITURGY AND THE SOCIAL SCIENCES

Nathan D. Mitchell

A Liturgical Press Book

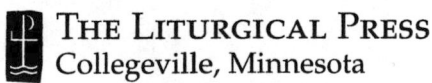
THE LITURGICAL PRESS
Collegeville, Minnesota

2	3	4	5	6	7	8	9

Library of Congress Cataloging-in-Publication Data

Mitchell, Nathan.
    Liturgy and the social sciences / Nathan Mitchell.
       p.   cm. — (American essays in liturgy)
    "A Liturgical Press book."
    Includes bibliographical references.
    ISBN 0-8146-2511-8 (alk. paper)
    1. Ritual.   2. Catholic Church—Liturgy.   3. Religion and the social sciences.   I. Title.   II. Series: American essays in liturgy (Collegeville, Minn.)
BX1970.M583   1999
264'.02—dc21   98-34981
                                                                  CIP

Contents

1 The Search for Ritual's Roots in Anthropology

Introduction

In his first collection, entitled *Harmonium*, Wallace Stevens, the Hartford Insurance executive who became arguably America's most important poet in the first half of the twentieth century, published a now-famous poem entitled "Thirteen Ways of Looking at a Blackbird." Critics have called this early poem a symbolist "collage" of images; Stevens himself insisted that it was a random "collection of sensations" rather than a sequence of thoughts or ideas. The point of the poem (if it can be said to have one) is not cognitive or logical, but embodied and sensory. Interestingly, the imaginative sources of Stevens' poem were both ancient and modern. From antiquity, Stevens sought inspiration in long-established traditions of Chinese landscape painting and Japanese poetry (especially haiku). From modernism, he drew upon images created by post-impressionist painters like Pablo Picasso. In his Cubist period, Picasso invited viewers to dance around an object (recall the astonishing large eyes that appear in Picasso's profiles), and to discover in a single work multiple perspectives, perceptions, sensations. The Cubists liked to describe painting as "a horde of destructions" because their art seemed to explode familiar objects into unfamiliar, prismatic fragments. "The effect," writes critic Michael Benamou, "was one of complexity; the picture became a simultaneous enumeration of related aspects."[1]

[1] Michael Benamou, *Wallace Stevens and the Symbolist Imagination* (Princeton: Princeton University Press, 1972) 9.

So it was with Stevens and his blackbirds. The sumptuous tapestry of the whole human sensorium is the implied landscape of the poem—the dance of images, the explosion of perceptions and perspectives. "I know noble accents," Stevens wrote, "and lucid, inescapable rhythms; / But I know, too, / That the blackbird is involved / In what I know."[2] He knew—as every artist (and possibly every blackbird!) does—that to create a work of art is to utter a great "cry against the twilight." The creation of art is a protest against extinction, as Dylan Thomas suggested in his line, "Rage, rage against the dying of the light." Small wonder, then, that Stevens thought of poetry as an essential human enterprise. "To help people live their lives," he wrote, "is the poet's function."[3] This function is fulfilled, he felt, chiefly by creating a "supreme fiction," a new and compelling myth that can fill the emptiness, the void left when "too many waltzes have ended."[4] In a word, Stevens understood that art is a passionate outcry against the encroachments of death—and that death is thus "the mother of beauty."[5]

Like the poetic logic of Stevens' "Thirteen Ways of Looking at a Blackbird," the ritual logic of Christian public prayer and sacrament is primarily embodied and sensory, imagistic and experiential, rather than cognitive or intellectual. Like art, ritual can be imagined as a protest against extinction; an outcry against annihilation; a challenge to the dying of the light, the ending of the waltz. Of course there are many more than thirteen ways of looking at ritual, whether as a species of human behavior with anthropological interest or as a species of Christian behavior with theological interest. In this chapter, I want to describe the consensus that seemed to emerge after the Second Vatican Council among many liturgists (chiefly Roman Catholic) who use anthropological data or categories to interpret Christian ritual. In subsequent chapters, I will attempt to show how this consensus has recently been challenged both by developments within the field of anthropology and by new approaches within the emergent field of ritual studies.

[2]Wallace Stevens, *Collected Poems* (New York: Knopf, 1978) 94.

[3]See Wallace Stevens, *The Necessary Angel: Essays on Reality and the Imagination* (New York: Knopf, 1951) 29.

[4]Wallace Stevens, "Sad Strains of a Gay Waltz," in *Collected Poems*, 121. See James S. Leonard and Christine E. Wharton, "Art as a Cry Against Extinction in the Poetry of Wallace Stevens," *The Wallace Stevens Journal* 5:3-4 (Fall 1981) 37.

[5]Wallace Stevens, "Sunday Morning," *Collected Poems*, 68.

Richard Gaillardetz has written that we are living in an era when people want either "community without transcendence" or "transcendence without community."[6] Those who seek "community" seem to want liturgies that are warm, intimate, hospitable, laid-back, user-friendly: in short, devoid of the ceremonialism that characterized Roman Catholic worship during the centuries that followed the appearance of the "Tridentine" Missal of Pius V (1570). Those who seek "transcendence" seem to want liturgies that display decorum, dignity, reverence, mystery, awe, otherness: in short, celebrations that challenge the comforting American culture of affluence, intimacy, individualism, and membership in approved groups. The communitarians argue that liturgies must mirror the people that celebrate them. The transcendentalists seem more comfortable with the idea that culture should be adapted to liturgy—not liturgy to culture. Gaillardetz suggests that this conflict can be resolved only if we understand Christian rituals as events that celebrate the unity of "communion with God" and "communion with one another":

> This liturgical rift can only be healed by a return to the Trinitarian and Eucharistic foundations of the Christian faith and the liturgy. The formal and social dimensions of liturgical life, when properly celebrated, remind us that human connectedness is written into the very structures of our personal existence and that when we realize ourselves as persons who live the life of communion with others we are, at the same time, living the life of communion with God. The celebration of the liturgy is the privileged ritual expression of what is in fact true every moment of our lives: every authentic act of human communion is by that fact communion with God.[7]

Gaillardetz's proposal will sound quite plausible to most readers of this essay. It is based on the familiar assumption—derived, it is often said, from the research of anthropologists—that ritual confers basic psychological and/or social benefits upon the individuals and communities who participate in them.[8] Rituals, it is said, are a

[6]Richard Gaillardetz, "North American Culture and the Liturgical Life of the Church: The Separation of the Quests for Transcendence and Community," *Worship* 68:5 (1994) 403–16.

[7]Ibid., 416.

[8]For a brief critique of this assumption, see John Stoddard, "'Performative Utterances' in African Rituals," *History of Religions* 13:1 (1973) 34–35.

vital means of negotiating a community's identity, of guaranteeing its social cohesion; they enunciate, embody and enact a people's most cherished meanings and values. But how did this view of ritual develop? And why did it gain such widespread acceptance, especially among Catholic liturgists? It will be the task of this chapter to propose some answers to these questions.

Beginnings

In a now-famous open letter written to the organizer of the Third German Liturgical Congress held at Mainz in April 1964, Romano Guardini spoke of the many "ritual and textual problems" that would inevitably accompany the postconciliar reform of the Roman Catholic liturgy.[9] "The question," Guardini wrote, "is whether the wonderful opportunities now open to the liturgy will achieve their full realization, whether we shall be satisfied with just removing anomalies, taking new situations into account, giving better instruction on the meaning of ceremonies and liturgical vessels, or whether we shall relearn a forgotten way of doing things and recapture lost attitudes."[10] The "forgotten way of doing things," as the rest of Guardini's letter makes clear, is precisely corporate ritual activity. Full, conscious and active participation in Christian worship is, he felt, contemplative yet corporate, personal yet public, internal yet incarnate. As Genevieve (Jennifer) Glen has noted, what Guardini called "the liturgical act" is in fact a layered paradox that simultaneously embraces contemplative action (itself an oxymoron) and community performance.[11] Christian ritual is not the contemplative act of an individual but of the assembly, the whole community gathered in faith and prayer in obedience to Jesus' command. The question is whether people (and presiders) can relearn such a way of "doing." As Guardini himself put it, "How can the act of walking become a religious act, a retinue for the Lord progressing through the land, so that an 'epiphany' may take place?"[12] One should be able to "read" a ritual act simply by doing it, simply by looking, simply by performing "without being theatrical and

[9] Romano Guardini, "A Letter," *Herder Correspondence,* Special Issue (1964) 24–26.

[10] Ibid., 24.

[11] See Jennifer Glen, "Twenty Years Later: A Reflection on the Liturgical Act," *Assembly* 12:4 (1986) 325–28.

[12] Guardini, "Letter," 25.

fussy."[13] That is the challenge facing Catholics as they attempt to implement *Sacrosanctum Concilium*.

Guardini's impassioned plea for relearning "a forgotten way of doing things" quickly became a kind of talismanic text, especially among people working in the field of pastoral liturgy. The open letter to the Congress at Mainz had touched a nerve, not only because it focused attention upon the liturgical act itself (rather than upon the mechanics of reform), but also because it suggested the need to explore more deeply the human sources and cultural contexts of ritual activity. In brief, Guardini had challenged Catholics to reevaluate the roots and roles of ritual.

He was not, however, the first or the only person to do so. In the first chapter of *Rite and Man*, Louis Bouyer had written:

> With the help of the modern sciences that deal with man, we intend to examine what might be described as the anthropological antecedents to Christianity. From this study, the human character of Christianity should emerge with a clarity that would otherwise be hardly suspected. . . . Indeed, the more perfectly we know the human aspects of Christianity, the more perfectly we shall understand that part of it which is the result of divine intervention. This is not to say that the human and the divine should be found in it separated from one another. It is rather that the divine reveals itself in the transformation it effects in what is human.[14]

As Bouyer recognized, his own interest in the "anthropological antecedents" of Christian liturgy was indebted, in part at least, to work done by the Benedictine monks of Maria Laach, especially by Dom Odo Casel.[15] The work of Sister Aemiliana Löhr—Casel's disciple at the Abbey of Holy Cross, Herstelle—must also be mentioned.[16] Casel and Löhr made extensive use of scholarly studies of

[13]Ibid.

[14]Louis Bouyer, *Rite and Man*, trans. M. Joseph Costelloe (Notre Dame, Ind.: University of Notre Dame Press, 1963) 2; Bouyer's work had originally appeared in 1962, *Le Rite et L'Homme: Sacralité naturelle et Liturgie*, Lex Orandi 32 (Paris: Cerf).

[15]Casel's work is summarized in English in his *The Mystery of Christian Worship and Other Writings* (Westminster, Md.: The Newman Press, 1962).

[16]Löhr's scholarly work is, for the most part, not available in English. Some of her commentary on gospels appointed for the liturgical year may be found in Aemiliana Löhr, *The Year of Our Lord: The Mystery of Christ in the Liturgical Year*, trans. a monk of St. Benedict (New York: P. J. Kenedy & Sons, 1937).

religion in ancient cultures in order to understand the meaning of "mystery" in Christian cult. In effect, Bouyer's *Rite and Man* extended this investigation a step further by broadening the inquiry to include living cultures—as studied by anthropologists, sociologists, and representatives of the *Religionsgeschictlicheschule*. One can see this movement in *Rite and Man*, especially in the chapter entitled "Recent Developments in the History of Religions,"[17] which makes use of studies by Mircea Eliade,[18] by biblical archaeologists like E.O. James and W. F. Albright,[19] and by sociologists like Joachim Wach.[20]

But Bouyer did not stop with the archaeological or anthropological antecedents of Christian ritual. He also drew attention to the work of depth psychologists like Freud, Jung and Adler.[21] This was an important and needed move, in part because of a tendency, common among many psychologists earlier in this century, to treat repetitive ritual behavior as a neurotic symptom. Although Bouyer does not discuss it, Jung's famous essay "The Mass and the Individuation Process" should be mentioned here.[22] Jung's essay begins with this provocative comment:

> Viewed from the psychological standpoint, Christ, as the primordial man . . . represents a totality far exceeding and encompassing the ordinary human being, and which corresponds to the total personality transcending consciousness. . . . Just as on the more archaic level of the Zosimos vision the homunculus is transformed and exalted to the condition of Pneuma, the Eucharistic mystery transforms the soul of empirical man—who is only a part of himself into its totality, which is expressed by Christ. In this sense, therefore, the Mass can be defined as the *ritual of the individuation process.*[23]

[17]Bouyer, *Rite and Man*, 14–37.

[18]Mircea Eliade, *Patterns in Comparative Religion*, trans. Rosemary Sheed (New York: Sheed and Ward, 1958).

[19]E.g., the classic studies by E. O. James, *Christian Myth and Ritual* (London: J. Murray, 1933) and W. F. Albright, *From the Stone Age to Christianity: Monotheism and the Historical Process*, 2nd ed. (Baltimore: Johns Hopkins Press, 1946).

[20]E.g., Joachim Wach, *Comparative Study of Religions* (New York: Columbia University Press, 1958).

[21]See Bouyer, *Rite and Man*, chapter 3: "Recent Developments in Psychology," 38–52.

[22]C. G. Jung, "The Mass and the Individuation Process." See the authorized English translation by Elizabeth Welsh in *The Black Mountain Review* 5 (Summer 1955) 90–147. Jung's essay is part of a larger study that was published in *Von den Wurzeln des Bewusstseins* (Zürich, 1954).

[23]Ibid., 90.

For Jung, the process of psychological individuation was not simply a matter of becoming more distinctively human; it included, as well, an essentially numinous component. That is the reason why, in many cultures, the most critical phases of human maturation require the services of "the shaman and medicine man . . . the prophet and the priest . . . philosophy and religion."[24] As Jung saw it,

> The shaman's varied experience of illness, torture, being killed and healed contains on a higher level the thought of sacrifice, reestablishment of the totality, transubstantiation and the raising of the human being to the status of the pneumatic man, in short the apotheosis. The [M]ass is the sum total and quintessence of a development extending over thousands of years, which with the gradual expansion and deepening of consciousness causes the once isolated experience of a specifically "tuned" individual to become gradually the common property of a larger group. The basic psychic event remains a secret and is perceptually and impressively represented in corresponding "mysteries" or "sacraments," with the help of instructions, exercise, meditations and sacrificial acts, which plunge the mystic so deep in the sphere of the mystery that he is able to become to a certain extent conscious of his intimate connection with the mythical proceedings. Thus, we see for example in ancient Egypt how "Osirification," originally a royal prerogative [sic], gradually spread to people of distinction and finally, towards the end of ancient Egyptian tradition, to the single individual. The mysteries in the Greek sphere, originally closed and kept secret, likewise expanded gradually into collective experiences, and at the time of the Roman empire it had become so to speak a favourite sport among Roman tourists to be initiated into foreign mysteries. Finally Christianity, after a little hesitation, has made the celebration of the mystery into a public ceremony, for it was its particular concern to introduce the greatest number of people into the experience of the mystery. Man was then unavoidably handed the opportunity of becoming conscious of his own transformation and its necessary psychological condition, as for example the confession of sins and repentance.[25]

Jung insisted that his interpretation of the Mass was not a wholesale attempt to psychologize religious ritual. The modern psychologist, he wrote,

[24]Ibid., 130.
[25]Ibid., 130–32.

is aware that he can produce no more than a description of a psychic process, formulated in scientific symbols, whose real nature transcends consciousness just as much as the secret of life or that of matter. . . . Because a so-called metaphysical statement is looked upon as a psychic process it is by no means said that it is "only psychological," as my critics like to put it.[26]

Jung did not seek to reduce Mass to the level of therapy; his point, rather, was that individuation—the process of establishing the wholeness and autonomy of the individual self by integrating personal consciousness with the collective unconscious—is a precisely self-transcending activity aptly reflected in the ritual dynamics of the eucharist. In other words, Jung saw the psychological process reflected in the rite, not the rite as originating in some psychological process.

While few theologians or psychologists today would adopt this Jungian analysis without reservation, the essay on "The Mass and the Individuation Process" helped to promote a serious dialogue between psychiatry and religion.[27] It led many Catholic liturgists to acknowledge that ritual is not merely rubrics and ceremonial but a much more comprehensive process having vital psychosocial roots and repercussions. The publication of Erik Erikson's famous essay on the "Ontogeny of Ritualization in Man"[28] was an especially critical moment in this developing dialogue between psychologists and students of Christian ritual. "Ritualization in man," wrote Erikson, "seems to be grounded in the pre-verbal experience of infants while reaching its full elaboration in grand public ceremonies."[29] Perhaps the most important of these preverbal experiences is "the 'greeting ceremonial' marking the beginning of an infant's day," for it is this simple transaction that marks "the ontogenetic source of one pervasive element in human ritualization, which is based on a *mutuality of recognition*."[30] The face-to-face encounter between infant and parent affirms the "sense of a *hallowed presence*" and "contributes to man's ritual-making a pervasive element which we will call the

[26]Ibid., 132–33.

[27]See, for example, Victor White, *God and the Unconscious* (Chicago: H. Regnery Co., 1953).

[28]Erik Erikson, "Ontogeny of Ritualization in Man," in *Philosophical Transactions of the Royal Society of London*, series B, 251 (1966) 337–49.

[29]Ibid., 337.

[30]Ibid., 338.

'Numinous'."[31] In a classic passage, Erikson outlined the reasons why the "ritualizations in the nursery" and religious rituals are linked: "In adult ritual . . . infantile elements are both emotively and symbolically re-evoked; but both infantile ritualization and adult ritual are parts of a functional whole, namely, of a cultural version of human existence."[32] Having made this crucial connection between cult and culture, Erikson went on to enumerate those "elements of ritualization which we can already recognize in the first, the numinous instance."[33] Summarizing the effects of ritualized transactions between infant and parent, he writes that they are

> based on the *reciprocal needs* of two quite *unequal* organisms and minds. We have spoken of the periodicity of developing needs to which ritualization gives a *symbolic actuality*. We have recognized it as a highly *personal* matter, and yet as *group-bound*, providing a sense both of *oneness* and of *distinctiveness*. It is *playful*, and yet *formalized*, and this in *details* as well as in the *whole* procedure. Becoming *familiar* through repetition, it yet brings the surprise of *recognition*. And while the ethologists will tell us that ritualizations in the animal world must, above all, be *unambiguous* as a set of signals, we suspect that in man the *overcoming of ambivalence* as well as of ambiguity is one of the prime functions of ritualization. For as we love our children, we also find them unbearably demanding, even as they will soon find us arbitrary and possessive. What we love or admire is also threatening, awe becomes awfulness, and benevolence seems in danger of being consumed by wrath. Therefore, ritualized affirmation, once instituted, becomes *indispensable* as a periodical experience and must find new forms in the context of new developmental actualities.[34]

Toward the end of his essay, Erikson provided readers with a chart outlining his views about the ontogeny and evolution of ritualization from infancy through adulthood.[35] He concluded by saying that his research may not provide "a complete inventory" of the ritualization process and that

> At any rate, there can be no prescription for ritualization, for, far from being merely repetitive or familiar in the sense of habituation, any

[31]Ibid., 338–39.
[32]Ibid., 339.
[33]Ibid.
[34]Ibid.
[35]Ibid., 348.

true ritualization is ontogenetically grounded and yet pervaded with the spontaneity of surprise: it is an unexpected renewal of a recognizable order in potential chaos. Ritualization thus depends on that blending of surprise and recognition which is the soul of creativity, reborn out of the abyss of instinctual disorder, confusion of identity and social anomie.[36]

The first liturgical scholar to grasp the import of Erikson's study for interpreting Christian ritual was Aidan Kavanagh.[37] In his essay "The Role of Ritual in Personal Development," Kavanagh showed how Erikson's research on the ontogeny of ritualization is valid not only for individuals but also for social groups. If the sequence of ritual patterns which Erikson linked to normal personality development breaks down, the result, Kavanagh argued, will be not only destruction for the individual but dissolution for the group:

> When the whole sequence [of ritual patterns and correlative ritual elements] breaks down in the individual members of a group, the group itself is already well into social dissolution.

> Why is this so? Because, I think, the patterns of ritual repetitive behavior correspond to and, therefore, may be said to carry, the inchoate and largely incommunicable human experience of reality—for the most part in a non-verbal and always in a parabolic and nondiscursive manner. The whole purpose, as I see it, of assembly, of coming together for public ritual engagements, religious or not, is so that individuals may communicate those experiences that are most incommunicable, publicly, in standard symbolic patterns agreed on by the group so that those experiences can be entered into, "put on," affirmed, and appropriated by the group as a whole. Such standard symbolic patterns are richly ambiguous, but they are also invariably and rigorously judgmental. The point at which the group does, in fact, enter into, finally affirm without reservation, and wholly appropriate the incommunicable life-experiences of its members is that at which judgment falls away in the face of solid affirmation and conviction. It is at this point alone, I submit, that celebration becomes possible if we understand celebration as the single ritual enterprise that is subordinated to no further or subsequent ritual pattern.[38]

[36]Ibid., 349.

[37]See Aidan Kavanagh's "The Role of Ritual in Personal Development," in James Shaughnessy, ed., *The Roots of Ritual* (Grand Rapids, Mich.: Eerdmans, 1973) 145–60.

[38]Ibid., 158–59.

Note here how Kavanagh links the individual's experience of the incommunicable to the standard symbolic patterns of the social group precisely as these are ritually enacted. In other words, the fate of "incommunicable (i.e., ultimate, transcendent) experience" is indissolubly connected to what might be called the group's ritual competence. That competence is defined and demonstrated by a process of reviewing and renewing values which Kavanagh outlines earlier in his essay:

> This process of *reviewing and renewing* values for the sake of group survival here and now is what gives the group continuity and cohesiveness in space and time, in the real order, in history. . . .
>
> This process of review and renewal of group values is what I understand tradition to be. . . .
>
> I must insist that *tradition* is the process by which values are communicated in human society; that *authority* is a central agent of that communication process; and that *myth and ritual*, the components of *cult*, are the enactments by which that communication of values takes place on the deepest and most critical level for the future survival of society itself.[39]

In a nutshell, what is at stake in ritual behavior—as it develops in individuals and is ritually enacted by groups—is nothing less than the survival of the social order. Or to put it in slightly different terms, culture cannot be defined apart from cult. When confronted by internal stress or external pressure, a group will inevitably seek to reconceive (review) and reenact (renew) its central meanings and values. "The conceiving aspect," Kavanagh writes,

> I take to be myth, and the enactment aspect I take to be ritual. Both myth and ritual thus appear to me as strictly correlative and inseparable functions: their reciprocal union is what I mean by cult. *The outcome of cult, so understood, is what I understand as culture*—what Margaret Mead has called "the systematic body of learned behavior which is transmitted from parents to children," or what I would prefer to call the continuous and cohesive life-style by which a particular group conceives and enacts what its values mean, thus to survive intact the stresses and threats of existence in the real order of space and time.[40]

[39]Ibid., 148, 151.
[40]Ibid., 148–49.

It is clear that both Kavanagh and Erikson seek to rehabilitate ritual by removing it, once and for all, from the sphere of "obsessional behaviour consisting of repetitive solitary acts with highly idiosyncratic meanings."[41] It is equally clear that Kavanagh extends Erikson's categories beyond the field of psychology and into the emerging discipline of ritual studies, where data from the social sciences—chiefly anthropology and sociology—must be taken into account. In effect, Kavanagh's essay was a boldly innovative call for a new discipline, for what one might term a "political science" of ritual behaviors—a systematic study of how human societies insure their cohesion and survival through the ritual appropriation of meanings and values, regularly reviewed and renewed.

Nothing quite like this had ever been attempted before, so Kavanagh and his colleagues sought a theoretical basis for this new discipline in the already established social sciences, particularly anthropology and sociology. What they found there—and more particularly, how they made use of what they found—will be the subject of the sections that follow.

Ritual: Definitions, Characteristics, Purposes, Strategies

Christopher Crocker defined ritual as "a statement in metaphoric terms about the paradoxes of human existence."[42] Ritual is, Crocker continues,

> essentially communication, a language in which societies discuss a variety of matters. It deals with the relationships a man has to other men, to institutions, spirits, and nature, and with all the various permutations of which these themes are capable. Our immediate problem thus becomes, exactly what is ritual communicating? How do we discover what a savage [sic] is saying, to himself and his fellows, when he parades about in feathers and paint, or what we mean when we use a fork to eat certain vegetables but our fingers to deal with corn-on-the-cob? Moreover, ritual not only says something; it also does things: it changes one season into another, makes boys become men, transforms ill persons into healthy ones, and the ghosts of the dead into the souls of the ancestors. Anthropologists agree that these functions of ritual are merely various perspectives of a nondifferenti-

[41]Erikson, "Ontogeny of Ritualization in Man," 337.
[42]Christopher Crocker, "Ritual and the Development of Social Structure: Liminality and Inversion," in Shaughnessy, *The Roots of Ritual*, 47.

ated, dynamic whole, but differ as to how communication relates to transformation and the mechanisms involved for both.[43]

Crocker may have overestimated the degree of unanimity among anthropologists about the meaning and mechanisms of ritual, but he was surely correct to note that many of them do regard ritual as a kind of social language whose grammar and usage is part of what field work attempts to discover. Perhaps the most famous example is to be found in Clifford Geertz's classic "Deep Play: Notes on the Balinese Cockfight."[44] Geertz looks at the entire competitive event not as an exercise in social *mechanics* but as an example of social *semantics*.[45] As a symbol system, the cockfight thus constitutes a *text* that, among other things, helps us to understand how societies may use "emotion for cognitive ends."[46] Geertz's work was extremely important because it signaled a fundamental "metaphorical refocusing" of the anthropologist's task:

> [I]t shifts the analysis of cultural forms from an endeavor in general parallel to dissecting an organism, diagnosing a symptom, deciphering a code, or ordering a system–the dominant analogies in contemporary anthropology—to one in general parallel with penetrating a literary text. If one takes the cockfight, or any other collectively sustained symbolic structure, as a means of "saying something of something" (to invoke a famous Aristotelian tag), then one is faced with a problem not in social mechanics but social semantics. For the anthropologist, whose concern is with formulating sociological principles . . . the question is, what does one learn about such principles from examining culture as an assemblage of texts?[47]

In other words, Geertz felt it might prove useful—and illuminating—if anthropologists were to extend the notion of "text" beyond written material, beyond the merely verbal, so that cultural forms could be seen as "imaginative works [texts] built out of social materials."[48]

[43]Ibid., 49–50.

[44]Clifford Geertz, "Deep Play: Notes on the Balinese Cockfight," in *The Interpretation of Cultures* (New York: Basic Books, 1973) 412–53; first published in *Daedalus* 101 (1972) 1–37.

[45]Ibid., 448.

[46]Ibid., 449.

[47]Ibid., 448.

[48]Ibid., 449.

> [T]o treat the cockfight as a text is to bring out a feature of it (in my opinion, the central feature of it) that treating it as a rite or a pastime, the two most obvious alternatives, would tend to obscure: its use of emotion for cognitive ends. What the cockfight says it says in a vocabulary of sentiment—the thrill of risk, the despair of loss, the pleasure of triumph. Yet what it says is not merely that risk is exciting, loss depressing, or triumph gratifying, banal tautologies of affect, but that it is of these emotions, thus exampled, that society is built and individuals are put together. Attending cockfights and participating in them is, for the Balinese, a kind of sentimental education. What he learns there is what his culture's ethos and his private sensibility (or anyway, certain aspects of them) look like when spelled out externally in a collective text; that the two are near enough alike to be articulated in the symbolics of a single such text; and—the disquieting part—that the text in which this revelation is accomplished consists of a chicken hacking another mindlessly to bits.
>
> Every people, the proverb has it, loves its own form of violence. The cockfight is the Balinese reflection on theirs; on its look, its uses, its force, its fascination.[49]

Note, incidentally, that Geertz saw his textual interpretation of cultural forms as a methodological alternative to treating them as rituals—a point that has perhaps been lost on Christian liturgists who attempt to make use of Geertz's categories. For him, the Balinese cockfight was not a social ritual, but "a Balinese reading of Balinese experience, a story they tell themselves about themselves."[50]

> What sets the cockfight apart from the ordinary course of life, lifts it from the realm of everyday practical affairs, and surrounds it with an aura of enlarged importance is not, as functionalist sociology would have it, that it reinforces status discriminations . . . but that it provides a metasocial commentary upon the whole matter of assorting human beings into fixed hierarchical ranks and then organizing the major part of collective existence around that assortment.[51]

What Geertz proposed was nothing short of an earthquake in anthropology. Prior to the publication of his work on the Balinese cockfight, the metaphor used by many anthropologists was *somatic:* the body and its boundaries supply the metaphoric light that illumines the principal codes of social structure and social change. For

[49]Ibid.
[50]Ibid., 448.
[51]Ibid.

example, as anthropologist Mary Douglas wrote in the preface to her book *Natural Symbols:*

> Most symbolic behaviour must work through the human body. . . . The human body is common to us all. Only our social condition varies. The symbols based on the human body are used to express different social experiences. . . .
>
> I will argue that the range of situations which use the human body for expression are fairly limited. They derive essentially from the quality of social relations. . . . [T]hese relations are structured according to two independently varying criteria which I have called grid and group. Group is obvious—the experience of a bounded social unit. Grid refers to rules which relate one person to others on an ego-centered basis. Grid and group may be found together. . . . [T]he most fundamental assumptions about the cosmos and man's place in nature are coloured by the socially appropriate image of the human body. . . . For if group is strong and grid weak, the idea of a cherished bodily form vulnerable to attack from without tends to be transferred from one context to another. It can serve as a theory of misfortune by pinning blame on hidden enemies of society; it can serve as a guide to action, requiring the enemies to be unmasked and disabled; it can serve as a philosophy of being, by distinguishing the forces of good from the forces of evil and identifying the inside of the body as the area under attack: inside becomes good and outside evil.[52]

In an introduction written for a new edition of *Natural Symbols*, Douglas clarified her position by noting that while the use of somatic metaphors and bodily processes provides a *basis* for symbol systems in a culture, the *meaning* of those systems is actually derived "from social experience."

> The starting-point of the argument in this book is that systems of symbols, though based on bodily processes, get their meaning from social experience. They are coded by a community with a shared history. Because of their hidden origins and community background, many such symbols seem to be more natural than language, but they are culturally learned and culturally transmitted. To the preliminary starting-point for this argument , one may add that there are no natural symbols; they are all social.[53]

[52]Mary Douglas, *Natural Symbols: Explorations in Cosmology*, new ed. (New York: Pantheon Books, 1982) vii–ix.

[53]Ibid., xix–xx.

Still, somatic symbols shape our fundamental experience and perception of social order or disorder—and hence contribute heavily to our definitions of dirt, disease and pollution. This is especially true when such symbols are enacted ritually:

> [S]ymbolic enactment . . . provides a focusing mechanism, a method of mnemonics and a control for experience. To deal with focusing first, a ritual provides a frame. The marked off time or place alerts a special kind of expectancy, just as the oft repeated "Once upon a time" creates a mood receptive to fantastic tales.[54]

Ritual's framing function is not merely convenient; it is indispensable, for social relations are not possible without symbolic acts—and symbolic acts require ritual performance:

> As a social animal, man is a ritual animal. If ritual is suppressed in one form it crops up in others, more strongly the more intense the social interaction. Without the letters of condolence, telegrams of congratulations and even occasional postcards, the friendship of a separated friend is not a social reality. It has no existence without the rites of friendship. Social rituals create a reality which would be nothing without them. It is not too much to say that ritual is more to society than words are to thought. For it is very possible to know something and then find words for it. But it is impossible to have social relations without social acts.[55]

Similarly, society defines dirt—and takes ritual steps to defend itself from it—as a transgression of those "ordered" social relations symbolized by social acts. Thus, as Christopher Crocker comments:

> [O]ur notions of "dirt" are really statements that things are out of place, disorganized—they are no longer ordered through the proper categories. Pollution results when such anomalous "dirt" is spread about, which is why so much primitive ritual seems designed to restore things to their proper categorical place. The products of the human body— hair, fingernails, saliva, blood, excrement, and so forth—are in this view very much liminal products. They are products of the body but not part of it; they express its boundaries and may threaten its integrity.[56]

[54]Mary Douglas, *Purity and Danger: An Analysis of Concepts of Pollution and Taboo* (Baltimore: Penguin Books, 1970 [1966]) 78.

[55]Ibid.

[56]Crocker, "Ritual and the Development of Social Structure," 70–71. Douglas develops this theme of dirt as disorder, pollution as contagion, in the first three chapters of *Purity and Danger*.

In brief, dirt is a violation of order; pollution arises from a confusion of categories. Both these powerful ideas are derived from a vision of social life rooted in the somatic metaphor. But perhaps the most significant result of Douglas's work came about not from her use of bodily metaphors to understand social experience, but from her critique of "anti-ritualism" in modern cultures.[57] This was a theme eagerly seized upon by liturgists. As applied to human behavior, Douglas notes,

> [R]itual, defined as a routinised act diverted from its normal function, subtly becomes a despised form of communication. Other symbolic acts accurately convey information about the intentions and commitments of the actor: ritual does not. The ritualist becomes one who performs external gestures which imply commitment to a particular set of values, but he is inwardly withdrawn, dried out and uncommitted. This is a distractingly partisan use of the term. For it derives from the long history of religious revivalism.[58]

Douglas goes on to identify "three phases in the move away from ritualism." First, she notes, "there is the contempt of external ritual forms; second, there is the private internalising of religious experience; third, there is the move to humanist philanthropy. When the third stage is under way, the symbolic life of the spirit is finished."[59] The "Bog Irish" living in London provided Douglas with a memorable example of how anti-ritualism erodes both social cohesion and religious identity. For these Irish immigrants, symbolic and ritual enactments like the traditional Friday abstinence from meat was in fact "the core rule of their religion: it is a taboo whose breach will bring automatic misfortune."[60] Postconciliar reformers utterly failed to understand this—and so they also failed to understand what makes most "uneducated believers" tick. The antidote to such misunderstanding is, Douglas suggests, a return to "ritualism":

> I shall take ritualism to signify heightened appreciation of symbolic action. This will be manifested in two ways: belief in the efficacy of instituted signs, sensitivity to condensed symbols. . . .

[57]See especially her chapter "Away from Ritual," in *Natural Symbols*, 1–18.
[58]Ibid., 2.
[59]Ibid., 7.
[60]Ibid., 3.

Ritualism is most highly developed where symbolic action is held to be most certainly efficacious. . . . Where symbols are highly valued and ritualism strong, then the idea of sin involves specific, formal acts of wrong-doing; where ritualism is weak, the idea of sin does not focus on specific external actions, but on internal states of mind: rituals of purification will not be so much in evidence. . . .

The devotion to the sacraments, then, depends on a frame of mind which values external forms and is ready to credit them with special efficacy. It is such a general attitude which commits the ritualist to sacramental forms of worship. And vice versa, a lack of interest in external symbols would not be compatible with a cult of instituted sacraments. Many of the current attempts to reform the Christian liturgy suppose that, as the old symbols have lost their meaning, the problem is to find new symbols or to revivify the meaning of the old ones. This could be a total waste of effort if, as I argue, people at different historic periods are more or less sensitive to signs as such.[61]

Whether she intended to or not, Douglas had handed Roman Catholic liturgists (and others identified as members of the "high church" camp) precisely the ammunition they had been seeking in their battle against the trivialization of ritual behavior (through a cult of pseudo-intimacy, individualism and cheap sentimentality) that had emerged in some quarters after the Second Vatican Council. Liturgists quickly found an ally for Douglas' "ritualist" position in the work of another anthropologist, Victor Turner. In an appendix to *Image and Pilgrimage in Christian Culture*,[62] Turner proposed a definition of ritual that epitomizes the work of an entire generation of Christian liturgists. Ritual, he wrote, is

formal behavior prescribed for occasions not given over to technological routine that have reference to beliefs in mystical beings or powers. . . . Observation of the rubrics of the ritual is deemed essential, for only by staying within the channels, marked out by custom, through which the collective action should flow . . . will the peace and harmony typically promised to ritual participants finally be achieved. . . .

Ritual [the definition continues, Turner now quoting Ronald Grimes] is . . . "transformative performance revealing major classifications, categories, and contradictions of cultural processes. It is not a bastion

[61]Ibid., 8–9.
[62]Victor Turner, *Image and Pilgrimage in Christian Culture* (New York: Columbia University Press, 1978).

of social conservatism whose symbols merely condense cherished cultural values. Rather it holds the generating source of culture and structure. . . . Hence, ritual is by definition associated with social transitions, while ceremony is linked with social states. Performances of ritual are distinct phases in the social process, whereby groups adjust to internal changes and adapt to their external environment.[63]

This carefully crafted definition provides a short summary of what was to become, among many Roman Catholic liturgists, the prevailing consensus about ritual's *origins, characteristics and purposes*—a consensus that many would call the "high church" view. Note that the definition sees ritual as both an enculturated "symbol system" and a social (or socializing) system. This means, of course, that ritual deals with both metaphysics and social mechanics; beliefs and behaviors; transcendent meanings and cultural structures; religious traditions and human transitions ("rites of passage"). It means, too, that rituals are thought to confer important psychological and sociological benefits upon the individuals and communities who enact them.

It may not, however, have been Turner's definition of ritual that influenced liturgists as much as his provocative essay of 1976 "Ritual, Tribal and Catholic."[64] A scathing jeremiad against the "hackwork of contemporaneous improvisation" that Turner believed the postconciliar liturgy had become, in effect, this essay argued, for the *ritual* superiority of the old Latin Mass (the "Tridentine" eucharistic liturgy as enshrined in the 1570 Missal of Pius V). Writing as a "Catholic by faith and anthropologist by profession," Turner complained that the new rite

---

[63]Ibid., 244. Compare Turner's definition with what Mark Searle wrote in 1985: "Christian liturgy is and has always been . . . the prayer of the community. It is also ritual prayer, characterized by the repetition of the same acts, rehearsing the same words, celebration of the same symbols and singing of the same chants. . . . Liturgy is characteristically traditional, though not necessarily uniform. . . . What the keepers of the tradition always knew . . . was how the structure was to be observed and how the variable elements were to be used in due order. The preconciliar Roman liturgy is not to be idealized . . . but it was usually celebrated whole and intact. In the postconciliar period this taken-for-grantedness of traditional ritual forms and of the fixed repertory of assigned texts and chants appears to be declining." Mark Searle and David Leege, "The Celebration of Liturgy in the Parishes," Report No. 5 (August 1985) *University of Notre Dame Institute for Pastoral and Social Ministry*, 4.

[64]Victor Turner, "Ritual, Tribal and Catholic," *Worship* 50:6 (1976) 504–26.

has been conceived, rather after the manner of Durkheim, Radcliffe-Brown and the now obsolescent functionalist schools of anthropology and sociology, as a suitable "expression" or "reflection" of contemporary social structures and processes, even fashions and fads. Rituals which represent the *fine fleur* of generic human experience understood in the light of the gospel have been jettisoned in favor of sometimes jaunty verbal formulations which are thought to be "relevant" to the experiences of "contemporary man," a blurry image contradictorily contrived by the communications media. Behind all this is the notion that the "ordinary faithful" can only appreciate the "sacred" when it is packaged in "secular" wrappings. This goes clean counter to all anthropological experience. . . . One advantage of the traditional Latin ritual was that it could be performed by the most diverse groups and individuals, surmounting their divisions of age, sex, ethnicity, culture, economic status or political affiliation. The liturgy stood out as a magnificent objective creation, a vehicle for every sort of Christian inferiority. . . . Now one fears that the tendentious manipulation of particular interest groups, prestigiously and strategically situated in the Church, is liquidating the ritual bonds which held the entire heterogeneous mystical body together in worship.[65]

Turner thus claimed to provide liturgists with a legitimate *anthropological* critique of the ritual reforms that followed Vatican II. Few seemed to notice the rather implausible *historical* basis of Turner's argument (his laudatory and uncritical citation, for instance, of Adrian Fortescue's bromide that the Tridentine liturgy represented "the most archaic service of the Holy Eucharist in Christendom").[66] Douglas's complaints against modern "anti-ritualism," coupled with Turner's views in "Ritual, Tribal and Catholic," thus became boiler-plate, repeated often by liturgists seeking a *serious anthropological* basis for their criticisms of what passed for "good postconciliar liturgy" in many parishes across the United States.

The Emergence of a Prevailing Consensus

Gradually a consensus based on an inventory of "what anthropologists (are believed to) think about ritual" emerged, especially (though not exclusively) in the "high church" liturgists' camp. It embraced these characteristics:

[65]Ibid., 524–25.
[66]Ibid., 509–10. For a penetrating critique of Turner's analysis, see Catherine Bell, "Ritual, Change, and Changing Rituals," *Worship* 63:1 (1989) 31–41.

- Ritual is neither an obsessive neurosis nor an artificial construct imposed on life from the outsider; rather, ritual is expressive, formalized, traditional, authoritative, nonutilitarian, symbolic, invariable, repeatable behavior whose remote roots are closely linked to the ontogenetic development of the human person.

- Although individuals may engage in idiosyncratic "rituals" of their own devising, the term is best reserved for actions that are public, social and collective (rather than strictly personal or private) in nature.

- Ritual embodies and transmits vital cultural information and processes (meanings, values, categories, classifications, contradictions) that support the collective identity and social cohesion of participants.

- Ritual does not merely reinforce already existing symbols and social structures; it may also generate or promote the emergence of new, transformative structures.

- Ritual is often (but not only) linked to social transitions (to rites of passage or life-crisis events).

- While its primary intention is to promote social cohesion and identity, ritual may sometimes encourage or legitimate social change and adaptation.

- Rituals preserve and represent archaic acts, ancestral memories and so provide access to the historic past—hence, a community without rituals is a community without a memory.

- A ritual's power is rooted in repetition and familiarity rather than unexpected novelty or innovation.

- Rituals are rehearsals both of who a community is (in its present life) and of what it means to become (in its eschatological future).

- Ritual orders and regulates social life, and thus it characteristically resists radical change, experimentation or improvisation.

In a word, ritual is essentially a way to regulate social life; to shape personal and corporate identity; to review and renew values; to express and transmit meaning in symbolic word and act; to preserve tradition; and to insure cultural cohesion and continuity. It is not an "efficient" or "utilitarian" way of acting. On the contrary, ritual acts are characteristically ambiguous, septic, multiple in meaning (and hence, not instantly clear or intelligible). For the most part, rituals are nonverbal deeds, not texts; they are "performances done by heart," without intrusive explanation or commentary. Moreover, the ritual version of reality is considered normative not only for participants' beliefs (doctrine), but for their behaviors as well (ethics).

This "orthodox consensus" about ritual—based (so it was believed) on "the best anthropological research"—seemed to find impressive confirmation in the work done by sociologists like Robert Bellah and his colleagues, as reported in their influential study *Habits of the Heart: Individualism and Commitment in American Life.*[67] One can easily detect the influence of these anthropological and sociological currents in "The Notre Dame Study of Catholic Parish Life," as summarized and reported by Mark Searle at the 1986 meeting of the North American Academy of Liturgy.[68] Early in his summary, Searle noted that in the parishes whose liturgical practices had been researched, "there is little evidence of ceremony and ritual splendor in the Masses," and that "the opportunities offered by the rite for solemnizing the liturgy are not much used in this country, even at the main parish Mass."[69] He suggested, further, that "the information given us by our observers points to the continuing victory of pragmatism over symbolism in American Catholic churches," and that "while there were some remarkable exceptions in our sample, the overall impression created by the liturgies we observed was one of mechanical and listless performance. Rarely was there an atmosphere of deeply prayerful involvement."[70] In short, Searle claimed to find in his data the very "anti-ritualism" and "hackwork

[67]Robert Bellah et al., *Habits of the Heart: Individualism and Commitment in American Life* (Berkeley: University of California Press, 1985).

[68]Mark Searle, "The Notre Dame Study of Catholic Parish Life," *Worship* 60:4 (1986) 312–33. The "Notre Dame Study" of parish liturgy was part of a $400,000 sociological study funded by the Lilly Foundation. It should be noted that this study did not claim to provide a comprehensive picture of "American Catholicism." As far as liturgy is concerned, Searle wrote, "It is a study of non-Hispanic American Catholics in the context of parish affiliation. The data provided by the study relate primarily to the thirty-six parishes involved and to the members of those parishes who are actually registered on parish lists. Consequently, one must be careful about generalizing to all U.S. Catholics" (312).

[69]Ibid., 317.

[70]Ibid., 317, 319.

improvisation" that anthropologists Mary Douglas and Victor Turner had predicted will result if rituals lose their historic connections to "distinctive social structure and correlated symbolism"[71] or to the close-knit "tribal community" created by the Roman Catholic Church over the centuries.[72]

But perhaps the most revealing portions appear in the final section of Searle's report, where the conclusions of anthropologists like Mary Douglas and Victor Turner are linked to those of sociologists like Robert Bellah. Searle suggests that "anti-ritualism" (Douglas, Turner) has combined with rampant "individualism" to put post-conciliar Catholic ritual on the rocks:

> Bellah sees *individualism*—that is, *the self-serving as final criterion of what is good, true, valuable, moral*—as characteristic of Western, *especially North American* culture. . . . [E]ven where evidence of individualism does not occur directly, the question casts a shadow over much of our data. When people say, for example, that they go to Mass because they enjoy being with God or they enjoy taking part in the liturgy, rather than out of a sense of duty, is that a step forward or a step backwards? In the study as a whole . . . *there is strong evidence that American Catholics are in process of becoming more characteristically American than characteristically Catholic. In other words, cultural assimilation appears to be occurring at the expense of a distinctive Catholic identity. In their moral, political and social attitudes, Catholics are becoming indistinguishable from the rest of the population.* Where liturgy is concerned, this means a growing alienation from precisely that sense of collective identity and collective responsibility which the liturgy might be thought to rehearse. It is a *threat to the integrity of the liturgical act.* Far from being able to inure Catholics against the negative aspects of their wider culture, *the liturgy may actually be succumbing to such influences.*[73]

[71]Douglas, *Natural Symbols*, 6. Cf. her remark: "[W]hen the social group grips its members in tight communal bonds, the religion is ritualist; when this grip is relaxed, ritualism declines. And with this shift of forms, a shift in doctrines appears" (13).

[72]Turner, "Ritual, Tribal and Catholic," 525.

[73]Searle, "The Notre Dame Study of Catholic Parish Life," 332–33; emphasis added. It should be noted that Bellah and his colleagues did not necessarily draw the same conclusions Searle did about the dire effects of "rugged American individualism" on ecclesial life. "Religious individualism," they wrote, "[I]s no more going to go away than is secular individualism. Ours is a society that requires people to be strong and independent. As believers we must often operate alone in uncongenial circumstances, and we must have the inner spiritual strength and disciplines to do so. . . . It would seem that a vital and enduring

The italicized portions of this quotation bristle with unspoken assumptions derived from a rather narrow reading of the research about ritual and religious commitment. Much of what is said in Searle's summary seems "soft," based more on *obiter dicta* than on hard anthropological data or sociological fact. For example, how does one prove that "North American" culture is statistically more self-serving than, say, the cultures of modern Europe or Asia? Indeed, can such sweeping generalizations about culture be made at all? In the United States alone, many cultures and subcultures coexist (not always comfortably), and although one may speak loosely of "American culture," it makes a huge difference whether one is referring to urban life in New York's Greenwich Village or to small-town life in rural North Dakota. Again, Searle remarks that "in their moral, political and social attitudes Catholics are becoming indistinguishable from the rest of the population."[74] This may—or may not—be true, but surely the comment requires nuance. What does it mean, for instance, if reliable public opinion polls "prove" that a majority of Catholics in the United States think church leaders should approve the use of artificial birth control methods—or that schools should make condoms available to sexually active teens and young adults? To a career curial official in the Vatican, such views may well sound "more characteristically American than Catholic," but to churchgoers in a Chicago suburb, they may sound like good common sense or healthy maturity in the faith.

Like many liturgical scholars in the "high church" camp, Searle borrowed a socio-anthropological category (cultural assimilation) in order to make an ecclesiological point (American Catholics are becoming a mere voluntary association rather than a traditional church).[75] In short, the critique of postconciliar liturgy (dull, me-

---

religious individualism can only survive in a renewed relationship with established religious bodies. Such a renewed relationship would require changes on both sides. Churches and sects would have to learn that they can sustain more autonomy than they had thought, and religious individualists would have to learn that solitude without community is merely loneliness" (Bellah, *Habits of the Heart*, 247–48).

[74]Searle notes that when "generalizing" comments about U.S. Catholics are made, the Notre Dame Study relied not upon data it had gathered but rather upon the "General Social Survey undertaken by the National Opinion Research Center in Chicago" (Searle, 312).

[75]One might point out here that, at its origins, the church was precisely such a "voluntary association" comprised of those who came to believe the

chanical and listless, hackwork improvisation) quickly became a critique of contemporary culture. "Particular interest groups" that "manipulate" the liturgy are thus accused of destroying what had once been "a magnificent objective creation," that "could be performed by the most diverse groups and individuals, surmounting their divisions of age, sex, ethnicity, culture, economic status or political affiliation."[76] These pernicious effects, so the argument continues, result whenever one adapts "liturgy to culture" rather than "culture to liturgy."

A spirited example of "liturgical-criticism-become-cultural-critique" appears in Aidan Kavanagh's essay, "Liturgical Inculturation: Looking to the Future."[77] Kavanagh chides the "middle-class piety" that "draws its power more from civil religion (which is itself the detritus of inculturated Western Christianity) than from the gospel."[78] He argues that such a piety amounts to a re-inculturation of the gospel to "new middle-class values . . . values such as comfort in affluence, participation in approved groups, consumerism, and a general optimism which seems to have lost its grip on reality."[79] Such a consumerist culture will, Kavanagh warns, produce liturgies that are shallow, verbose and fundamentally hostile to a sense of sacramentality:

> Some signs of this in the churches of my own country are the tendency to "ministerialize" the middle-class laity; to turn the entry rite into an act of gathering and hospitality conducted by such new ministers so as to produce the approved sort of community which celebrates middle-class values of joining, meeting, and "speaking out"; to use these two endeavours as means to "create community" . . . to move away from the art of ceremony and symbol towards verbalization as the assembly's main medium of communication within itself. Iconography is disappearing in our new church buildings, giving way to potted plants and shopping-mall-like spaces. These tendencies obscure a sense of sacramentality and of the divine presence as something distinct from and transcending the community at worship. When one

---

message of Jesus, the Risen One, and who celebrated that belief in word and sacrament.

[76]Turner, "Ritual, Tribal and Catholic," 525.

[77]Aidan Kavanagh, "Liturgical Inculturation: Looking to the Future," *Studia Liturgica* 20:1 (1990) 95–106.

[78]Ibid., 102.

[79]Ibid.

adds to this the understandable if often aggressive and ill-considered attempts unilaterally to alter liturgical language and the ways it names God . . . the liturgy becomes perceived by many as less an obedient standing in the alarming presence of the living God in Christ than a tiresome dialectical effort at raising the consciousness of middle-class groups concerning ideologically approved ends and means.[80]

In many respects Kavanagh's critique of culture expands and updates Turner's "anthropological" arguments in "Ritual, Tribal and Catholic." Both scholars seem convinced that the "ritual bonds which held the entire heterogeneous mystical body together in worship" are in serious danger of dissolution because of the combined "disintegrative forces of personal religious romanticism, political opportunism and collective millenarianism."[81] But Kavanagh goes further by suggesting that such results happen whenever culture is allowed to trump cult. The problem, he suggests, is not in the methods and mechanics of liturgical reform, but in the uncritical acceptance, by Christians, of a culture that has "a very sedated way of life . . . a short memory, a tendency towards the dialectically abstract, and no taste for the astonishingly radical demands of the gospel."[82]

It may be suggested that this tendency to transform a "critique of liturgy" into a "critique of culture" has its roots in Catholic reaction to the Enlightenment. Since at least that time, the church's officialdom has doggedly resisted modernity in all its forms, cultural and cultic. When, for example, the Synod of Pistoia (1786) attempted to reform certain features of Catholic liturgy, its decrees were condemned by the papal bull *Auctorem fidei*.[83] Now, two centuries later, it seems obvious that the challenges of modernity remain an Achilles heel for the Roman church. As philosopher Albert Borgmann writes,

> The Roman Catholic Church has suffered terribly under modernism. For the first time in her history she was unable to appropriate and sanctify the surrounding culture. At first she fell back on medieval

[80]Ibid.

[81]The phrases are Turner's, "Ritual, Tribal and Catholic," 525–26.

[82]Kavanagh, "Liturgical Inculturation," 102.

[83]Among other things, the synod of Pistoia had urged that there be only one altar in each church, that only one parish Mass be celebrated each Sunday, that the vernacular be permitted in liturgical services. *Auctorem fidei* was issued by Pope Pius VI on 28 August 1794.

styles of thinking and building, holding the secular at arm's length while surrendering her administration to the aggressive and methodical tendencies of modernism. In the second half of this century, she threw away what cultural substance she had left while proving herself unequal to the task of accepting and redeeming democracy within her own communal order.

The hierarchy of the Roman Catholic Church wants to hold onto divinity while avoiding reality and slighting community. Hence the church is ailing at the center and surviving mainly at the periphery and in the diaspora.[84]

There is, Borgmann suggests, a way out of this impasse—and some courageous congregations, like the Episcopal Cathedral of Saint John the Divine in upper Manhattan, seem to have found it. In this inclusive and welcoming community, focal reality[85] lives in the arts, in liturgical celebration, and in care for the surrounding community:

The people at St. John's have seen that divinity must become real and that art, once the daughter of religion, can now be her sister. Genuine art is the disclosure of focal reality, which is in itself divine, however tentatively. Hence the arts are housed in the cathedral and are part of the liturgy. There are companies of dancers and musicians; there are artists in residence and workshops of artisans.

Divinity and reality inspire community. . . . When we have been invited and invigorated by sacred celebration, we want to help the weak get up on their own two feet and join in. Opening the door is not enough when so many cannot walk. . . . Accordingly, the people of St. John's feed the hungry, shelter the homeless, build housing for the poor, and care for the young, whether they worship at the cathedral or not.[86]

[84]Albert Borgmann, *Crossing the Postmodern Divide* (Chicago: University of Chicago Press, 1992) 145.

[85]By "focal reality," Borgmann refers to those persons, objects and events that "have engaged mind and body and center our lives. Commanding presence, continuity with the world, and centering power are signs of focal things. They are not warrants, however. Focal things warrant themselves. Things can be focal only in the care of human practices—a wilderness in hiking; a horse in grooming, training, and riding; a rod in fishing. Focal reality is alive in the symmetry of things and practices—of nature, craft, and art entrusted to the care of humans. Human skill commensurates with the commanding presence of a thing, and human devotion corresponds to the profound coherence of the thing with the world." (Borgmann, *Crossing the Postmodern Divide*, 119–20, 121).

[86]Ibid., 145–46.

What Borgmann calls "focal reality" thus becomes a means whereby Christians may negotiate modernity—without harm to either the gospel or modern life. "The renewal of Roman Catholicism in this country," he concludes, "depends on whether it comes to terms with democratic equality and contemporary culture. This is what the postmodern spirit, the holy spirit, calls us to do."[87]

Summary

The connections between the "critique of liturgy as critique of culture" position (represented by Mark Searle and Aidan Kavanagh) and the "mainline" anthropological perspective on ritual (represented by Victor Turner and Mary Douglas) are reasonably clear. Tradition; authority; the review and renewal of group values (and their symbolic enactment in cult); the public communication of ineffable experience; the agreed-upon, repetitive, invariable and rigorously normative nature of ritual patterns; ambiguous symbols as the means of appropriating ultimate reality—in the "consensus" views of the "high church" camp, all these characteristics have come to define ritual as both an anthropological category and a liturgical one.

These scholars all seem to assume that ritual's primary purpose is the social production of meaning through a culturally conditioned system of symbols. These meanings are encoded in rites (and hence available through ritual symbols)—yet ultimately, they lie beyond the participants' power to manipulate or control. In this fundamental sense, liturgical ritual is canonical, to use the term employed by University of Michigan anthropologist Roy Rappaport. This means that its meanings are authoritatively encoded in the invariable, repeatable patterns of liturgy. As Rappaport has written,

> [T]o view ritual as simply a way to fulfill certain functions that may as well or better be fulfilled by other means, or as an alternative symbolic medium for expressing what may just as well—or perhaps better—be expressed in other ways is, obviously, to ignore that which is distinctive of ritual itself. . . . [R]itual is not simply an alternative way to express certain things . . . certain things can be expressed only in ritual.

> I take ritual to be a form or structure, defining it as the performance of more or less invariant sequences of formal acts and utterances not encoded by the performers.

[87]Ibid., 146.

> The term "liturgical order" . . . include[s] not only the fixed se-
> quences of words and acts providing forms to individual ritual
> events, but also . . . to the fixed sequences of rituals that lead men
> around circles of seasons, along the straight paths that depart from
> birth and arrive at death, through the alterations of war and peace or
> along the dream tracks that cross Australian deserts.[88]

For Rappaport, ritual is *the* basic social act. Intrinsic to ritual's structure, therefore, are the "social contract, morality, the concept of the
sacred, the notion of the divine, and even a paradigm of creation."[89]
Thus, while some of ritual's messages may be indexical (consisting
of variable, transitory information transmitted by participants *about*
themselves—e.g., their current physical, psychic or social conditions—*to* themselves and others), its deepest and most stable messages are canonical (consisting of messages concerned with ultimate
realities not visibly present but conveyed through symbols). Canonical messages are never invented or encoded by participants; they
are "found" or "discovered" as already given in and by the rite.

Kavanagh strongly adheres to such a position. To say that
liturgy is canonical

> means that the liturgy is an art constrained by rule. . . . Every litur-
> gical system in existence, Christian or not, is based on this principle
> simply because so highly complex a social art as liturgy must main-
> tain a defined order of regular expectations lest it fail to be a partici-
> pated event. . . . To ignore these canons or rules runs the highest
> risk of leading the assembly into idiosyncratic dead ends, no matter
> how appealing these may appear to be at the moment.[90]

Ritual meaning is thus symbolic, enduring, invariable, and ultimately independent of human agents. It is neither produced by participants, nor defeated by their emotions, nor exhausted by
repetition. True, ritual symbols and styles are historical and hence are
shaped by cultural variation and change. Nevertheless, Kavanagh
warns, we should "adapt culture to the liturgy rather than liturgy to

[88]Roy A. Rappaport, "The Obvious Aspects of Ritual," in *Ecology, Meaning and Religion* (Richmond, Calif.: North Atlantic Books, 1979) 174–76.

[89]Ibid., 174.

[90]Aidan Kavanagh, *Elements of Rite: A Handbook of Liturgical Style* (New York: Pueblo, 1982; Collegeville: The Liturgical Press, 1990) 55; see also Roy A. Rappaport, *Ecology, Meaning and Religion*, 179.

culture. . . . Liturgy either dies at the hands of the Trendy, or it slays them."[91]

Such, in sketch, is the consensus arrived at by the "high church" camp of Roman Catholic liturgists in their search for the roots of ritual in the research of anthropologists. These views have not, of course, gone unchallenged. Chapter 2 will explore criticism of the "high church consensus" by students of ritual studies (like Ronald Grimes), by scholars in the field of family systems (like David Kertzer), and by historians (like Professor Talal Asad).

[91]Kavanagh, *Elements of Rite*, 56, 103–4.

2 Critiquing the "Classic" Consensus

A Ritual Wasteland?

Toward the end of her chapter "Impersonal Rules" in *Natural Symbols*, Mary Douglas writes that "the secular world view is no modern development, but appears when group boundaries are weak and ego-focussed grid is strong."[1] Douglas likens the anti-ritualist atmosphere of many modern cultures to the famous "cargo cults" of New Guinea, which like other millennial movements discard "existing rituals" while looking "for a radical new rite which will usher in a golden era."[2] Nevertheless, the cargo cults have one crucial, distinguishing mark: "Most millennial movements reject the material values of society and seek to transform it into something quite other. But the cargo cult explicitly accepts the current material values, these especially, and seeks to provide for its followers a means of achieving them." As Douglas goes on to observe,

> The cargo cult is to be seen as a specially potent rite which dissolves all existing commitments and relationships for the sake of establishing a new, more profitable set of links. Nor surprisingly, in view of what we have seen about the tendency to reproduce a social situation in bodily symbolism, shaking, frenzy and sexual promiscuity accompany many cargo cult rituals. . . . My own hypothesis is that a

[1]Mary Douglas, *Natural Symbols: Explorations in Cosmology*, paperback edition, with new introduction by the author (New York: Pantheon Books, 1982 [1970]) 139. Note that for Douglas "group" refers to the "experience of a bounded social unit," while "grid" refers to "rules which relate one person to others on an ego-centered basis" (viii).
[2]Ibid., 137.

society so strongly centered on a structure of ego-focussed grid is liable to recurrent breakdown from its inherent moral weakness. It cannot continually sustain the commitment of all its members to an egalitarian principle that favours a minority. It has no way of symbolizing or activating the collective conscience. . . . Thus the cargo cult and its prototypes would be cults of revolt against the way the social structure seems to be working, but not of revolution against the traditional structure itself.[3]

In other words, the cargo cults (and similar anti-ritualist movements) want to maintain material advantages (and the social structures that produced them) while rejecting traditional commitments, moral restraints and relationships (and the rituals that sustained them). These twin goals are incompatible; they inevitably result in cultural chaos, followed by social dissolution. Using historical and anthropological data of this kind, Douglas argues, one may outline the principal sources of anti-ritualism, ancient and modern.[4] These include (1) rapid social change, an obvious source that needs little comment; (2) conversion, even "conversion to a ritualist belief";[5] (3) violence, which will result whenever the socially oppressed or disenfranchised are treated as objects and automatons, not as persons;[6] and (4) fallout from protest movements that reject rituals of *differentiations* even as they honor rituals of *enthusiasm*.[7] Douglas concludes by observing that "the apparent anti-ritualism of today is [in actuality] the adoption of one set of religious symbols in place of another."[8]

A great deal can said in favor of Douglas's conclusion—namely, that anti-ritualism is really the substitution of new and improved

[3]Ibid., 138–39.

[4]Ibid., 140–55.

[5]The new viewpoint that results from conversion "produces a revulsion against dead ritual. Whichever way a person has moved . . . there is a burden of old, irrelevant rituals to be laid aside. . . . So the more social change, the more radical revision of cosmologies, the more conversion phenomena, and the more denigration of ritual," ibid., 145.

[6]See ibid., 146–55.

[7]See ibid., 154–55. Recall Aidan Kavanagh's criticism, outlined in chapter 1, that among Roman Catholics in the United States, much postconciliar liturgical practice seeks to obliterate ritual distinctions by "ministerializing" the middle-class laity and so by transforming entry rites into liturgies of hospitality and welcome that promote approved values of belonging, joining, and meeting.

[8]Douglas, *Natural Symbols*, 166.

symbols for older (now despised or discredited) ones. More often, however, one hears the argument that Americans live in a culture stripped of public rituals—and of the potent myths and symbols such rites might be thought to rehearse and embody. The dangers of such a "ritual wasteland" were discussed in the popular PBS series "The Power of Myth," hosted in 1988 by Bill Moyers and mythographer Joseph Campbell. In the United States, Moyers and Campbell noted, there are no ancient, agreed-upon "rites of passage"; hence, adolescents have no clear way to negotiate ritually the perilous transition from puberty into young adulthood. Ours is a culture crippled by the devastating effects of ritual deprivation: fractured families, violent crime, gang rule, drug use, and racial conflict.

But how accurate is this picture? Professor David Kertzer, a family therapist at Bowdoin College, argues that while the problems facing young Americans are deep, real and troubling, our society is not quite the ritual wastelands Moyer and Campbell make it out to be. Kertzer maintains that modern Americans have in fact developed a rich repertoire of rituals, although many of these no longer rely on traditional symbolism derived from Judaeo-Christian tradition:

> A look at American society today hardly reveals the kind of ritual-less society described by Moyers and Campbell. Even in the case of the transition to adulthood, rather than witnessing the demise of rites of transition, we see the continued central role played by such rites. The high school [or college] graduation ritual [for example] . . . provides a key reference point for many of the country's youth, publicly signalling their change of status while celebrating a variety of both official and unofficial values.[9]

Indeed, Kertzer notes, public rituals have actually grown more elaborate as American culture has become larger and more complex. When societies become more mobile (as ours has in the fifty-plus years since the end of World War II), ritual becomes more important (not less so) as a tool for maintaining solidarity among nonresidential kinship groups.[10] This is particularly true among Roman Catholics in the United States. Unlike many of their immigrant forebears, most of these Catholics no longer spend their entire lives

[9]David Kertzer, "Lasting Rites," *The Family Therapy Networker* 13:4 (1989) 22.
[10]Ibid., 25–26.

in a single urban working-class neighborhood. Nor are they "baptized, married and buried" in the same (often ethnic) parish. Nor is permanent residence in their parents' home city and state a top priority. The structure of the traditional nuclear family has been fundamentally altered by postwar economic and social mobility. Moreover, divorce (even among Roman Catholics) creates an ever-increasing number of separated families and single-parent households. Today, more than ever before, the whole kinship system in the United States depends not on geographic proximity or marital stability, but on a well-defined cycle of ritual occasions to which scattered family members are periodically summoned: weddings, baptisms, first communions, bar or bat mitzvahs, anniversaries, funerals, Thanksgiving dinner, Christmas, Hanukkah, etc. Failure or refusal to attend these gatherings signals a choice to "redefine oneself outside the family group."[11]

In a word, family and kin today are no longer defined simply by blood ties, by physical proximity, or by participation in traditional occupations and careers (farming, factory work, medicine, law). Rather, family membership is defined by voluntary participation in ritual events that bring people together on occasion, often from great distances. Willing involvement in these rites embodies and expresses one's relation to a particular kinship group. Ironically, in "ritually deprived" America, ritual bonds have become thicker than blood.

A New Category: "Emerging Ritual"

If David Kertzer's argument is accurate, it may well be that modern cultures seem ritually impoverished only to academics who insist that ritual be defined, exclusively, by the formal, the collective, the traditional, the repetitive, the invariable, the symbolic, and the canonical. Such a narrow definition, however, ignores the growing body of ethnographic and psychological data that points to a contemporary proliferation of ritual especially among marginalized people, families in therapy, and individuals or groups facing intergenerational or intercultural transitions. Far from being dead, ritual seems to be alive and well wherever people seek critical and creative responses "to radically altered social configurations."[12] What seems to be emerging is not a ritual

[11]Ibid., 24.
[12]See Ronald Grimes, "Reinventing Ritual," *Soundings* 75:1 (1992) 21.

wasteland nor a ritually depleted culture, but a new understanding of the social conditions and pressures that give rise to rituals in the first place. A new understanding of how rituals originate and evolve is coming into view. It is an understanding that directly challenges many of the cherished conclusions that were formulated by liturgists searching for the roots of ritual in the research of anthropologists.[13] Some key characteristics of this new view of ritual may be summarized here.

- *Rituals* (as Kertzer notes) *grow more elaborate—not less so—as cultures become more complex and diverse.* Increasingly, in multicultural societies like the United States, family affiliation is chosen rather than imposed. Genetics and ethnicity alone do not determine the social or ritual significance of kinship. Under these conditions, seasonal or life-cycle rites often become the essential means of creating bonds among families whose ties are no longer determined by factors like geography and bloodline.

- *Rituals create and confirm membership in a group (e.g., a family). They may thus generate social solidarity even in the absence of shared beliefs.* Many American Jews, for example, celebrate the traditional Passover seder with their families, even if not all participants agree on its precise religious meaning. Similarly, Christmas has become an inculturated, family-centered, festive season that extends from Thanksgiving through New Year's Day. Its many public rites—the boozy office party, the ritual meal of ritual foods (e.g., turkey and trimmings), the quiet holiday dinner with old friends—may or may not coincide with a Christian's view of what the Church celebrates in the mystery of the Incarnation on December 25. Nevertheless, "Christmas rituals—whether in the form of the rowdy excesses of carnival or the more tender excesses that surround the Christmas tree—have long served to transfigure our ordinary behavior in an almost magical fashion, in ways that reveal something of what we would like to be, what we once were, or what we are becoming despite ourselves."[14] Ironically, in the absence of shared beliefs, ritual may be more important, not less so.

- *Rituals encourage us to interpret reality in very specific ways.* In the not-too-distant past, the logistics of a formal dinner—who eats

---

[13]See chapter 1.
[14]Stephen Nissenbaum, *The Battle for Christmas* (New York: Knopf, 1996) xii.

what with whom—provided a ritual portrait of socially brokered power (insiders and outsiders, haves and have-nots, dominance and submission). In my farm family, Sunday dinner was almost always formal and usually festive—a joyful occasion where parents and grandparents, siblings, aunts, uncles and cousins were all present. There was also little doubt about who belonged where. When my mother and dad hosted the gathering, they typically shared the meal's "presidency," each of them taking a prominent place at opposite ends of a many-leafed table. They occupied the "better" chairs: the ones that had arms. In short, ritual "presidency" and "placement" demonstrated not only my parents' control of the occasion (the meal) but also their view of marriage (a partnership of equals). If either was absent, the chair stayed empty—no other family member would have usurped it. They were in charge; everybody else was subordinate. Not inferior; subordinate. Not always; but on occasion. Today, such traditional dinner scenes may be dinosaurs, but their power to impose a version of reality can hardly be doubted.[15]

• *Rituals link smaller groups (e.g., families) to larger ethnic or cultural ones.* "In America," notes David Kertzer, "we can scarcely separate symbols of ethnic affiliation from the rites of family life. To be Italian-American is to use certain ritualized patterns of speech to refer to certain relatives *(nonna, nonno, zia, zio)* . . . and to eat pasta at family dinners. In short, the rites that provide family identity are not separate from the rites that provide ethnic and other forms of identity."[16] An illustration of Kertzer's point can be found in the film *Moonstruck*, which shows how vital the kitchen table is to an Italian family's life.

• *Religious rituals are the products of family rites—not vice versa.* Thus, as Freud surmised, the first "religious" ritual may simply have been a family dinner. Perhaps that is why, early on, the Is-

---

[15]Sometimes, for example, domestic rituals promoted views about gender-relations that few people today would accept or support. Among the families of rural Wayne County, Indiana, where I grew up in the 1940s and 1950s, "men-only" meals often characterized the busy haymaking and threshing seasons. (It was customary for farmers whose lands were adjoining to work together to get the crops harvested.) At noon, on these occasions, a huge meal was prepared by the farmers' wives, who started cooking, literally, at dawn. But only the men actually sat down at table; the women served—and ate their meal later, after the men had returned to the fields.

[16]Kertzer, "Lasting Rites," 24.

raelite priest appears to have been simply head of a family or tribe—not a cultic figure whose primary duties are religious or ceremonial.[17] *Theological* and *sacerdotal* interpretations of secular rites emerged *later,* when the need arose to justify existing social arrangements by linking the historical present to a sacred past. Consider, for instance, the way Israel's archaic Bedouin and agrarian rituals (Pesach, Mazzoth) were reinterpreted, fused into a single feast of national identity and deliverance for an increasingly *urban* community with its cultus centralized in the Jerusalem temple.[18] The rituals of Passover (with their twin themes of exodus from slavery and entry into the Promised Land) thus began not as public cult, but as a spring celebration among families and tribes whose livelihood depended on the fertility of flocks and fields. The family celebration came first; the theological rationale followed.

• *Rituals may be potent vehicles for social change.* Once again, this is the case even when the rituals in question do not represent a shared system of belief. Perhaps the most obvious example of ritual potency in our national life was felt during the freedom rallies and protests of the early 1960s. On the streets of Selma—and on the mall in front of the Lincoln Memorial on August 28, 1963—blacks and whites, Protestants and Catholics, Jews and gentiles, the devout and the doubting, joined in demonstrating a solidarity to the landmark civil rights legislation of 1965. The nonviolent rituals of protest promoted by Dr. Martin Luther King, Jr., were "friendly" to people of religion, *but they did not require religious affiliation for their effectiveness.* Hence, ritual potency does not necessarily derive from a structured belief system to which all participants adhere.[19]

---

[17]See Nathan Mitchell, *Mission and Ministry,* Message of the Sacraments 6 (Wilmington: Michael Glazier, 1982; Collegeville: The Liturgical Press, 1990) 19–23.

[18]Exod 12:1–13:16 suggests that "Passover" developed after the spring animal sacrifice (mentioned in Exod 12:2-13) was joined to the seven-day spring festival of unleavened bread (see Exod 12:14-20).

[19]One might note here, that many of the social rituals of the 1960s (some linked to civil rights, others to the antiwar movement) engendered meanings and values that were quite real, quite inclusive, and quite effective (as agents of social change), even though their roots in authority and tradition were often quite vague and difficult to define. This shows, perhaps, that the *authoritativeness* of ritual is not necessarily derived from rigid, authoritarian strategies and traditions. It may emerge, instead, from a loosely federated group of people

These six elements characterize what scholars like Ronald Grimes sometimes call *emerging* ritual. Emerging ritual is what happens, for example, when the women of a Roman Catholic community gather to celebrate their life as church, their call to ministry, their struggle for recognition. No official liturgy for such a purpose exists, nor, perhaps, are the participants able to articulate their intentions through traditional ritual categories. They are groping forward, looking for honest ways to express and enact their experience as women of faith in a church where men still cling to power. What is taking shape among these women is not so much protest or paraliturgy, but emerging ritual. After all, in order to be valid and effective, rites do not need to exist from time immemorial, nor do they have to last forever. Potent rituals may be improvised, practiced for a limited time, for limited purposes—and then discarded. Indeed, there is something *invented*, about all rituals, even those that endure. This is the conclusion reached by the late Barbara Myerhoff after her study of homemade rites of graduation for senior citizens in a religious-studies program:

> *All* rituals are paradoxical and dangerous enterprises, the traditional and improvised, the sacred and secular. Paradoxical because rituals are conspicuously artificial and theatrical, yet designed to suggest the inevitability and absolute truth of their messages. Dangerous because when we are not convinced by a ritual we may become aware of ourselves as having made them up . . . Our ceremonies, our most precious conceptions and convictions—*all are mere invention,* not inevitable understandings about the world at all but the results of mortals' imaginings.[20]

All rituals are *dangerous,* Myerhoff suggests, because ultimately all of them are human *improvisations.* I noted above that emerging ritual erupts especially on a society's margins. It is thus not surprising to discover abundant (if informal) rites among groups which "respectable" culture stigmatizes as menacing, marginal, sick, morally degenerate, disreputable or out of the mainstream. Twelve-step programs—especially those that deal with drug or alcohol addiction such as Alcoholics Anonymous—provide well-known

---

driven by common instincts about the need (say) for justice, equality, and the dignity of all persons. Sometimes, it seems, ritual is its own warrant.

[20]Barbara Myerhoff, *Number Our Days* (New York: Simon and Schuster, 1978) 86.

examples. Among the marginalized participants in recovery groups emergent rites rarely imitate the hierarchical, highly structured, formal, invariant, repetitive, canonical, authoritative strategies of "high church" ritual. Instead, these are *un*authorized acts, often characterized by an extraordinary freedom, creativity, playfulness, informality and even irreverence. A brief look at the ritual structure of an AA meeting will illustrate these points.

The Twelve Steps of Alcoholics Anonymous constitute a compact course in conversions.[21] Defined as "guides to spiritual progress" by the "Big Book" (AA members' affectionate title for their charter text), the steps are practical suggestions (not laws or rules) whose intent is to lead alcoholics into ever-deepening levels of recovery by helping them "step backward" into "the universal heart of humankind" (as AA co-founder Bill W. used to say). Thus the Steps confront alcoholics with the need for ego-deflation, self-surrender and belief in a Higher Power (steps 1–3) through acts of rigorous self-evaluation, "confession," restitution and reconciliation (steps 4–9). The hoped-for result is a radical change of heart (steps 10–11) and a readiness to share the message, with others who still suffer from alcoholism (step 12). What is sought in the steps is thus a spiritual awakening, a profound personality change, a "new state of consciousness and being, the beginning of 'true kinship' between persons and God."[22]

While alcoholics are advised to "practice these principles in *all* their affairs" (step 12), the methods and goals of recovery are *ritually* focused in the AA meeting (which many members attend daily—or at least several times a week). While all AA meetings abound in ritual elements, each gathering remains quite fluid in format, length and style of leadership. Each AA group is free to structure meetings as it sees fit. Typically, a member volunteers to "chair" the meeting, but that individual is never considered the "presider." AA has no authoritative overseers, no priesthood, no hierarchy. Leadership is simply a specific and limited act of service; it carries with it no juridical role or office. In AA, power is freely shared by all, not bestowed on a few. In short, the AA group is quite literally a discipleship of equals.

<hr>

[21]For these Twelve Steps, see the first edition of the book *Alcoholics Anonymous* (New York: Works Publishing Co., 1939) chapter 5, "How It Works."

[22]E. Sellner, "What Alcoholics Anonymous Can Teach Us about Reconciliation," *Worship* 64:4 (1990) 331–48; here, 337.

In the AA context, ritual space is ordinarily a rented meeting room, quite often a church basement. AA as such owns no property. Each group—which must be entirely self-supporting through voluntary contributions from its members—is expected to find and pay for its own meeting place. By long-standing AA tradition, all donations from outside sources are declined. Seating is never reserved or assigned; members come in and choose a spot around a long, rectangular table.[23] A podium may be set up if a speaker is to present his or her story, and baskets are ordinarily provided to collect donations from members, but there are no required ritual objects at an AA gathering. Meetings may be "open" (to any person interested in alcoholism or spiritual growth) or "closed" (restricted to persons who identify themselves as alcoholics). Coffee is usually served; indeed, it functions as a kind of sacred beverage among members. Typically, a meeting may follow this format:

- After a brief introduction, the leader calls for a moment of silence, followed by the "Serenity Prayer."[24]

- After a member recites the "AA Preamble,"[25] a portion from the Big Book—usually "How It Works," the beginning of Chapter 5—may be read. Persons celebrating anniversaries of sobriety may be recognized and applauded. Occasionally, readings from other AA literature follow.

- A topic for discussion is announced or a speaker is introduced. A discussion meeting—loosely organized around a Step or spiritual theme—permits all present to reflect upon their lives and experiences, before and after recovery. Occasionally, there are Step meetings that focus on the reading of relevant portions from *Twelve Steps and Twelve Traditions*.[26] Similarly, a Big Book meeting studies a text from *Alcoholics Anonymous*

[23]The table is not essential. Some groups simply arrange chairs in a circle or semicircle. At "speaker meetings" (where an individual alcoholic tells the story of his or her addiction and recovery) members may sit in rows facing the speaker.

[24]"God grant me the serenity to accept the things I cannot change; courage to change the things I can; and wisdom to know the difference." The prayer is attributed to Reinhold Niebuhr.

[25]The text of this preamble may be found inside the front of any issue of the *AA Grapevine*, published monthly by AA World Services in New York.

[26]*Twelve Steps and Twelve Traditions* (New York: Alcoholics Anonymous World Services, 1960). This book is a kind of semiofficial commentary on the meaning of the steps for AA members.

with members offering reflection based on their experience. A speaker meeting highlights the experience of a single individual whose story describes what it was like (the drinking life), what happened (crisis, bottoming out, recovery); and what it is like now (the sober life).

The ritual repetition of stories is the central, essential dynamic of AA, for this action permits members to identity with one another; to share "experience, strength and hope"; and to embody AA's primary purpose: to stay sober and to help other alcoholics achieve sobriety.

- Volunteers for the next meeting (to chair, make coffee, greet newcomers, etc.) are solicited, and the gathering concludes, characteristically, with members joining hands to recite the Lord's Prayer.

Although they may appear to be hopelessly haphazard, AA meetings are potent, internally regulated rituals that repeatedly offer members support, moral guidance and critique, nurture, healing and reconciliation. The extemporaneous shared stories are, in fact, ritual structures punctuated by familiar ritual phrases (such as "This too shall pass," "Keep coming back," "Easy does it," "Live and let live"). Meetings are thus both heavily ritualized and radically egalitarian. They consist of symbolic actions done by heart which, nevertheless, do not exclude the stranger or the newcomer.

In AA the dominant metaphor for understanding alcoholism is not sin but sickness—and this fact shapes ritual behavior both inside and outside meetings. Members like to say, "We're not bad people trying to get good; we're sick people trying to get well." This is particularly evident in the way recovering alcoholics approach step 5: "[We] admitted to God, to ourselves, and to another human being the exact nature of our wrongs." This step is not so much a confession of sin as a fearless reappraisal of life that leads to reconciliation. The purpose of step 5 is not ego-deflation but "an exegesis of tears": a sifting through one's suffering in order to find there the God who is never defeated by pain or failure. The goals of the Step are release from the compulsion to drink, from the bondage of self-centeredness, and from the hegemony of fear.

This "exegesis of tears" is neither a solitary self-appraisal[27] nor an exercise in self-pity, but a rigorous ritual exploration of one's

[27]*Alcoholics Anonymous*, 84.

whole existence, carried out in the presence of God and another person. One takes step 5 with a trusted partner: one's sponsor (AA guide or mentor), a skilled counselor, doctor or psychologist, a member of the clergy. The step usually begins with a brief prayer, continues with a thorough review and discussion of one's assets and liabilities (often lasting several hours), and concludes with affirmative words and gestures from the person who has "heard" the step. The alcoholic is then encouraged to spend an hour or so in quiet solitude, humbly seeking the willingness to have God remove all defects of character (step 6). This period of reflection concludes with the prayer of step 7: "My Creator, I am now willing that you should have all of me, good and bad. I pray that you now remove from me every single defect of character which stands in the way of my usefulness to you and my fellows. Grant me strength, as I go out from here, to do your bidding. Amen!"[28]

These examples, drawn from David Kertzer's research and from the ritual repertoire of Twelve Step groups like AA, show that the "high church consensus" about ritual's origins and characteristics outlined in chapter 1 often neglects potent emerging rituals that arise in both secular and religious contexts, and in both mainstream and marginal cultures. As these examples illustrate, such rituals may rely more upon unstructured improvisation than upon the fixed patterns of traditional, "authoritative" ritual. To summarize, one may note these qualities of emerging ritual tradition:

• Ritual tradition is *a fully cultural, historical and embodied process—and so is characterized to a remarkable degree by inventiveness, creativity, change and variability.* As Ronald Grimes writes, "Tradition must be understood not merely as cultural inertia but also as a mode of active construction."[29] "Classicist" anthropology of the high church variety often soft-pedals this point, seeking instead to define tradition as "essentially a process of formalization and ritualization characterized by reference to the past."[30] Against this rigid view, Grimes proposes an understanding of the relation between ritual and social tradition that is more interactive:

> Body and culture, self and society, are not merely opposites; they are dialectical pairs. Taking seriously one term in each pair always leads

[28]Ibid., 88.
[29]Grimes, "Reinventing Ritual," 25.
[30]Eric Hobsbawm and Terence Ranger, eds., *The Invention of Tradition* (Cambridge: Cambridge University Press, 1983) 4.

to the other term. For this reason I reject much that is assumed about ritual and the individual, for example, that ritual is by definition collective. It is necessarily collective only in the sense that anything human is: nothing, not the body, not the self escapes culture. And culture has its most persistent root in the human body itself.[31]

As Grimes explains in "Reinventing Ritual,"

> Just as language is always being invented in the process of using it, so ritual is always in the process of being created as ritualists enact it. The history of any rite known to us always reveals it as changing, and these changes are typically congruent with others, which suggests that ritual is a fully historical, fully cultural process.[32]

- The most fertile location for ritual development is a culture's *margins, not its mainstream.* Ritual inventiveness more commonly characterizes the socially, politically and religiously disenfranchised— not the people who hold power. To say this is to challenge two widely held consensus views about ritual: (a) that ritual is inherently collective, and (b) that it is received (as part of a tradition) rather than invented. As Grimes observes,

> Much contemporary ritualizing is focused on the body and is articulated using the rhetoric of the self. This focus and rhetoric give emergent ritual a distinctively individualistic ethos that sets it in opposition to the standard scholarly view of ritual as a group-oriented phenomenon that is essentially collective and necessarily social.[33]

For the most part, however, the growing body of North American literature on individualism and self-culture[34] fails to take seriously the "ritual manifestations of individualism. Consequently, many students of ritual overlook or reject ritualizing on definitional grounds ('It's not really ritual') or moral and psychological grounds ('It's neurotic and narcissistic')."[35] These attitudes often prevent theologically

[31]Ronald Grimes, "Emerging Ritual," *Proceedings of the North American Academy of Liturgy* (1990) 25.

[32]Grimes, "Reinventing Ritual," 24.

[33]Ibid., 26.

[34]For example, see Christopher Lasch's popular analysis of North Americans as narcissists in *The Culture of Narcissism: American Life in an Age of Diminishing Returns* (New York: Warner, 1979). See also Robert Bellah et al., *Habits of the Heart: Individualism and Commitment in American Life* (Berkeley: University of California Press, 1985).

[35]Grimes, "Reinventing Ritual," 27.

or anthropologically trained critics from understanding that a great deal of ritual (whether traditional or contemporary) is concerned with negotiating the relation between self and society. For even the self—that narcissistic *bête noire* that Christian liturgists and theologians love to hate—is in fact a cultural construction. So one can, notes Grimes, "easily argue that self-generated rites are a form of social expression. There is no such thing as an unsocialized individual, therefore no such thing as an asocial rite."[36] In sum,

> Theorists of ritual too often set ritual on the collective side of an individual/collective split, but we should reject the dualism this action presupposes, because taking seriously either term in the self society pair always leads to the other term: bodies are enculturated and cultures are embodied. For this reason it is necessary to reject much that is assumed about ritual and the individual, for example, that private ritual is inherently neurotic or that all ritual is by definition collective. It is necessarily collective only in the sense that anything human is: nothing escapes socialization. Societies have their most persistent root in the human body itself, and the body is always—no matter how closeted or private—socially inscribed.[37]

• *Rituals are always incarnate, embodied deeds.* As a ritual agent, however, the body is not a mindless hulk; it is a personal subject with its own unique ways of probing, questioning, arguing, asserting, thinking. Skin has a mind of its own, a mind always at work in ritual. Thus, researchers who adopt the "high church consensus" may sometimes fail to appreciate "the creative, cognitive, critical functions of the ritualizing body. . . . The body is cognitive, not stupid; and conversely, the mind is embodied."[38]

• *In ritual, the presence of mystery is not incompatible with critical, self-conscious awareness.* Even ritualists of the high church camp recognize the historical role of ritual inversions such as the medieval feast of fools, or the burning flax that accompanied the words once uttered to a pope during his coronation: "Sancte pater, sic transit gloria mundi."[39] Such half-humorous, self-critical inversions were a way of keeping communities and individuals honest about the link-

---

[36]Ibid.
[37]Ibid.
[38]Ibid., 32
[39]"Holy Father, thus passes the glory of the world."

age between liturgy and life. Scholars like Ronald Grimes emphasize that such criticism is essential for all healthy ritual.[40]

* *The meanings of ritual unfold from within the ritual action itself; they are not imported from outside the ritual event.* Rituals are not necessarily meaningful, if by the term meaning one implies access to a set of codes (references) found beyond or outside the ritual performance itself. Rituals are meaningful not by reason of what they refer to, but in virtue of what they actually do, individually and socially. For this reason, ritual symbols are evocative rather than referential. They invite response, not explanation or decoding. Their meaning is in their performance, not in some secret hidden truth or doctrine. "Ritual symbols," writes Ronald Grimes, focus our "attention and evoke memory; they do not leave us with religious ideas or political statements that constitute their meaning."[41]

Such, in brief, is an outline of emerging ritual, the principal category used by many scholars today in their critique of the "high church consensus" about ritual's roots and ramifications.

Reevaluating Victor Turner

As I noted in chapter 1, the recent history of the relation between liturgy and the social sciences—especially anthropology—cannot be written without considering the impact of Victor Turner's work. In large part, I suspect, Turner's influence derives from his feisty 1976 essay "Ritual, Tribal and Catholic" and not his justly famous book, *The Ritual Process* which, despite its title, does not have very much to say about ritual.[42] Rather, *The Ritual Process* examines the ways in which the liminal condition of persons caught in critical social transition (e.g., from puberty to adulthood, from illness or old age to death) is reflected "both within ritual and within society as a whole."[43] The main contribution of *The Ritual Process* lay in its

[40]See Ronald Grimes, *Ritual Criticism* (Columbia: University of South Carolina Press, 1990). See also *Liturgy Digest* 1:1 (Spring 1993), Lexicon entry "Ritual Criticism," 111–14, which discusses Grimes' position and provides a brief bibliography for further research.

[41]Grimes, "Reinventing Ritual," 36.

[42]See Martin Stringer, "Liturgy and Anthropology: The History of a Relationship," *Worship* 63:6 (1989) 508; also, Victor Turner, *The Ritual Process: Structure and Anti-Structure* (Chicago: Aldine, 1969).

[43]Stringer, "Liturgy and Anthropology," 509.

emphasis upon "our need to keep the marginal people in our society in their traditionally sacred position and not to oppress them or simply to ignore them."[44]

As an anthropologist, therefore, Turner focused upon the unfolding identity (individual and social) of persons involved in the ritual process rather than upon the process itself. He pointed to the distinctive kind of "antistructural" bond *(communitas)* that unites liminal persons—and to the ways their condition is symbolized in social contexts (whether actual or remembered).[45] What made Turner's work on liminality, *communitas*, and social drama so relevant to liturgy was the way it loosened ritual from its calcified past. "Before Turner," writes Grimes, "ritual was [treated by theorists as] static, structural, conservative. After Turner, it is imagined as flowing, processual, subversive. In effect he reinvented ritual."[46] Or, as Grimes wrote in a perceptive essay published some twenty-one years ago:

> So pervasive is Turner's sense of the liminal [the "threshold" condition of persons in process of social transition], that he deviates radically from the ways many anthropologists do ritual studies. Ritual is no longer a Durkheimian collective representation which reflects and insures social solidarity. Ritual is not a bastion of social conservatism whose symbols merely condense cherished cultural values. Rather it is the generating source of culture and structure. Hence, ritual is by definition associated with social *transitions,* while ceremony is linked to social *states:* "Ritual is transformative, ceremony confirmatory.[47] . . . . In such a manner he rather radically challenges the usual assumptions of social anthropologists and historians of religion . . . who would interpret ritual and myth solely as presentations of static

[44]Ibid.

[45]See especially "Appendix A: Notes on Processual Symbolic Analysis," in Victor Turner and Edith Turner, *Image and Pilgrimage in Christian Culture* (New York: Columbia University Press, 1978) 243–55. There, Turner defines *communitas* as "social anti-structure"; its bonds are "undifferentiated, egalitarian, direct, nonrational, existential, I-Thou (in Buber's sense). *Communitas* is spontaneous, immediate, concrete, not abstract. . . . It does not merge identities; it liberates them from conformity to general norms, though this is necessarily a transient condition if society is to continue to operate in an orderly fashion. It is the *fons et origo* of all structures and at the same time their critique" (250).

[46]Grimes, "Reinventing Ritual," 22.

[47]The reference is to Turner's *The Forest of Symbols: Aspects of Ndembu Ritual* (Ithaca, N.Y.: Cornell University Press, 1967) 95.

paradigms, rules, grammars, or structures. . . . Ritual is usually interpreted in the light of its *conserving* function; Turner wants us to perceive its *creative* function. . . .

Ritual cannot be divorced from the becomingness which is society, so it shares society's "processual," dramatic form. To be sure, there is pattern in the flow, but the patterning occurs as a phasing process, not as a set of systemic grids.[48]

Thus, Turner roundly rejected asocial and atemporal methods in the study of ritual. As he wrote in his book *Dramas, Fields and Metaphors:*

The social world is a world in becoming, not a world in being (except insofar as "being" is a description of the static, atemporal models men have in their heads), and for this reason studies of social structure *as such* are irrelevant. They are erroneous in basic premise because there is no such thing as "static action." . . . Such a view violates the actual flux and changefulness of the human social scene. Here I would look . . . to Bergson rather than . . . to Descartes, for philosophical guidance.[49]

Still, there is a noticeable tension in Turner's work between the temporal and the atemporal, the culturally conditioned and the virtually unconditioned. "Turner has rejected aculturalism and atemporalism in method," writes Grimes, "only to rediscover it in liminal phenomena, which not only are experienced as 'moments in and out of time,' but are cross-cultural, universally human. Liminality is transcultural. Of course, Turner knows quite well that what is liminal today will be part of the status system tomorrow. . . . But despite his recognition of the temporariness of liminality-*communitas*, he still views experiences of such as essentially the same in widely differing times and places."[50]

Thus, despite his acknowledgment that "the social world is a world in becoming, not a world in being," and despite his conviction

[48]Ronald Grimes, "Ritual Studies: A Comparative Review of Theodore Gaster and Victor Turner," *Religious Studies Review* 2:4 (October 1976) 20.

[49]Victor Turner, *Dramas, Fields and Metaphors* (Ithaca, N.Y.: Cornell University Press, 1974) 24.

[50]Grimes, "Ritual Studies: A Comparative Review," 21. Today, of course, most anthropologists would be very reluctant to speak of "cross-" or "transcultural" anything. They are aware of how easily ethno- and Eurocentric grids can be imposed upon the distinctive elements of other cultures.

that ritual is characterized by motion, flow and creativity, Turner often spoke in cross-cultural, transtemporal generalizations.[51] For example, when writing about the use of white symbols in Ndembu ritual, Turner compares them to the whiteness of the whale in Melville's novel *Moby Dick* and to the dazzling white of the angel's garments in Matthew's account of Jesus' resurrection (28:3):

> One of the marks of a viable ritual symbol may be said to be its capacity to move from society to society without marked change in form but with many changes in meaning. Though referents are lost in transference, new referents are readily acquired. Certain symbols arouse an almost universal response, much as music does.[52]

Here one can detect a theme that Turner will return to a decade later in "Ritual, Tribal and Catholic": namely, the notion that ritual symbols are (or should be) transculturally portable, capable of moving from one society to another "without marked changed in form." Note, however, that in *The Forest of Symbols*, Turner admitted such transference will result, inevitably, in "many changes of meaning." In this, Turner seems to have harkened back to an older "essentialist" view among anthropologists, that regards ritual symbols as a rigid system of references which point to encoded meanings.

In sum, then, Turner "quite often pursues a dominant symbol through its ritual context, to the wider context of the whole cultural system of symbols, then through a whole culture area, and finally toward a cross-cultural assessment. Such a method is possible, he thinks, because dominant symbols have a kind of autonomy."[53] Many anthropologists today would be very reluctant to make such vast claims for *any* symbol system, even one hallowed by centuries of tradition and use in many cultures. Perhaps, later in his life, Turner might have shared their reluctance. In any case, it is clear that Turner's understanding of ritual and symbolic structures continued to evolve right up until his death in 1983. In 1979, for instance, he wrote,

> Cartesian dualism has insisted on separating subject from object, us from them. It has, indeed, made voyeurs of Western man, exaggerating sight by macro- and micro-instrumentation, the better to learn the

[51]Ibid.
[52]Turner, *The Forest of Symbols*, 291.
[53]Grimes, "Ritual Studies: A Comparative Review," 21.

structures of the world with an "eye" to its exploitation. The deep bonds between body and mentality, unconscious and conscious thinking, species and self have been treated without respect. . . .

With the renewed emphasis on society as a process punctuated by performances of various kinds, there has developed the view that such genres as ritual, ceremony, carnival, festival, game, spectacle, parade and sports event may constitute, on various levels and in various verbal and nonverbal codes, a set of intersecting metalanguages. The group or community does not merely "flow" in union at these performances, but, more actively, tries to understand itself in order to change itself. This dialectic between "flow" and reflexivity characterizes performative genres: a successful performance of any transcends the opposition between spontaneous and self-conscious patterns of action.[54]

Texts like this reveal that Turner's evolving thought about ritual was sometimes at odds with the way he defined it.[55] By the time of his death, he was emphasizing ritual's inherent *inventiveness* (even in archaic, pre-industrial societies).[56] He had begun to prefer thinking about ritual "essentially as performance, enactment, not primarily as rules or rubrics."[57]

The rules "frame" the ritual process but the ritual process transcends its frame. A river needs banks or it will be a dangerous flood, but banks without a river epitomize aridity. The term "performance" is, of course, derived from Old English *parfournir*, literally "to furnish completely or thoroughly." To perform is thus to bring something about, to consummate something, or to "carry out" a play, order, or project. But in the "carrying out," I hold, something new may be generated. The performance transforms itself. True . . . the rules may "frame" the performance, but the "flow" of action and interaction within that frame may conduce to hitherto unprecedented insights and even generate new symbols and meanings, which may be

[54]Victor Turner, "Dramatic Ritual/Ritual Drama: Performative and Reflexive Anthropology," *The Kenyon Review* (New Series) 1:3 (1979) 92–93. This essay is reprinted in Victor Turner's *From Ritual to Theatre* (see note 58 below) 89–101.

[55]In several works, Turner defined ritual as "prescribed formal behavior for occasions not given over to technological routine, having reference to beliefs in invisible beings or powers regarded as the first and final causes of all effects" (*The Forest of Symbols*, 19).

[56]See Tom Driver, *The Magic of Ritual*, Appendix B, "Some Points in Criticism of Victor Turner" (San Francisco: Harper, 1991) 237.

[57]Ibid.

incorporated into subsequent performances. Traditional framings have to be reframed—new bottles made for new wine.[58]

Turner's insistence here that "traditional [ritual] framings have to be reframed—new bottles made for new wine" seems a far cry from his anguished plea, at the end of "Ritual, Tribal and Catholic," not to "dynamite the liturgical rock of Peter" nor to abandon the Roman rite "to the disintegrative forces of personal religious romanticism, political opportunism and collective millenarianism." So too is his comment, published posthumously, that ritual may be "a kind of collective 'autobiography,' a means by which a group creates its identity by telling itself a story about itself, in the course of which it brings to life 'its Definite and Determinate Identity' (to cite William Blake)."[59] But perhaps the most telling evidence of a shift in Turner's thinking can be found in the introduction to the book *From Ritual to Theatre,* where his debt to Dilthey's philosophy of experience is explicitly acknowledged:

> The positivist and functionalist schools of anthropology in whose concepts and methods I was first instructed could give me only limited insight into the dynamics of social dramas. I could count the people involved, state their social status-roles, describe their behavior, collect biographical information about them from others, and place them structurally in the social system of the community manifested by the social drama. But this way of treating "social facts as things," as the French sociologist Durkheim admonished investigators to do, gave little understanding of the motives and characters of the actors in the purpose-saturated, emotional, and "meaningful" events. I gradually gravitated, with temporary pauses to study symbolic processes, theories of symbolic interaction, the views of sociological phenomenologists, and those of French structuralists and "deconstructionists," towards the basic stance delineated by the great German social thinker . . . Wilhelm Dilthey (1833–1911). This stance

[58]Victor Turner, *From Ritual to Theatre* (New York: Performing Arts Journal Publications, 1982) 79.

[59]See Victor Turner, "Epilogue: Are There Universals of Performance in Myth, Ritual, and Drama?" in Edith Turner, ed., *On the Edge of the Bush: Anthropology as Experience* (Tucson: University of Arizona Press, 1985) 293–94. In this passage Turner is commenting on the value of Barbara Myerhoff's notion of "definitional ceremonies." It may be noted that the idea of ritual as "collective autobiography," as a means "by which a group creates its identity by telling itself a story about itself," could cover both traditional liturgies (e.g., those of the Easter Triduum in the Roman rite) and "emergent rites" (e.g., those of an AA group).

depends upon the concept of experience (in German, *Erlebnis*, literally "what has been lived through"). . . .

Structures of experience, for Dilthey, are not the bloodless "cognitive structures," static and "synchronic," so beloved of the "thought-structuralists" who have dominated French anthropology for so long. . . . Thought clarifies and generalizes lived experience, but *experience is charged with emotion and volition, sources respectively of value-judgments and precepts*. Behind Dilthey's world-picture is the basic fact of the total human being (Lawrence's "man alive") at grips with his environment, perceiving, thinking, feeling, desiring. As he says, "life embraces life. . . ."

For me, the anthropology of performance is an essential part of the anthropology of experience. In a sense, every type of cultural performance, including ritual, ceremony, carnival, theatre, and poetry, is explanation and explication of life itself, as Dilthey often argued. Through the performance process itself, what is normally sealed up, inaccessible to everyday observation and reasoning . . . is drawn forth—Dilthey uses the term *Ausdruck*, "an expression," from *ausdrucken*, literally, "to press or squeeze out." "Meaning" is squeezed out of an event which has either been directly experienced by the dramatist or poet, or cries out for penetrative, imaginative understanding . . . An experience is itself a process which "presses out" to an "expression" which completes it. A performance, then, is the proper finale of an experience.[60]

As his own life drew to a close, Turner seemed to sense that ritual was a spiraling process of negotiation rather than an exact, repetitive pattern. Thus, he objected to the idea that ritual is always "rigid, stereotyped, obsessive," arguing that this is a "peculiarly Western European" prejudice, "the product of specific conflicts between ritualists and anti-ritualists, iconophiles and iconoclasts, in the process of Christian infighting. Anyone who has known African ritual knows better—or Balinese or Singhalese or Amerindian."[61]

Such flexibility in Turner's later work has led some scholars to propose an amended definition of ritual that avoids the rigidity of earlier statements ("ritual is prescribed formal behavior") and pays greater attention to the performative character of rites.[62] Thus, for

[60]Turner, *From Ritual to Theatre*, 12–13; some emphasis added.
[61]Victor Turner, *The Anthropology of Performance* (New York: Performing Arts Journal Publications, 1988) 26.
[62]See Driver, *The Magic of Ritual*, 238.

example, Bobby Alexander makes use of his research on rituals in African-American Pentecostal churches, to argue that a better Turnerian definition of ritual would be "planned or improvised performance that effects a transition from everyday life to an alternative framework within which the everyday is transformed."[63] As Alexander notes, "The greatest misreading of Turner is the view that he presents ritual as essentially conservative."[64] Or as Turner himself wrote,

> Ritual is a transformative performance revealing major classifications, categories, and contradictions of cultural processes. It is not, in essence, as is commonly supposed in Western Culture, a prop for social conservatism whose symbols merely condense cherished values, though it may, under certain conditions, take on this role. Rather does it hold the generative source of culture and structure, particularly in its liminal stage.[65]

There is, then, a strange appropriateness about the way Turner's own passing was ritualized. Frederick Turner has written the following description of how the great anthropologist's family and friends celebrated his funeral:

> Turner staged African and Dixieland weddings, pilgrimages, curing rituals, even funerals. The last one in which he participated was his. It was a full-scale Ndembu funeral for a chief, with drum music, masked dancers, a seclusion hut for the widow, communal dancing, much drinking, tears, laughter and reminiscence. It was put on at Turner's house by his friends, family, students, and colleagues in anthropology, religious studies, and the performing arts. . . . The absurdity of this strange event, the curious element of comedy that we all felt in it, was entirely in the spirit of the Ndembu ritual itself, which partly consists of the personification of the deceased's death as a grotesque and absurd figure, and a comic mocking of it until it is subdued and made familiar . . . .

[63]See Bobby C. Alexander, "Pentecostal Possession and Grotowski's Ritual Projects as Social Protest: A Critical Assessment of Victor Turner's Theory of Ritual Anti-Structure as an Interpretive Tool" (Columbia University, unpublished doctoral dissertation) 21.

[64]Bobby C. Alexander, "Correcting Misinterpretations of Turner's Theory: An African-American Pentecostal Illustration," *Journal for the Scientific Study of Religion* 30:1 (March 1991) 26.

[65]E. Turner, ed., *On the Edge of the Bush*, 171.

Skeptics might well object that this ritual was inauthentic because it was done consciously and reflexively, in a "meta" mode, so to speak. But Turner's research had showed that all live human rituals are already "meta"; reflexivity is not just a feature of the sophisticated postmodernist work of art . . . but is the normal condition . . . of the major human rituals. This may have been one of Turner's greatest insights: that there never were any innocent unconscious savages [sic.], living in a state of unreflective and instinctive harmony. We human beings are all and always sophisticated, conscious, capable of laughter at our own institutions, inventing our lives collectively as we go on, playing games, performing our own being. This is our specialization as animals, our nature.[66]

It is inaccurate, therefore, to treat Turner's work as though it constituted some irreformable, conservative manifesto against ritual inventiveness and social change. As a scholar immersed in many cultures—some archaic and traditional, some modern and transient—Turner understood that society is a process punctuated by performances, that rites are not rubrics, that ritual frames must always be reframed, that ritualizing is a group's collective autobiography, that human beings invent their lives as they go along, playing games, performing their being.[67]

What follows is a short summary of some of Turner's mature views about the relation between religious ritual and anthropology.

• *Anthropology must respect the autonomy of religion.* Religion must be understood on its own, distinctively religious terms; it cannot be dismissed by reductionist definitions (e.g., the functionalist attempt to define religion as little more than "society worshipping itself "[68]). For Turner, religion is not simply "practices or feelings," it

[66]Frederick Turner, "Hyperion to a Satyr: Criticism and Anti-structure in the Work of Victor Turner," in Kathleen Ashley, ed., *Victor Turner and the Construction of Social Criticism* (Bloomington: Indiana University Press, 1990) 155–56.

[67]One suspects that, in spite of his rhetoric, Turner's objections to postconciliar Roman Catholic ritual were less anthropological than aesthetic. He seems to have been offended by the speed and carelessness with which rites of centuries' duration were cast aside in favor of a "reforming puritanism." Even in this atypical essay, Turner recognized that ritual is "a symphony of expressive genres," "many-leveled" and "capable of creative modification on all or any of its levels." (Victor Turner, "Ritual, Tribal and Catholic," 505–6).

[68]This formula has its roots in the work of French sociologist Émile Durkheim (d. 1917).

is "a set of beliefs."[69] These beliefs deal not just with human behavior and the social order, but with the very nature of the cosmos. Religious cosmologies are not hostile to (or incompatible with) the conclusions of modern science.[70]

- *Religious ritual is not only an irreducible reality per se, it is also irreducibly human.* This means, first, that ritual cannot be defined as either neurotic obsession or collective divinizing (in which society objectifies itself, then worships what has been objectified). Secondly, it means that play is always a "dialectical dancing partner" with ritual.[71] Play thus becomes an indispensable component in the process by which ritual restructures culture and redefines reality. The human brain's limbic system, where the roots of play reside, seems endowed with a kind of carnivalesque capacity to mock the established order and subvert business as usual. As ritual's dancing partner, play "makes fun of people, things, ideas, ideologies, institutions, and structures . . . it is partly a mocker as well as a mimic and a tease, arousing hope, desire or curiosity without always giving satisfaction

---

[69]Robert Segal, "Victor Turner's Theory of Ritual," *Zygon* 18:3 (September 1983) 328–29.

[70]An example of the way Turner demonstrated the basic compatibility of religion and modern science appears in his essay "The New Neurosociology," in *On the Edge of the Bush,* 275–89. There Turner discussed similarities and differences between his own work as an anthropologist studying myth and ritual and the work of biogenetic structuralists like Eugene d'Aquili and Charles Laughlin. For example, whereas d'Aquili and Laughlin tended "to stress myth as the expression of *conceptual* models through the medium of language," Turner himself saw "myth-telling as a subgenre of *ritual* performance." He went on say that "Myth is the whole brain, recent and archaic, playing or performing itself to itself, using the costumes, props, and masks of particular cultures, the products of social experience in specific habitats, but revealing the contours of its own topography and the traces of its own intersecting movements" (287–88). In short, myth (like ritual, a feature of religion in many—if not most—cultures) is a kind of "brain map," a "highly colored map of brain neuroanatomy." Myth is thus compatible with the brain's cognitive structures—and may even express them—but *it is not limited to them.* (Note, again, Turner's insistence on the irreducibility of religious phenomena.) Myth is "as fully charged with the interplay of language, imagery and music across the bridge from the left and right halves of the . . . brain, as it is with cognitive structures or charters [that validate] extant social structures." (288).

[71]This notion is developed in Victor Turner, "Body, Brain and Culture," *Zygon* 18:3 (September 1983) 221–45.

. . . play can deceive, betray, beguile, delude . . . dupe, ho_ ___ik, bamboozle and gall."[72]

Because of its unique ability to subvert customary ideas and social structures, play can create new definitions of reality. It can recombine familiar elements of experience into new, unfamiliar and even arbitrary patterns. Turner referred to this capacity of play as "ludic recombination" and saw it as a richly creative force within cultures and individuals. It may be noted that this intrinsic connection between play and ritual is also relevant for understanding liturgical structures. In liturgy, ritual "rewires" familiar experience, enabling it to create new patterns and definitions. In this way, ritual also "rewrites" those who participate in it. Consider, for example, how the eucharistic prayer "rewires" Jesus' history and so radically rewrites our relation to it. An event that should have consigned Jesus to the past (namely, his death and burial) instead makes him a living presence—fully, bodily, personally accessible to us in Word, in bread and wine, in care and service of the least and neediest among us.[73] As Marianne Sawicki writes,

> We may theorize worship as replications of the pattern of Jesus' relationship with God in multiple media. In sacramental communication, God's offer of reconciliation and its human acceptance in Jesus Christ become available through effective interpretation in the media of song, gesture, speech, textiles, sculpture, architecture, water, bread, fire, incense, oil, salt, and wine. Worship is scripted and inscribing artifact.[74]

As ritual's dancing partner, play makes liturgy's redefinitions possible and plausible.

• *Religious ritual is both cognitive (affecting how and what participants think) and social (shaping how participants live).* Robert Segal has argued that Turner (along with Clifford Geertz and Mary Douglas) saw religious ritual as a universal phenomenon, not one restricted to archaic or "primitive" cultures. "They can be universal," Segal writes, "exactly because they do not rival science and so do not get superseded by it. Rather than either explaining or controlling the world, ritual . . . serves to give human beings a place in it. Ritual does so

---

[72]Ibid., 234.

[73]See Marianne Sawicki, *Seeing the Lord: Resurrection and Early Christian Practices* (Minneapolis: Fortress, 1994) especially 334–36.

[74]Ibid., 336.

by conveying information: by describing that place."[75] The "place" that ritual provides for participants is both cosmic and social. "On the one hand," Segal explains, "society becomes part of the cosmos, which thereby both explains and justifies it. On the other hand the cosmos gets manifested through society, which thereby verifies it."[76] For Turner, then, the cognitive and social functions of ritual coincide.

• *The notion of "social drama" is essential to understanding how ritual works in groups of people.* "This . . . 'drama'," Turner once wrote, "is crucial to the understanding of ritual. Both in its plot and in its symbolism, a ritual is an epitome of the wider and spontaneous social process in which it is embodied and which ideally it controls."[77] As social drama, however, ritual does more than "simply effect a 'cathartic' discharge of socially dangerous impulses" (in the manner, say, of classical Greek drama).[78] Rather, ritual utilizes "the power or energy" of social conflict (hostility, disagreement) and redirects it, remobilizes it, placing it in the service of reunification. "Ritual, then, invests with that energy the quintessential symbols of the solidarity of the widest effective social group. . . . The dramatization, or symbolization, of conflict is the means wherewith such symbols are endued with warmth and desirability."[79] Still, as critics like Segal point out, Turner does not explain just *how* ritual accomplishes its representations and resolutions of the social drama.[80] Perhaps the fairest thing to say is that in his earlier work, Turner was concerned to show how in "static, primitive" societies (if such actually exist), ritual serves "to reinforce both existing society and the existing places of human beings in both it and the *cosmos*."[81] Later, Turner paid closer attention to "dynamic, modern" societies, and set out to demonstrate that "ritual, as part of culture, serves to alter

[75]Segal, "Victor Turner's Theory of Ritual," 329–30.
[76]Ibid., 330.
[77]*The Drums of Affliction* (Ithaca, N.Y.: Cornell University Press, 1968) 273–74. One may note here that Turner's view of ritual as "an epitome of the wider and spontaneous social process" is, finally, not all that different from Geertz's view (discussed in chapter 1) of the Balinese cockfight as a *text*, "a Balinese reading of Balinese experience, a story they tell themselves about themselves."
[78]Ibid., 268.
[79]Ibid.
[80]Segal, "Victor Turner's Theory of Ritual," 333.
[81]Ibid., 334.

both society itself and the places of human beings in both it and the cosmos."[82]

But even this shift of emphasis in Turner's thought leaves some basic issues unresolved. As Catherine Bell has observed, neither of these two approaches—ritual as a "mechanism of continuity, a way of countering change," or ritual as "affording change via adaptation or integration"—provides a satisfactory theoretical basis for understanding the basic dynamics of ritual.[83] Bell writes,

> It is possible that ritual is not intrinsically concerned with resisting or embracing change. A more useful approach would incorporate the many insights of Turner's . . . work, while not similarly restricting ritual's social role. Such an approach would attempt to identify dynamics intrinsic to ritual that, on the one hand, enable it to serve unchanging tradition or cultural adaptation, while on the other also make apparent the logic by which rituals are altered.[84]

Summary

The "classic consensus"—what Catherine Bell labels "the reigning scholarly assumptions about ritual and its social role"—was formulated, as argued in chapter 1, as part of a bold strategy to create something never before attempted, a sort of "political science" of ritual behavior: a systematic study of how human societies insure their cohesion and survival through the ritual appropriation of meanings and values, regularly reviewed and renewed. The beginnings of such a new science are evident, I suggested, in the work of Aidan Kavanagh (and, to a lesser degree, in the writings of Mark Searle). Thus, in his introduction to *Elements of Rite*, Kavanagh critiques portions of the Constitution on the Sacred Liturgy, especially paragraph 34, with its insistence that the reformed rites be "short, clear . . . unencumbered by useless repetitions."

> One cannot . . . think in a ritual context of the living and the dead (that is, historically) without soon realizing that human rituals are

[82]Ibid.

[83]Catherine Bell, "Ritual, Change, and Changing Rituals," *Worship* 63:1 (January 1989) 33.

[84]Ibid., 34. Bell's own attempt to formulate a "social-analytical approach to ritual dynamics" may be found in her book *Ritual Theory, Ritual Practice* (New York: Oxford University Press, 1992).

rarely short, clear, and without repetition. They are more often long, richly ambiguous, and vastly repetitive. This is so because many people participate in them simultaneously. This takes time, requires repetition, and embraces many different facets of meaning the participants bring with them to the act. *A liturgy without this time-consuming repetition is one without rhythm; one without rhythm allows little or no active participation; one without participation will communicate little or no crucial meaning.* For these very reasons, ritual is *a system of symbols.* . . . Symbols coax one into a swamp of *meaning* and require one to frolic in it.[85]

One can detect in Kavanagh's comments a connection to Turner's notion of "ritual as social drama," a means by which societies represent conflict and restore unity through a symbol system that embodies and transmits meanings. In this chapter, I have attempted to show how Turner's own views about ritual evolved and expanded, especially toward the end of his life, and how both recent research (by scholars like Kertzer, Grimes and Bell) and the observable facts of "emerging ritual" among marginalized groups (e.g., the AA meeting) have necessitated a change in anthropology's account of ritual's roots and roles. The "reigning scholarly assumption" insists that rituals are a "symbol system" aimed at producing "meanings." Chapter 3 will reveal that this assumption is no longer taken for granted by anthropologists—and indeed, that ritual might even be imagined as one of Michel Foucault's "technologies of the self."

[85]Aidan Kavanagh, *Elements of Rite: A Handbook of Liturgical Style* (New York: Pueblo, 1982; Collegeville: The Liturgical Press, 1990) 5; emphasis added.

3 New Directions in Ritual Research

At the conclusion of chapter 2, I noted that, among many Christian scholars, the reigning academic consensus about the "anthropological" roots and roles of ritual has been linked to the conviction that traditional liturgies constitute a symbol system providing references that point to encoded meanings. This ritual encoding, as anthropologist Roy Rappaport argues, is derived from a "more or less invariant sequence of formal acts and utterances" that are "given," i.e., not determined or prescribed by the participants in the ritual:[1]

> Liturgical orders are public, and participation in them constitutes a public acceptance of a public order, regardless of the private state of belief. Acceptance is, thus, a fundamental social act, and it forms a basis for public orders, which unknowable and volatile belief or conviction cannot.[2]

For Rappaport, a liturgical order is by definition a public one that provides the correct categories (about nature and cosmos, social structure, moral rules) which participants are expected to impose upon their private processes. The very performance of the liturgical order establishes a publicly accepted obligation to conform to the rite's rules, norms and values. These obligations, accepted in the liturgical performance, are not nullified by subsequent disbelief or violation. Thus, liturgical orders establish and preserve the conventions they encode, in spite of the vagaries of usage

[1] See "The Obvious Aspects of Ritual" in Roy A. Rappaport, *Ecology, Meaning, and Religion* (Richmond, Calif.: North Atlantic Books, 1979) 173–221.
[2] Ibid., 194.

and the real possibility of insincerity or failure on the part of the participants.[3]

Such has been the "classic consensus" about the nature of those rituals we commonly call "liturgical orders." As we have seen, it is a consensus challenged widely today by a substantial number of critics. David Kertzer's work with families subverts the myth of a ritually deprived America; Ronald Grimes demonstrates the importance of emerging ritual, especially among marginalized groups and individuals; Catherine Bell questions the adequacy of the theoretical basis for this anthropological consensus and suggests that ritual is not intrinsically about either preserving tradition or promoting change. In the present chapter, my task is to sketch for readers some of the new directions ritual studies is taking among anthropologists and sociologists, and to show how these might reshape our understanding of the rituals of Christian liturgy.

Ritual and the Technology of the Self

The first of the new approaches that I want to examine flows from the research of Talal Asad, a British scholar who, for two decades or more, has been studying the distinctive contribution of Western monasticism to our understanding of religious ritual.[4] In medieval Benedictine monachism, Asad argues, ritual was not primarily a symbol system aimed at the production of meaning but a *technology*—an acquired aptitude or embodied skill—aimed at the production of a "virtuous self," i.e., of a person who is obedient, humble, chaste, charitable, compassionate, hospitable, and wise.

Asad's discourse about ritual technology is connected to the work of Michel Foucault. Foucault's project had been, in his own words, "to sketch out a history of the different ways in our culture that humans develop knowledge about themselves: economics, biology, psychiatry, medicine, penology."[5] He wished not simply to accept this knowledge at face value, but to look at the sciences just

---

[3] See ibid., 197.

[4] I am indebted to Dr. Fred Roberts, professor of anthropology at Michigan State University, for alerting me to Talal Asad's work and for showing me its relevance to the field of ritual studies.

[5] Luther H. Martin, Huck Gutman, and Patrick H. Hutton, eds., *Technologies of the Self: A Seminar with Michel Foucault* (Amherst: The University of Massachusetts Press, 1988).

mentioned as "'truth games' related to specific techniques that human beings use to understand themselves."[6]

These techniques (technologies) fall into four fundamental categories: (1) technologies of production, "which permit us to produce, transform, or manipulate things"; (2) technologies of sign systems, "which permit us to use signs, meanings, symbols, or signification"; (3) technologies of power, "which determine the conduct of individuals and submit them to certain ends or domination, an objectivizing of the subject"; and finally, (4) technologies of the self, "which permit individuals to effect by their own means or with the help of others a certain number of operations on their own bodies and souls, thoughts, conduct, and way of being, so as to transform themselves in order to attain a certain state of happiness, purity, wisdom, perfection, or immortality."[7]

To speak about a technology of the self is thus to discuss "the history of how an individual acts upon himself," along with the interactions between self and others as these are driven by strategies of domination or power.[8] Note that this technology of the self is not an autistic, idiosyncratic or isolated process. Indeed, the phrase is closely connected to what early Christian writers called *cura animae*, "care of the soul (self)."[9] This *cura* is deployed and exercised chiefly through the practices of asceticism (e.g., discipline, control, penance, prayer, and purification). But if self-care is personal, it is also, for Christians, inherently and decisively social. It comes as no surprise, therefore, that the ascetic practices of *cura animae* inevitably involve ritual. Thus, technologies of the self include both the "rites" practiced by individuals and the "ritual construction" of the whole social order.[10] The reason is that Foucault sees the human

[6]Ibid., 18.

[7]Ibid. Foucault notes that these technologies rarely function separately. Each of them, moreover, "implies certain modes of training and modification of individuals, not only in the obvious sense of acquiring certain skills but also in the sense of acquiring certain attitudes."

[8]Ibid., 19.

[9]See the examples Foucault cites from writers like Gregory of Nyssa; ibid., 20–22.

[10]See Catherine Bell, *Ritual Theory, Ritual Practice* (New York: Oxford University Press, 1992) 97–98. Note her critique of Foucault: Even though Foucault "consistently chooses the nomenclature of 'ritual' to evoke the mechanisms and dynamics of power," he is not "concerned to analyze ritual per se or even to generate a description of ritual as an autonomous phenomenon," 98, 201.

body not simply as a private possession but as "a political field."[11] As Catherine Bell describes it,

> For Foucault, the body is "the place where the most minute and local social practices are linked up with the large scale organization of power." The body is a political field: "Power relations have an immediate hold upon it; they invest it, mark it, train it, torture it, force it to carry out tasks, to perform ceremonies, to emit signs." The body is the most basic and fundamental level of power relations, the "microphysics" of the micropolitics of power. Ritualization, Foucault appears to imply, is a central way that power operates; it constitutes a political technology of the body.[12]

Ritual is thus a way of inscribing the body personal, the body politic and their complex, inevitable interactions. Foucault's work (and that of feminist thinkers like Julia Kristeva) has helped us form a new image of the body. No longer is the body a stepchild, "the mere physical instrument of the mind; it now denotes a more complex and irreducible phenomenon, namely, *the social person.*"[13] This new image is inescapably linked to ritual:

> For Foucault, the "body" emerged in the late seventeenth century as the arena in which more local social practices were linked to the larger scale organization of power. With examples that range from marking the body with torture to confessional routines and the control of space, Foucault has suggested how "rituals of power" work to forge a specific political "technology" of the body. As the medium of the play of power, he argued, the body came to be linked to a new political rationality specifically rooted in the technologies of "biopower." This historical emergence of the body as a focus, moreover, would constitute a new level of analysis located between biology and the institutional vehicles of force, and giving rise to the human sciences themselves.[14]

In a real sense, this modern reappropriation of the body—its new image as an arena for the ritual negotiation of power and politics—

---

[11]Ibid., 201.

[12]Ibid., 202. It might be noted here that Foucault's project—to produce a history of the "political technology of the body"—is not so vastly different from what (as I suggested in chapter 1) Aidan Kavanagh was aiming at with his call for a kind of "political science" of ritual.

[13]Ibid., 96.

[14]Ibid., 97.

is what made the modern human sciences such as anthropology and sociology possible.

Technologies of the self thus have roots (and consequences) that are both ancient and modern. Two familiar axioms of the ancient world were "know yourself" and "take care of yourself." But as Foucault notes, "there has been [in modern life] an inversion between the hierarchy of the[se] two principles. . . . In Greco-Roman culture knowledge of oneself appeared as the consequence of taking care of yourself. In the modern world, knowledge of oneself constitutes the fundamental principle."[15]

In many Western cultures today, therefore, self-knowledge is supreme, while "taking care of yourself" is regarded with suspicion. Foucault summarizes the situation this way:

> [T]here has been a profound transformation in the moral principles of Western society. We find it difficult to base rigorous morality and austere principles on the precept that we should give ourselves more care than anything else in the world. We are more inclined to see taking care of ourselves as an immorality, as a means of escape from all possible rules. We inherit the tradition of Christian morality which makes self-renunciation the condition for salvation. To know oneself was paradoxically the way to self-renunciation. . . .
>
> We are [also] the inheritors of a social morality which seeks the rules for acceptable behavior in relations with others. . . . Therefore, it is difficult to see concern with oneself as compatible with morality. "Know thyself" has obscured "Take care of yourself" because our morality, a morality of asceticism, insists that the self is that which one can reject.[16]

But it is not only the hierarchical relation between self-knowledge and self-care that has been altered in modern life. As Foucault observes, the course of Christian history shows a close correlation "between *disclosure* of the self, dramatic or verbalized, and the *renunciation* of self."[17] Self-disclosure—i.e., showing the truth about oneself—has taken two main forms, each of them a "technology" rooted in the church's emerging penitential discipline. The first form is what both Greek and Latin Christian literature called *exomologesis* (ἐξομολογησις, usually translated "confession"), "a dra-

---

[15]Martin et al., eds., *Technologies of the Self*, 22.   *How society views practice)*
[16]Ibid.
[17]Ibid., 48.

matic expression of the situation of the penitent as sinner which makes manifest his status as sinner."[18] Christianity, Foucault noted, is not only a "salvational" religion but a "confessional" one as well.[19] It imposes "very strict obligations of truth," not only about doctrine but about the *self*.

Each person has the duty to know who he or she is, that is, to try to know what is happening inside oneself, to acknowledge faults, to recognize temptations, to locate desires, and everyone is obliged to disclose these things either to God or to others in the community and hence to bear public or private witness against oneself. The truth obligations of faith and the self are linked together.[20]

Exomologesis was thus a means of discovering and deciphering the terrible truth about oneself. It was an exercise in the "recognition of fact," a "ritual of recognizing oneself as a sinner and penitent."[21] Note that *exomologesis was not* primarily verbal behavior; rather, it was "the dramatic recognition of one's status as a penitent."[22] Thus, for example, the Christian Latin writer Tertullian paraphrased the Greek term with the Latin phrase, *publicatio sui*. By it, he meant not a verbal or mental analysis of thoughts and deeds (as practiced by the Stoics, for example), but a *somatic and symbolic* activity.[23] *Publicatio sui* was a not a way to explain one's sin but to show and present oneself as a sinner. "Exposé," therefore, "is the heart of *exomologesis*."[24] Christian penance constituted a kind of voluntary "ritual martyrdom," a complete "rupture with self, past, and world," a means of showing "that you are able to renounce life and self, to show that you can face and accept death."[25]

Thus, the ritual technology embedded in the early Christian penitential system was *not* aimed at establishing or maintaining a personal or corporate identity (the typical goals of ritual as interpreted in the "classic consensus"). Its purpose, rather, was "the re-

[18]Ibid., 40.
[19]Ibid.
[20]Ibid.
[21]Ibid., 41.
[22]Ibid. On the historical roots of penance as a Christian ritual, see J. A. Favazza, *The Order of Penitents: Historical Roots and Pastoral Future* (Collegeville: The Liturgical Press, 1988).
[23]See Martin et al., eds., *Technologies of the Self*, 42. As Foucault notes, "What was private for the Stoics was public for the Christians."
[24]Ibid.
[25]Ibid., 43.

fusal of self, the breaking away from self."[26] It represented "a break with one's past identity. . . . Self-revelation is at the same time self-destruction."[27] Foucault thus summarized the differences between the Christian ritual of *exomologesis* and the (Stoic) tradition of self-examination in this way:

> [I]n the Stoic tradition examination of self, judgment, and discipline show the way to self-knowledge by superimposing truth about self through memory, that is, by memorizing the rules. In *exomologesis*, the penitent superimposes truth about self by violent rupture and dissociation. It is important to emphasize that this *exomologesis is* not verbal. *It is symbolic, ritual, and theatrical.*[28]

Within the context of Christian monasticism, however, the penitential ritual of *exomologesis* changed. As noted above, the older notion of penance as *publicatio sui* aimed at the *ritual* "showing forth of oneself as a sinner." But in monasticism, a different ideology took hold, an ideology of obedience and contemplation. Personal autonomy—symbolized, in the *Rule of Benedict*,[29] by "the vice of private ownership" (*RB* 33)—was disallowed. Anything done without permission was tantamount to stealing: stealing back the freedom, the control which monks renounce and surrender when they enter the monastery.[30] Moreover, the goal of monastic life was understood to be contemplation. "It is the obligation of the monk," wrote Foucault, "to turn his thoughts continuously to that point which is God and to make sure that his heart is pure enough to see God."[31]

Both these factors meant that the technology of the self, as it developed in monasteries, took on distinctive characteristics. Dominated by the ideals of obedience and contemplation, monastic ideology focused more upon thought than upon action. As Foucault comments,

> Since the monk must continuously turn his thoughts toward God, he must scrutinize the actual course of this thought. This scrutiny thus has as its object the permanent discrimination between thoughts which lead toward God and those which don't. This continual concern with the present is different from . . . memorization of deeds and their

[26]Ibid.
[27]Ibid.
[28]Ibid., emphasis added.
[29]Hereafter *RB*.
[30]Martin et al., eds., *Technologies of the Self*, 45.
[31]Ibid.

correspondence with rules. It is what the Greeks referred to with a pejorative word: *logismoi* ("cogitations, reasoning, calculating thought").[32]

The monk's life is a continual scrutiny of conscience, a supreme effort "to immobilize consciousness, to eliminate movements of the spirit that divert one from God."[33] Here, we are brought to the beginnings of the "Christian hermeneutics of the self" that emphasizes "the deciphering of inner thoughts" and implies "that there is something hidden in ourselves . . . that we are always in a self-delusion which hides the secret."[34]

Precisely because of the danger of self-delusion, there is only one way for monks to be certain that their thoughts are spiritual and pure—and that is by telling absolutely *everything* to one's director or superior. Note that this process of self-examination and "confession" is verbal and analytic. If early Christian penance relied on a strategy that was symbolic and dramatic (ἐξομολόγησις = *publicatio sui*, which was the ritual revelation of oneself as sinner), monastic self-examination stressed the constant need to verbalize one's inner thoughts in obedience to a spiritual "superior" (ἐξαγόρευσις = verbal "exegesis" of the self through statements made to another). Foucault notes that these two strategies have

> one important element in common: *You cannot disclose without renouncing. Exomologesis* had as its model martyrdom. In *exomologesis*, the sinner had to "kill" himself through ascetic macerations. . . . In *exagoresis*, on the other hand, you show that, in permanently verbalizing your thoughts and permanently obeying the master, you are renouncing your will and yourself.[35]

This theme of self-renunciation (through either the ritual martyrdom of penance or the verbal/analytical martyrdom of monastic

---

[32]Ibid.

[33]Ibid., 46. To illustrate, Foucault appeals to three of the analogies used by John Cassian, who describes how monks must "care for themselves" through the exercise of constant scrutiny. Commenting on Cassian's analogy of the "money changer," Foucault notes, "Conscience is the money changer of the self. It must examine coins, their effigy, their metal, where they came from. . . . As there is the image of the emperor on money, so must the image of God be on our thoughts. We must verify the quality of the thought: This effigy of God, is it real? What is its degree of purity? Is it mixed with desire or concupiscence?" (47).

[34]Ibid., 46.

[35]Ibid., 48.

*self-examination and confession) has had vast influence on Christian life.[36] Of the two techniques that promote it, the second (verbalization) eventually became the most important, not only within Christianity but within the emerging "human sciences." "From the eighteenth century to the present," Foucault notes, "the techniques of verbalization have been reinserted in a different context by the so-called human sciences in order to use them without renunciation of the self but to constitute, positively, a new self. To use these techniques without renouncing oneself constitutes a decisive break."[37] Thus the older Christian "technology of the self"—and its monastic corollary, the "hermeneutics of the self"—have been reappropriated and reinterpreted by modern sociology and anthropology. The focus is no longer the renunciation of self (as it was in classical Christian asceticism), but the creation of a new self, the formation of a new identity.

As the research of Talal Asad shows, however, the Western monastic tradition, especially *RB*, combined the older Christian emphasis (self-disclosure as self-renunciation) with a view akin to the "modern" focus (self-disclosure as creation of a new identity). Asad notes that in *RB*, ritual is not yet recognized as a separate mode or specialized category of human behavior (the way modern liturgists and anthropologists might like to think of it).[38] Monastic liturgy and ritual are not yet seen as formal activities that are inherently "symbolic, structured, canonical, invariable, non-technical, traditional, and repetitive" in nature. Indeed, *RB* seems to think of the monks' three principal daily occupations—chanting the Divine Office *(opus Dei)*, manual labor, and "holy reading" *(lectio divina)*—as the same kinds of activity requiring roughly the same amount of time.[39] Nor

---

[36]Ibid.

[37]Ibid., 49.

[38]Asad would not quite agree with the opinion of scholars like Catherine Bell who see ritual fundamentally as "a way of acting that distinguishes itself from other ways of acting." He writes, "it does not seem to me to make good sense to say that ritual behavior stands universally in opposition to behavior that is ordinary or pragmatic, any more than religion stands in contrast to reason or to (social) science." See his essay "On Discipline and Humility in Medieval Christian Monasticism," in Talal Asad, *Genealogies of Religion* (Baltimore: Johns Hopkins University Press, 1993) 167. Asad is also critical of Clifford Geertz's view of religion and ritual. See "Anthropological Conceptions of Religion: Reflections on Geertz," *Man* (NS) 18:2 (1983) 237–59.

[39]See *RB* 47 and 48.

is *opus Dei* spoken of as though it were some kind of *symbolic* action that was opposed to manual labor and *lectio*. Writing about the idea of monastic "liturgy" in *RB*, Asad observes:

> The liturgy is not a species of enacted symbolism to be classified separately from activities defined as technical but is *a practice among others essential to the acquisition of Christian virtues.* In other words, the liturgy can be isolated only conceptually, for pedagogic reasons, not in practice, from the [rest of the] monastic program. . . . In the *Rule* all prescribed practices, whether they had to do with the proper ways of eating, sleeping, working, and praying or with proper moral disposition and spiritual aptitudes, are aimed at developing virtues that are put "to the service of God."[40]

The virtues of a monastic man or woman were thus formed by cultivating the ability to behave, bodily, in certain ways (humbly, obediently, compassionately)—no matter what the particular activity might be. This is clear from *RB*'s description of the "twelfth step of humility":

> The twelfth step of humility is that a monk always manifests humility in his bearing no less than in his heart, so that it is evident at the Work of God [the Divine Office], in the oratory, the monastery, or the garden, on a journey or in the field, or anywhere else. Whether he sits, walks or stands, his head must be bowed and his eyes cast down.[41]

✷ In *RB*, ritual is thus perceived as bodily inscription, as embodied practice, rehearsal, routine. It is a way of acting equally applicable to work in the garden, to a business trip outside the monastic enclosure, or to chanting psalms in the oratory. Obviously, such an understanding of ritual has nothing to do with ceremonial grandeur, solemnity or "canonicity" (in Rappaport's sense of the term as applied to "liturgical orders"). It aims, rather, "at the apt performance of what is prescribed, something that depends on intellectual and practical disciplines *but does not itself require decoding*. In other words, apt performance involves not symbols to be interpreted but *abilities to be acquired* according to rules that are sanctioned by those in authority: it presupposes no obscure meanings,

[40]Talal Asad, "Toward a Genealogy of the Concept of Ritual," in *Genealogies of Religion*, 63; emphasis added.

[41]*RB* 7.62–63. Translation in *RB 1980: The Rule of St. Benedict in Latin and English with Notes*, Timothy Fry et al., eds. (Collegeville: The Liturgical Press, 1981) 201.

but rather the formation of physical and linguistic skills."[42] In *RB*, ritual means "thinking" with the skin, "speaking" with the whole human sensorium. Ritual's role is to teach the body how to develop spiritual virtues by material means. Ritual competence is thus bodily competence, for the body is "an assemblage of embodied aptitudes, not . . . a medium of symbolic meanings."[43] Strictly speaking, monastic rituals are cognitively "empty" and "meaningless."[44] Their significance is acquired and interpreted by the body. Their "meaning" is inscribed on the skin, borne by the blood, carved in the bone.

According to *RB*, then, the ability to enter into communion with God and others is a function of bodies that have learned how to behave ritually, of bodies that "practice" virtue in much the same way that a pianist's hands practice music and bring it to life in performance.[45] Early Benedictinism saw ritual as a "technology of the self" with roots in early Christian *exomologesis* (ritual presentation of self as sinner), in monastic *exagoresis* (self-examination and its verbal expression), and in what modernity calls "the creation of a new identity." In *RB*, self-renunciation leads not to martyrdom or self-destruction, but to the creation of a new being. This new monastic identity is not bestowed through a single sacramental stroke; instead, it is gradually gathered through the patient learning of skills inscribed on the body. If ritual rules seem to govern virtually every aspect of life in *RB* (eating, working, walking, sleeping, praying), they are aimed at neither regimentation nor ostentatious display.[46] Rather, the ritual structures provide the social means—the "institu-

[42]Asad, "Toward a Genealogy of the Concept of Ritual," 62; emphasis added.

[43]Ibid., 75.

[44]See Frits Staal, "The Meaninglessness of Ritual," *Numen* 26:1 (1979) 2–22. "A widespread but erroneous assumption about ritual is that it consists in symbolic activities which refer to something else. It is characteristic of a ritual performance, however, that it is self-contained and self-absorbed. The performers are totally immersed in the proper execution of their complex tasks. Isolated in their sacred enclosure, they concentrate on correctness of act, recitation and chant. Their primary concern, if not obsession, is with rules. There are no symbolic meanings going through their minds when they are engaged in performing ritual" (4).

[45]Asad, "Toward a Genealogy of the Concept of Ritual," 76.

[46]See Staal, "The Meaninglessness of Ritual": "Ritual, then, is primarily activity. It is an activity governed by explicit rules. The important thing is what you do, not what you think, believe or say" (4).

tional resources of organized community life"—that make the "production of a virtuous self" possible.[47] This virtuous self *is* the new identity disclosed—slowly, perhaps painfully—through the technologies of confession and self-examination, as well as through the myriad rules and rites that accompany work (manual labor), prayer *(opus Dei)* and reading *(lectio divina)*.

In sum, "ritual" in *RB* is a *quality* that characterizes communal behavior,[48] rather than a separate species or category of human action. It is closer, perhaps, to Herbert Fingarette's description:[49]

> Rite brings out forcefully . . . the inherent and ultimate dignity of human intercourse; it brings out also the moral perfection implicit in . . . dealing with others as beings of equal dignity, as free coparticipants in *li*. . . . [T]o act with ceremony [i.e., with *li*] is to be completely open to the other; for ceremony is public, shared, transparent; to act otherwise is to be secret, obscure and devious, or merely tyrannically coercive. It is in this beautiful and dignified, shared and open participation with others who are ultimately like oneself that man realizes himself. This perfect community of men . . . becomes an inextricable part, the chief aspect, of Divine worship. . . .
>
> Instead of being a diversion of attention from the human realm to another transcendent realm, the overtly holy ceremony is to be seen as the central symbol, both expressive of and participating in the holy as a dimension of all truly human existence.[50]

This is also the basic attitude toward ritual in *RB*. Rite is not the formalized presentation of condensed corporate symbols that encode canonical meanings, and guarantee social cohesion. Rather, rite is a technological means of acquiring a new self—one defined by solidarity with all others as "beings of equal dignity" and by participa-

---

[47]See Talal Asad, "Notes on Body Pain and Truth in Medieval Christian Ritual," in *Genealogies of Religion*, 83–124.

[48]One might even say that in *RB*, ritual is what renders human behavior (even if practiced individually) communal.

[49]Herbert Fingarette, *Confucius—The Secular as Sacred* (New York: Harper Torchbooks, 1972) 16. Fingarette is commenting on the Chinese notion of *li* (usually translated "holy rite" or "sacred ceremony"). He argues that ultimately this notion refers not to any "ritualism" but to the idea that we engage in the art of becoming human by learning the ritual repertoire of the human community, i.e., by dealing with all others as "beings of equal dignity."

[50]Ibid., 16–17.

tion in a life that "in its entirety finally appears as one, vast, spontaneous and holy Rite."[51]

This is not to say that the Western monastic understanding of ritual lacks roots in the traditions of renunciation and self-surrender (what Foucault called the element of martyrdom). The rituals that *RB* attaches to actions like prayer, work and reading are ascetic ones, and cannot be learned without pain—mental pain, spiritual pain, even bodily pain—not because the body is evil and should be punished; not because Christians should "suffer like Jesus"; but because the human self is always (if sometimes involuntarily) in bondage to competing feelings, demands and desires. That is why, in the literature of Christian asceticism, physical pain (e.g., the distress of fasting, the weariness of vigils, or the discomfort of denying the body's urge for sex and satisfaction) is viewed as an ordinary, inevitable aspect of the ritualized "technology of the self." That is also why this link between ritual and pain is extremely unfashionable today. For many North Americans, pain is pathological. Our analgesic cultures encourage us to greet even the mildest discomfort with horrified denial; with medication or sedation. We feel there is nothing to be learned from pain's presence.

But Christian history reveals a different attitude. The distress and discomfort that inevitably result when one is learning how to inscribe the body with rituals of compassion, hospitality and graciousness (washing the feet of the poor, welcoming the stranger, caring for the sick, lifting the leper, listening to the garrulous) are also *the* way of embodying "holy rite as a metaphor of human existence." Perhaps that is why, near the end of Matthew's gospel, these uncomfortable rituals of service and self-surrender are the actions that will form the basis for God's judgment. Ritual is not only a way Christians negotiate their access to the Sacred; it is also their way of editing experience, "rewriting" personal history, and appropriating a new identity.[52] Inescapably, such activity will pose a substantial degree of danger and discomfort. For ultimately, the performance of

[51]Ibid., 17.

[52]Asad explains in one of his essays how the ritual character of medieval chapter sermons (such as those given by Bernard to the monks of Clairvaux) helped new monastic recruits (adults) to "rewrite" their experience, to reinterpret it in light of a self undergoing the profound change of monastic conversion. See Talal Asad, "On Discipline and Humility in Medieval Christian Monasticism," in *Genealogies of Religion*, 125–67.

ritual is the way we discover how and what we *think*. Thus, as Foucault notes, the Christian rituals connected with chastity aim not at inhibition but at openness:

> the opening up of an area . . . which is that of [embodied] thought . . . with its images, memories and perceptions, with movements and impressions transmitted from the body to the mind and the mind to the body. This has nothing to do with a code of permitted or forbidden actions, but is a whole technique for analyzing and diagnosing thought, its origins, its qualities, its dangers, its potential for temptation and all the dark forces that can lurk behind the mask it may assume.[53]

In other words, the goal of all ascetic ritual is purity of heart. The author of *RB* knew that human beings (including monastic recruits) are not just mildly misinformed—they are tragically and radically *self-deceived*. From birth, we humans are addicts, and our deepest addiction is to a mistaken identity, to a false self. We insist on living someone else's life, not our own. In Genesis, the great temptation was not about sex; it was about living someone else's life. "Eat of this tree," the serpent said, "and your eyes will be opened! You will be like gods who know good from evil!" The temptation was and is to forget that "even in heaven there are ants,"[54] to forget the painful facts of our human vulnerability and failure, of our lies and liabilities. That is why the chapter on humility in *RB* proposes a series of rituals designed to counter our human habit of "forgetting," of running away, of pretending to be someone else. Forgetting feeds addiction. So *RB* 7.10 warns that we must "resolutely shun oblivion" if we hope to reach the life with God that creates a new self. To become pure of heart, to discover the terrible truth about oneself, is thus to *remember*, to "keep the fear of God always before one's eyes, and never to forget it."[55] It also means what Tertullian called *publicatio sui*—ritually revealing the exact nature of one's life and thoughts to oneself, to God, to another human being.[56]

Thus the goal of the whole battery of ascetic rules and disciplines that comprise *RB*'s "technology of the self" is to replace ritu-

---

[53]Michel Foucault, "The Battle for Chastity," in *Politics, Philosophy, Culture: Interviews and Other Writings, 1977–1984* trans. Alan Sheridan et al., ed. Lawrence D. Kritzman (New York: Routledge, 1988) 239.

[54]See Staal, "The Meaninglessness of Ritual," 2.

[55]*RB* 7.10.

[56]See *RB* 7.44–48.

als of denial with rituals of remembrance. Remembering permits recovery of our real human identity, our original face and form, our true name and nature. <u>Memory gives us our own lives back</u>. Moreover, memory is not merely the mind's habitat; it also belongs to the *body*. *RB* knows that our deepest memories are buried in the skin, borne on the blood and breath, bred in the bone. That is why *RB* 7.9 insists that the "ladder" of humility (by which we "return" to paradise) is "our whole life on earth," built by the *body* as well as the soul.[57]

Thus, as Asad's research suggests, the goal of Western monastic ritual is an *embodied* "spiritual awakening." The ritually inscribed body becomes the place where God's presence and power are known. It becomes the place where the cosmos comes to consciousness. As the great Estonian-American architect Louis Kahn wrote: "All material in nature, the mountains and the streams and the air and we, are made of Light which has been spent, and this crumpled mass called material casts a shadow, and the shadow belongs to Light."[58] The ritually inscribed body is the place where truth is brought to light and the self's true identity is restored, in a ritual "process in which [bodily] pain and discomfort [are] inescapable means."[59]

To summarize, the ritual technology associated with the Western ascetic tradition (of which *RB* is a prime witness) emphasizes these six points:

- *The body's passions play an indispensable role in acquiring virtue*, in "diagnosing *thought*, its origins, its qualities, its dangers, its power of seduction."[60] Ritual action gives rise to thought—not the other way around. The body is the essential clue for recovering the self's identity. As *RB's* chapter 4 on "the tools for good works" suggests, one acquires humility not by thinking about it, but by ritually embodied acts (washing another's feet, drying another's tears).

---

[57]See *RB* 7.9: "We may call our body and souls the sides of this ladder, into which our divine vocation has fitted the various steps of humility and discipline as we ascend."

[58]Quoted in John Lobell, *Between Silence and Light: Spirit in the Architecture of Louis Kahn* (Boulder, Colo.: Shambhala, 1979) 5.

[59]See Asad, "Notes on Body Pain," 311.

[60]Foucault, *Politics, Philosophy, Culture*, 239.

- *The ritualized body is the privileged place where God's presence and power continue to be visible in human history.* That may well be why Tertullian, an early Christian exponent of asceticism, placed such strong emphasis on the visible, dramatic presentation of oneself as a penitent in *exomologesis*. God's power to forgive and reconcile is revealed in the ritually inscribed body of the penitent.

- *The ritual process is the ritual content.* In the ascetic tradition, ritual is not a "score" to be performed, but the performance itself. Thus, for example, the ritual technology that teaches the body how to behave humbly is the meaning of humility.[61] As performance, ritual redefines the self by embodying thoughts and emotions never before known, risked or felt. These coincide with (rather than are shaped or evoked by) the ritual performance. This point is paramount. As the British art historian R. G. Collingwood once put it: "The expression of emotion is not, as it were, a dress made to fit an emotion already existing, but is *an activity without which the experience of that emotion cannot exist. Take away the language, and you take away what is expressed.*"[62] To put the matter another way, a ritual's "spiritual content" cannot be separated from bodily performance. "The meanings of conventional [everyday] performances and the feelings and intentions of performers are not sharply separated," writes Asad. "On the contrary . . . it is precisely their interrelation that is central."[63]

- *The Rites found in Western ascetic sources like* RB *do not claim to be representative of broad cross-cultural patterns found in virtually all human societies, as an earlier generation of anthropologists*

[61]Note the ritual provision in *RB*: If one wishes to "know" the content of humility, one must "embrace suffering" (*RB* 7.35); one must bow the head and lower the eyes (*RB* 7.63); at times one must lay the body down at the entrance of the oratory, begging forgiveness from all who pass by (cf. *RB* 44.1–31). If one wants to know the content of "being hospitable," one must wash a guest's hands and feet (*RB* 53.12,14) and welcome a stranger "with all the courtesy of love" (*RB* 53.3). If one wants to know the content of "compassion," one must console the grieving and never lose hope in God's mercy (cf. *RB* 4.19, 74). In *RB*, the "content" and "meaning" of virtue emerge not from the grammar of thought or theology, but from the grammar of ritual performance.

[62]Talal Asad, "On Discipline and Humility in Medieval Christian Monasticism," in *Genealogies of Religion*, 130–31, n. 6; emphasis added.

[63]Ibid., 130.

claimed to be true of many rituals (e.g., rites of passage). Rather, they ritualize "historically specific emotions that are structured internally and related to each other in historically determined ways."[64]

- *The ritual repertoire represented by the Western ascetic tradition does not belong to the "rites of passage" category.* For instance, the rites and rules of *RB* do not, in fact, ritualize passages that every (Christian) human being experiences (e.g., the transition from puberty to adulthood, or youth to old age, or life to death). Novitiate is not catechumenate; monastic profession is not a "life-crisis rite" in the way initiation or marriage may be; the election of an abbot or abbess is not ordination. Rites of passage use encoded symbols to produce meanings that will support specific definitions of reality, reinforce social identity and cohesion, and guarantee the "success" of critical human transitions. But the rituals of asceticism do not try to produce meanings. They are, as Frits Staal suggests, "primarily activity. . . . The important thing is what you do, not what you think, believe or say."[65] Moreover, life-crisis rites are, by definition, terminal. They have an obvious beginning, middle and end. What the ritual doesn't finish, nature will. By contrast, ascetic rites are open-ended. They lack both the social drama of a life-crisis event (like marriage) and the high symbolic stakes of a sacrament (like initiation or eucharist). Furthermore, life-crisis rites attend to involuntary transitions (like the onset of menstruation or the coming of death), while ascetic rites are chosen and voluntary. The ritual technologies of a monastery are thus voluntary routines whose goal is embodied virtue. These virtues are not values ritually reviewed and renewed, as the classic anthropological consensus might have it, but acts aimed at unselfconscious goodness. They are similar to the deeds praised by the Chinese sage Chuang-Tzu in his chapters on the *Tao Te Ching*:

> [I]n the world of perfect peace, no value [is] placed upon exalting the wise, or putting the capable . . . in positions of power. The ruler [is] like the top of a tree (unconsciously there), and the people live like the deer of the forest. Doing right, they do not know it is called justice. Kind to one another, they do not know it is called humanity.

[64]Ibid., 134.
[65]Staal, "The Meaninglessness of Ritual," 4.

They are upright and do not know it is called faithfulness. They are proper and do not know it is called honesty. They move about and call to one another for help, and do not call it favor. Therefore their actions leave no trace and their deeds leave no record.[66]

• Finally, *the models typically used by anthropologists to interpret ritual negotiations of power* (ritual as catharsis, rhetoric, persuasion or metaphysical theater) are *not especially helpful for interpreting the kind of power being negotiated in ascetic rituals.* The ritual strategies of *RB* do not claim to represent, symbolically, the ultimate nature of reality or to justify power among a hierarchical elite. Rather, they are "essential *to* the disciplined development of the self."[67] In this sense, the gradual formalization of rites in monasteries (especially in the medieval epoch) did *not* signify the increasing domination of inferior subjects by repressive, superior leaders. In fact, as Asad's research shows, it was precisely those persons *excluded* from full participation in monastic rites such as "lay brothers" and peasants attached to the monastery's lands or businesses who were most likely to suffer repression and exploitation. Even when formalized, ritual was not viewed as an activity inherently symbolic or canonical. In the monasticism envisioned by *RB*,

> The liturgy is not a species of enacted symbolism to be classified separately from activities defined as technical but is a practice among others essential to the acquisition of Christian virtues. . . . It presupposes no obscure meanings, but rather the formation of physical and linguistic skills.[68]

Ritual competence is bodily competence, for the body is an ensemble of *"embodied aptitudes, not . . .* a medium of symbolic meanings."[69]

Ritual, Religion and "Critical" Anthropology

The innovative studies of scholars like Talal Asad are but one example of the revolution that has been taking place in the fields of so-

---

[66]*The Wisdom of Laotse,* trans. Lin Yutang (New York: Modern Library, 1948) 57; text slightly altered.

[67]See Asad, "On Discipline and Humility in Medieval Christian Monasticism," 134–35.

[68]Asad, "Toward a Genealogy of the Concept of Ritual," 63, 62.

[69]Ibid., 75.

cial and cultural anthropology over the past quarter-century. This revolution has important repercussions for the way Christian liturgists make use of anthropological data, as I hope to show in this final section.

Of course, anthropology has been changing throughout the twentieth century. The introduction of field method, early in this century, marked a major shift in the way anthropologists go about collecting data.[70] Gone was the anecdotal, "armchair" approach to the study of other cultures, ancient or modern; in its place came direct inquiry and participant observation. The anthropologist's task was to describe in detail a culture or society, "to record as accurately as possible the modes of life of other people."[71] This approach to ethnography—with its emphasis on actual experience and accurate recording—was a welcome improvement, but it also suffered limitations. "The chief experience of ethnographers was that of 'culture shock,'" writes John Saliba, "which was obviously not shared by the indigenous people."[72] Moreover, anthropologists often seemed more eager to discover "what anthropology is" than, for example, "what this ritual means to the life of an Eskimo village." "In a sense anthropologists were studying only one culture—the culture of anthropology."[73]

In reaction, therefore, a new ethnography (a "cognitive anthropology") emerged, one whose aim was not to formulate a grand unified theory of culture (as advanced by the older ethnographers), but to concentrate on competent descriptions of *particular* cultures and their cognitive systems.[74] The ethnographer's task is "to discover how different peoples organize and use their own cultures" by seeking answers to two basic questions: (1) What phenomena are most important to the people who share a common culture?, and (2) How do the people organize these phenomena? This newer approach sought, above all, "to avoid imposing on an alien culture a preconceived order [and] to elicit that culture's own semantic categories."[75] In short, the goal was to describe cultures from the inside out rather than from

[70]John Saliba, "The New Ethnography and the Study of Religion," *Journal for the Scientific Study of Religion* 13 (1974) 145.

[71]Ibid., 146.

[72]Ibid.

[73]Ibid. The quotation is from Stephen Tyler's edited collection, *Cognitive Anthropology* (New York: Holt, Rinehart and Winston, 1969) 203.

[74]Saliba, "The New Ethnography and the Study of Religion," 146–47.

[75]Ibid., 147.

the outside in. Both questions and answers must come from the culture of the people under investigation—and not from some preexisting order (usually Western) imposed by the ethnographer.[76]

While these changes were happening within the field of anthropology itself, new developments in the ethnoscientific study of religion were also underway. First, researchers began to see that Western categories for what constitutes "religion" or "religious experience" are not universally applicable, and hence cannot be applied indiscriminately.[77] Secondly, they began to question their use of the familiar, contrasting categories commonly applied to religious phenomena (sacred/profane, natural/supernatural). These, again, may be of some relevance to the study of Western Christian practices, but they are not very useful for understanding the native religious experience of indigenous peoples in Asia or Africa. Thirdly, researchers began to realize that religious experience cannot be fully or accurately described simply on the basis of official texts or surveys. As John Saliba notes,

> The primary lesson of ethnoscience for the study of religion is the emphasis on field work. If religious experience has to be stressed, then one cannot really base one's conclusions on sacred books or statistical surveys. . . . Up to now fieldwork, as understood by anthropologists, has not as a rule been diligently pursued by those historians of religions whose main area of study is contemporary religious beliefs and rituals.[78]

Recently, moreover, anthropology's landscape has begun to change again—partly as a result of critique from feminist scholars, and partly because of new challenges posed by the anthropology of science, technology and economics.[79] Some would argue that the disci-

[76]The "new ethnography" did not abandon the field method, but it did propose a newer way of getting at the native point of view through "controlled eliciting." The ethnographer is thus trained "to elicit from [native persons in the culture] the relevant questions they ask about themselves and the world around them. . . . [T]he ethnographer must be prepared to listen to his informants and to let them do most of the talking; to allow them to choose, as often as possible, the topics of conversation and to discuss the issues they have in mind" (ibid., 148).

[77]Ibid., 151.

[78]Ibid., 154.

[79]See David J. Hess, "The New Ethnography and the Anthropology of Science and Technology," *Knowledge and Society* 9 (1992) 1–26.

pline is suffering an identity crisis from which it may never recover. Others argue that the changes are needed in order to restore balance to a discipline long dominated by patriarchal, Eurocentric and colonialist assumptions. While it is not possible to chronicle all of the changes in anthropology over the past quarter-century, four of the major ones are noted here:

- First, *the "starting point" for anthropology is changing.* It was noted above that the new ethnography of the 1970s emphasized the importance of eliciting questions and answers from the native peoples under investigation. Today, as David Hess observes,

> The idea of the "native's point of view" should not be taken too literally or too narrowly. As in the term "native New Yorker," the natives . . . are often quite cosmopolitan and well-educated; these "natives" include artificial intelligence researchers, space scientists, or the inventors of new bio- and reproductive technologies. . . . The term "natives," then, is a less formal way of referring to the Other, the members of a society or social group who have a culture or perspective different from one's own, even if the Other is merely a different segment of one's own society (because anthropologists are studying with greater frequency groups within their home societies). Furthermore, it may be better to speak now of the starting point of the anthropologist's task as interpreting the natives' *points* of view.[80]

Anthropology today "retains a thoroughgoing skepticism of most universalistic statements about human beings and their social world."[81] But this does not mean that the modern ethnographer is paralyzed by what conservative critics derisively describe as "political correctness." Ethnography continues to practice participant observation. This does not suggest merely "watching people's behavior"; rather, it means "talking to and interacting with people, and ultimately attempting to understand their symbolic worlds and *social action.*"[82]

- Second, *anthropologists are finding it increasingly necessary to critique the assumptions and conventions of their craft.* This necessity has led Clifford Geertz to complain that exaggerated scrupulosity may soon render the anthropologist aphasiac. He speaks of a "pervasive nervousness" that hovers about his field today:

[80]Ibid., 2–3.
[81]Ibid., 3.
[82]Ibid., 4.

What is at hand is a pervasive nervousness about the whole business of claiming to explain enigmatical others on the grounds that you have gone about with them in their native habitat or combed the writings of those who have. This nervousness brings on, in turn, various responses, variously excited: deconstructive attacks on canonical works, and on the very idea of canonicity as such; *Ideologiekritik* unmaskings of anthropological writings as the continuation of imperialism by other means; clarion calls to reflexivity, dialogue, heteroglossia, linguistic play, rhetorical self-consciousness, performative translation, verbatim recording, and first-person narrative as forms of cure. . . .

Both the world that anthropologists . . . study, which once was called primitive, tribal, traditional, or folk and now is called emergent, modernizing, peripheral, or submerged, and the one that they . . . study it from, academia, have vastly changed . . . The end of colonialism altered radically the nature of the social relationship between those who ask and look and those who are asked and looked at. The decline of faith in brute fact, set procedures, and unsituated knowledge in the human sciences . . . altered no less radically the askers' and lookers' conception of what it was they were trying to do.[83]

Because his field keeps changing, Geertz wonders whether the very "right to write" ethnography is not now at risk.[84] In less combative moments, however, he admits (as many of his colleagues surely would) that ethnographic texts are *"made, and made to persuade."*[85] In other words, one must recognize that in anthropology there is (and has ever been) as much art as science. Anthropology is a work of the *imagination*, "like quantum mechanics or the Italian opera."[86] To say this is not to deny that ethnography deals also with the actual, the factual, with what Geertz calls "vitality phrased."[87] The art of persuasion should not, therefore, be dismissed as mere drama or deception:

This capacity to persuade readers . . . that what they are reading is an authentic account by someone personally acquainted with how life proceeds in some place, at some time, among some group, is the

[83]Clifford Geertz, *Works and Lives: The Anthropologist as Author* (Stanford, Calf.: Stanford University Press, 1988) 130–32.

[84]Ibid., 133.

[85]Ibid., 138; emphasis added.

[86]Ibid., 140.

[87]Ibid., 143.

basis upon which anything else ethnography seeks to do—analyze, explain, amuse, disconcert, celebrate, edify, excuse, astonish, subvert—finally rests. The textual connection of the Being Here and Being There sides of anthropology, the imaginative reconstruction of a common ground between the Written At and the Written About . . . is the *fons et origo* of whatever power anthropology has to convince anyone of anything.[88]

In other words, the call to critique assumptions should not be construed as a call to abandon the anthropologist's art. What is needed is greater honesty about what anthropology is (craft, persuasion, rhetoric, art, science) and how it is practiced and written. Unquestionably, imperialist and colonialist assumptions *have* sometimes comprised the integrity and results of field work. Nor can anyone doubt that "dispassionate science" is sometimes only political ideology. In an effort to be more self-critical about their work, modern anthropologists have proposed new methods and metaphors. With Claude Lévi-Strauss, for instance, "the metaphors of society shifted from biological ones, the analysis of society in terms of the functional integration of organs/institutions, to musical and informational ones: the analysis of society as the decoding of ciphers."[89] With Clifford Geertz, a different metaphor appears: the ethnographer is "a *reader*" who examines native rituals as "cultural *texts*" that can be read through a variety of lenses: "political, economic, psychological, status/local, and aesthetic."[90] The point is that, while no science is utterly free of assumptions, honesty about their nature and presence is a first step toward overcoming the limits they impose.

• Third, *anthropology today seeks what some call a "dialogical" or "polyphonic" ethnography.* This means, to some degree, "surrendering authorship of the ethnography to one's informants or . . . surrendering large spaces of the ethnographic text to direct . . . transcriptions of the informants' voices."[91] There is, of course, a potentially serious shortcoming in such efforts to respect native informants. Informants bring assumptions and prejudices of their own to descriptions of their

[88]Ibid., 143–44.
[89]Hess, "The New Ethnography," 7.
[90]Ibid., 7–8. As Hess notes, some critics have accused Geertz of simply "reinscribing in the ethnographic text the colonial relationship between anthropologist and informant," 8.
[91]Ibid., 9.

culture and social world. They may be as blind as the alien anthropologist to "oppressive systems of imperialism, race, class, and gender."[92] As feminist scholars note, culture is never neutral; it "is composed of seriously contested codes of meaning . . . language and politics are inseparable, constructing the 'other' entails relations of domination ."[93]

• Finally, *there is widespread recognition among anthropologists that their art must be both reflexive and critical—though not everyone agrees how this should be accomplished.* Many insist that "because values and politics will be inscribed in texts," anthropologists should "self-consciously decide what their politics are and contribute to the critique of knowledge-power-technology systems that are bound up with (and legitimate) structures of oppression."[94] Virtually everyone agrees that anthropology needs to provide room for *second voices* or *other* voices that might never get heard. This will necessitate a regular review—a "political and theoretical critique"—of every anthropologist's "discipline and discourse."[95]

These changes in the way anthropologists understand and practice their craft also have a bearing on their views of religion and ritual. Until recently the majority of anthropologists tended to place religion generally—and ritually specifically—in the category of symbolic or expressive action (as opposed to natural/biological or technical actions).[96] As Talal Asad comments,

> Studies of the social functions of religion tend to be either reductionist ways of arriving at its meanings, or (more usefully) ways of describing social consequences which, although brought about by religious institutions, may also be secured by "secular" ones. Religion itself is rarely approached in terms of "technical action"—that is to say, the disciplining of the body, of speech, which is used to produce religion in its variety.[97]

To put it another way, religious reality (including ritual) must be allowed to be itself, and not simply a system of symbols that points to something else. Moreover, one cannot assume that the meaning of

[92]Ibid., 10.
[93]Ibid., 10–11.
[94]Ibid., 11.
[95]Ibid., 18.
[96]Talal Asad, "Anthropological Conceptions of Religion: Reflections on Geertz," in *Genealogies of Religion*, 251.
[97]Ibid.

religion (and hence, of ritual) is absolutely univocal, and thus constant from one historical epoch to another. Religion, argues Asad, is usually linked to *power*, not merely power in the political sense, but "in the sense in which power constructs religious ideology, establishes the preconditions for distinctive kinds of religious personality, authorizes specifiable religious practices and utterances, produces religiously defined knowledge."[98] But over the course of history, such power is deployed and distributed differently, to achieve quite different goals and purposes.[99]

This is the case even if discussion is confined to a single religious tradition, e.g., Christianity. It is widely assumed that, for Christians, ritual provides a symbolic means of negotiating power (just as it does in other social groups). Obviously, this does not mean that ritual is mere artifice designed "to disguise the crude instruments of power" or coercion.[100] The power linked to ritual cannot simply be defined, then, as political manipulation or as the violent oppression of the weak by the powerful. Indeed, there are two distinct sets of questions that need to be raised about the relation between ritual and power: (1) What *kind* of power does ritual create, possess, or transmit? and (2) How does religious power, ritually expressed, create religious *truth*?

The first of these questions has been cogently formulated by Catherine Bell. "If ritual is not merely a *mask* for power," she asks, then "[H]ow does ritual do what we keep saying it does: How does it actually inculcate cultural or political values, converting beliefs about another world into facts about this one and vice versa, and 'inventing' traditions even as it purports to be transmitting them?"[101] Traditionally—as is evident from the "classic consensus" *liturgy* arrived at by Christian liturgists using anthropological categories— ritual is seen as an *instrumental* agent, as a way to impose social control by celebrating canons of correct belief and behavior (*lex orandi, lex credendi*) and by transmitting tradition (meanings and values). But today, many anthropologists will argue that ritual is neither an instrument of power "nor does it refer, express, or symbolize anything outside itself."[102] Political rituals, for instance, "do

[98]Ibid., 237.
[99]Ibid., 238.
[100]Bell, *Ritual Theory, Ritual Practice*, 194.
[101]Ibid.
[102]Ibid., 195.

literary (handwritten marginal note)

not *refer* to politics . . . they *are* politics. Ritual is the thing itself. It *is* power; it acts and it actuates."[103] In a word, ritual is not a "referential instrument," not a "functional mechanism or expressive medium in the service of social solidarity and control."[104] Rather, ritualization is "a strategic mode of practice" that "produces nuanced relationships of power, relationships characterized by acceptance and resistance, negotiated appropriation, and redemptive reinterpretation of the hegemonic order."[105]

But if ritual power is not instrumental or political or coercive or authoritative, *what is it?* Bell suggests that we try to answer this question by returning to the work of Michel Foucault. "For Foucault," she notes, "power is contingent, local, imprecise, relational, and organizational."[106] In other words, Foucault broke with the long-standing Western tradition that sees power as substantive, centralized, sovereign or hypostasized (e.g., in the person of a monarch). Instead, power is distributed all over the social body; it is "a matter of techniques and discursive practices that comprise the micropolitics of everyday life."[107] *Power is thus the way ordinary people define and negotiate the reality of their daily* lives—whether they're haggling over the price of a croissant at the corner bakery or staking a claim on a parking space in front of the apartment building. Power is, therefore, deeply embedded in the network of ordinary social relations. It is not something external to those relations, but rather, arises from within the local, "petty calculations of daily life."[108] Power of this sort always includes the potential for conflict, resistance, confrontation, struggle. It's the kind of power found, for instance, in the rituals of an Italian-American family around the kitchen table in the film *Moonstruck*. Rituals are *practices:* actions that act upon others.

Ritual is thus an imprecise way to organize the world of "local reality" by the seat of the pants, and so to construct *"particular* relationships of power effective in *particular* social situations."[109] This

---

[103]Ibid. Bell is alluding, here, to the position developed by Clifford Geertz in his *Negara: The Theatre State in Nineteenth Century Bali* (Princeton, N.J.: Princeton University Press, 1980).

[104]Bell, *Ritual Theory, Ritual Practice*, 197.

[105]Ibid., 196.

[106]Ibid., 199.

[107]Ibid.

[108]Ibid., 200.

[109]Ibid., 202.

way of acting is closely linked to Foucault's notion of the body as a "political field" (a point noted in the previous section of this chapter). "Power relations," he writes, "have an immediate hold on [the body]; they invest it, mark it, train it, torture it, force it to carry out tasks, to perform ceremonies, to emit signs."[110] Or, as Bell comments, "The body is the most basic and fundamental level of power relations, the 'microphysics' of the micropolitics of power. Ritualization, Foucault seems to imply, is a central way that power operates; it constitutes a political technology of the body."[111] Thus,

> It is in ritual—as practices that act upon the actions of others, as the mute interplay of complex strategies within a field structured by engagements of power, as the arena for prescribed sequences of repetitive movements of the body that simultaneously constitute the body, the person, and the macro- and micronetworks of power—that we can see a fundamental strategy of power. In ritualization, power is not external to its workings; it exists only insofar as it is constituted with and through the lived body, which is both the body of society and the social body. Ritualization is a strategic play of power, of domination and resistance, within the arena of the social body.[112]

The power of ritual is thus far more local, strategic, messy, imprecise, ordinary, flexible, ambiguous, and indeterminate than the high church liturgist might wish us to believe.

But if this is the case, how does religious power, ritually expressed, create religious truth (the second of the two questions posed above)? Can ritual make any claims to truth? The question cannot be answered (or dismissed) simply by arguing that the effectiveness of rites are independent of those who use them, or that truth always transcends (flawed) performance. After all, as Asad points out, "a deeply committed Christian surely cannot be unconcerned at the existence of 'truthful' religious symbols that appear to be largely powerless [or irrelevant] in modern society."[113] One cannot respond adequately to this situation by appealing to a theological defense of ritual effectiveness (to the rite's "objective efficacy," apart from a minister's worthiness or a participant's intentions). Ritual (as I argued

---

[110]See Michel Foucault, *Discipline and Punish: The Birth of the Prison*, trans. Alan Sheridan (New York: Vintage Books, 1979) 25.

[111]Bell, *Ritual Theory, Ritual Practice*, 202.

[112]Ibid., 204.

[113]Asad, "Anthropological Conceptions of Religion: Reflections on Geertz," in *Genealogies of Religion*, 242.

above) is practice—and the discourse of practice (the discourse that *is* practice) is not the same as discourse *about* practice (theology).[114]

Moreover, Christian history shows that the discourse which serves as an authorizing "model" for truth has varied enormously:

> [T]he ways in which authorizing discourses, based on a cosmology, systematically redefined religious spaces, have been of profound importance in the history of Western society. In the Middle Ages such discourses ranged over an enormous space, defining and creating religion: rejecting "pagan" practices or accepting them; authenticating particular miracles and relics . . . ; authorizing shrines; compiling saints' lives, both as a model of and as model for the Truth; requiring the regular telling of sinful thoughts, words, and deeds to a priestly confessor, and giving absolution to a penitent, regularizing popular social movements into Rule-following Orders (for example, the Franciscans), or denouncing them for heresy. . . . The medieval Church did not attempt to establish absolute uniformity of practice; on the contrary, its authoritative discourse was always concerned to specify differences, gradations, exceptions.[115]

Truth, in other words, was not authorized or guaranteed by a rigid uniformity of ritual practice. Rather, *truth emerged from a locally brokered ensemble of diverse practices, diverse discourses*—some of them overtly "pagan" (and thinly Christianized), some of them sacramental, some of them devotional, some of them juridical, some of them penal. All these competing discourses collectively constituted the religion and the ritual of the Middle Ages.

It cannot be argued on historical grounds, therefore, that the Christian churches have deployed rituals primarily as responses to our deeply human "dread of disorder."[116] Ritual is not an antidote to chaos—indeed, it often contributes to it. As medieval Christian history shows, local ritual variations were common and widespread; they were the norm, not the exception—and these variations produced a rich "polyphonic ritualism" rather than liturgical monody. It never seemed to occur to anyone in that period that ritual's claims to truth required absolute uniformity. Moreover, the authoritative imposition of a single rite upon all of Western Christendom was quite unthinkable prior to the invention of movable type.

[114]On this point, see ibid., 243.
[115]Ibid., 244.
[116]See ibid., 246.

Medieval Christianity understood instinctively that rituals do not contain meaning and truth in quite the same way that a vase contains water or a book contains "content." That is why the "stimulus-response model of how ritual works will not do."[117] Religious ritual is indeed, as Geertz suggests, a type of cultural performance, but it is one where claims to truth and meaning are *literally* played out in *practice*:

> [I]f we are to understand how this happens, we must examine not only the ritual itself, but the entire range of available disciplinary activities, of institutional forms of knowledge and practice, within which selves are formed, and the possibilities of "attaining to faith" are marked out. In other words, for the anthropologist to explain "faith" must be primarily a matter of describing a dependence on authoritative practices and discourses, and not of intuiting a mental state laying beyond them said to be caused by ritual.[118]

Ritual *does* embody religious dispositions, faith and truth—but it does so in a manner that is far more homely, local and imprecise than some anthropologists (and some liturgists) might assume. Religious ritual is a kind of *bricolage*, an act cobbled together from whatever is immediately at hand and available for use. It is not some heroic, Kierkegaardian leap of faith that beckons participants into a "framework of meaning which religious conceptions define, and the ritual ended, return[s] again to the common-sense world."[119] The stuff of ritual *is* the stuff of the common-sense world. On this point, the Christian liturgy has stubbornly insisted for almost two millennia. It is the stuff of spittle, salt, water, oil, bread, wine, light, fragrance, touch, taste, smell.

Ritual is not a source of truth independent of all the other practices, disciplines, dispositions, technologies and embodied inscriptions that, together, produce knowledge, faith, and social life (in both religion and the common-sense world). The ritual symbols of Christian liturgy inhabit precisely this common-sense world. Access to their truth does not require a leap into some other world. If it did,

[117]Ibid., 249.

[118]Ibid.

[119]Clifford Geertz, *The Interpretation of Cultures* (New York: Basic Books, 1973) 122. The result of this ritual leap, Geertz goes on to suggest, is that "a man is . . . changed. And as he is changed, so also is the common-sense world, for it is now seen as but the partial form of a wider reality which corrects and completes it."

the result would be not Christianity, but *gnosticism*—the idea that Truth can be known and measured only by privileged observers whose powers derive from another (alien and superior) culture, another world.

✳ In short, religion and ritual are precisely <u>*products*</u> of human culture. (Note that I did not say they can be "reduced" to human culture.) It is because of that, <u>ritual can make claims to truth</u>. Thus, instead of approaching religion "with questions about the social meaning of doctrines and practices, or . . . about the psychological effects of symbols and rituals," we need to study "the historical conditions (movements, classes, institutions, ideologies) necessary for the existence of particular religious practices and discourses."[120] In other words, as Michel Foucault and Catherine Bell might ask, "How does *power* create religion? How does it create ritual?" These questions can be answered only through a careful study of the social disciplines and forces "which come together at particular historical moments, to make particular religious discourses, practices and spaces possible." In other words, we must examine how each historical culture and society produces knowledge, including the knowledge and truth embodied in religion and ritual. In short, Christian liturgists and professional anthropologists must continue their dialogue.

For the fact is that in every human life and in every age—religion (like ritual) is woven together from an exuberant variety of sources, some official and authorized, some not. This entire ensemble, this riotously imperfect babble is what constitutes the several discourses of religious and ritual truth in any historical period. Medieval believers understood this, as do many modern ones. In his lovely essay "Sweet Chariot," Mark Doty explains how he grew up in "two religions."[121] The first and most enduring of these, a religion of images, he learned from his fundamentalist Christian grandmother:

> She would set me up on her lap and, rocking all the while, read Bible verses to me. I'm not sure if I remember especially her readings from Revelations, but it simply feels to me now, whenever I hear someone

[120]Asad, "Anthropological Conceptions of Religion: Reflections on Geertz," 252.

[121]Mark Doty, "Sweet Chariet," in Brian Bouldrey, ed., *Wrestling with the Angel* (New York: Riverhead Books, 1995) 1–10.

mention a phrase like "last days" or "apocalypse," that the scent of her—lavender and peppermint and clean old dresses—and the textures of her clothes and the Bible's leatherette cover and onionskin pages are forever commingled with those words; some essence of her imbues them. It was she who presented me with my first religion . . . the religion of images, and they were given to me in Bible verses and in the songs we'd sing on the porch swing, summer nights: the sweet chariot coming to carry us home, the moon turning to blood, the angels sounding the trumpet so that all the dead would clap hands and arise.[122]

This "ritual of the rocking chair" is a perfect example of how religion creates power and power creates religion. It happens summer evenings, on the front porch, in a beloved grandmother's lap, as much as it does during the solemn grandeur of a papal liturgy. For religion and ritual are always—and inevitably—polyphonic, as are societies, cultures and the human beings who create them.

[122]Ibid., 2.